T0201689

TITLES BY LORELEI JAMES

The Blacktop Cowboys® Series

Corralled
Saddled and Spurred
Wrangled and Tangled
One Night Rodeo
Turn and Burn
Hillbilly Rockstar
Wrapped and Strapped
Hang Tough
Racked and Stacked
Spun Out

The Want You Series

I Want You Back

The Need You Series

What You Need
Just What I Needed
All You Need
When I Need You

The Mastered Series

Bound
Unwound
Schooled (digital novella)
Unraveled
Caged

RACKED AND STACKED

A BLACKTOP COWBOYS® NOVEL

LORELEI JAMES

JOVE
New York

A JOVE BOOK
Published by Berkley
An imprint of Penguin Random House LLC
penguinrandomhouse.com

Copyright © 2018 by LJLA, LLC
Excerpt from *Spun Out* by Lorelei James copyright © 2019 by LJLA, LLC
Penguin Random House supports copyright. Copyright fuels creativity, encourages
diverse voices, promotes free speech, and creates a vibrant culture. Thank you for buying
an authorized edition of this book and for complying with copyright laws by not
reproducing, scanning, or distributing any part of it in any form without permission.
You are supporting writers and allowing Penguin Random House to continue to
publish books for every reader.

A JOVE BOOK, BERKLEY, and the BERKLEY & B colophon
are registered trademarks of Penguin Random House LLC.

ISBN: 9780593098073

Jove trade edition / August 2018
Jove mass-market edition / February 2020

Printed in the United States of America
3   5   7   9   10   8   6   4   2

Cover art by Aleta Rafton/Bernstein & Andriulli
Cover design by Colleen Reinhart

This book is dedicated, with thanks, to the men and women who climb into the cab of a truck every shift— long haul or short run—because they are the backbone of commerce in this country and the true heroes of the blacktop.

I'm lucky two awesome readers were willing to read sections of the manuscript and offer their expertise as professional truck drivers.

A huge shout-out to my longtime James Gang member Jeramy Zwiefelhofer, for making sure that Riss—and I—got the details and the lingo right.

Thanks also to Tony (and Kristen!) Eckard, for the input, technical suggestions and quick turnaround.

That said . . . any errors are mine alone . . .

Chapter One

❧

*L*arissa Thorpe prided herself on the fact that she'd never cried at a wedding.

And her tomboy reputation had nothing to do with it.

Truthfully, she couldn't remember the last time she'd cried over anything. She wasn't prone to dramatic outbursts—unless she was pissed off—and yelling was more her style.

"For godsake, Riss, would you pay attention?" Ike hissed in her ear.

Speaking of pissing her off . . .

Riss ignored the impulse to jam her elbow into his ribs. They were on day sixty-one of their truce—the last day—and she wouldn't be the one to blow it.

Without making eye contact, she hissed back, "Shove a sock in it, Palmer. I *am* paying attention. The song is almost over."

She'd kept her focus on the bride and groom—although Jade and Tobin were so engrossed in each other that Riss doubted they'd notice when the soloist stopped warbling.

"Shove a sock in it?" Ike repeated. "Are you ending our truce?"

"Hell no. That was me being nice."

Ike mumbled something.

The singer finished.

Jade turned to Riss, handing over her bridal bouquet. As agreed, Riss and Ike stepped to the side, allowing the guests to watch the bride and groom repeat their vows.

There hadn't been a sneak peek at those vows at the rehearsal the night before. The minister's only advice was for them to speak loudly and clearly during the ceremony.

The first sign this wouldn't be the typical "'til death do us part" exchange was when Jade began to list the reasons why she fell in love with Tobin. Some funny. Some romantic. Some slyly dirty. Her words were such an intimate glimpse into the bond the couple shared as lovers, friends and life partners that Riss's nose began to itch.

A reaction she blamed on the flowers—gardenias always made her sneeze.

Then Tobin started his vows to Jade. Achingly sweet promises. Words of devotion that Tobin wasn't the least bit self-conscious about sharing in front of everyone. Inside jokes that had Jade laughing through her tears.

Riss kept it together until Tobin slipped the ring on Jade's finger. "I never believed in soul mates even when I secretly hoped for one of my own. When you came into my life . . . my head, my heart and my body went wild for you. And finally my soul was at peace. It was whole for the first time because you are my other half, Jade. And this love—who we are together, what we bring to each other, the life we're building—was so worth the wait."

At that point, Riss didn't bother to hide her tears. So much for her "not crying" record.

Not that anyone was paying attention to her anyway— as it should be.

Sniffles echoed behind her. She chanced a glance at Ike. The lump in her throat hardened as she silently willed him not to look at her.

He didn't.

Not when the preacher pronounced Jade and Tobin husband and wife.

Not when Tobin kissed Jade with a passion that was unnerving to witness.

Ike ignored her until Tobin yelled, "Hot damn! Me'n Mrs. Hale will be a little late for the reception, but y'all go ahead," and swept Jade into his arms, then raced out of the room.

No one said a word.

Even the minister seemed shocked.

Then Garnet Evans, wearing a sequined *Grandmother of the Bride* sash, stood up in the front row and addressed the wedding guests. "Well, you heard my new grandson. Let's get this party started."

The minister insisted that Ike and Riss dismiss the wedding guests one row at a time.

That's when they exchanged a "WTF?" look and Riss realized they were meant to employ a delaying tactic.

After the first row exited, Riss muttered through her smile, "You coulda warned me that Tobin planned to bolt with the bride as soon as the ceremony ended."

"I had no idea, but the minister knows what's up."

Riss nodded to Bran and Harper Turner. "Do you remember the last time he said they'd be 'a little late' to us?"

"They caught the final fifteen minutes of that shitty movie *we* didn't want to see." He dipped his chin to the Lawsons—Abe and Janie, and Hank and Lainie—as they shuffled out. "And the time before that—"

"We ended up watching the demolition derby by ourselves because they didn't show up at all." She nodded to Renner and Tierney Jackson. "They'd better not pull a no-show at their own wedding reception."

"We're already stuck delaying the guests. What else can we do?"

"Find them ASAP." Riss nudged him with her shoulder. "Bet you thought bein' best man meant just showing up in a suit and handing over the rings."

"Yep."

"I say we check the laundry room first. The vibrating machines only set Tobin back a couple of quarters. And who washes clothes at a resort on a Saturday night?" Since nearly all of the wedding guests were local, it'd been business as usual for the Split Rock Ranch and Resort, the wedding venue. Resort guests were being treated to a closed-door, catered dinner in the lounge during the short wedding ceremony in the main lodge.

"Nope. Too public for Tobin. I'd guess they're in one of the offices."

The last two rows of guests exited and the maintenance crew immediately started moving chairs.

"We would've seen him hoof it up the stairs." She faced him. "The barns are too dirty. The kitchen is filled with the catering staff. The bar is brimming with resort guests."

"It's freezin' outside so they ain't fogging up the windows in his truck."

They said, "The clothing store," at the same time.

Ike led the way at a quick clip with Riss right behind him.

After turning the corner, they noticed the horny couple had left the glass door to Wild West Clothiers ajar.

Dumb-asses.

In the hallway leading to the dressing rooms, Riss and Ike heard the *thump thump thump* of movement against a solid surface. Their eyes met for a moment when female moans and male grunts escalated.

Yay. They'd arrived in time to hear the big finish.

"Lucky us, huh?" Ike drawled.

Lucky Jade.

For the briefest moment, Riss wondered if she'd ever experience that kind of devoted urgency. Sure, she'd had her share of lustful encounters, but that burning need never lasted beyond a night or two.

So it wasn't as if she didn't believe lust, love, respect and a lifelong commitment was possible with one man. She'd seen it happen to several of her friends; Riss just lacked faith that it'd happen to her.

"Hey," Ike yelled, pounding on the wall, scaring the crap out of her—and evidently the newlyweds, because Jade screamed. "Quit fucking around and get your horny asses to your damn wedding reception."

Silence.

Then Tobin bellowed, "Did you *follow* us?"

"Someone had to," Riss chimed in. "Better us than—"

"Your mom and dad," Ike inserted. "Or your—"

"Grandma Garnet," Riss added, grinning at Ike. "Although, the Mud Lilies *would* get a huge kick out of finding you two cracking the plaster in the dressing room."

"They'd probably take pictures," Ike said. "Miss Maybelle does have that fancy new camera—"

"And it would add those juicy details everyone wants when she writes up the wedding announcement in the *Muddy Gap Gazette.*"

Jade's gasp was soothed by Tobin's low, reassuring rumble. Then he said, "Come on, guys. Give us five more minutes."

"Five minutes and that's it," Riss shot back. "And Jade better not have sex hair, Tobin. I mean it."

"Fine! Now will you two just go?"

Riss dragged Ike out of the store.

Laughing, Ike held his fist out for a bump. "That went well."

"They are lucky we found them before anyone else did." Riss slumped against the wall. "We're through the easiest part. How many hours you reckon we have left?"

"Hell if I know." Ike looked at her curiously. "What do you mean we're through the easiest part?"

"The wedding itself. Now we gotta make sure no one monopolizes the bride and groom's time. Plus there's the toasts, cutting the cake, the first dance . . ."

"Stuff I haven't thought about, since I just showed up in a suit with the rings," he said drolly.

"Yep. Which is why if the Mud Lilies get out of hand, you're dealing with them. They tend to get liquored up at an open bar."

"So does someone else I know."

Riss shook her head. "No, sir. I promised Jade I'd be on my best behavior."

Ike looked skeptical.

That annoyed her. "I keep my promises, Palmer. Besides, there aren't any hookup possibilities. You, me, Tobin's brother Streeter and the Mud Lilies are the only singles here."

"Why are you discounting Streeter?"

"Beyond the fact he's a traumatized widower with an equally traumatized young daughter? That's a pass for me. A *hard* pass."

"Too much trouble?"

"The guys I pick know the score. Streeter doesn't. It wouldn't be fair to pretend I'm interested in more than one go-around just to get my hands on that banging body of his."

"You're not one of them women who wants to heal him?"

"Uh . . . no. I can't fix myself; I'd never be cocky enough to assume I understand what he needs. Especially when I doubt he knows himself."

When Ike didn't respond and she felt him staring at her, she snapped, "What?"

Ike shrugged. "Just surprises me when you prove you got a brain beneath them mean red curls."

She snorted. "A backhanded compliment skirts the borderline of a truce-breaking comment."

From the moment they'd crossed paths two and a

half years ago, Riss and Ike had maintained an antagonistic relationship. It started after Ike had gotten her brother Lloyd fired from his first postmilitary job. The Thorpe family held the "all for one" mentality, so if all three of her brothers hated Ike, then Riss did too . . . even when she kind of suspected that Ike wasn't entirely responsible for Lloyd getting canned.

But Ike hadn't helped matters by acting toward her like the asshole that her brothers claimed he was. With everyone else, he personified cowboy charm, even earning the nickname Palmer the Charmer. So when Riss's BFF Jade got engaged to Ike's BFF Tobin, and they started seeing even more of each other—besides just occasionally working together—they decided to put their past behind them and forge a truce. Which turned out to be easier than Riss had imagined.

"Admit you can't wait to end this truce," Ike prompted.

"You admit it first, ass—I mean sassafras."

"Ooh. You almost blew sixty-one days of not-horrible behavior," Ike taunted her.

"Horrible behavior? Think they're talkin' about how rude and downright mean it was to interrupt us?" Tobin said behind them.

"They do seem a little smug, don't they?" Jade said.

Riss whirled around to give Jade a once-over. "You look spectacularly fucked, Mrs. Hale."

"I am." She kissed Tobin's jaw. "For now."

"Come on, tiger." Tobin's gaze flicked between them. "We owe you for that. Big-time."

Riss waited until the couple was out of earshot before she said, "Did that sound like a threat?"

"Vaguely. But it's not in the same league as the threats you've given me."

"*Used* to give you," she said sweetly. "Do you miss those threats?"

"Nope." He grinned. "But they were creative as hell. I will admit that much. So feel free to direct those insults at anyone else to keep me entertained tonight."

Riss pretended to wipe away a tear. "That's the nicest thing you've ever said to me."

As they reached the main lobby, Ike said, "Think Boy Scout and Sweetie Pie will ditch their wedding reception again?"

Her former nemesis had a sly sense of humor. Calling Tobin "Boy Scout" and Jade "Sweetie Pie" always made her laugh because his descriptions of their BFFs were dead-on. "They can *try*. It's up to us to stop them."

Ike groaned.

She patted his cheek. "Smile, cowboy. The night is all uphill from here."

Chapter Two

⧖

One hour later . . .

"It was just a blow job."

Ike froze outside the doorway when he recognized Riss's voice.

So much for her being on her best behavior.

"It was a stellar blow job, hot stuff, and you know it," the unseen male responded hotly.

"It was ages ago."

"I think about it all the time. And seein' you here . . . I consider it a sign since I'll be workin' in Casper for a few months. I'd sure like to get together again. Take you out on a real date this time."

Ike cringed. *Oh, buddy, wrong thing to say.*

"Not interested."

"Come on. Just one date."

"I told you before. I don't date."

"Ever?"

"Never ever ever ever."

"Why not?"

Christ on a cracker. Why wouldn't this guy just take a hike?

"Lemme spell it out. The ratio of men to women in this state is four to one. That's way too many partners for me to pass up."

"So you're happy just whorin' your way through Wyoming a blow job at a time?" the guy demanded.

"Yep."

Then Riss emerged through the doorway, head held high.

Never a dull moment around her.

When Ike turned the corner, he was face-to-face with the recipient of Riss's oral expertise.

The man—still smarting from Riss's smackdown—glared at Ike. "What do you want?"

He pointed at the bathroom. "To use the can. You in line?"

"Nah. It's open." Recognition dawned on the guy's face. "Hey. I know you. Ike, right? Cattle broker with Stocksellers?"

Instead of correcting him with *former cattle broker* or *I got shitcanned*, Ike said, "Yeah, that's me. Remind me again where I should know you from?"

"Ryland Johnson. I work at the Blackwood sale barn."

Although Ike had zero recollection of this guy, the salesman in him surfaced. He offered his hand and a smile. "Now I remember. What're you doin' out here?"

"Me'n my buddies signed up for a private hunt."

"The Split Rock has great guides. You're sure to get your money's worth. Nice seein' you again. Take care." Ike sidestepped him.

But Ryland blocked the door. He jerked his chin toward the private banquet room. "Are you at the same wedding as Riss Thorpe?"

"Yep. Why?"

"What's the deal with her? Is she dating anyone?"

She just told you she ain't the dating kind, jackass. "Do you know her?"

"I'd like to get to know her better. This is the first time I've seen her since we . . . ah . . . hooked up a few months ago."

"And you were lookin' for a repeat?"

"Yeah."

Ike shook his head. "Look elsewhere. Riss is the 'one and done' type."

"More like blow and go," Ryland grumbled. "Maybe if I—"

"Don't even try to change her mind unless you want your balls kicked into your throat and a fat lip."

The mouth breather immediately bristled up.

"Not a threat from me, buddy. I'm just warning you that's what *Riss* will do to you if you keep bugging her."

Ryland looked skeptical. "I'll keep it in mind."

When Ike returned to the wedding reception, he sidled up to Riss standing at the bar. "A funny thing happened on the way to the bathroom . . ."

"I've heard this joke before," she deadpanned.

"Not a joke. I ran into a friend of yours."

Riss faced him, her green eyes narrowed with suspicion. "What friend?"

"Guy named Johnson." Ike took a plastic cup of beer from the man tending the keg and nodded his thanks. "He claims you're familiar with—"

"His Johnson?" she inserted. "Unfortunately." She snagged the shot glass off the bar top, downed it, and signaled to the bartender for another.

"Whoa there, partner. You promised Jade you'd be on your best behavior and you're doin' shots?"

"I promised her no tequila. This is rum."

He raised a brow. "Like that is somehow better?"

"For me? Yes. So what'd he say to you?"

"He asked if you were dating anyone. He seemed a little put out that you wouldn't . . ." He grinned. "Well . . . put out."

"Christ. Suck a guy's dick one time and suddenly he's in love."

Ike choked on his beer.

Laughing, Riss slapped him on the back. "You oughta be used to my lewd and crude mouth by now, Palmer."

"Not when your goal is maximum shock value with minimum effort, Thorpe."

She shrugged. "Some people consider my vulgar vocab my most charming attribute."

"Really? Name *one* person."

"Jade."

"She's from New York. Nothin' shocks her, so she don't count."

"Whatever. I know you're dying to hear the dirty details about me'n the big Johnson."

"Why would I give a damn about how you handled that tool?"

"Because you, Ike Palmer, are as snoopy as a fifteen-year-old girl." She poked him in the chest. "Don't deny it."

He couldn't. "Fine. Get it off your chest if you have to, so I can immediately scrub it from my brain."

"Four or five months ago I drove a load of cars to a junkyard in Nebraska. I had to spend the night and ended up in the local bar, where I met Ryland. We had some shots, some laughs, and I figured what the hell, I was horny, and he was there. I blew him in the parking lot and he lasted like a minute, setting off my bad-sex warning bells, so I cut my losses and went to bed alone."

"You assumed he'd be a lousy lay because he was quick on the trigger?"

"Uh, yeah. Stamina is a good thing." She cocked her head. "Oh no, cowboy. Did I hit a nerve? Are you and Johnson packing the same kind of fast-shootin' gun?"

"No," he scoffed.

"Sure you aren't." She patted his shoulder. "Belly up to the bar and tell Doc Riss about your stamina issues."

"That's never been an issue for me. I'm just saying that your aggressiveness probably caught him off guard since most guys don't get blow jobs from women they just met unless they're paying for it. I doubt the poor SOB had had many encounters with a woman like you."

"And that, my friend, is exactly why I bailed."

While watching her tongue circle the rim of the shot glass, Ryland's claim *It was a stellar blow job* echoed in Ike's head.

"Besides, the guy couldn't kiss for shit. That's the best indicator of how good *his* tongue game is."

His *don't ask* mantra vanished instantly. "Seriously?"

"Yep. I did us both a favor by walking away."

Ike leaned in. "He don't see it as a favor and I suspect he'll try to corner you again even when I warned him off. So if you need me to—"

"He gets out of line, I'll handle him. I've never been a damsel and I ain't about to start acting like one now." Riss pushed her red curls off her damp forehead. "Keep an eye on the horny duo. It's hotter than balls in here and I need to get some fresh air."

"It's four degrees below zero outside," he reminded her, watching that curvy ass twitch as she exited the side door.

Grumbling about hardheaded women, Ike headed to the back of the room, where he intended to perfect his wallflower impression as he watched for the bride and groom to try to make a break for it. He'd never imagined this would be part of his best man duties.

It'd surprised him when Tobin had asked him to be his best man, since Tobin had two brothers and Renner Jackson had been more than just Tobin's boss. Then again, as the remaining bachelors in their group of friends, in the last few years he and Tobin had spent their free time together.

Until Jade entered the picture. Then Tobin was one hundred percent about his new love. That hadn't been a surprise. Tobin had always been looking for a serious relationship.

Not Ike. He liked the single life. Usually weddings were a great place to hook up, but as Riss had pointed out, the only single women at this one were the Mud

Lilies—a seventy-plus set that included Jade's grand-mother—and the blow job queen, Riss.

"So what's this I hear about Hugh staying on the West Coast?"

Ike looked at his longtime friend Bran Turner, who'd snuck up on him. With a beer in his hand and no sign of his three rambunctious boys, the rancher appeared more relaxed than Ike had seen him in a few years. "Wouldn't you stay where palm trees blow in the ocean breeze?"

Bran smirked. "Point taken. What's he been up to?"

"Meeting with rodeo committees to convince them to use Jackson Stock Contracting for their events. There's a huge market and hasn't been much competi-tion. Seems a lot of them use the same stock contractors and have for years." *Sometimes my ability to bullshit around the truth surprises even me.*

"I can see why." Bran took a swig of his beer. "It's a big area to cover. The price of hauling premium rodeo stock has to be somewhat cost prohibitive."

"Could be. But contestant complaints have led the Cowboy Rodeo Association to investigate events where the scores have been consistently low. We're lookin' for opportunities to fill in as temporary contractors—and show our versatility and top-notch rough stock." If they could ever get any takers. They'd been pounding the blacktop for a year and a half on behalf of their new business endeavor and so far few rodeo committees had followed through with their promise to partner with them. But as Ike had done his entire professional life as a salesman, it was all about how you spun it. And the last thing he wanted was for anyone to realize that under his co-ownership, Jackson Stock Contracting was spiraling toward failure. He hadn't even told Riss how bad things were after they'd used her as a driver. Like an asshole, he'd led her to believe they'd been using another trucking company to transport their livestock to events . . . instead of admitting the truth that they hadn't added any new events at all.

"I'm glad you're doin' something you like. But, man, I hate to think of the day when you'll be too busy to deal with my cattle sales."

That day had arrived more than a year ago, but not due to his busyness. Now wasn't the time for Ike to confess he'd been fired from his previous job and signed a no-compete clause, so he'd bought into the stock-contracting business to save face. He had months to suggest another broker before this year's calves would be saleable. Ike gave him a considering look. "You draw the short straw to bring this up with me?"

"Yeah." Bran sighed. "You've always gone above and beyond for the Lawsons and me. Same for Renner, Kyle and Eli. I suspect you're still dealing with the Hales' sales even when that's become a clusterfuck."

"You don't know the half of it." Ike did a quick scan of the room. He still couldn't believe that Dan and Driscoll Hale—Tobin's father and oldest brother—had skipped Tobin and Jade's wedding. Even though Dan Hale had been the first rancher to sign on with Ike years ago when he'd first started in the cattle-brokering business, even if Ike still had his job with Stocksellers, he would've ended his association with Dan.

"I don't wanna know the ugly particulars, but now that Streeter is workin' for Renner at the Split Rock full-time, I'm hearin' them anyway, since my wife loves to gossip."

So do you. Ranchers were a nosy lot. Everyone in the county knew everyone else's business—or they thought they did.

A shit-eating grin creased Bran's face. "Hot damn. My wife has that look in her eyes, so I gotta go." Bran clapped Ike on the shoulder. "See ya."

And he was gone.

Ike saw the couple slip out the side door.

First lesson he'd learned when he started doing business at the Split Rock? Never open any door without knocking first. That included the door to the storage closet and the walk-in cooler. His married friends apparently snuck in a quickie whenever they had the chance.

"Who're you hiding from?" Riss asked, causing him to jump, since she'd snuck up on him.

"You."

She snickered. "And here I am again, just like a bad penny." Then she nudged him. "Scoot over so we're both in the shadows."

"Why? Did Johnson try to corner you outside again?" he said sharply.

"No. But us both bein' in the shadows is a stealthy way to bust Tobin and Jade."

That didn't sound right. He squinted at her. She'd lost some of that sexy swagger he secretly found appealing. "You sure that's the only reason?"

"It's just . . ." She glanced down before meeting his gaze. "These formal dresses suck. I'm sure I look as awkward in it as I feel."

No, freckles, you look awful damn cute.

Cute. Right. She'd kidney-punch him if he ever called her cute to her face.

Normally Riss wore baggy and stained coveralls, or painter's pants, paired with an equally baggy hoodie.

But she had cleaned up very well for this wedding. She'd tried to tame her crazy red curls into a ponytail. Leaving her neck exposed accentuated the ivory tone of her skin. She'd used eyeliner that made the green hue of her eyes even more arresting—the color ranging between pale green and peridot, depending on her mood. Her emerald-colored bridesmaid's dress molded to her, reminding him—and every other male—that she'd been blessed with a truly magnificent body, especially her tits.

"Why are you staring at me?" she demanded. "It's sure takin' you a long damn time to come up with an insult."

"Truce, remember?" Ike allowed his gaze to encompass her face, as if he was truly seeing her for the first time. "You don't look awkward, Riss. You look really pretty." Before he could stop himself, he ran the back of his knuckles down her cheek, from her temple to the tip of her chin. "It pains me—"

"To admit that?"

"No. And stop interrupting me. It's a pain to see that you covered up your freckles."

She blinked at him. "Why?"

He shrugged. "I like them. They're just . . . you." *That sounded like a come-on.* He backtracked. "Besides, makeup hides your level of anger so I can't see your face getting red."

"Then that means you can't see me blushing either."

"Why would you be blushing?"

She blushed even deeper. "Because you said I looked pretty."

He barely kept his jaw from dropping. This woman could babble about blow jobs in public without batting an eye, but a compliment brought heat to her cheeks? He didn't know what the hell to even say to that.

"Genuine flattery from Palmer the Charmer is enough to make any woman swoon."

She did a shimmy-shake with her shoulders—was that supposed to convey a swoon?—sending her enormous breasts swaying, and Ike's avid gaze tracked every shift of flesh against fabric. "At least you were looking at my face." Another shimmy-shake sent her breasts bouncing. "Not that you are now. It's hard to look away from the girls when they're out of captivity, isn't it?"

Jesus. "How long do we have to stick around after the newlyweds are allowed to leave for real?"

Surprisingly, she didn't needle him about the rapid subject change. "I'm not sure. I know Jade's mom and dad are staying until the last guest leaves. I thought the Mud Lilies would be whoopin' it up tonight and chase everyone away, but they've been on their best behavior."

"I suspect Jade demanded obedience from them the same as she did from you."

"Me obedient? Never. My toned-down behavior is strictly voluntary."

Ike preferred wild Riss. She had a spontaneity he lacked. "Like that's a shocker."

"I am shocked that none of the Mud Lilies have stalked you and demanded a dance."

"Me too. I figured since they were behaving they'd track me down and regale me with stories about the wild bachelorette party you threw," Ike said.

Riss rolled her eyes. "You really think that Garnet would let anyone else plan a night of debauchery for her only granddaughter? She barely let me host a bridal shower for her."

"That's strange, ain't it?"

"You don't know the half of it. Garnet's cronies have called dibs on throwing Jade a killer bachelorette party."

"They do understand that a bachelorette party is supposed to take place *before* the wedding, right?"

"Not in the Mud Lilies' universe. According to Jade, the only way Tobin would agree to let them plan a party was if it took place *after* the wedding and the honeymoon."

His eyebrows rose. "Tobin is usually putty for them old gals."

"Not when he overheard Garnet and Miz Maybelle discussing the 'ultimate Vegas girls' weekend,' which included a trip to a gun range, a skyscraper zipline challenge and an overnight stay at the Desert Dreams Dude Ranch. He forbade them from taking Jade out of Wyoming. Not fun for him to fly to Vegas to bail them all outta jail."

"Luckily for him the law around here is very familiar with the ladies' shenanigans," he said with a laugh.

"And so are the bail bondsmen. I'm pretty sure Tobin believes the Mud Lilies will forget about it and move on to something else."

"I hope so. I hate Vegas."

Riss tipped her head back and looked at him. "Seriously? Why?"

"Besides the fact I don't gamble?"

"Dude. There's lots to do in Vegas besides gamble." She studied him. "Isn't Vegas a stock contractor's dream? Standing on the podium at the national finals in December? Aren't the national finals an annual destination for all the folks who put on rodeos across the country? I'd think you'd be jumping at the chance to do a meet and greet there. Especially since Hugh is based not more than four hours away in Cali, right?"

She'd totally busted him. Now he had to backtrack. "Hugh couldn't get meetings with the event coordinators he'd been in touch with throughout the year. So we opted not to and decided to push harder for meetings next year, after we've got a few successful events under our belts." Ike shifted to face her. "Will you be bummed if you don't end up in Sin City for a belated bachelorette party?"

"Yes. And no. I mean, most people have that 'what happens in Vegas' mind-set only when they're on the Strip. I prefer to put half-truths into everyday life." She laughed at his alarmed expression. "You don't do that?"

"Do what?"

"Mess with people? Strangers mostly, but sometimes even friends?"

"Explain 'mess with,' Thorpe."

"Say you're out of town and you're in a C-store to feed your craving for Funyuns, Reese's peanut butter cups and Fanta grape soda. You're in line to check out, and the woman behind you says, 'Bad breakup?' So instead of telling her to mind her own business, you complain good-naturedly that you wish, but the truth is your wife is pregnant with twins and she gets ridiculous cravings late at night. That you're glad not to be buying something super weird like last time, when she craved stewed tomatoes and Three Musketeers and ate them together."

Ike couldn't believe how fast Riss had whipped up that story.

She poked him in the chest. "See? Even you're intrigued about that weird-ass craving. So the Nosy Nelly who began the conversation will either ignore you from that point on, or she'll start telling you about what she craved during pregnancy."

"And if I run into Nosy Nelly again?" he prompted.

"You won't."

"So you just flat-out lie to people?"

"I prefer to call it creating an altered reality."

"In other words . . . you lie." Ike leaned closer and caught a whiff of Riss's coconut perfume. How in the hell wasn't he supposed to imagine oiled-up bodies in tiny bikinis when that damned tropic aroma teased him?

She poked him in the chest again. "Oh, lose the judgmental look. You used to be a salesman—a *professional* creator of alternate reality, whereas I'm merely an amateur."

He couldn't pull off indignant so he laughed. "Have you ever created an altered reality with me?"

"Besides this whole 'truce' thing? No. Are we messing with our friends by not telling them about our truce? Absolutely."

"Is that how you ended up with the big Johnson? Created an altered reality and he bought into it?"

Riss groaned. "I wish. That's a perfect example of why I should always veer away from using my real name."

"I don't want to know how many times you've created an alternate reality, do I?"

"Probably not. But you could tell me the most spontaneous thing you've ever done." She tugged on his tie. "Bonus points if it's a dirty sexual scenario."

"No judgment?"

"None."

"Coming up with the idea of buying out Renner Jackson and taking over JSC," he said in a rush, not having the guts to add that it was the worst idea he'd ever followed through on.

"Interesting." She toyed with the ends of his bolo tie. "Your answer is business related and it hasn't been about business between us for months."

He chucked her under the chin until her gaze collided with his. "I wish I had done something spontaneous and cool in my life to wow you with, Riss."

"It's not too late." Her vivid green eyes issued a challenge. "The next time you have a chance to act out or act up . . . don't hesitate. Be impulsive."

"And if I don't have the balls to follow through with it, then I should lie my ass off to you anyway?"

Riss smirked. "Now you're getting it, Palmer."

A throat cleared behind him. Ike turned to see Tilda, the tiniest and flightiest of the Mud Lilies studying them suspiciously. He said, "Hey, Miz T, what's up?"

"I was sent to bring you over to our table so you can settle a bet."

"No can do. Tobin warned me about them pixie dust shots. And as far as I know, the bartender ain't supposed to be serving them to any of you—regardless if Garnet is the grandmother of the bride."

"Oh pooh. Our question isn't about booze. It's about sex."

Chapter Three

❧

*I*ke's deer-in-the-headlights look . . . Priceless.

No way was Riss letting him get out of this.

"Go on." She nudged him hard and smiled at Tilda. "He'd love to help out. He just needs a little encouragement."

"Aw, it's sweet that he's shy," Tilda said.

"Shy?" he sputtered. "I ain't shy. Not at all."

"Here's your chance to prove it." Then, over Tilda's head, she mouthed, "Be spontaneous, remember?"

A wolfish smile creased Ike's face. "Now, darlin', what kind of man would I be, leavin' you here to fend for yourself?"

She waved him off. "I'll be fine."

"No. Really. I *insist* you come along." Ike snagged Riss's hand.

Tilda took a step back. "We don't want no trouble because of you two."

"*Because* of us? Like we're trouble?" Riss demanded.

"The two of you *together* spells trouble. Don't pretend you're unaware of your reputation for combustible behavior around each other," Tilda retorted.

"It's in the past," Ike assured her with a smile. "We've dealt with the issue maturely and privately. So I can promise that you ladies will want *input* about sex from the woman around these parts most likely to *put out*, won't they, sweet cheeks?"

Damn punny man. She'd argue that point . . . but it was true. "I don't want to horn in where I'm not wanted, sugar pie."

"Didn't stop you earlier."

"Didn't stop *us* earlier. I'm not takin' all the blame for that." She scanned the crowd. Speaking of the bride and groom . . . "Did you see where they went?" she said to Ike.

"Nope. Dammit. Should we—"

"You should come to our table right now." Tilda urged them both to huddle down and stage-whispered, "Fair warning. The discussion might get a little steamy."

"Nothin' fazes him," Riss confided with a wink. Then she smiled at Tilda. "Lead the way."

Ike said, "Jesus, you're a menace," under his breath as he followed her.

The Mud Lilies' table was farthest from the main door and closest to the bar. Vivien, the youngest of the bunch, smiled graciously. "Lovely that you could join us also, Riss."

"Ah bloody hell. You ain't gonna rat us out to Bernice?" Pearl demanded.

"Why would you ask that?" Riss demanded. "What did she say about me?"

"Nothin'," Pearl retorted. "Just gotta CMA." She elbowed Garnet. "CMA means cover my ass."

"We know what it means," Garnet, Tilda, Vivien and Miss Maybelle said simultaneously.

"I am *not* a snitch."

Ike's fingers—which were somehow interlaced with hers—squeezed in warning and he murmured, "Easy, darlin'."

"Besides. Aunt B ain't here. Vegas rules apply."

"Hot damn," Miz Maybelle said with glee. "Pop a squat."

Once they were seated, Ike said, "Tilda said you want me to settle a bet?"

"Actually . . . first we have some questions."

"About?"

"Oh, a lot of stuff, sonny, so get comfy. You're gonna be here a while," Garnet said.

Pearl said, "Hush up, Garnet, you'll scare him off." Then her focus zoomed back to Ike. "Them online dating places. They're not really for finding a date. They're for finding sex."

Oh boy.

"Sign up and sex is guaranteed, right?"

Ike opened his mouth, and then closed it.

Twice.

Riss took pity on him and answered. "Maybe you should clarify for us which online dating sites. Like eHarmony? Match.com? Matchmaker?" *Sexy Singles over Seventy? Was there even such a site?*

"No, no and no," Garnet said. "We're talkin' about phone apps. Where you punch in your location and it tells you if any horny honeys are in the same vicinity. Like that Tingle one."

"For the tenth time, Garnet, there's no app called Tingle. It's *Tinder*," Vivien retorted.

"Well, it oughta be called *Tingle* if your girlie bits want male attention that makes them tingle," Garnet volleyed back.

"There's one called Grindr and I think that says what we all want," Pearl said. "Some hot grinding action."

Riss couldn't have held back her grin even if she'd tried. "Hate to burst your bubble, ladies, but Grindr is for gay men."

Miz Maybelle slapped the table and pointed at Pearl. "I *knew* them guys were too hunky to be straight. Lord, even the old fellas were wearing banana hammocks in their profile pictures."

Do not glom onto that mental image, Riss. Leave. It. Be.

"Is there a lesbian dating site?" Tilda asked. "Only seems fair. But it's probably got a name like Strap-on. Or Nipplr."

"Or Foxy Taco," Garnet tossed out.

Ike heaved a sigh beside her. "Ladies . . . I think—"

"This is a lot to process," Riss inserted. "Ike and I could both use a fresh drink before we get into the down-and-dirty details."

"Excellent idea." Garnet placed her fingers in her mouth and whistled loud enough to wake the dead.

The bartender practically came running. "Yes, ma'am?"

"Champagne. The good stuff in the back cooler. And seven glasses. Real champagne flutes. None of them plastic ones."

"Right away."

Then five pairs of eyes zipped to Riss.

"Do *you* use them dating apps?" Miz Maybelle asked.

Ike murmured, "Ironic, isn't it, that they're askin' for dating advice from the woman who doesn't date? This oughta be fun. Your advice oughta be real helpful."

She kicked him under the table.

"Well, that was a dumb question." Pearl snorted. "Just look at her, Maybelle."

Riss froze.

Just look at her.

. . . she's a red-haired freak.

. . . she's a tomboy.

. . . she's a dyke.

. . . she's a two-bagger.

. . . she's a fatty.

. . . she's butt-ugly.

Her stomach churned with memories of those words flung out like poisoned arrows. Words that had hit the bull's-eye and burrowed in, annihilating any chance of building self-confidence in her younger years. Words that retained power over her today.

"A girl with rockin' hair like that? And with that kinda cleavage and curves bustin' outta the seams of her dress? And the don't-take-crap-from-anyone attitude? Lord, I'll bet she has her pick of men, don't cha, sweetheart?"

She was so floored she couldn't speak.

Shoot, she might actually bawl again.

"They got you down pat, don't they?"

Automatically she turned to glare at Ike, but she realized he wasn't being sarcastic.

That was freaky. And a little unnerving. Just like earlier when Ike had said she looked pretty. He seemed as shocked that he'd said it as she'd been to hear it.

Didn't mean she hadn't liked the heated look of male appreciation in his eyes, though.

She sent Pearl a smile. "Thanks for that. But the truth is, I don't really . . . date. I'm more the 'hump and dump' type."

Silence.

As usual she'd taken it a step too far.

Tilda leaned over and whispered, "You done it now."

"What? Offended them?"

"Heck no. Now they're gonna want all of your humping secrets. And they ain't above plying you with money and booze to get us some action."

The champagne arrived.

Vivien raised her glass for a toast. "Here's to our future. May we all swipe right at least once."

"Even if he dresses left," Pearl added with a snicker.

Ike choked on his drink.

She sipped her champagne. Damn. They were keeping the good stuff for themselves.

"So hit us with your best nondating dating advice," Miz Maybelle said to Riss.

"There's an app called Bumble. It'd be a good fit for all of you."

"Why? Is it for old folks who are bumbling around with this computer dating junk?" Garnet asked.

"It's an app where women make the first move, first contact, whatever you want to call it."

"Ike, you wanna jump in and share your experience?" Vivien said.

"That's easy. I don't have any experience. I'm more old-school. If a woman catches my eye, I approach her right then. You might say . . . I *swipe* her off her feet."

"That's boring," Miz Maybelle chided. Then her gaze turned shrewd. "Unless you avoid apps because you're technologically challenged?"

"What? No. I know how to use them . . . I mean, I don't *have* to use them, but I could if I wanted to." His knee nudged Riss's under the table in a plea for help.

Rescue him or let him flounder?

He's been complimentary to you tonight. You owe him.

"I've seen Palmer the Charmer in action, ladies. Trust me. Within fifteen minutes this smooth-talking hottie with more charms than Pandora has lined up his options and backups to his options."

"Does that make you jealous?"

Why would Tilda ask that? Weird. "Jealous that Ike's been blessed with that type of sexual magnetism? Yes. Some of us have to work harder for it. So, I'll admit . . . I've used Tinder when I'm on the road."

"Does it really work?"

Riss nodded at Tilda. "It does for me, since I'm only looking for a night or afternoon or morning of hot sex."

"And is that the real reason that you don't date?" Vivien asked.

What the hell? "Excuse me?"

Then Miz Maybelle jumped in. "Or maybe you're telling everyone you don't date because you're already involved with a guy and you're keeping it a secret."

"I . . . have no idea what you're talkin' about."

"A guy everyone thinks you despise," Vivien added.

"The same guy feigns that he can't stand you either. It's all an act, isn't it?"

How much had these ladies been drinking? Because they weren't making any sense.

Pearl gestured between them. "We wanna know what the devil is goin' on with the two of you. So spill it, sister."

"The two of us?" she repeated. "As in . . . me and Ike?"

"Yes, you and Ike. Listen, girlie. We got eyes. We see the sparks fly between you. Heck, I saw the two of you yelling at each other in the parking lot of the Prickly Cactus last summer and it sure as shootin' looked like a lovers' quarrel."

Riss and Ike exchanged a startled look.

Then Ike said smoothly, "Why was a classy lady such as yourself hanging out in a dangerous dump like that?"

"Don't you never mind," Pearl said prissily. "We all got our little secrets. This is about you two."

"We're snoopy old broads," Garnet confided, as if that was a secret. "We wanna know if you two are nasty to each other because you're *doin'* the nasty."

"We're not *that* nasty to each other!" Riss protested.

Every single one of those women laughed.

Ike shrugged. "You have called me some nasty names in the past, sweetheart."

Jerk. Next time she'd let him flounder. She started to say he'd done the same to her, but dammit . . . that just proved the point.

Vivien delicately drummed her fingers on her champagne glass. "I consider myself hip to the language of today, but can you explain the term 'douche canoe'? You yelled it at Ike in the Buckeye parking lot."

"And define 'twatwaffle' while you're at it," Tilda inserted. "I'd never heard it before you used it, but I'm pretty sure it has nothing to do with breakfast food."

"Lilies." Pearl tapped the center of the table. "We're getting off track."

"So give up the goodies," Garnet said, rubbing her hands together. "Because I've got a thousand bucks riding on this bet."

"The one I told you we needed you to settle," Tilda reminded Ike when he looked confused.

"Wait." Ike still seemed confused. "The bet *wasn't* on whether certain dating apps guaranteed sex?"

"Nope," Tilda said gleefully.

"Well, sonny, we really *were* curious about that and we wanted the truth from the horse's mouth, so to speak," Miz Maybelle said.

"I hear a 'but' in there, so someone start talkin'," Ike said.

"I got you both over here under false pretenses," Tilda blurted out. "Sorry."

"Dadgummit, Tilda. You're always the first one to crack!"

"But I did it exactly like I was told to and they're both here, aren't they? I don't think *you* could've done any better."

Riss snapped her fingers. "Enough! Out with the truth about this bet."

Silence.

Their expressions were part guilt, part mutiny.

Then Ike drawled, "You'll find I'm not as patient as Tobin. Or as nice."

"Ike. That is not helping," Riss said.

"Like 'out with the truth' is getting results?"

"You dragged me into this, Palmer!"

"See! They're acting exactly like Jade and Tobin, hating on each other. Told ya they're a couple," Garnet crowed, lifting her hands above her head in victory. "Pay up, suckers."

"That's what you're betting on?" Ike demanded. "Whether me'n Riss are a couple?"

"Yes. But we've all got theories on why you are or aren't together, and some of 'em are real doozies." She rubbed her hands together. "And you will listen as we share them."

Riss muttered, "Kill me now."

"So you heard Garnet's theory," Vivien said. "Who's up now?"

"Me." Pearl wore a smug look. "My theory is the fightin' between you two is real . . . but there's a whole lotta hot hate sex goin' on afterward."

Ike started to sputter, but Vivien cut him off. "You'll get your turn to confirm or deny after you've heard all the theories." She nodded at Miz Maybelle. "We're next."

"Me'n Viv have the same theory. After one night of bed-frame-breaking sex, Ike fell hard for Riss. But she's a *playa*, who'll never settle down. Now he has to pretend to hate her so she won't guess the truth that she broke his heart."

"Poor baby," Riss whispered to Ike. "Sorry I stomped on your heart. I was aiming for your nuts."

"For the love of god, woman, you are gonna pay for that."

"Ssh," Vivien said to Ike. "You'll get your turn. Tilda, honey?"

"I'm a romantic. I believe you two like to play games. Me'n my husband used to spice things up with role-playing. I'd dress up as Little Red Riding Hood and he'd be the Big Bad Wolf. My favorite was the swash-buckling pirate and he was my virgin captive."

"We've heard about your dirty fairy-tale games a million times, Tilda," Miz Maybelle said crossly. "This is about them."

The ladies argued among themselves and Ike moved closer to murmur, "This is bizarre, right? It's not just me?"

"It's beyond bizarre, so it's not just you."

"So which theory is right?" Pearl demanded. "The stakes are high, people. You've been too quiet, Ike, so spill it, mister."

"All of them were downright fascinating theories, weren't they, sweet cheeks?" He flashed Riss a panty-dropping smile. "I'll admit that Larissa has the part of a foul-mouthed trucker down pat. But it's not role-playing for her; it's who she is."

"What about you? What role do you play?" Tilda asked.

"Maybe I'm the charmingly roguish cowboy who de-lights in shutting her up with a hungry kiss. Or maybe it's wishful thinking that I could be the guy who tames her wildness . . . without usin' a rope, although that's always fun." He paused and met their gazes one at a time. "But didn't you just remind me that we've all got our little secrets? So what makes you think we'd tell you the truth about ours?"

The Mud Lilies were speechless for a good fifteen seconds.

And Riss was completely impressed. He'd told them nothing about their relationship, but damn if he hadn't gotten her thinking about all the fun ways he might try that taming-with-a-rope thing.

Then, as one, the ladies looked to her for confirmation or denial.

Riss shrugged. "It's weird that you're betting on what is or isn't goin' on with us. Don't you all have better things to do with your time?"

"Of course we do. This 'are they or aren't they' game wasn't our idea," Vivien protested.

Ike lifted his hand. "Hold up. Was this a bet? Or a game?"

"It's a game with betting. Like *Wheel of Fortune*," Tilda said.

"Not that one," Miz Maybelle argued. "It's like poker. Plunk your money down and figure out who's bluffing."

"Wrong!" Pearl said. "It's like Clue, where you gotta strategize to come up with a theory. Where I say I heard Riss and Ike fighting in the library, but Vivien says she saw them kissing in the kitchen. You figure out who's lying."

"You're all lying," Ike said.

All eyes moved to him.

"Whose idea was it to make us play a game, or settle a bet, or whatever this is?"

Five women blinked at him with manufactured innocence.

So Riss focused on the one who looked ready to bolt. "Tilda?"

"It was Jade and Tobin!"

"Dadgummit, Tilda! You're as easy to crack as a pistachio," Garnet complained. "We weren't supposed to tell them. We were just supposed to distract them."

Ike scanned the reception area and glanced at his watch. "Wanna take bets on what the bride and groom have been doin' while we've been sitting here?"

Those bastards. Sneaking off to play another round of hide the sausage.

Riss rested her forehead on Ike's shoulder, not caring if it looked lovey-dovey. "Low five, best man. We failed in our wedding party duties."

"Aw, now, don't be too hard on yourselves," Tilda said. "It's their wedding night. They just wanted some time alone."

Some time. Hah. Riss doubted the Lilies knew that she and Ike had stopped the horny couple from sneaking off three other times during the reception.

"Gotta hand it to you ladies. Helluva distraction." Ike chuckled. "I still ain't sure exactly what we were talkin' about with all the conversation switcheroos."

Pearl looked smug. "Bait and switch. It's all about strategy so they could steal away for a moment to become one with the person they've pledged their life to."

"That pull is so strong." Vivien wore a bittersweet smile. "If we had it to do all over again, we'd say to hell with the reception and sneak off like them too."

The ladies all nodded.

It broke Riss's heart to see how well they all understood love and loss.

Ike reached for her hand under the table and squeezed.

Sometimes he could be so sweet. She squeezed back and sent him a soft smile.

"Larissa?"

Riss turned to face Jade's mother.

"Jade sent me to find you."

"Duty calls, ladies."

Ike stood before Riss did and offered his hand to help her up. She kept a hold of him until they were out of sight. Let the Mud Lilies gossip about that.

An hour later, after the bride and groom were off on their honeymoon, Riss and Ike were watching the DJ pack his equipment and the guests retrieve their coats.

Riss heaved a sigh. "I'm whupped. Bein' the maid of honor was stressful."

"It's certainly been an entertaining night," Ike said.

"Coulda been better."

"How so?"

"It doesn't really feel like a Wyoming wedding unless at least one fistfight breaks out."

"Just say the word, sweet cheeks, and I'll track Ryland down and punch him in the face for you."

"Aw, lookit you, Palmer. Showing your chivalrous side." She cocked her head. "Or are you just itchin' for a fight because it's a Saturday night and you're a cowboy?"

"I'm thinkin' a concussion might erase the mental image of what profile pics the Mud Lilies intend to post on Tinder."

"And Bumble."

"You certainly went the extra mile for them." He paused. "Why?"

"Even though they were distracting us, they wanted

advice or they wouldn't have asked. Besides . . . I feel for them. Imagine outliving your husband after being married for so long. Sounds like they were used to getting it regular, and then *wham*! They ain't getting any at all and they miss it. Maybe it's unusual that they're not looking for companionship—they've already got that with each other. It takes guts to try something new to reignite their sexuality. A need for intimacy is a human thing, not an age thing. I hope I still crave that lovin', touchin', squeezin' when I'm past what society considers my prime."

Ike was quiet for a beat before he said, "You never fail to surprise me."

Riss didn't break the moment by asking if that was a good or a bad thing. Instead, she said, "And with that . . . I best be getting home. I have a drop-off tomorrow."

"You okay to drive?"

"Yep." She pushed her chair back. "Been an hour since that glass of bubbly." She paused and debated bringing up the subject they'd mutually avoided.

Those eerily beautiful blue eyes locked on to hers. "What?"

"Truth time: I'm all for extending this truce."

Ike's back straightened and his face turned stony. "Meaning?"

"Meaning, we need to seriously talk about my future runs with Jackson Stock Contracting. Last year didn't shape up how I expected it—and we didn't discuss it. So I'm not sure if I somehow didn't measure up to JSC standards. Now we've proved that we can be civil to each other, so I'd like to know JSC's plans for this year."

He granted her that insincere salesman's smile. "I promise I'll e-mail you a preliminary schedule next week."

Sure you will.

"And just so you know . . ." He seemed unsure whether to continue before he did. "I've had a blast doin' all this wedding party stuff with you."

"Really? I thought it sucked."

His eyebrows shot up. "You did?"

"Nah. Just razzing ya. It's been fun in a way I never thought it'd be."

Ike unfolded that long lean body out of the chair, then stood close enough to cast her in shadow.

"What now?"

"Gimme a damn hug."

Her heart pounded and that made no sense. "Why?"

"Because I suffered through your blow job philosophy, deflected rumors of our secret sexcapades, helped offer senior citizens hookup advice and interrupted our buddies consummating their marriage . . . all in the past four hours. I'm feelin' vulnerable and I need a damn hug."

"Whatever will people think?"

"Probably that we're both hammered."

Riss laughed. "Come here, baby, and let me make it all better."

Ike wrapped her in his arms.

Oh yeah, the man gave great hugs. And he smelled amazing too. So maybe she held on a little longer than was polite.

But Ike wasn't inclined to let her go either.

Then his breath teased the top of her ear. "Bet this'll get tongues wagging all over town."

"Kneeing you in the groin would stop the gossipmongers."

"Always with the violence." He kissed her right cheek, then her left. "You'll hear from me soon."

Chapter Four

Two weeks later . . .

Ike and Tobin were sitting in Tobin's living room, watching the Avalanche getting their asses handed to them, when an old-fashioned ringtone echoed from the kitchen.

"I got it!" Jade raced out of the music room and past them.

"I'm surprised you still have a landline," Ike said. "Didn't Garnet take her phone number with her when she moved?"

"Yep." Tobin snorted. "But Miz New York City decided we needed a house phone because she loved the retro look of Garnet's old phone. But I swear she only uses it to call her cell, since she loses it at least three times a day."

Ike laughed.

Then the Canadiens scored on a power play and they tuned back in to the game.

So when Jade returned and stood directly in front of the TV, visibly shaken, Tobin hit pause. "Jade? What's wrong?"

"When was the last time you talked to Riss?" she asked Ike.

"Talked to? At the wedding. We e-mailed back and forth early last week." He paused. "Please tell me she didn't just call you to bitch about the fact I haven't responded to her last e-mail yet."

She shook her head. "That wasn't Riss."

"Then who called?" Tobin asked.

"Riss's oldest brother, Lonnie."

"What'd he want?"

"He's probably askin' which loser the wild child holed up with last night," Ike joked.

Jade snapped, "Lonnie knows exactly where Riss is. She's at his house recovering."

All the blood drained from Ike's face. "Recovering? From what?"

"An accident."

"A car accident?"

"No, the accident happened at her house."

"Is she okay?"

"No. She broke her right arm. Like, in three places."

"Holy shit. This happened today?"

"Lonnie said it's been five days. Three of those days she spent in the hospital in Casper."

"We're just hearing about it *now*? Did she break her damn fingers, so she couldn't dial a phone?"

"Yes. Her hand is in a splint too."

Shit. What the hell had she been doing? He scowled. "She should've called me."

"Why would she call you? You and Riss aren't friends."

Good point. He and Riss didn't hang out together unless they were with mutual friends.

"Lonnie knew we were on our honeymoon," Jade continued. "Today was the first day he tried to get in touch with me."

"Did Lonnie say why she isn't recovering at her place?" Tobin asked.

"Because the pipes in her trailer are frozen—that's the cause of the accident. She was under the trailer trying to fix—thaw—them or whatever."

"Of course she was," Ike said hotly. "Damn woman has to do everything herself, regardless of how dangerous it is."

Jade set her hand on his arm. "I hear you, Ike. Her I-don't-need-help attitude drives me crazy too. But getting mad at her, berating her? That is not what she needs right now. She needs sympathy and understanding. I remember when my friend broke her arm in high school she couldn't do anything while the bones and ligaments were mending. Immobilization the first two weeks is crucial to recovery. That's why Riss is staying at her brothers' place."

"So they haven't fixed the issues with her trailer?" Ike couldn't imagine just saying "oh well" and forcing his injured sister to deal with a major problem.

Jade shook her head. "That's the Thorpe brothers' way of keeping Riss where they can watch her—by refusing to make her trailer habitable."

"Lonnie *told* you that's how they're handling it?"

"None of them trust her to stay by herself because she'll ignore all doctor's orders."

Ike whistled. "Makes sense, but man . . . that is harsh."

"And unfair." Jade turned to Tobin. "You've heard Riss refer to her brothers' place as the Triple L Whorehouse and Gaming Emporium. I've met her brothers and I know that moniker fits. Riss claims Lonnie used to run gambling tables in the house when they were short on funds. Her brooding middle brother, Lloyd, always has a harem of women hanging around trying to fix him. And Louie is the life of the party; he'd have the house packed to the rafters with people every night. The kicker is all three of the Thorpe brothers are ridiculously good-looking and women flock to them. So how is she supposed to rest and recover amidst all that? She can't. It'll be pointless."

That didn't sound good.

"I can't imagine how much this sucks for her." Jade flopped onto the sofa. "She can't drive, she can't work and she can't go home. And Lonnie said she's completely out of contact with her friends because she doesn't want pity." Her chin wobbled. "I hate this for her. And yet I'm mad that she believes no one will step up and help her."

"No tears, tiger." Tobin pulled Jade into his lap. "We'll step up. Riss can recover here for as long as she needs a place to stay."

"You'd do that for her?" she said softly.

"Of course."

Ike knew Tobin wasn't doing it for Riss; he was doing it for Jade.

"Call Lonnie back," Tobin continued. "Tell him we'll have a place set up for Riss tomorrow."

"Thank you. You're the best."

Tobin's gaze caught Ike's. With Jade's face nestled against Tobin's chest, only Ike could see the conflict in his eyes. Although Tobin and Jade had lived together before their marriage, they just returned from their honeymoon and deserved this time as newlyweds.

Given what Ike knew of Riss's brothers, even Miss I Hate Being Dependent on Anyone would take Jade's offer.

But Riss would run roughshod over Tobin and Jade. She wouldn't mean to, but Tobin and Jade were too damn nice and would let her become the houseguest from hell.

He, however, would not hesitate to make her toe the line. He'd raised three younger sisters and was wise to female manipulation, girl drama and sheer orneriness. Plus, he'd dealt with his sister Lea when she'd broken her arm, so he understood the limitations, even if it sounded as if Riss's situation was more serious.

Besides, it wasn't like his job consumed much time. Having Riss around would give him a chance to pick her brain about a few things.

So hell yeah. He could step in and save the day.

Before Ike considered all the logistics, he said, "I can't let you guys do that, although I'm sure Riss would jump at the chance to crash here. But you both have jobs, and this place is pretty far out of town if something were to happen when you weren't around. Riss needs someone to keep an eye on her full-time, so she should move in with me until she's back on her feet."

Both Tobin and Jade gaped at him as if he'd lost his mind.

Maybe he had.

"Ike. Buddy," Tobin said slowly. "Need I remind you—"

"That Riss and I are usually at odds with each other about something?" he supplied.

"At *odds* with each other about something?" Jade repeated. "More like you're at odds with each other about *everything* and trying to verbally annihilate each other before weapons are chosen for physical combat."

"Hey, it's not that bad."

"Uh, yeah . . . it is," Tobin said. "So while I appreciate you offering to step in, unless Riss is so drugged up that she ain't aware of what's goin' on, we all know she'll say *hell no*."

"More like she'll *scream* hell no, before laughing hysterically at you for even suggesting that option," Jade added.

"Thanks for your input, smart-asses, but Riss and I managed to be civil—hell, even nice to each other—for sixty-two days straight during our truce."

Tobin's eyes narrowed. "What truce?"

He'd blown that secret. Well, the cat was out of the bag now. "Riss and I agreed to a truce during the prewedding stuff since we'd be forced to spend more time together. Our . . . unique style of communicating sets people on edge and we didn't wanna stress you two out."

"Why is this the first we've heard of it?" Jade demanded.

"Because . . ." He laughed self-consciously. "To be honest, we weren't even sure if we could pull it off. But we did."

Then Tobin and Jade looked at each other and started laughing.

"What?"

"That explains it." Tobin patted Jade's ass. "And that means you lost the bet, little wifey of mine, so get ready to pay up."

Now Ike was confused. "What am I missing?"

"During those months before the wedding we noticed you and Riss were being obnoxiously nice to each other," Jade said. "I suspected you guys were secretly sleeping together."

"I disagreed," Tobin said. "I figured you two had a rip-roaring fight and were killin' each other with kindness to see who would crack first."

"Jesus. Really? You bet on that?" Then it clicked. "So that insane hour we spent with the Mud Lilies at your wedding reception . . . ?"

"Was them gathering intel for us." Jade giggled. "Man, they were all over that idea of getting you and Riss to confess something juicy—not that either of you did."

"And it kept them ladies occupied and out of the booze for a while," Tobin added.

Well, well. Boy Scout and Sweetie Pie weren't averse to manipulation. Maybe he should let them deal with Riss. Then again, Riss was on a whole other level. And he wanted to see if he was up to the challenge.

"I give you props for that. But I'm giving myself even bigger props for surviving sixty-two days of forced bliss with Riss." He smirked. "So I'm positive that Riss and I could make it another week or two."

"I don't know, Ike. It'll be different if you're in the

same space twenty-four/seven. You can't escape each other."

"Riss is bound to be cranky as hell bein' all busted up," Tobin added.

"And she has dependency issues—as in, she hates being beholden to anyone. For anything. So no offense, but there's no way she'll accept your help, Ike."

Tobin nodded.

"I'm gonna prove you both wrong. By the end of the workday tomorrow, Riss will be staying with me. Voluntarily."

"How do you hope to accomplish that?"

Good question. "With my irresistible natural charm."

"So you plan on bluffing your way through it?" Tobin asked. "Or bullshitting?"

"I reckon I'll have to use both. And if that don't work, I'll fall back on my tried-and-true sales tactic."

"Which is what?" Jade asked.

Lying my ass off—or, in Riss's terminology . . . creating an alternate reality. He winked at her. "Now, darlin', that's a trade secret."

Tobin muttered, "Twenty bucks says he's screwed."

"You're on."

Ike grabbed the remote. "Now that I've decided to do my good deed for the year, can we finish watching the game?"

∞

Early that evening Ike called Hugh Pritchett, his partner in Jackson Stock Contracting. "What's up, California Dreamin'?"

"Still not funny after the hundredth time you've said it, Ike."

"Dang, partner, that hurts. And speaking of hurting, Riss broke her arm."

"What? How'd that happen?"

"Not sure. Something to do with fixin' pipes under her trailer." Ike had zero mechanical skill and even less aptitude for explanations.

"So what's that mean for us?"

After Ike said his piece, he waited for Hugh to organize his thoughts. The man was a deliberate thinker. It used to drive Ike crazy, but he'd gotten used to it over the years.

Finally Hugh sighed. "I hate to say this, but at least Riss's accident happened when there's just one event scheduled in Gillette."

"I was hopin' to hear you'd picked up a couple down your way."

"I've been workin' on it. Nothin' new to report."

"It's hard not to get discouraged with the 'wait and see' attitude, isn't it?"

"Yeah. Some've talked a good game about hiring us, then it falls back on an unseen committee that doesn't want to outright fire a local stock provider."

"I'm startin' to wonder if Renner was right in scaling back this side of the business and if we were fools to take it on," Ike said.

"We knew expanding Jackson Stock Contracting would take time and patience, especially since we're cold-calling venues that haven't heard of us. We just have to push the fact we've got two generations of rank bulls in our rough stock arsenal."

"I hear you, Hugh. It's just frustrating as hell. It's been a year and a half and we're still nowhere. You're still in California, which I thought would be temporary."

"It gets more permanent every day."

That tipped off his radar. "Something else goin' on you wanna tell me about, partner?"

"It's fuckin' expensive to live in California."

"And? That's not news," Ike said.

"And we agreed to draw a minimal salary until we had some money coming in."

Ike hadn't been drawing a salary at all—a fact he'd managed to keep from his partner. The bank account couldn't afford to pay them both, so Ike had been living off his personal savings, which had dwindled down to nothing.

"So while the building maintenance job I'm working in our apartment complex lowers our rent and pays me a decent wage, I'm gonna need more money." A pause, then Hugh blurted out, "Harlow is pregnant."

Ike's stomach dropped.

"I know what you're thinkin', Ike."

"You do? You've become one of them psychic Californians reading my aura and my energy along with my mind?"

"Piss off. I'm serious. You're worried I'm gonna pull a Renner."

"With all due respect, Hugh, you *don't* know how things will play out once you and Harlow are holding the precious kid in a few months. Heck, you don't even know if you can handle leaving Harlow alone while she's pregnant."

"So you're sayin' that now ain't the time to talk about it."

Seemed they never talked about anything real. They spoke in circles and in terms of potentials.

But a baby was as real as it gets.

Ike honestly didn't know what to say. He cleared his throat. "I guess congratulations are in order."

Hugh snorted. "While on one hand we're thrilled, on the other . . . this wasn't something we planned, so we're both in shock."

"Harlow has told Tierney and Renner?"

"Yeah. Tierney wants Harlow back in Muddy Gap after the semester ends, so she can keep an eye on her during the pregnancy, since their mom . . . had preterm and postterm problems." He blew out a breath. "I can't even wrap my head around the life-and-death issues my woman might be facing because I knocked her up. That's scary shit, man."

"Obviously Harlow's health is the most important thing."

"And?" Hugh prompted.

"And I'd do an Irish jig complete with heel kicks if the two of you moved back here. It'd be easier to run the business from one location." That sounded offhand and supportive and not panicked as all get-out.

"I know that, Ike. For now, we're in a holding pattern. Harlow just started the spring semester and that puts us at the second week in May before she's finished. If all goes well, she'll be in the last trimester of her pregnancy. Sounds as weird as hell saying that."

"Better get used to it."

"So back to Riss . . . you'll keep me and Harlow updated on how she's doin'?"

"Sure, no problem."

"You sure you two ain't gonna kill each other bein' in the same place for more than five minutes?" Hugh asked.

"Nope. But it'll be a damn sight harder for her to take a swing at me with a broken arm."

"Don't put it past her if you piss her off . . . which you've been known to do on occasion."

The warnings about their knockdown, drag-out fisticuffs were wearing on him. "I have no idea what you're getting at."

"I'm getting at that I don't know if you'd come back from bein' smacked upside the head with a cast since the girl has a wicked uppercut."

"I'll handle her like I handle everything else in my life."

"And how's that?"

"Dodge and weave, my friend, dodge and weave."

Chapter Five

❧

Squeak. *Squeak. Squeak. Squeak. Bang.*

Groaning, Riss squinted at the clock on the coffee table.

Two a.m.

Seriously? It was the middle of the damn night. They were supposed to be sleeping, not fucking.

Again.

It was the second time she'd been jarred out of a deep sleep by the horny duo.

Maybe she needed a higher dose of meds.

No, you need to get the hell out of here.

Yeah, well, that was easily wished for and harder to accomplish.

The squeaks got progressively faster and louder, as did the voices coming from her brother Louie's bedroom.

"Yes, yes, yes! Drill me harder."

For fuck's sake.

Riss couldn't cover her head with a pillow fast enough before Louie's bedmate began moaning like a porn star, which was only marginally better than hearing her brother grunting.

When it finally—*finally*—went quiet, Riss lamented the fact she couldn't clap on account of her mangled hand.

Lucky thing her mouth worked just fine.

She yelled, "I give you fuckers a six out of ten for sexual stamina and a seven out of ten for wakin' up the household with your jungle howls." Then Riss started laughing even though she doubted her brother and what's-her-face would find it funny.

Sure enough, twenty seconds later, a bedroom door banged open. Stomping footsteps echoed down the hallway.

The lights came on, practically blinding her.

"You think it's funny to horn in on a private moment?" Louie demanded.

"Well, stud, it *wasn't* a private moment, that's the point," Riss shot back.

"Then stop bein' a little pervert and don't listen!"

"I'm not a pervert, asshole. I'm sleeping on the couch right outside your bedroom! It's after two o'clock in the morning, Lou, and this is the second time your sexcapades have woken me up tonight."

"Oh, boo-fucking-hoo. Deal with it, sis."

Another bedroom door opened.

"This *is* how I'm dealing with it since you all insisted I stay here when I'm supposed to be recovering. So the least you could do is fuck quietly."

"I agree. It's bullshit we're up because of your *bow-chicka-wow-wow* times."

Riss looked at her brother Lloyd . . . and immediately wished she hadn't. At least Lou had put on boxers; Lloyd was buck-ass naked.

"For fuck's sake," Lou hissed, "put some damn pants on."

"Why? I ain't got nothin' to hide."

"That's beside the point. I don't want my hookup wandering out here lookin' for me, only to see your dick."

"Afraid of the comparison?"

"Fuck you, Lloyd. It ain't the size of the tool that matters, it's how well you use it."

"Then why don't you invite her out, Lou, so she can compare tool sizes."

"Great idea, since we're all up anyway," Riss said with false enthusiasm. "Here's some advice: with the way your hookup was screeching, she definitely needs more lube."

Lloyd laughed.

Lou did not.

Especially not when his lady friend—fully dressed and sporting some seriously awesome sex hair—stormed into the living room.

"A *hookup*?" she emphasized snottily. "That's all I am to you?"

"Baby, you know that's not true."

Baby. The term her man-whore brother used when he couldn't remember his hookup's first name.

"I thought you were different."

Lou moved closer to her—mainly to block her view of Lloyd. "Baby, I *am* different."

"Prove it."

He murmured something about proving it for a third time, but she wasn't falling for his sweet bullshit.

"No, prove it by saying my name," she retorted prissily.

Oh man. Seeing Lou backed into a corner was totally worth lost sleep.

"Uh, it's . . . Carly, right?"

"*Carly?* You think my name is *Carly*?"

Louie kept sinking deeper. "No, baby, I was kidding. Of course I know your name."

"Then what is it?" she shouted.

"Ah . . . Charley?"

"No!"

"Marley?" he offered. "No, wait. It's Harley."

"Omigod! You really don't have a clue."

Lou's puppy dog eyes were wasted on her; she'd already booked it to the coatrack by the front door.

"I'm such an idiot. I thought we had a connection."

"You did connect at least two times from what I heard," Riss interjected, "so maybe—"

"Maybe you should stay the hell out of this!" Louie snapped at Riss.

Carly/Charley/Marley/Harley glared as she donned her outerwear. "Don't ever contact me again, Louie Thorpe."

"Not a problem, since he doesn't remember your name, *baby*."

"Go to hell. All of you," the woman said and slammed the front door behind her.

"You just had to go there, didn't you?" Lloyd said to Riss, shaking his head.

"I'd go *anywhere* else if I could, but I can't."

"Just great, Riss. I can't fucking believe you did that!"

"How is this *my* fault?"

Before Louie started in on her, Lloyd jumped in. "Don't get pissy at Riss because you woke up the whole house in the middle of the damn night."

Lou and Lloyd argued until a shrill whistle sliced through the air—the Thorpe family warning signal that shit was about to get real.

Lonnie, Riss's oldest brother, wandered into the living room, his hands signaling time out. "Enough. You and you"—he pointed to Louie and Lloyd—"go back to your rooms. Finish this fight in the morning." When they both hesitated, he said, "Go," in that sharp tone no one argued with.

Bedroom door number one slammed.

Riss fought a snicker. Louie had been way more dramatic growing up than she had.

Lloyd's door closed with a soft click.

Now she and her big, bad oldest bro were alone.

Her hope that Lonnie would return to bed without lecturing her . . . yeah, she should've known better.

He studied her with that I'm-the-law, spill-your-guts-*now* half squint.

And yep, she cracked. She always did. "What?"

"I know exactly what you've been doin', sis."

She squirmed to resituate her body on the lumpy couch. But her feet were tangled in the afghan and her pillow had somehow lodged itself under her ass.

Lonnie pulled the afghan free. Then he tugged at the pillow and replaced it at the end of the couch. Being mindful of her cast, he gently tucked the afghan around her.

Say thank you. Don't tag it with a defensive phrase like you're capable of taking care of yourself because you're obviously not. "Thanks."

"You're welcome. And reverting to bein' our bratty little sister ain't gonna work."

She opened her mouth to deny it, but Lonnie just shook his head.

"You've been baiting Louie. You've tried that with Lloyd and me, attempting to piss us off so we'll send you packing. That ain't happening, Riss, because you've got no place else to go."

Way to point that out, jerkface.

Just because she didn't want to hear Lonnie's tough-love declaration didn't make it any less true. But he could just fuck the fuck off because her eyesight was getting blurry.

"Hey, now. Don't cry."

"As if." She sniffed. "I'm just frustrated and miserable and exhausted because I can't sleep here. Anytime I move my arm it starts throbbing."

"Want me to contact the doc about upping your pain meds?"

She bristled. If she needed stronger meds, *she'd* call the doctor. She hated when he treated her like a twelve-year-old. "No, I hate bein' out of it. I hate bein' here. I know you were obligated to take me in because we're family, but this is a jail sentence."

"Sucks for you, but you're here for the duration, or until the doc tells me at your next appointment that you'll be okay staying on your own."

Riss still couldn't believe her bad luck and the bizarre accident that had landed her in the hospital.

The pipes under her trailer had frozen. She'd gathered the necessary tools to start the thawing process—a process she was all too familiar with—and slipped on a patch of ice. In the act of falling on her ass, she attempted to right her balance and fell into the ladder leaning against the side of the house. The ladder bounced and knocked her down, directly onto her large metal toolbox. She heard the bones in her arm break as she face-planted into the snow.

The doctor figured she'd knocked herself out since she'd come to disoriented and cold. When she tried to get up, she couldn't move. That was when she noticed the ladder's grooved left foot was lodged beneath the trailer's metal skirting, pinning her down. Using her left arm, she attempted to jerk the ladder free. But she yanked too hard and the ladder skidded across the ice, catching her right hand between two rungs as the ladder unlatched and smashed into her already broken arm and the top of her head.

Evidently that pain knocked her out again.

Thankfully her mailman found her before she'd frozen to death. In the ambulance on the way to Casper, the paramedics called Lonnie, her emergency contact.

When the X-rays revealed severe damage to her arm and hand, the doctor referred her to an orthopedic specialist, who scheduled her for surgery the following day.

They kept her doped up while waiting for the surgical swelling to stabilize before the cast application. She awoke to see all three of her brothers in her hospital room, holding vigil. But as she found out a few hours later, they were worried about her reaction to her sole recovery option: living with them.

"You've already zoned out on me, so I'm done with the brotherly advice," Lonnie said, dragging her attention back to him. "I have to be up in a few hours."

Since the living room and kitchen were essentially one "great room"—aka her bedroom—she'd be up too.

Instead of shuffling back to his room, Lonnie paused.

"What now?"

"It's okay to clean yourself up tomorrow."

When Riss heard his door close, she let go of the tears she'd been holding back.

She needed a shower . . . except she couldn't shower with the cast on and she couldn't shower by herself anyway.

She needed clean clothes . . . but her brothers had yet to take her home and no way in hell was she sending them to paw through her dresser drawers.

She needed to wash her hair . . . but the gash on her head that had required stitches would be impossible to avoid when she used her left hand. In the shower. That she couldn't take.

In essence, she was a mess. Dirty hair, stuck taking a whore's bath and wearing her brother's old clothes. No wonder she hadn't told any of her friends what had happened.

The last thing she needed was anyone to see her like this.

That depressing thought was her last before she drifted off to sleep.

∞

The doorbell rang at nine a.m. the next morning.

Louie answered the door. "What the fuck are you doin' here?"

Riss immediately shot upright to see who it was and

winced in pain when she remembered she wasn't supposed to do that. She secretly hoped that Carly/Charley/Marley/Harley chick had shown up to rip Lou a new one.

But Ike Palmer stepped into view.

Ike?

Wow. This was some weird-ass dream.

Wasn't it?

"I didn't say you could come in, Palmer," Louie snapped.

"Yet here I am inside," Ike replied.

Whoa. Not a dream.

Ike sauntered over with the cowboy swagger that both irritated and fascinated her.

She brazenly took his measure. A bright blue wool cap covered his blond head, drawing attention to his vivid blue eyes, which were studying her with equal scrutiny. He wore a light tan leather and shearling coat that added bulk to his lean frame, accentuating his broad shoulders. Dark jeans and boots completed his outfit. The man could've stepped out of an advertisement for rugged western wear.

His stride stayed confident even if his plastered-on smile hinted at nervousness.

Ike "the Charmer" Palmer nervous? Get out. She had to be seeing things.

"How did you know I was here?"

"Aw, sweet cheeks, I missed you too." Then he was right in her face. "Seventy-eight days we've been together. And yes, I kept adding to the total even after that stupid postwedding fight when you demanded I give you some space. But finding out from Jade that you had a serious accident that resulted in surgery and a hospital stay? Five days after it happened? I'm so god-damned mad I can barely see straight. I may never let you out of my sight again, understand?"

No. She didn't understand. Not at all.

Ike read her confusion and put his mouth on her ear. "Play along."

"Why?"

"Because I'm bein' spontaneous and breaking you outta this jail."

"Ike—"

"You dared me to create an alternate reality the next time I got the chance, so I'm doin' it."

Riss fought the urge to argue. Or laugh.

But the look on Ike's face when he was nearly nose-to-nose with her? Those striking blue eyes weren't twinkling with amusement, but were seriously intense.

Seriously hot.

Seriously sexy.

Ike curled his hand around the side of her face and pressed his mouth to hers. At first just a tease, a brush of his pillowy soft lips across hers. Almost . . . chaste and achingly sweet. Then his tenderness vanished and he was kissing the breath out of her in a tongue-dueling, head-shifting, hungry, openmouthed kiss that sent her head spinning, her reason fleeing and kick-started her libido from idle to full-speed-ahead, pedal-to-the-metal lust.

She whimpered and arched closer, only to have him freeze mid-kiss.

Then, clearly shocked by the chemistry that had ignited between them, Ike retreated, abruptly changing the tenor of the kiss to sweet and flirty.

Holy fuck.

She couldn't believe Ike Palmer, her nemesis, could kiss like this. She never imagined his laid-back persona masked such extraordinary passion. Being charming was one thing, but that trait didn't necessarily translate into sexual potency. But the self-assured way his mouth took hers—owned hers—left no doubt in Riss's mind that the man would be a dominating force in bed.

He rested his forehead against hers, his fast breaths fanning across her damp lips. After whispering a reminder to play along, he backed off, and then, loud enough for Louie to hear, he said, "I'm sorry I wasn't here for you. But I'll make it up to you."

Riss blinked at him. Jesus. That life-changing liplock was Ike . . . acting? That soul-stealing kiss meant nothing to him?

"Been a while since my kisses gotcha so het up you can't even speak, baby," he teased.

Baby. That mean-nothing term of endearment men used was a dash of cold reality that allowed her to regain some semblance of normality and control. "Well, one incredibly hot kiss won't make me forget why I was pissed off at you in the first place, *baby*."

Louie stopped at the end of the couch, his gaze pinging between them.

When Riss saw Louie's expression of shock, she decided payback was in order for the sleep she'd lost due to his sexcapades. He'd look like a total dumb-ass to their brothers when he tried to convince them that she and Ike Palmer had been in a secret relationship all along . . . because that stupid kiss had nearly convinced her.

But no way would she let Ike Palmer one-up her in the alternate reality game. No. Freaking. Way.

"Sis, you wanna tell me what's goin' on?" Louie demanded.

Ike reached for her good hand and kissed her knuckles. "Just tell him the truth."

"Does that mean we're telling your sisters the truth about us too?" she cooed back.

"Sweet cheeks, I've wanted to shout it to the world since that first time you rolled out of my bed."

Lord. The Charmer was laying it on thick, but Louie was totally buying it when he gasped, "You two are a couple?"

Sucker.

Riss smiled coyly at Ike. "Maybe the fact we've kept it to ourselves is why it's working for us."

Pressing her hand against his cheek, Ike said, "Come home with me. I'll take good care of you."

"Promise?" she said on a breathy whisper.

He crossed her fingers over his heart and kissed them. "Promise."

Good thing she was immune to his sweet bullshit, because it'd be easy to buy into his act. "Then take me."

That startled Ike for a brief moment before he flashed that cocky grin and stood. "Where's your suitcase?"

"I don't have one."

"Fine. Got a garbage bag to put your stuff in?"

"My brothers didn't bring anything from my trailer, so there's no stuff."

His eyes narrowed. "You've got nothin' here?"

"Nothin'? She's got us," Louie said with a huff.

Ike scowled at Louie, then said gently to Riss, "Darlin', you don't have *any* clothes or toiletries?"

Riss blushed. "They bought me a new pack of underwear and a toothbrush when they filled my prescriptions at the drugstore. For clothes . . . I've been wearin' theirs."

The anger in Ike's eyes wasn't feigned. "How is that takin' care of you? Is one of them helping you shower?"

She shook her head. "I haven't showered since I left the hospital."

Ike walked to the coatrack and snagged her Carhartt. "Which ones are your boots?"

"The Hi-Tecs with the blue soles."

He brought her outerwear over and set it next to her.

Riss had the ridiculous urge to giggle when Ike pulled a Prince Charming, dropping to his knee so he could put her boots on.

"Where are all your meds and medical instructions?" he asked tersely.

"In that plastic bag on the table with the 'RX' on the outside."

Ike stood to grab it and Louie immediately confronted him.

"Hey, ass-wipe! What part of 'you ain't takin' her anywhere' is confusing to you?"

"What part of 'you suck as her caretaker and I'm getting her the hell out of here right now' is confusing to you?"

Nose-to-nose, Louie and Ike were the same height. They had similar attitudes, which meant there'd be a lot of pushing and shoving before one of them took the first swing.

Ike couldn't have timed her escape any better, showing up when he did. Lou would bitch the entire time she prepared to leave, but he *would* let her go. Lloyd and Lonnie would not. They'd gleefully take turns tossing Ike off the porch.

"She ain't getting what she needs to recover here. Christ, she's sleeping in the living room, wearing men's cast-off clothing, eating whatever crap you fix her"—he tipped his head toward a bag of Cool Ranch Doritos—"not to mention you three guys are completely unaware of a woman's . . . hygienic needs."

She winced out of pride, but Ike had a point.

"And you're an expert on a woman's 'needs' because of all the notches in your belt?" Lou said with a sneer.

"I'm an expert because I raised three younger sisters. I'm willing to help Riss in ways—the most basic human hygienic ways—that you as her brothers are obviously avoiding." He paused to let that sink in. "We done now?"

Lou threw up his hands. "Yeah, man. Fine. Whatever. But expect to be hearin' from Lonnie and Lloyd about this."

"Good. I got plenty to say to them too." He offered his hand to Riss. "Let's go, sweet cheeks. You're all mine now."

Chapter Six

❧

On the drive to Riss's trailer the dingy gray clouds reinforced the ugliness of January in Wyoming.

It matched Ike's dark and gloomy mood.

He felt sorry for Riss—not that he'd tell her that. No wonder she was a tomboy; her brothers treated her like another brother.

No wonder the Thorpe boys were still bachelors if they were that clueless about women.

You're still a bachelor, a little voice in his head prompted, which he ignored.

One of her brothers should've given up his room so Riss had a quiet, private place to recover. But no, instead they dumped her on the couch.

One of her brothers should've realized that Riss needed her own things, not just to wear but to give her a feeling of familiarity in a situation where she had zero control.

One of her brothers should've figured out a way to wrap her cast so she could shower. They should've also called their aunt Bernice, who owned Bernice's Beauty Barn in Muddy Gap, about pitching in.

At the very least, one of her brothers should've asked *Riss* what she needed.

It bothered him that the always-feisty Riss had just accepted what little they'd offered her.

Ike knew he'd done the right thing by intervening. Even if that spontaneous kiss—what the fuck had he been thinking?—blew his ever-loving mind.

"So, seriously. How did you find out I was stuck at Chez Thorpe? Jade called you? Or Tobin told you?"

"I was over at their place yesterday when Lonnie called."

"That fucker. I'd say I can't believe he went behind my back, but I know why he did."

"Why didn't you want anyone to know about the accident?"

Riss didn't answer.

"You scrambled your egg good if you believed your friends would judge you for havin' an accident, Riss."

"They can judge me for dragging them into my miserable world, which I tried to avoid. Injured, homeless, helpless and broke is not a good way to start the New Year." She stared out the window, huddled in the blanket wrapped around her since her coat hadn't covered the cast.

She looked so damn small and he hated that. This woman defined "larger than life."

He turned into her driveway and parked. Off to the right side of her trailer was a stand-alone metal carport.

Her rigs were lined up by size: a horse trailer, a box truck, a flatbed, a stepdeck, a semitrailer and a bull hauler.

Wait a second. Another vehicle was parked sideways behind the flatbed. He started to ask why she needed a dump truck, but she spoke first.

"Why?"

"Why what? Why am I helping you?" *Or why did I kiss you?*

She nodded.

"Because it sucked when my youngest sister broke her arm. She was such a brat. She couldn't do nothin'. Hell, the first week she couldn't even wipe her own ass."

When Riss didn't retort *no way are you ever wiping my ass*, Ike knew she wasn't herself.

"Plus, Jade worried you'd do more damage to yourself attempting to escape from your brothers."

Riss made a growling noise. "That's why you're helping me? Because of your experience playing Florence Nightingale to a bratty girl? How hard did Jade have to beg you to *volunteer* to take me in?"

"Careful, darlin', that bratty side of yours is showing." He ignored her harrumph. "I volunteered out of the goodness of my heart."

Her skeptical look didn't waver one whit.

"Fine. There is something else I could use your help with. A work thing."

"A work thing," she repeated.

"Look, I don't gotta tell you Jackson Stock Contracting is havin' some issues getting rolling. Everyone says you're great at figuring out unique solutions to various problems."

"*Everyone* says that? Like who?"

"Well, Jade says that. Anyway, all the JSC paperwork is at my house, so once you're feelin' up to it, I could use your help and advice."

The longer she stared at him the more he sweated out her response.

"What?" he said irritably.

"You wanna explain that kiss?"

Ike considered lying and just outright ignoring the question. But he opted for the truth. "I have no fucking idea. I was in the moment. And, darlin', I can see where it'd be easy to get carried away when playin' a part in an alternate reality. But you don't have to worry that it'll happen again."

"You're sure?"

Fuck no. "Yep. It'd be the ultimate dick move for me to take advantage of the situation when you're homeless, popping pain meds and relying on me . . . to wipe your ass." He smirked. "You can't even take a decent swing at me with a broken wing, so really, where's the challenge?"

That brought a wan smile. "I'm sorry for making you defend yourself for bein' nice to me, Ike."

"We seem to jump to the worst conclusion first when it comes to each other, don't we?"

"Yeah. But you were the last person I expected to waltz in this morning and give me a glimmer of hope."

He chuckled. "That's me, darlin', a stealthy bright beam of hope, shining over the rainbow of happiness, ridin' to the rescue on my sparkly unicorn when you least expect it."

"I'd punch you for that smart-ass comment . . . except . . ." She jerked her chin at her arm.

"See? You're already getting back to normal. You'll be yelling at me before you know it."

"How long you think you can stand havin' me around?"

"How about we give it two weeks? If it sucks, after that you can leave."

"I'll take it. Thank you."

"Now that that's settled, where are your house keys?"

"In my purse, in the house. I didn't see the need to drag a handbag with me when I was crawling under the goddamned trailer with a blowtorch." She paused. "Live and learn, right? But I'll be damned if I'll take my purse with me everywhere as my brothers have demanded."

"Your brothers gave you grief about that?"

"Of course they did."

"They were probably scared shitless, seein' Larissa the Invincible busted up." He gestured to her cast, which stretched from the knuckles on her right hand to the top of her biceps. "I wasn't expecting it to be that big."

"You forget I'm big boned."

He grinned at her off-the-cuff cheekiness. "So how are we getting in?"

"There's a spare key under the orange flowerpot. I'll show you." She reached for the door handle.

"Uh-uh. Stay put."

"You don't know where anything is in my house, Ike. It'll take twice as long to get what I need if you don't let me come inside with you."

"Fine. But you do nothin' besides point out the

things you'll need. Promise me, girl who swears she always keeps her promises."

Riss raised two fingers. "Scouts honor."

"I'll come around to your side and help you out."

She squirmed.

Ike let her.

"This is a test, isn't it?" she asked grumpily. "Whether I'll do what you ask without arguing."

He held up a sheaf of papers he'd picked up next to her meds. "I gotta trust that you'll follow doctor's orders at all times, Riss, whether I'm with you or you're alone at my house. The one smart thing your brothers did was keepin' you under a watchful eye at all times."

"All right."

"Second thing. You have to let me help you. Fightin' me is fightin' healing."

She let her head fall back into the headrest. "I really hate this."

He silently asked the universe to grant him more patience—no doubt he'd need it.

The front door to her trailer hadn't even been locked—just another thing that her brothers had neglected to check that pissed him off. Inside was almost as frigid as outside, so Ike didn't dawdle as he followed her down the dark hallway to the back of her trailer. In her bedroom, he filled two suitcases. One with clothes. The other with toiletries, the pillow from her bed, a fleece blanket . . . her vibrator.

He opened his mouth to ask if that was really necessary, but he snapped it shut, half-fearful of Riss taunting him that if she didn't have it, it'd be up to him to keep her sexually satisfied.

Riss took his silence as judgment. "I know you've seen a vibrator before. And I can go lefty with that one when I'm needing a little self-love."

"Jesus, Riss. TMI."

"Better grab my laptop bag. That has my e-reader, computer, log books and assorted cords." She smirked. "And extra batteries."

∞

During the drive to Ike's house, Riss retreated into total silence again.

After he parked in his driveway, she angled her head to peer at the two-story structure. "This is a lot of house for one guy."

"It's not the first time you've seen it," he reminded her.

"But it's the first time I'll be invited inside it," she retorted.

He tried not to feel guilty, telling himself they'd been frenemies, not friends.

"It looks new."

"It's not. I got a good deal when I built it about ten years ago."

"You've lived here by yourself that long?"

"After raising my sisters, I wanted my own place. I hired my buddy Holt Andrews, who'd just started his construction company, to build it."

"If you grew up in Rawlins, why did you build a home in Muddy Gap?"

Ike shrugged. "The lot was cheap. Holt had other jobs around here so it would've taken longer to finish if I'd chosen Rawlins. I liked the sense of community my buddies who lived here had. My new neighbors were happy to keep an eye on my place since I traveled out of town so much."

"You made the right choice. Great house, great location." She frowned. "That said . . . it's a little too close to Bernice's Beauty Barn for me."

"But Bernice is your aunt."

"Technically . . . yes. Her husband, Bob, and my dad were stepbrothers. Dad and Uncle Bob were pretty close, but Bernice wasn't the type of aunt who'd host family gatherings during the holidays or on birthdays. Her clients at the hair salon know her far better than I ever have. So I do my best to avoid her because she's Judgy McJudgerson with me."

"Well, sweet cheeks, you ain't got that option today."

Riss stared at him until he met her glare. "What did you do?"

"Set up an appointment for you with Bernice."

"Why in the hell would you do that?"

Ike's cheeks heated. "I thought she could give you some tips about washing your hair one-handed and other girl grooming stuff."

"But . . ." Her bottom lip quivered. Her eyes glistened with tears. "I thought *you'd* be washing my hair every night. And then you'd comb it in front of a crackling fire while we sipped wine and gazed longingly into each other's eyes while we listened to soft rock classics."

His stomach clenched, until he caught that devilish look in her eyes. "Woman, you are a menace. You almost had me worried there for a moment."

"The trembling lip was too much?"

Too much temptation. Since he'd kissed her just an

hour ago, he'd discovered a new fascination with her lips.

You promised no more kissing, so quit gazing dreamily at her mouth.

"Ike?"

He refocused on her eyes. "The tears were over the top. You're not the type of woman to pout if you're upset."

"More likely I'll start throwing shit." Her face sobered. "As far as Bernice . . . that was a thoughtful gesture, but I'm not up to facing her or her beauty shop cronies."

"That's why she's coming to my house instead of you goin' over there."

"She's making a house call? Gotta be a slow gossip day at the Beauty Barn."

"Or maybe, she's worried about you and will do whatever it takes to help you."

Riss rolled her eyes.

After Ike helped Riss into the house and removed her outerwear, he started guiding her toward the guest bedroom.

Her pale skin and the pinched set to her mouth indicated pain. She didn't make it past the couch.

For the first time, Ike wondered if Riss crashing here was a good idea. The only women he'd lived with for more than two days were his sisters. How was he supposed to act around her? Since after that kiss, he couldn't deny there was serious chemistry lurking below the surface, but his relationship with Riss wasn't intimate.

Then she said, "Could I get some water? I need to take my meds."

"Sure."

Riss already had her pills in hand when he returned. After she popped them in her mouth, she said, "What time is Bernice coming over?"

"After the shop closes. Rest."

"Is that an order?"

"Yes. Get used to it. I'll be down the hall in my office."

She returned to her prone position. "Do you have a bell I can ring if I need something from you?"

"A bell? You wish." Ike snorted. "This ain't Downton Abbey. Just holler if you want me."

"You know how loud my voice is, so remember you said that."

Chapter Seven

❧

*R*iss woke up completely disoriented.

These damn drugs. She couldn't wait to be done with them.

"I heard you rustlin' around in here."

She barely withheld a scream when Ike's face appeared above her.

"How you feelin'?"

"Groggy. Dirty. Embarrassed because I'm sure I smell like a sewer. I need a shower."

He crouched down. "A bath would be easier."

"I'm all ears on how we can accomplish that, cowboy."

"Best way would be to wrap your cast in plastic. While you were sacked out I cut some garbage bags to size and I'll tape them around the plaster until it's covered. Probably won't be the most comfortable bath, keepin' your arm on the edge of the tub the whole time."

"I don't care as long as I can get clean." She slowly sat up. "Can we do it now? Please, please, please?"

"Sure." He stood and crossed the room. "But I'll hafta take your shirt off first."

Riss groaned. "I hate that I can't even get undressed by myself. But at least it's you undressing me. It's not like you haven't seen the girls bouncin' free a time or two before."

When Ike faced her, his cheeks were pink.

"What? You'd be lyin' if you said you hadn't looked that night at the Phillipsburg Rodeo when I got a little wild and crazy."

"Oh, I looked, all right. But seein' you tipsy on tequila and topless on the back of a steer, in front of an arena full of drunken fools is way different than seein' your girls up close and personal as I'm waterproofing your cast in my house."

Usually she'd snap back with a lewd retort, but damn . . . she couldn't think of a single response for that.

Then he flashed her that cocky cowboy grin. "But that don't mean I'm gonna look away this time either."

She tried—and failed—not to blush.

"Come on, smelly. Let's get you cleaned up."

∞

As Riss lounged in the bathtub, she tried to think of something other than Ike Palmer's gentleness. That he had a softer side hadn't thrown her as much as how much she'd needed someone to show her tenderness.

She'd kept up her screw-you attitude with her brothers, because admitting to being in pain wouldn't have changed anything. They'd expected her to suck it up so she had.

While her arm had a persistent gnawing pain, the aches all over her body were worse. She'd fallen down twice. Then a ladder body-slammed her, so she had bruises everywhere. Her skin resembled a spotted cow.

And she hadn't known how bad she looked until she'd seen the horror on Ike's face.

Thank god she hadn't gotten naked until after he'd wrapped her cast. Even the pieces of stiff plastic were gently warmed and conformed by his patient hands. He began the wrap at her wrist, looping the strips up as if he was mummifying her. When he reached the top of her biceps with the wrap, the back of his hand grazed the side of her breast. After the second layer of plastic, he'd stopped apologizing whenever his hand connected with her breast. But he hadn't stopped watching how her nipples hardened at his every accidental touch, nor had he apologized—not that she expected it. Her body's re- action was her issue, not his.

She waited to strip until the tub had filled.

But she couldn't push the sweats down past her left butt cheek. "Dammit. I can't do this."

Ike's murmured, "That's why I'm here. Let me help you," resulted in her gripping his shoulder while he slipped his fingers beneath the waistband of her sweats. The scrape of his fingertips on her bare skin led to an explosion of goose bumps across her entire body. After she stepped out of her sweatpants and underwear, she glanced down at him and witnessed his horrified look.

Getting naked had never been a big deal for her. Yeah, she was a little chubby. So what. Yeah, where her skin wasn't lily-white, it was covered with freckles. So what. She'd made peace with her body years ago. She refused to let anyone—male or female—body-shame her. Same with slut-shaming. She liked sex. Denying herself pleasure because of someone else's archaic moral standard? Nope. The way she saw it, she had one life and she'd live it on her terms.

So Ike's distress wasn't because her naked body disgusted him. His distress came from seeing the brunt of her injuries up close and personal.

When he spread his palm across her bruised rib cage, with a whispered, "Gorgeous girl, that looks painful," she didn't bat his hand away. She didn't move—she scarcely breathed when he continued to inspect every mark on the front side of her battered body.

And Ike probably would've given her backside the same treatment, but he had a flash of remorse for his intimate examination and abruptly stepped away with a gruff, "Get in. The water's getting cold."

For the next step, climbing into the tub, Ike was more concerned with keeping her from falling than gawking at her bouncing breasts and ass.

After she'd assured him she'd be fine and careful alone in the tub, he'd bailed.

That was when the tears came.

Tears of gratitude for him reminding her that it was okay to let someone take care of you. A reminder that showing kindness and tenderness shouldn't be considered a burden.

Her stomach roiled with the awful suspicion that her brother had called Jade in hopes of ridding himself of the burden of taking care of her. Lonnie counted on Jade being the sweet, loving, loyal friend who'd insist that Riss recover at her house. Riss had no doubt Jade had offered.

So how had she ended up staying with Ike Palmer? Tobin would've done whatever Jade asked of him, including welcoming Riss into their home. So had Tobin asked for Ike's intervention? Or had Ike been telling the truth about volunteering to take her in?

Their personal issues aside, Ike was a good guy. But this situation went beyond letting a buddy crash at your place for a few days. And she hadn't even taken into account how that amazing kiss could change things between them.

No way was that just acting. No freakin' way.

But with his promise it wouldn't happen again . . . she'd have to forget about it too.

It wasn't like she didn't have other more pressing things to worry about. How much this accident would cost her with hospitalization and surgery, not to mention rehab. Not only were her out-of-pocket medical expenses a concern, but so were her lost wages. Her reputation for being a reliable driver meant steady work. If she had to lose three or four months to recovery, would she have to work twice as hard to get back to the position of seniority where she'd been just a week ago?

All these questions made her head pound.

Plus, there was the issue of her trailer. Letting it sit there unattended with no heat and no water for weeks during the winter was a terrible option, but the only one she had until she could be on-site. Then she'd have to make some tough decisions to stay financially afloat.

One decision in particular weighed on her, but chances were good that the *work thing* Ike wanted to discuss would make that decision easier.

Easier. Right. As if anything in her life was ever easy.

Everything was fucked.

She sank deeper into the tub, using her toes to turn the handle for the hot water.

At least she had this moment of bliss.

Two loud raps sounded on the door.

She said, "Come in," expecting Ike.

But Bernice answered. "Lord, child. Lookit you."

"I know. I'm beat to shit. And it's my own fault so can you just get the lecture over with?"

"Why am I not surprised that's the first thing that came outta that mouth?"

"I'm sorry." She paused. "Thanks, Aunt Bernice, for takin' time out of your busy day to help me out. I appreciate it."

Bernice flipped on the bathroom fan before she settled on the toilet next to the tub. Then she held a slim metal e-cigarette to her frosted lips and took a long pull.

"Ike won't like that you're smokin' in here."

She exhaled—and the "smoke" immediately dissipated. "He ain't gonna know. This is cherry scented."

"I thought you quit."

"I quit buying tobacco cigarettes. Now I vape." She inhaled again. "All the cool kids are doin' it."

For as long as Riss could remember, her aunt had looked the same. Same pale red teased hair. Same apple-shaped body. Same polyester clothes. Same row of bracelets up her arm. Same beringed fingers with perfectly manicured nails. "How is it you never seem to age?"

"I was born an old soul."

She'd buy that.

"But it might've put a few years on my face when I found out what happened to you." She pointed with the e-cig. "From someone outside the family."

"Lonnie didn't let you know?"

"No. So I'm mad as hell, girl. You oughta know that up front."

"I figured you would be."

Aunt B cocked her head. "Did you ask Ike to call me?"

Riss shook her head.

"You're stubborn as a goddamned mule."

"That's not exactly news."

"Point taken. You about done with your leisurely soak?"

"Yeah. The water is getting cold."

"You'll be colder yet by the time I get through with your shampoo and set. Drain the tub and skootch over so I can see the stitches."

Bernice lowered to her knees and bent over the edge of the tub. Her fingers tenderly brushed the hair away from the gash on her scalp. "Does it hurt?"

"Not as much as my arm."

"I'll be gentle, sweetheart. But I will have to scrub a bit to get the dried blood off. I brought baby shampoo, so I'm hoping it won't sting in that cut."

"I'd put up with it stinging my eyes if it meant I could have clean hair."

"I hear ya. Now tip your head back and close your eyes."

Riss shivered. Her arm ached from holding it up without support.

"Shit. Sorry. I forgot Ike gave me a board here for you to rest that on." She slid a two-by-four from the tub's edge to the wall. "Try that."

"Much better. Thank you."

Aunt B clucked her tongue and muttered as she shampooed. Rinsing was the worst. She filled up a gallon-sized ice cream pail and poured it over Riss's head. Again and again.

"That's probably good."

"Tellin' me how to do my job?"

"No. By all means, continue torturing me."

"You're the one torturing this hair. Lord, girl, do you need conditioner."

"It doesn't seem to tame these frizzy damn curls, which I inherited from my mother's genetics, not my dad's."

"As I'm aware. But you did inherit your dad's tendency to skirt the truth, so I've got a bone to pick with you."

"What did I do now?"

"Put me in a bind with my Mud Lilies pals."

Riss bristled. "How so?"

"You convinced them during that wedding game that there's nothin' romantic goin' on between you and Ike. Then a few weeks later, you're livin' in his house? Sounds like there's something goin' on and them ladies are gonna grill me for details."

"You can handle it."

Bernice released a husky laugh. "You don't give an inch, do you, girl? I'm askin' if you pulled one over on them, because Louie said Ike laid a tonsil-scratching kiss on you today and claimed you two are a couple."

"Louie has a big mouth." Riss slowly cranked her head around and looked her aunt in the eye. "My brother just called you outta the blue to gossip about me?"

"You'd hate that, wouldn't you, sugar?" She gently turned Riss's head back to where it'd been. "But I actually called *him* to check on you."

"Oh."

"So what is the deal with Ike?"

"I don't know." Riss filled Bernice in—not that there was much to tell.

Bernice said, "This does seem a little screwy that he'd show up and spirit you away, even takin' into account your truce. But I'd much rather have you here under his supervision than have you dealin' with what your brothers consider care." She paused. "That said, if this doesn't work out with Ike, my door is open to you, Riss."

Since when?

"Now hold still. I know you're cold, but I need to do your comb-out where I can see and not tear into your stitches."

"Thank you. I feel a million times better."

Aunt Bernice hugged her from behind. "Then I did something right with you for a change."

This day just kept getting weirder and weirder.

After helping her out of the tub and drying her off like she was a child, Bernice wrapped a long bath sheet around her. "I brought you some tops. They're not your style, but the arms are stretchy enough to fit over your cast."

"Thanks, Aunt B. That's super thoughtful. This is all so unexpected . . ."

Sadness passed through Bernice's blue eyes. "That's the sad thing, sugar. We're family. It shouldn't be unexpected, it should be given without thought. My damn pride . . ." She shook her head. "This ain't about me, it's about you, and we'll save that for another time."

"Okay."

Bernice attempted to smooth out Riss's curls. "You'll probably wanna wash your hair in three days. Text me to set up a time. Meanwhile, I brought dry shampoo for you to use between washings."

Bewildered by her aunt's positive attention, Riss just stared at her.

"Get a move on, girl. Pick something to wear. You can't be parading around nekkid. You'll catch your death of cold."

There was her brusque, bossy aunt. "You better not have tried to pawn off the ugly-ass shirt that looks like electric vomit onto me, Aunt B."

"I love that damn shirt, smart-ass." A loud crack echoed when Bernice snapped a towel behind her. "Your arm's broken, not your feet. Move it. I ain't got all night."

After Bernice bailed, Ike tried to interest Riss in dinner.

"No offense, but I don't feel like eating. I think I'll just go to bed."

"This is not a negotiation. You need fuel to heal and you're not supposed to take painkillers on an empty stomach, so you *are* eating."

"Already getting off on bossing me around, aren't you?"

"Yep. Get used to it." Ike's eyes softened. "Seriously, Riss. You'll sleep better with food in your belly. So sit tight and I'll make you a peanut butter sandwich."

"With jelly—grape jelly. And the crusts cut off."

"Don't push it."

Riss could barely keep her eyes open. She managed to eat half the sandwich and drink a glass of milk. "I'm sorry. I'm just so tired."

"It's been a stressful day."

"It's been a stressful week," she countered with a yawn.

"Come on, let's get you tucked in."

In the guest bedroom, Ike had folded back the bedding on the queen-sized bed.

Riss slipped between the flannel sheets and sighed. "This is heaven. It's quiet. It smells nice. It's warm. Wake me up in two months."

He rearranged the placement of the pillows three times. Even through her exhaustion she recognized he was stalling.

"Ike. Quit fussin' like an old lady. I'm fine."

"It's been a while since I had anyone to fuss over."

"I'm sure your girlfriends appreciated that. I, however, do not."

He tugged the blanket higher. "Never bothered with girlfriends. I'm talkin' about my sisters. The youngest in particular. She loved bein' babied. Still does."

Riss scowled. "I hated that. I *still* hate it because my brothers treat me like I'm twelve."

"Then I'll refrain from givin' you a good-night noogie."

Then Ike did the oddest thing: he placed a lingering kiss on her forehead. "I'll check on you later."

"I promise to be more sentient tomorrow and we'll talk about that work thing."

Chapter Eight

❧

*B*ut they didn't talk the next day.

Or the day after that.

Or even the day after that.

Riss slept.

Ike brought her food in bed after she'd fallen asleep during dinner and almost slipped off the chair.

So while she easily drifted off into slumber, Ike remained restless.

Pacing. Waiting . . . for what? He didn't know.

He'd also fielded phone calls from her family and friends.

Her oldest brother, Lonnie, hadn't shown up like Louie had warned him. Instead he received a terse text, addressed to *him* on Riss's phone:

LT: WATCH URSELF WITH RISS, CAUSE WE R WATCHING U.

LT: SHE GETS HURT, U GET HURT

All caps might've been overkill. At least he hadn't added a bunch of threatening emojis.

Jade called every day.

So did Bernice.

So did Hugh and Harlow.

So did some guy named Tito who claimed he worked with Riss.

By phone call number seven, Ike wasn't real friendly to the dude named Ron who also claimed a workplace connection.

But the truth was . . . Ike had no idea what Riss did on a day-to-day basis. He knew at one point she'd worked as a lube jockey. She'd mentioned that her past work history included selling farm equipment, slinging drinks, cleaning cars, stocking groceries. But the loads and runs she'd talked about recently? She could've been delivering rocks, furniture or elephants, for all he knew.

Didn't it make him a self-involved jackass that he hadn't bothered to ask her about it?

Has she *asked* you *how you spend your days?*

No. Thank god for that.

Jade had been busy, rallying Riss's friends in a show of support.

Garnet sent a sling decorated in rhinestones.

Miz Maybelle and Tilda sent flowers.

Pearl and Vivien sent DVDs.

Susan and Sherry from Buckeye Joe's dropped off a bottle of Gentleman Jack, Kentucky's finest whiskey. He hadn't known that Riss even liked whiskey. There was a lot he didn't know about her.

Even the gals from Riss's book club sent cards.

No doubt the woman was well liked.

The weirdest thing that had happened so far was that Ike's buddies' wives—Lainie Lawson, Tierney Jackson, Harper Turner, Janie Lawson, Tanna Fletcher and Celia Gilchrist—checked on Riss via phone calls, as if he and Riss were a couple. Which he assured them they were not.

So he didn't try to guess which one of Riss's friends had sent another delivery when his doorbell rang midafternoon.

It shocked him to open the door and see his sister on his porch.

"Jen? What's wrong? Did something happen to Kay or Lea or the kids?"

"No, everyone is fine."

"Then . . . why are you here?"

"Can't a girl just swing by and say howdy to her big brother?"

"Swing by? It's eighty miles round trip. And you've done that twice in ten years, both times when you freaked out about bein' pregnant."

"Rub it in. I'm sorry I'm a crappy sister."

Ike glanced at the clock. "Besides, isn't this when you pick the kids up from school?"

She rolled her eyes. "Always micromanaging me."

Someone needs to.

"I'm here because no one has heard from you since Sunday morning. We didn't know what to do with ourselves without your daily big brother check-in, so we worried you were sick."

"Jesus. I don't call every day. As you can see, I'm fine."

Jen stamped the snow off her boots. "It's bum-freezin' cold out here. Move so I can come in."

"Uh, now is not a good time."

"Why? Did I interrupt a little afternoon delight?"

While he didn't appreciate her sarcasm—as if that wasn't a real possibility—Ike didn't take the bait. He just sighed and stepped aside.

Once inside, Jen shed her boots, her coat, her scarf and her gloves—right where she stood—and stepped over the pile. She'd always been the messiest of his sisters and he forced himself not to pick up after her even now.

Then she propped her hands on her hips and attempted to intimidate him.

At five foot nothin' and six years younger than him, it'd never worked, but that hadn't stopped her from trying.

"Seriously, Ike. What is goin' on with you? You're never out of the family loop for more than a day or this secretive."

"Drives you three crazies crazy, doesn't it?"

"Yes!"

"Welcome to my world. What goes around comes around. If the three of you weren't keepin' secrets from me, you were tellin' me lies."

"Hardly. You always busted us." Her gaze homed in on Riss's panda-themed purse on the counter. "Speaking of busted. That handbag is a little whimsical for you."

"Funny. It's not mine."

"No shit. Whose is it?"

"It ain't a gift for any of you, so quit eyeballin' it."

"As if." She sniffed with derision. "I'm wondering who'd buy that hideous thing."

Truth time. "It belongs to Riss."

"Riss." She blinked with uncertainty. "Riss. As in . . . Riss, the truck driver? Riss, the woman I've heard you bitch about? Riss, the shrew whose brother bad-mouthed you? Riss, the chick who threatened to castrate you at a branding last spring? *That* Riss?"

"One and the same," Riss said cheerfully as she entered the room. "But I believe you forgot to call me the foul-mouthed bane of your brother's existence. That one used to be his favorite, huh, honey buns?"

Jen's mouth hung open.

"Riss, this is my sister Jen. Jen, this is Riss, the feisty she-devil I've mentioned a time or two."

"Nice to meet you." Riss pointed at her arm. "Excuse me for not bein' up to my usual loutish, shrewish, devilish self. It's hard to manage a forked tail *and* a cast."

"What happened to your arm?" Jen asked.

"Oh, this little ol' thing? I got tromped during my last bull ride. I held on for the full eight seconds, but all anyone remembers is that damn bull doin' a two-step on my arm, not the ninety-two-point ride."

Ike groaned. "For the love of god, Riss, really?"

"What?" She went goggle-eyed with phony innocence. "Does she have a weak stomach? Because I purposely left out the parts about the blood and mud and the sound of my own bones cracking."

"You must be feelin' better if you're back to tellin' such a whopper of a lie."

"I prefer to call it creating an alternative reality, remember?"

"Wait." Jen's gaze swung between them. "You *didn't* get that injury from bull ridin'?"

Riss sighed. "Nope. It's not as exciting as that. It's sort of embarrassing, which is why I stretched the truth a tad."

Stretched the truth. Ike snorted.

"So what really happened?"

"Sex injury. See, me and"—she sent Ike a coquettish look—"um . . . this *guy* were goin' at it against the corral, and my foot slipped—"

Jen held up her hand. "You win. It's none of my business."

Wait for it . . . because Ike knew his sister wouldn't leave it at that.

"But I will ask why my brother's supposed nemesis looks as if she just tumbled out of his bed."

Ike quelled Riss's retort—most likely another lie—with a sharp look and addressed his snoopy sister. "Riss is stayin' with me while she heals up."

"Staying with you . . . as in . . . sharing your house? Or sharing your bedroom?"

"That, little sis, ain't none of your business either."

Jen leveled a glare at Riss as if that'd scare her into talking.

But Riss mimed zipping her lip and throwing away the key.

Ike laughed. "Woman, you are such a pain in my ass."

"Oh, hush. I liven up your staid life, stud."

Yeah, she was definitely feeling better.

"Omigod. It's like *I* stepped into an alternate reality." Jen hastily snatched up her outerwear. "One where you actually have a life, Ike."

"Thanks for that, Jen." He didn't look at Riss to see her reaction to his sister's sad-but-true comment.

"Kay and Lea won't believe this."

"But you can't wait to tell them, can you?"

"Nope. Later days, dude."

Her phone was in her hand before she shut the door.

"Some days I wonder where I went wrong with her."

"She seems normal to me, if a little gullible." She snickered. "It'd be fun to put her and Louie in a room and see how much crap we could get them to believe."

"Pass." Ike moved toward her. Her color looked good. Her eyes were clearer. She'd call him a pervert if she realized how closely he'd watched her the past two days. But the woman was a noisy sleeper. He'd be sitting in the living room and hear gasps, groans and even laughter drifting out of the guest bedroom, so naturally he'd race in to check on her. Her animation even in sleep fascinated him.

"Before you ask . . . I feel much better. Although the last couple days have been a blur."

"You mostly slept."

She wrinkled her nose. "I'm a sucky houseguest, huh."

"A popular one. All your buddies have been callin', askin' to talk to you."

"Probably just making sure that you haven't killed me yet."

"It'd shock the hell out of them to see us getting along, wouldn't it?"

"It's easy to avoid conflict when one person sleeps all the time."

"True." Ike couldn't tear his gaze away from her.

"Stop staring at me. I look like hell. I haven't had makeup on for days—"

"You don't need it. And you don't look like hell. I hate it when you say that, so knock it off. You look fresh faced and feminine and rested." Ike stopped there before he confessed he'd spent way too much time pondering her subtle natural beauty, and comparing it with the brash, tomboyish Riss he thought he knew.

Riss seemed tongue-tied.

"Now that you're up and around, I'll fix you an early supper."

"I should probably return some phone calls."

"Nope. Food first. March yourself into the kitchen."

She lifted an eyebrow. "Were you this bossy with your sisters?"

"Way worse. Especially with the youngest because that girl questioned everything."

"Then she and I would probably get along like gangbusters."

"Wrong. You'd get annoyed with her dependency within two minutes." He nudged her. "Food. Now."

"I'm not hungry."

Her stomach rumbled loud enough they both heard it. Ike merely pointed to the kitchen.

"Fine. I'm goin'."

Chapter Nine

❧

*R*iss decided she could easily watch Ike cook all day.

The smooth way he moved from counter to counter. The almost sensual way he used his hands when he chopped vegetables. Then how he washed and dried his hands with deliberate care as he listened to her speak.

In her pain-filled haze, she hadn't noticed specific things about Ike beyond that he was right there when she needed something. Given time to study him as he multitasked, she noticed his laid-back nature. From his casual clothing—a long-sleeved black T-shirt, faded gray sweatpants and a Jackson Stock Contracting ball cap he wore backward—to the relaxed set of his shoulders, to the scruff on his face. He smiled more, which made him look younger. He talked less, which meant she filled the dead air with chatter. But for all she knew, maybe that sexy little smile indicatcd he'd tuned her out.

They ate the minestrone soup—he'd prepared from scratch—at the breakfast bar dividing the kitchen and dining room. He had good manners too. No slurping or burping—disgusting habits her brothers displayed at home and probably in public.

His dining room table was covered with clutter, same as hers. When he caught her staring at it and started to explain, she said, "I can't eat on mine either."

"Mine's always been a horizontal shit collector. I figure I'm doin' good if I can confine the paper mess to one place."

"Do you work out here more than in your office?"

"More than I'd like to. My PC is in my office, but I'm only in there if I'm printing something out. I prefer my laptop. The Internet is faster, the screen is bigger, but I can't seem to give up the desktop since I've got years' worth of information stored on it. Why?"

"Just wondered where we're having the long-overdue business discussion." She smiled. "As soon as we're finished eating."

Riss's cell rang and she switched it to speakerphone. "This is Riss Thorpe."

"Riss! I was starting to worry I'd have to sic the sheriff on your cranky male nurse since he refused to put you on the phone."

Cranky male nurse. "Not his fault, Tito. I've slept like the dead."

"You sound good." A pause filled the air. "So how about we switch to FaceTime? I miss seein' that pretty face of yours, Red."

She forced a laugh. "Dude. I have serious bed-head, I'm not wearing makeup and I'm still in my damn pajamas. If you saw me like this, you'd drop your phone."

"I'm worried about you, chica."

"And I appreciate that. So what's up?"

"Look, I know you've got a broken arm, and no pressure, but any idea when you'll be back behind the wheel?"

"Jesus. Are you fucking serious?" Ike snapped. "She's dealin' with way more than just a broken arm, buddy. She's had surgery and—"

"Tito, hang on a second." Riss poked the mute button and got in Ike's face. "Don't do that again. You have no right to blab my private business to my boss."

Ike scowled. "Your boss?"

"Yes. Tito owns the trucking company that lines up seventy percent of my jobs. And I do not need you"— she drilled her finger into his biceps—"fucking that up for me. If Tito understood the extent of my injuries, he'd write me off. I worked too damn hard to get in with his company to allow that to happen."

"Riss. He's gonna know something is up when you turn down every job for the next two months."

"There's nothin' saying that the doc won't release me early. And until I know for sure I can't drive anything, anywhere, for anyone, I *am* keeping my options open. So back off." She started to leave the room.

But Ike stopped her. "Uh-uh, *chica.* I'll keep my mouth shut, but I wanna hear every word of what this guy expects from you and what *alternative reality* you're willing to tell him to keep him on the hook."

"You get one warning from me. Stay out of my business."

Riss locked her gaze to Ike's and pasted on a smile before she clicked off mute. "Sorry, T. My cranky male nurse is pissy because I've asked for my third sponge bath today." She lowered her voice. "He's starting to suspect I like havin' those big, rough hands of his all over me all of the time."

The muscle in Ike's jaw flexed, but he stayed mum.

Good boy.

"I'm sure he's enjoying it too. Anyway, I've got a couple of short runs comin' up. Nothing too taxing. Deliveries you could do in your sleep. You interested?"

She said, "Always," and hoped Tito didn't hear Ike's snarl.

"Awesome. Take care of my girl and I'll call next week with the deets."

"Thanks, Tito. Have a great weekend." She hung up just as Ike exploded.

"What the fuck, Riss? Did you not hear anything I said? You are on medical restrictions. There is no way—no way in hell—I'm letting you take those runs!"

"*Letting* me? First off, *I* make my own choices. And secondly, let me repeat, *I make my own choices.*"

Ike's nostrils flared. His eyes darkened with fury. Somehow he kept his hands on his hips even as he loomed over her.

And . . . wow. The man was one sexy beast.

How hadn't she noticed that before?

Normally, she'd get nose-to-nose with him. But if she ventured any closer, she might be tempted to see if his angry kisses were as intoxicating as his sweet kisses. And his erotic kisses. Or any kisses at all, really.

She took a step back and put a lid on the lust. "Now. Can we have a civilized discussion?"

"No." He flashed his teeth at her. "I'll be upstairs working off this goddamned mad."

And then he was gone.

Okay. She realized this was the first time she'd truly been alert and alone for a week. It was ridiculous she didn't know what to do with herself.

Since her pain was manageable, she skipped the pain meds and opted for a beer. She snagged her phone and called Jade.

"Is this really you, Riss? Or Ike calling with an update?"

"It's me."

Jade squealed. "I've been so worried, but I didn't want to bother you. I need to see your face. Hanging up to FaceTime you."

The call ended.

What the heck was up with people needing to see her? She looked like hell.

Ike's sweet compliment about her looking fresh faced and feminine popped into her head. It seemed out of character for him. During their truce they quit insulting and taunting each other, but they hadn't tossed out random compliments.

The FaceTime icon appeared. She propped the phone up and hit accept call.

Jade's gorgeous face filled the screen. Her almond-shaped eyes zeroed in on Riss's cast. "Omigod! I didn't think it'd be that big!"

"Ain't that what you said the first time your husband dropped his pants?"

"Yes, and your continued jealousy about that awesome fact is so unbecoming." Then Jade scrutinized Riss's face. "Scratch that. You look good, Riss. Better than I expected."

"I've done nothin' but sleep. It sucks. Today is the first day I've gotten out of bed except to pee."

"Lovely visual. GG said that Bernice left the shop early to help you with 'lady stuff.' Please tell me it wasn't to wax your hoo-ha."

"Dude. No. That's gross. Aunt B washed my hair. It was weird as fuck."

"Why?"

"Because she didn't volunteer."

"Then how'd she know?"

"I guess Ike asked her to come."

Jade made a shooing motion offscreen. "Go away, perv. I'm FaceTiming with Riss."

"Hey, Riss." The side of Tobin's face came into view as he placed a loud kiss on Jade's cheek. "Tell Ike I said hey."

"Yeah, I'll get right on that."

"Speaking of Ike . . . how are things going with you two sharing close quarters?"

Riss waggled her beer. "I'm drinkin' downstairs and he's punching the shit outta something upstairs."

Jade winced. "That bad, huh?"

"Actually, it hasn't been bad. We just had a . . . disagreement."

"Think it'll blow over?"

"Like a lead balloon."

"I'm happy to see you're back to your ornery self." Jade shot a quick look over her shoulder. "You can always move in with us if you and Ike keep butting heads."

"Thanks, but you're a newlywed. All that happiness and constant loud sex would be way worse for my mental health than Ike running hot and cold with me."

"What's that mean . . . running hot and cold?"

Riss swigged her beer. "It's weird. I don't want to strangle him all the time. And no, I can't blame that abnormal reaction on pain meds because it started when Ike and I agreed to a truce before your wedding."

"Omigod, Riss. Have you fucked him?"

It threw her when Jade dropped the rare f-bomb. "No."

"Blown him?"

"No."

"Then why is it weird?"

"Because it doesn't freak me out to imagine doing those things with him." Holy shit. What possessed her to admit that? She glared at her beer like it'd morphed into some kind of freaky truth serum.

"That's it! He's brainwashed you, or overmedicated you, or dick-charmed you, and I won't stand for it. Pack a bag. I'll be there to get you in twenty."

Riss laughed. Dick-charmed. "I appreciate the concern, but this . . . situation has been building between me'n Ike for a while. It's time we dealt with it."

"So it is personal?"

"Mostly business."

"Fine. I'll let it go. But keep me posted, okay?"

"You'll probably get sick of hearin' from me, sweet cheeks."

Jade grinned. "That's so cute."

"What's cute?"

"How you've picked up Ike's idioms. But the only person I've ever heard him call that is . . . you, *sweet cheeks*."

"Piss. Off."

Jade laughed again. Then she pressed her lips to her fingers and touched them to the screen. "Love you. We'll swing by soon. With honeymoon pictures."

Yay.

Riss closed her eyes. A whirring noise and the steady *slap slap slap* of athletic shoes hitting a rubber treadmill echoed down the stairs.

You can't run away from me any more than I can run from you, buddy.

She finished her beer and picked up the list of callers Ike had jotted down. She crossed Tito and Jade off the list. Next she dialed Ron's number on speakerphone.

"Desert Plains Distribution, how may I direct your call?"

"Ron Fiora's office, please."

"Thank you. Please hold."

Crappy Muzak was the worst part of being on hold.

A click, then, "This is Ron."

"Ron. Riss Thorpe."

"Riss! How are you? You seemed a little out of it the last time we spoke."

"I was. Blame it on the post-op pain meds."

"How's your recovery going?"

"I seem to be sleeping through it."

He laughed. "Well, you sound like you're getting back to normal."

There won't be a normal for me for a long damn time.

Fuck. She did not want to lose this job, but maybe honesty would pay off and the loss would be temporary. "That's the thing, Ron. It'll be a couple months until I'm back to normal. Eight weeks is the doctor's best guess-timate before the cast comes off. Then PT at least twice a week for god knows how long after that."

Ron said nothing.

"With my other job . . . I can find drivers to take my runs until I'm back on my feet. I'm aware that is not an option with Desert Plains."

"No, it isn't. I'm sad to be losing such an exemplary driver. We don't get many applicants willing to deliver to the state penitentiary."

"I was grateful for the opportunity. If you don't fill the position in the next three months, would you consider calling me so I can reapply for it when I'm at full recovery?"

"Absolutely. I'm putting a reminder on my calendar right now."

"Thank you."

"My pleasure." He paused. "HR will mail your last paycheck to the address on file."

"Perfect."

"Take care, Riss, and good luck."

As soon as the call ended, Ike bellowed behind her. "Are you shitting me that you've been workin' at the state pen in Rawlins?"

"Go away, Ike. I cannot deal with you right now."

"Tough. Shit." The chair next to hers spun out. Then she and the big sweaty cowboy were sitting knee to knee.

Except his knees were bare. And muscled. And covered in golden hair.

Did she mention muscled?

"Start talkin'."

Riss raised her head and deflected his glare with one of her own. "I can't discuss it. I signed a bunch of NDAs."

"Because you worked in a fucking prison filled with rapists, murderers and pedophiles."

"No. I worked for a distributor that delivered supplies to a fucking prison filled with rapists, murderers and pedophiles."

"Cut the sarcasm." He leaned in. "Since it sounded like you just turned in your resignation, then the NDAs don't apply. So I wanna know why you'd agree to be a prison delivery girl, when you started and what you delivered."

"I hate that you're bein' this way."

"What way?"

"Your usual way—a self-righteous bossy prick who believes he has the right to question *my* decisions about what jobs I've taken so I can pay my bills."

His eagle-eyed gaze never strayed from her face.

"It was hard as hell passing the screening process for that job, but I'm damn proud I did it and I will not let you shame me for it. So just to shut you up about it, I can say that I started workin' for them two years ago. It's a state government contract and I was legally bound not to disclose my employment. When I made deliveries I never had contact with more than four inmates. They unloaded the truck. I remained with the guards. So yeah, workin' as a *prison delivery girl* paid extremely well and was by far one of the easiest jobs I've ever had and it blows donkey dick that I have to quit."

"Riss—"

"And I don't even wanna think about how I'll replace that income." She turned to walk away.

"Wait."

She did.

"I'm sorry. I was out of line."

A quick apology . . . not what she expected from him. "Ya think?"

"I wasn't shaming you. It just tripped all of my triggers when I imagined them inmates staring at you, hating that they probably fantasized about doin' sick things to you."

She faced him. "Would it ease your overactive imagination if I told you I wore a shapeless uniform that gave no indication that I was female?"

"Darlin', nothin' masks the fact you're all woman, all the time." His focus dipped to her chest and skated down to her belly, across her hips and back up to her mouth. "World-class curves, baby. You own that shit."

"You flattering me to get out of the doghouse?"

He cocked his head and gave her puppy dog eyes. "Is it workin'?"

"A smidge."

"I really am sorry I let my mouth run unchecked."

"I believe you."

"But?"

Riss shook her head. "Let's leave it at that."

"I can't. You need to know why the prison is a hot-button issue for me."

This couldn't be good.

"My dad was in there." He ran his hand through his hair. "I was probably five when he was sentenced to six months for possession. My mom used to take me on visitation days and I hated the way the other inmates leered at her and made crude comments and lewd gestures."

"In front of you?"

Ike nodded.

"That's awful." It churned her stomach to imagine sweet-faced, towheaded, innocent Ike in such an ugly situation.

"Anyway, my dad got out of jail long enough to knock my mom up with my sister Jen. He also made new prison friends, and just for fun, they robbed a bank. Or should I say *tried* to rob a bank because they got caught. My mom wised up and divorced him. We never saw him again. So for all I know, he could still be in there, or maybe he died, or maybe he got transferred or released. I've never cared enough to find out."

"Ike. I'm sorry."

"So I can't wrap my head around you bein' there, no matter how well it pays." He clenched his hands into fists.

"Since it's a state contract, I also deliver to the women's prison in Lusk and to various military installations. And so I have the experience to admit I'd rather deliver to the prisons. Way less hassle than the bullshit the government puts me through."

"I didn't know you had regular runs, Riss. That made me realize there's so much I don't know about you." Ike's gaze sought hers. "And so much you don't know about me."

Clearly he was embarrassed about his self-involvement. Or maybe he expected her to say something snarky about his dad being in prison. The only way he'd know she didn't give a damn about his father's past was to show him all she cared about was the here and now. "The only way to fix that is to get to know each other better, right?"

"Right."

"So let's hang out and watch a movie." *Do not suggest* Escape from Alcatraz, *Riss, not even in jest.*

Ike granted her a crooked smile.

"What?"

"It's killin' you not to toss out any prison break movies as options, isn't it?"

"Yes!" She laughed. "I sorta hate that you can see past my poker face."

"Then we're definitely playing cards tomorrow night. But first . . ." He erased the distance between them. "Gimme a damn hug."

"You need a damn hug from me a lot, Palmer."

"I've gotten used to them on the regular, Thorpe."

Ike repositioned her cast before he wrapped his arms around her.

She could get used to this too.

Chapter Ten

❧

*E*arly the following afternoon Riss slung her laptop bag over her left shoulder and headed to the kitchen. Given Ike's reluctance to talk business now, coupled with him avoiding her the months prior to their truce, she knew this meeting wouldn't be the good news she needed.

The moment Ike saw her, he jumped up and skirted a pile of boxes to take her laptop bag. "Where's your sling? You're not supposed to—"

"It was digging into my shoulder when I took the nap you forced on me. I need a break from it." That was when she noticed he'd cleared off the dining room table. "Are you cooking me a fancy-schmancy dinner later?"

"I'll be happy if you're just speaking to me after this."

"Maybe you'd better break out the beer."

"In a minute."

He settled across from her. He wasn't wearing the

cowboy armor she'd expected. His head was bare—no hat, no ball cap. His blond hair stuck up like he'd been pulling on it. He'd swapped his usual form-fitting dress shirt for a seen-better-days Denver Nuggets jersey.

"Riss. Honest to god, I don't even know where to start."

"Rip the bandage off—worst news first and we'll go from there."

His eyes met hers. "Jackson Stock Contracting is failing."

Fuck. She knew it. "How did this happen?"

"A combination of inexperience and unrealistic expectations. See, those few weeks we were on the road that summer? Everything went so well it just seemed like that's what me'n Hugh oughta be doin'. Rollin' from town to town. Basking in the praise about JSC's excellent stock. Signing on to provide rough stock for every rodeo that'd have us." He paused. "How do you remember it?"

"Stressful."

Ike smiled. "Ain't that the truth."

"And boring."

His smile fell. "Seemed I didn't have time to turn around, let alone time to get bored."

"That's because you were busy behind the chutes or schmoozing with the rodeo people. I either had a lot of downtime to fill or was behind the wheel. So while traveling had its moments, I realized I'd romanticized life on the rodeo circuit. Short trips were okay. When you guys were talkin' about trips to California? No, thanks. I'm not interested in the long haul—in any aspect of my life."

He frowned. "So why'd you agree to work with us?"

Because I had a big ol' girl crush on you, Ike Palmer. With your rugged looks and smooth ways, I dreamed of long hot nights between the sheets, sating our mutual hunger and kink. Afterward we'd laugh about fooling everyone with our daily snipefest, because for us, loathing was the ultimate foreplay.

"Riss? We agreed to total honesty, remember?"

Maybe not *total* honesty. "Because if I would've said no, I'd look petty. People would've thought I refused out of orneriness or to antagonize you."

"That doesn't sound like the 'I don't give a shit what people think of me' Riss that I know."

"A large part of that is just an act. Besides, Hugh vouched for me out of desperation and I'm a sucker."

Ike's eyes widened.

"He wanted to get back on the road no matter what. So when Hugh approached me, I already had the time off."

"You never mentioned that."

She shrugged. "It never came up. Anyway, I'd planned on hitting the Phillipsburg, Kansas, rodeo. When I learned that was one of the stops, I figured what the hell, and turned it into a workin' vacation." She swallowed a drink of beer. "So lemme ask you something. When you and Hugh pitched the proposal to take over JSC, did you know Hugh was movin' to Cali?"

"This is where I bring up the problem—mine mostly—of inexperience and bein' naive. Hugh had worked in the business with Renner. So if Hugh said we could double down by running JSC outta two locations, I believed him without hesitation."

"And now?"

"Now? Him movin' out West was the worst fuckin' decision for the company. No one knows us in Cali. Why would they hire a contracting outfit from Wyoming? We'd have the same attitude if a California contractor tried to move in on our territory."

"I wondered when one of you would come to that conclusion."

"I did early on. I don't know that Hugh has come to that realization even now. It's a mess. Yeah, at one time JSC had a great rep for providing top-notch stock. But with Tobin bowing out of the breeding program, we're stuck with what we've got. And it ain't like we ever had Chad Berger's success rate for breeding rank bulls and parlaying that into a contracting business."

"Ah-ah." Riss pointed with her beer bottle. "But at one time Chad Berger was an unknown bull breeder from North Dakota."

"Maybe Hugh's vision of success was built on that idea. But hopin' your vision will pan out by makin' cold calls to rodeo committees ain't getting it done. *Hugh* is the guy with the personal contacts in the Midwest. *He* oughta be hittin' the blacktop up here where it might actually result in . . . results." Ike sighed and ran his hand through his hair. "We've got one event lined up. One. That won't pay the bills. And now that Harlow is pregnant—"

"Whoa. Harlow is pregnant? No one told me."

"I only learned about it the day before I moved you in here."

"Jesus, Ike. That's a complete game changer."

He threw up his hands. "Thank you, voice of reason! I told Hugh the same thing, but he's taking the 'wait and see' tack. Which is what we've been doin' for a year and a half. We can't both draw a salary. Food and shelter for bulls and broncs don't come cheap."

"Back up. Hugh is takin' a salary?"

"Yeah."

"Are you?"

Ike squirmed.

Riss angled across the table. "No bullshit, remember?"

"No, I'm not getting paid."

"Does Hugh know that?"

"Nope."

"But he has access to the bank statements and payroll records?"

"Of course. I don't know that he's bothered to look at the books beyond the bottom line."

"Well, that's just stupid. He should be questioning you on all expenses, including lack of them." She pointed at him. "Not that I'm letting you off the hook. You let this go on too long. Partners mean equals. If Hugh is getting a check, so should you."

"Don't know that it'd make that much difference since I'm close to broke."

This was way worse than she'd thought.

"Go ahead and give me some of that Riss Thorpe tough-love speech, because I obviously need it."

"You think I'd do that, Ike? Kick you when you're down?"

His head shot up. "I'm serious. I need someone to light a fire under my ass because it's pretty damn obvious I'm not a self-starter."

Riss bit back the question, do you even want to be a self-starter? Not everyone did.

Not everyone was capable of it either. She'd have to tread lightly while she figured out where Ike fit. She'd save the brutally honest talk for then.

She got up from the table. "Since you're bein' completely unreasonable in my recovery, not allowing me to move furniture, would you scoot my chair closer to yours so we can put our heads together and figure something out?"

"Sure." Ike stood. Rather than grabbing the chair, he gently wrapped his arms around her, tugging her against his body, her back to his chest.

Her heart beat double time with Ike's strong arm banded across her waist. His warm, hard body cradling hers immediately turned her thoughts toward how easy it'd be to tilt her head to the side, offering him her neck, the most vulnerable place on her body, as he spoke of his own vulnerabilities. But Riss understood arousal wasn't Ike's intent . . . even when his breath stirring her hair caused her skin to tingle, sending her mind straight to images of mouths sucking and hands stroking, of body heat and slick skin sliding together, the physical need twisting them both up until they were lost in each other.

His voice, when he finally spoke, was a low-pitched rumble. "I've been scared shitless to talk to you about this."

"Why?"

"Because I'm admitting that I'm a failure, Riss. I've never failed at anything in my life." He groaned and the vibration sent gooseflesh rippling across her skin.

A wave of heat spread outward from her center, reminding her of how much she loved that initial rush of lust. How long it'd been since she'd felt it. How it didn't seem wrong that she was feeling it with Ike.

"That sounded cocky . . . until I confess I haven't failed because I haven't taken any risks. I'm a rule follower. Hell, maybe I'm just a follower, period. Tell me what to do and I'll get it done. But when I'm in unfamiliar territory, I freeze. When I can't figure out what to do, well, I do nothin'. That's been my life of late. Doin' a whole lotta nothin' as the business I thought I'd be capable of runnin' spirals into nothin'."

Ike finally being this open with her, taking her into his home and his confidence while his life seemed to be in shambles, brought a new dimension to their relationship. They weren't merely playing house for a few weeks and then they'd go their separate ways with fond memories. "Thanks for telling me the truth, Ike."

"Thanks for not hightailin' it out the door." He chuckled. "Although the day's still young."

"I'm built of sterner stuff than that."

"Don't I know it." He released her and reached around to drag the chair closer.

Riss was rattled by these revelations, but equally determined not to show it. She pushed the notebook in front of him. "I can't write so you're gonna take notes."

"For what?"

"For me. I'm a list maker. And by the time I'm done with you? You'll be makin' lists too."

He scowled.

"Think of it this way: A list is a map. To get to your end destination you gotta make stops and turns. You'll pass familiar points along the way. But if you get lost, you return to the map—the list—see where you went wrong and reroute. A list forces focus on one thing at a time. In order. A focused person is an organized person. An organized person is more likely to be a self-starter."

Ike wore an expression she hadn't seen before.

"What?"

"Smart Riss is sexy as shit." He flashed that roguish grin. "I'm a little turned on hearin' you talk about the power of lists."

She rolled her eyes. "Pen in hand, perv. Now while I grab us another beer, you write down three things you need to accomplish before you go to bed tonight."

"Just three?"

"Start small. A twenty-item list is daunting. That results in panic, and panic results in forced disinterest, which results in plopping in front of the TV to binge watch Netflix and forget the list entirely."

"Jesus, you're a hot-talkin' mama. Do you have a pair of them smart-girl glasses? Because I'd be all over that role-playin'. Hot librarian takes the class troublemaker to task."

Although her thoughts raced with all the delicious ways she could take him in hand, Riss played it cool. "You wanna convince me to play dirty games with you, cowboy?"

"Like you wouldn't believe."

She hadn't expected such vehemence. Or such heat in his eyes. "Here's the deal: if you accomplish today's list, I'll consider letting you pencil it in for tomorrow's list."

"Tomorrow? Not later tonight?"

"Sugar pie, Lola the Librarian is a hard-ass taskmaster. You wanna play in her world? You gotta do things *exactly* by the book."

His sexy groan of frustration caused her pulse to spike.

As she walked into the kitchen, Ike said, "Can you have Lola wear one of them skintight skirts?"

"I'll add it to the list."

"Now you're just bein' mean."

Without thinking, she used her right hand to jerk open the refrigerator door.

Immediately pain exploded in her fingers and shot up her arm in a searing bolt of fire that knocked her to her knees.

Somehow, even in the flash of agony, she clapped her left hand over her mouth to cover her gasp. She closed her eyes against the wooziness and the urge to vomit.

She remained that way, left hand over her mouth and her forehead resting on the cool metal of the fridge door, praying that Ike was so engrossed in completing his list that he hadn't noticed.

Then she heard, "Riss? You okay?"

Guiltily, she scrambled to her feet, taking care not to knock her arm into the fridge door. "I'm fine," she lied. "Just giving you time to work on your list."

"Is that so?" he said directly behind her. "You were on your knees prayin' to the god of refrigeration, thanking it for the cold beer?"

Shit. "How did you know?"

"Jesus, woman, I can see into the kitchen. One moment you were standing there, the next, on your knees." He paused. "I waited for you to ask me for help."

Riss forced herself to look at him.

"But you didn't."

"What could you have done besides cluck around me like an angry mother hen, showing annoyance at my moment of forgetfulness?" she snapped. "Been there, done that with my brothers, Ike. I don't need it from you."

Both eyebrows rose. "*Cluck* around you? You should know that insulting me won't stop me from giving you the what-for you deserve. You only rely on me to help you when it suits you. Here we are on day four, havin' the same issue we had on day one."

"Trust."

"No. Your issue is that you need independence above all else. Regardless of the situation, your biggest concern is that you'll have to depend on someone. Well, guess what? We're past that. You *are* dependent on me for as long as you're here."

She didn't cry from that shock of pain, she certainly wasn't gonna bawl when Ike pointed out a major character flaw that she was fully aware of.

But a whimper escaped anyway.

"Riss."

She shook her head.

Ike moved in and cupped her jaw, tilting her head back to look into her eyes. "How bad does it hurt?"

No words pushed past the lump in her throat, just a sharp gasp.

"C'mere." Ike just took over.

And she let him.

He insisted she take a pain pill. Then he practically carried her to the couch. He pulled her into his lap, cradling her to his chest, nestling her face in the curve of his neck as he propped her cast on a pillow.

"You don't have to coddle me."

"I'm not. I'm *cuddling* you, sweetheart. Big difference. Just think of this as a really long hug, since I haven't gotten my damn hug from you today."

Crazy man and his insistence on hugs. "I don't want this cuddling to keep you from doin' other things."

He sighed. "Here I thought you were paying attention when I told you I sit around doin' nothin' ninety percent of my day. Which is why I volunteered to be your caretaker; I got nothin' else to take care of."

"Lucky me." When he tensed, she said, "I wasn't bein' sarcastic. I do feel lucky that you're looking out for me. Thank you."

"My pleasure. Now take a few deep breaths and relax. Let the pain pill do its job."

"I'm still expecting you to finish your list."

"Lola *is* a taskmaster," he murmured against the top of her head.

Someone needs to be, with you.

"I say the same thing to my sisters all the time."

Whoa. She hadn't said that out loud, had she?

"Quit fidgeting."

With his warm lips on her temple and his soothing caress on her skin, Riss could easily become addicted to this feeling of contentment.

The meds kicked in, the pain faded and she drifted into sleep.

Chapter Eleven

Once again, Riss jolted awake, disoriented.

Very disoriented, since she couldn't remember the last time she'd awoken with her face nestled into a warm neck and male scruff tickling her cheek.

"Do you ever wake up slowly," Ike murmured next to her ear, "or do you prefer to scare yourself awake?"

"It's those pain pills. Drops me like I've been KO'd and I wake up the same way, lookin' around in a panic for who knocked me out." She struggled to free herself from the temptation of burrowing deeper into him.

His arms fell away. "Guess I should consider myself lucky that you didn't wake up swinging."

"That'd be hard to do since you've got me locked down." She inhaled a deep breath and let it out. "I do feel better."

"I told you that you needed that pain pill."

Riss shifted to look at him.

"What?"

"You sound like my brothers with the 'neener neener, I told you so' response."

"And you were acting like my baby sister with the 'you're not the boss of me' attitude," he retorted.

"Baby sister," she scoffed. "How old is she?"

"Lea is twenty-nine."

She smirked. "I hit the big 3-0 last year."

Ike smirked back. "I will hit the big 4-0 this year."

"Just think . . . if you got married this year, you and the little wifey would be together for twenty-five years when you retired."

"Jesus, Riss. I don't know what scares me more. The thought of bein' with a woman that long or retiring from a business that ain't even got off the ground yet."

"How long were you a cattle broker?"

"I worked for the same company for twenty years." Ike pushed her hair over her shoulder. "Does that seem pathetic I was always a company man, loyal to the very end?"

By the casual, almost absentminded way he touched her, Riss knew his thoughts were elsewhere. Maybe she could get an honest answer out of him—the man was a master at deflection—because pieces of his story didn't line up. "Seems odd a proclaimed 'company man' would simply walk away."

"Oh, trust me; there wasn't anything simple about it."

She waited for him to explain that statement, but he just kept twining the same curl around his index finger over and over.

So she tried a different tack. "What really happened between you and my brother Lloyd?"

"What did he tell you?"

"Just that you got him fired."

Those piercing blue eyes met hers. "So you hated me because Lloyd told you to?"

"Sounds stupid when you say it that way. But I am loyal to my brother, which is why his anger and resentment toward you when he lost his job became my anger and resentment toward you."

"Even if Lloyd was in the wrong?"

"I don't know that he was wrong, which is why I'm asking you what happened."

"Riss, I'm not sure—"

"I am." Her fingers circled his wrist. "Lloyd wouldn't be straight with me. When I pushed the issue, Lonnie made me back off."

"Too bad Lonnie ain't around now," Ike muttered.

"Lonnie said Lloyd would tell me when he was ready. It's been, what . . . three years? He should've gone into more detail than *don't trust Palmer; he has his own agenda* when he knew I'd be seeing you on a regular basis."

"That's all Lloyd said?"

"Well . . . he forbade me from workin' with you, and you know how well ultimatums go over with me."

Ike moved his arm, forcing Riss to let go of it. He scrubbed both hands over his face. "Yeah, I guess I can see where *my* motives would be suspect when Lloyd was workin' for a lyin' piece of shit like Zeke Toggles."

"Again, you're talking in riddles and I have no idea what the hell that means. All I know is that Lloyd took a job with Toggles right after he outprocessed from the air force."

His gaze caught hers again. "Why Toggles?"

"My brother wanted to work outside. Toggles needed a ranch hand so Lloyd hired on. None of us were happy he'd opted to live outside of Laramie instead of around Casper, but he was closer to the VA and veterans' services in Cheyenne."

"So he took a job with a man he knew nothin' about?"

"I think I've established that, Ike, so just get to the meat of the story," she said crossly.

"Fine. About a dozen years ago, Toggles inherited his uncle's ranch, but no cattle. So instead of getting a loan to buy stock, he decided to steal other ranchers' calves. He sold them on the black market and built up enough capital to fund his own herd."

Riss gave him a skeptical look. "You're saying Toggles was a cattle rustler?"

"Yep."

"In this day and age cattle rustling is still a thing?"

"With the acreage needed to sustain livestock out here, the herd gets isolated and it happens more often than it should. Lots of guys chalk up missing calves to animal predators—that's usually the easiest explanation. But one of Toggles's neighbors saw Toggles casing the herd a few days before four calves went missing. He called the sheriff but there wasn't evidence so Toggles wasn't ever charged, but everyone knew that Toggles was guilty. At Stocksellers, we were warned never to do business with him. All of our buying and selling had documentation and the company has an excellent reputation for quality and fair dealing. There were plenty of other cattle brokers around who didn't have the same moral compass, so Toggles didn't have a problem turning over his herd. But it stuck in his craw that Stocksellers refused his business. But he knew brokers are always lookin' for new business, so he had Lloyd pretend to be a new potential client. Lloyd called as the seller and set up an appointment for us to come out and evaluate his stock for a rapid sale."

"Seriously?"

"I don't doubt that Lloyd didn't know what Toggles was up to and Toggles lied to him. Stocksellers sent me to handle it and I knew as soon as I was within a mile of Toggles's place that we'd been set up. Problem was, with a rapid sale, I'd already contacted some of my clients who were looking to buy and I hated that I'd have to go back to them and tell them it'd been a misunderstanding. So I was good and pissed off by the time I got out of my truck. Of course, Toggles hadn't come; he'd sent Lloyd to meet me. I lost my shit, said a bunch of things, half of which I don't remember. And instead of Lloyd listening, he got mad. He said if he didn't close the deal with me then Toggles would fire him. I told him I didn't care."

Riss's anger bubbled up, but she slapped a lid on it.

"And I didn't. I walked away."

"That's it?"

Ike shook his head. "We both know Toggles fired him. Not my problem. So a couple weeks later I was at Summerfest and Lloyd waylaid me in the parking lot. I'd had enough to drink that I didn't appreciate him talkin' shit about me. So we got into it. After a few punches, we ended up rollin' in the dirt."

"I'm glad I wasn't there."

"You were the only member of the Thorpe family who wasn't there that night."

Her mouth dropped open. "Louie and Lonnie both jumped in? Three against one?"

"No, just Louie at first. When I started to beat his ass, Lonnie showed up."

She stopped herself from asking how much time Ike had spent in the hospital after tangling with Lonnie, because Ike would think she was joking. Lonnie didn't ever settle his differences the Wyoming way—aka with his fists—since he could go to jail for it. "I take it Lonnie broke up the fight?"

"Yeah. He warned me the next time the three of them crossed paths with me, just another scumbag cattle broker, I wouldn't be so lucky."

She snorted. That sounded like her big brother.

"His threat didn't make sense. Wasn't my fault that Lloyd lost his job because he bought into Toggles's lies. It was nearly *two years* before you and I met and that Thorpe family grudge remained in place. So what am I missing?"

"Lloyd didn't want—" Riss snapped her mouth shut.

"Don't you clam up on me now. Lloyd was hammered and said a bunch of random shit about low-life brokers destroying his family. What was that about?"

"Our dad."

Ike frowned. "What about him?"

"Dad supplemented the ranch income workin' as a mechanic. He was a piss-poor money manager. He got behind on the mortgage and to stave off foreclosure, he decided to sell his cows. A slick-talkin' cattle broker promised Dad he could get him top dollar. The broker loaded up the cows and no one ever saw him again."

"You're kidding."

"Nope. Then the bank foreclosed on the ranch. Instead of allowing us to become homeless, Bob, my dad's stepbrother, funded the down payment and cosigned the loan for the house that my brothers still live in now. Apparently the ranch loan had been in my mom's name and no one gave a shit what it did to her credit since Dad had always made payments and she wasn't even around."

Ike flopped back into the cushions and groaned. "Jesus. What are the odds? Seriously, Riss. Your dad . . . and your brother havin' bad luck at the hands of a cattle broker?"

"I don't know why those fuckwits didn't tell me what'd gone on with you and Lloyd. Wasn't like when I was a kid and I didn't know why we were moving away from the ranch. I didn't find out the truth until I was eighteen." She clenched and unclenched her fist. "I hate that they keep stuff from me, like I'm a weepy little girl who can't handle the truth."

"Hey." He grabbed her hand and brushed his mouth across her knuckles until she loosened her fist. "You're the toughest woman I know."

Ike's sweetness caught her off guard again.

"I hate that a simple conversation would've cleared this up," he said. "It probably wouldn't have ended the antagonism between us entirely, but it might've happened sooner."

"Maybe. Losing that stupid job was the best thing for Lloyd anyway. And for Lonnie. Lloyd moved to Casper and took the mechanic's job at the garage. With reliable help, Lonnie could finally buy the shop from Ricky Freytag."

"Do all of your brothers work together and live together?"

"They all live together, but just Lonnie and Lloyd work together. Lou is the shift manager at Crow's Truck Stop. He rotates first through third shift every six weeks. He's on nights now, so they had a babysitter for me during the day." Riss tipped her head back and looked at him. "Why am I telling you all this?"

"Because we're roomies and roomies swap stories and other stuff."

"Well, roomie, I'll take your word for it. But I draw the line at us painting each other's nails and gossiping about boys."

Ike wore a cute smile as he studied her.

"What?"

"My sisters never gossiped about boys with me either. Maybe if they would have, Jen wouldn't have gotten knocked up twice. By two different guys."

"Don't tell me you feel guilty about that?"

"No." He sighed. "Maybe a little. I love my niece and nephew. I just don't think Jen knew how hard it is to be a single parent."

"You do."

"Yeah." He pushed her hair away from her forehead. "Even when at times it feels like you don't get a minute to yourself, it's lonely. None of my friends understood what I dealt with every day, except for Abe Lawson. But Hank and Celia were older when their parents died. Lea was eight, Kay was ten and Jen was twelve. My options were suck it up and be a single guardian or split them up into foster care."

"Which wasn't an option. I get that. Lonnie faced the

same choice when our dad died. At age nineteen he became guardian to a seventeen-year-old, a fifteen-year-old and a twelve-year-old."

"Riss, darlin', where was your mom, if you don't mind me askin'?"

"She took off when I was five. Again, I don't have all the particulars," she said with a tinge of bitterness, "but once I overheard Dad and Lonnie talking about us kids bein' registered with the tribe and the monthly stipend per kid. Evidently that was her stipulation for signing away all her parental rights to Dad. She got every penny every month until we turned eighteen. So as you can imagine, things were a little tight for us."

"Man. No offense, but that is cold."

"I'm glad she left. She didn't even come back for Dad's funeral."

Ike continued stroking her hair. "You haven't seen her since you were five?"

The ugly memory came roaring back. Her haggard-looking mother showed up teary eyed, acting remorseful, and zeroed in on Riss, who at age sixteen had daily battles with Lonnie about everything. So naturally, Riss glommed on to her mom, believing her promises, seeking her advice and offering to help her out by begging Lonnie to let her stay with them. Looking back, Lonnie had made the smart move by agreeing to let their mom crash with them, because Riss was forced to see her all the time, not just short, happy times of her mother's choosing.

The first week things were great. Her mom had even purchased a prom dress for Riss. A hideous dress, but Riss had been secretly thrilled her mom wanted to be part of that moment in Riss's life. By week two, Mom went out partying every night and sometimes wasn't back by the time Riss left for school. By week three, Mom was snappish and mean, making fun of Riss or tossing out backhanded compliments.

But the kicker was the night Riss overheard Lonnie and Mom arguing about money. That had been the only reason she'd come back, to connive them out of cash or to steal it. Lonnie ordered her out of the house, and when she refused to go, he called the sheriff.

So the last time she'd seen her mother, she'd been spewing obscenities at Louie, hurling insults and lies at Riss and threatening Lonnie with legal action as the deputy shoved her in the back seat of a cop car. She'd never discussed the visit with her brothers. Neither had they known the nights she'd cried herself to sleep, feeling ashamed for getting tangled up in her mother's poisonous web.

"Riss?" Ike murmured.

"Sorry, I zoned out there for a moment."

"You okay?"

"Uh-huh."

Warm lips grazed her ear. "Liar."

Oh man. His breath in her ear sent tingles up her scalp, nearly setting her hair on end. She waited for him to say something else, but he appeared to be . . . sniffing her?

Nah. Couldn't be.

But then Ike trailed his nose down her neck and back up.

Her skin broke out in gooseflesh and she remained still to see what he'd do next.

"Christ, woman. You always smell like coconuts."

"It's my body spray. I can stop using it if it bothers you."

He chuckled against her neck. "It gets me bothered in a way I shouldn't be. It makes me wanna take a big bite outta you, see if you taste as good as you smell."

Don't arch your neck. Don't offer to let him taste you wherever he wants.

Wait a second. How had she gotten sprawled across the back cushions?

Ike lifted his head and gazed into her eyes. He didn't smile, but took his time studying every nuance of her face. "Not a look I ever expected to see you aiming at me, sweet cheeks."

"What look is that?" she said breathlessly.

"Like you wanna take a big bite outta me too."

"If I had the chance, the first part I'd start nibbling on are those sexy-ass lips of yours."

"Larissa." He half growled her name. "This can't . . ."

The doorbell rang.

He froze.

She froze.

The doorbell pealed again.

He muttered, "Saved by the goddamncd bell." He gently pushed away from her and perched on the edge of the couch. He finally looked at her as the doorbell dinged for the third time. "Sorry."

Then he stood and disappeared around the corner.

Riss closed her eyes, not sure if she should feel relieved by the interruption or annoyed by it.

From the entryway, she heard Ike say, "Bernice. I didn't know you were coming by today."

"Bob has a thing at the Moose Lodge tonight so I'm

checking on my niece. See if she needs anything." Bernice bustled into the room and stopped in front of Riss. Her eyes narrowed. "You look flushed. You feeling okay?"

"I accidentally used my arm today like I normally would and it reminded me why I'm not supposed to do that."

"Your caretaker didn't stop you before it happened?"

She shrugged. "My fault, not his. I took a pain pill and just woke up. Anyway, you're here to torment me because you're bored with Uncle Bob gone for the night?"

She grinned. "Maybe I'm telling Bob I'm here when I've got plans with the Mud Lilies. That way he won't worry about me when he's with his buddies."

Riss shook her finger at her aunt. "If he calls lookin' for you, Aunt B, I'm rolling on you."

Ike said, "And here you had me convinced you weren't a snitch."

"A snitch is if I called my uncle and told him she was whoopin' it up with her cronies. I don't plan on doin' that."

"Good. I've got time to kill before I meet up with the Lilies, so into the bathroom with you."

"But I didn't text you."

"I wasn't gonna wait around for that. Anyway, I got you on the schedule and I'm here. Now git movin'. Them bingo cards are calling my name." She offered her hand to Riss and gently pulled her to her feet.

"A bingo night is in your big, wild plans with your pals?" Riss snickered. "I imagined you all would be at a private survivalist training meeting, learning to make bombs out of simple household chemicals."

Bernice patted her hand. "That's next month. Tonight

we gotta earn the cash to pay for the private training. It's double payout at the senior center in Casper. Last time we played on a double payout night we cleaned 'em out."

Riss frowned at her. "Should you be bragging that you emptied the coffers at a senior citizens' community center?"

"Ain't like we're stealing it. We earned every penny of ka-ching by playing their game of chance. Besides, it's not like they're gonna complain, since each one of us buys eight bingo cards for each session." She winked. "Plus, the bingo caller is sweet on Tilda. She sneaks him nips from her flask during breaks."

"Honestly, that sounds like fun."

"I'd love to take you sometime." She shuffled down the hallway to the guest bathroom.

Ike's voice tickled her ear. "Poor Tilda. That bingo caller sees you? He'll be as sweet on you as I am."

The sexy way Ike said *sweet* wasn't sweet at all.

That annoyed her. Hadn't the man just apologized for getting cozy with her? And now he was flirting with her again? Talk about running hot and cold.

She put distance between them before she turned and said, "Make a list or make supper, but do something useful."

He had no retort for that.

Chapter Twelve

❧

*R*iss stormed into the kitchen and announced, "I have to leave the house today and that is not a goddamned request."

"It's an order?"

"Yes."

Ike glanced up from the newspaper. "If I refuse?"

"I'll start smashing my cast into the walls because I swear they're closing in on me."

"You sure you oughta go out?"

"Why? Is it below zero outside?"

"No. But accidentally using your arm yesterday had you out cold on the couch by eight o'clock last night."

"That wasn't my fault." She swiped his coffee and drained it. "*You* picked the snoozefest movie about fishing."

"*A River Runs Through It* ain't about fishing. If you

woulda stayed awake you'd know that." He pried the mug from her hand. "And get your own damn coffee."

Riss sighed. "The honeymoon period of you waiting on me hand and foot is officially over."

"Get up earlier if you want the full treatment, darlin'."

"What time did you roll out of bed?"

"When the alarm went off at five a.m."

"Why?"

He chuckled at her horrified expression. "To deal with the livestock."

"Oh. Right. I forget that's part of the gig with you cowboy types who love country livin'."

"I'll remind you I wasn't raised on a ranch. If I could find a reliable hired hand to spread hay and shovel shit, I'd happily pass it off."

"Then why don't you?"

Because I don't have a spare nickel these days.

"Because I'd take a rash of shit from Renner, Tobin, Hugh, Hank, Abe, Bran, Kyle and Fletch about bein' a pussy. Easier to do it myself than make myself a target for the real country types who do love country livin'."

"Sucks to be you, dude. Anyway, I'm ready to go."

His gaze slid over her. Damn. She looked fine today with her hair down and those corkscrew curls just begging for a man to twine them around his fingers. She hadn't bothered with makeup besides adding gloss to her lips. His perusal stopped at her neck. He didn't care what clothes she had on because he couldn't see past her smile. "Where am I takin' you?"

"Out of this house."

"How about Casper? We could grab lunch."

"Rawlins is closer." She sidled up to him. "Or are you embarrassed to be seen with me in your hometown?"

"No. Trust me . . . you look good enough to eat." Dammit, he'd promised himself he wouldn't say shit like that after their close call yesterday afternoon. "But I'm near guaranteed to run into one of my sisters if we're in Rawlins. They have an uncanny ability to find me and, sweet cheeks, I don't feel like—"

"Explaining me."

He smiled. "I'll start the truck."

The sun shone, giving the illusion of warmer temps than the mercury indicated. But it was a pretty morning. Even the snowdrifts had an extra sparkle in the sunlight.

They didn't speak, nor did Ike turn on the radio.

When they were within five miles of Casper, he said, "What's your favorite restaurant?"

"I usually eat at one of the truck stops."

"Not today. I've got a place in mind if you trust my judgment."

"You've been cooking for me all week so it's only fair that you pick the place and I pay."

He shook his head. "I pick. I pay."

"Fine. If those are the rules then I'll pick."

"Don't matter. I'll still pay."

"Ike."

"Larissa. You can't win, so give up."

She laughed. "And you claim *I'm* stubborn."

Ike chose Reuben's Diner. Couldn't go wrong with comfort food and cozy private booths.

After placing their orders, he caught Riss studying him. "What?"

"How many dates have you brought here?"

"A few. Why?"

She shrugged. "Just curious if you had a routine laid out. Dine at Reuben's. Catch a movie at the C-plex. Then rock the rocker panels getting down to funky-monkey business in the truck."

Christ. "Do you lie in bed at night and think this kinda stuff up?"

"Sometimes. So, tell me if I'm right."

"I'm thrilled to say . . . you're wrong."

"Shoot." She smirked. "Bein' wrong happens so rarely that you'll wanna write it on the calendar to mark the occasion."

He laughed. He never would've thought being with her would be so easy.

"What's your favorite thing to do in Casper?"

"There've been some great concerts at the Events Center."

"I can't do concerts. They crank the music so loud that my eyeballs pulse. FYI: Pulsing eyeballs? Not fun." She swirled her soda with a straw. "I'd rather go to the symphony. Too bad you missed Jade's debut. Her solo was amazing."

"No offense, but you don't seem like the type to dig classical music."

"My dad loved it. I used to tag along when he worked in the garage on the weekend. He amassed a ton of info on classical music, especially for a mechanic with grease-stained hands."

He didn't detect embarrassment that her father had been blue collar, which was a refreshing change from other women he'd hooked up with who were trying to outrun their pasts. "Class and culture don't have economic boundaries."

"Class doesn't, but culture absolutely does. He didn't have cash to pay someone to 'culture' him so he learned about music on his own." She looked up at him. "Which in some ways was better because it meant so much to him."

"You're so damn smart."

Riss gave him a cheesy wink. "Not bad for a chick with just a high school diploma and a Commercial Driver's License. So what about you?"

"What about me?"

"Did you go to college or trade school?"

He shook his head. "School of Hard Knocks. Right after high school I needed to work to support my sisters."

"Was there life insurance?"

"Yeah, but by the time I paid off the medical bills there wasn't anything left."

Riss threaded her fingers through his. "It's weird how we came from similar situations, but reversed birth order."

"Kindred spirits. That explains why we've always gotten along so well."

She laughed. "Smart-ass."

Their meals arrived.

After they'd eaten and had returned to the truck, Riss yawned. "Where to now?"

"Home. You'll be asleep five minutes after we're on the highway."

"No, I won't. I promise to stay awake, but you've gotta talk to me."

Ike sent her a sideways glance. "As long as we don't talk about JSC. At all."

"Fine, roomie. Let's see how similar our histories really are."

"Nope, nice try. But you haven't been lewd and crude for a couple of days, and I'm your captive audience, so I'm betting your questions will all be sex related, and I don't need to drive with a hard-on for the next hour."

"Just talking about sex will get you hard?"

Just talking about sex with you *will get me hard. Because then I'll imagine how hot the sex would be with you. What sounds you'd make with my mouth sucking your tits and my fingers fucking you.*

"Ike?"

"Gimme a sec, I'm coming up with a question."

Riss started humming the *Jeopardy!* theme song.

"Got it."

"Hit me."

"Favorite sport to play when you were a kid."

"Like, group sport? Probably kickball. There wasn't money for club soccer or hockey or volleyball." She looked at him. "Your turn."

"Football. I didn't do extracurricular either since cash was tight. In high school I joined rodeo club so I didn't have to pay to watch my friends compete."

"Smart." She tapped the console. "My turn. Who was your first big crush?"

"Like someone famous?"

"Sure."

He blurted out, "Anna Nicole Smith."

"Because . . . ?"

"Curvy body and those tits. Man." He looked at her. "Now you. Who were you crushing on?"

"Spice Girls. I wore out one CD entirely. I so wanted to be part of their posse. As far as guy crushes? Spike from *Buffy the Vampire Slayer*."

"Why him?"

"It was the first time I understood that people weren't all good or all evil. That you could be both and there'd be times in your life when one would overtake the other." She smirked. "Plus, I like blond guys."

Was she yanking his chain? He couldn't tell.

"Your turn, blondie," she said with a laugh.

Definitely yanking his chain. "How did you become a truck driver?"

"By chance. Casper High School had a test program my senior year with Sage Truck Driving School. Kind of an overview course of the different requirements for a Commercial Driver's License. No girls were on the list, which was bullshit, so I signed up. Anyway, after the course ended and I'd done well—better than any of my male classmates—they offered me an admission slot for the summer. I took it and haven't looked back. The only downside was bein' so young when I graduated. I had to take a lot of shit jobs—not just shitty driving jobs—to make a living. But it taught me self-reliance."

"So, I noticed when we picked your stuff up that you've added a dump truck to your fleet."

"Fleet. Hah. Hard to justify keeping any of the trailers since I don't own a semitruck. I tried the owner-operator route and it didn't work for me, nearly sent me into bankruptcy. I'm better off driving for someone else like Tito and Desert Plains. I own the bull hauler and the cargo van outright. The other trailers I co-own with Lonnie and Lloyd—including the dump truck. I found it at an auction and it needed an overhaul, which chases most bidders away. But I've got an ace in the hole with Lonnie and Lloyd both bein' mechanics, so we went halvsies on it. We'll probably put it up for sale this spring when construction is in full swing again."

"Riss, darlin', if you don't own a semitruck outright, then how did you plan to haul bulls for JSC?" It bothered him that she'd led them to believe she was fully equipped to work with them.

"The few times JSC hired me I rented the semi from Tito and hooked up my bull hauler. If there'd been any indication you'd need a full-time driver, I probably would've considered buying a semi. As it is now . . . I—we—make more money renting out the trailers to other drivers for short hauls."

When she rested her head against the window and remained silent for several long moments, Ike jostled her leg. "Hey. No sleeping."

"Then talk to me."

"Ask me a question."

"What's the most fun thing you ever learned how to do that you didn't get paid for?"

"That was random."

She shrugged. "It's on the same lines of how I got interested in driving. I didn't get paid to take that course in high school. In fact, I had to quit my waitressing job for six weeks because all of the training was after school and on weekends."

Ike didn't have a long list of employers and part-time jobs. He'd had little free time in the years he'd raised his sisters to learn new skills. He knew enough about basic mechanics to get by, but he wasn't interested in any skill that required a garage full of specialized tools. It wasn't that he didn't like getting his hands dirty—he dealt with livestock nearly every day and he'd spent numerous weekends fixing fence with his rancher buddies—he just wasn't interested in building shit from scratch.

Until he'd worked with Holt on his house. Something about the scent of fresh-sawn lumber, the rapid beat of hammers on wood and metal, the sense of accomplishment for his contribution, no matter how small, had given him a different perspective. And one he hadn't thought of in a long damn time.

"Ike?"

"Sorry. Helping Holt build my house was fun. I wasn't setting roof trusses or framing out windows or pouring concrete, but I saw it all done. It helped too that Holt didn't treat me like an idiot who oughta know the basics."

Riss reached for his hand. "Everyone needs a friend like that."

"Or better yet, we should try to be that type of friend." Ike felt her staring at him. "What?"

"Sometimes you say things that remind me you're more than a hot-bodied cowboy charmer with a ridiculous smile and super awesome hair."

He granted her a ridiculous smile. "Why, thank you, sweet cheeks."

His cell phone rang through his navigation system. The screen read: LEA.

He released Riss's hand and poked the ANSWER CALL icon. "Hello?"

"Ike, omigod, I'm so glad I caught you! Everything is

a disaster and I don't know what to do. First it was one thing and now it's like the universe is conspiring against me."

"Lea, slow down and tell me what's goin' on."

"The shower isn't draining. Water is running out the base and I've used all my towels to try and soak it up."

"You didn't notice the drain was plugged when you were standing ankle deep in water?" Lea took notoriously long, hot showers.

Riss snickered.

"Well, I guess I did. I was thinking about my test next week and time got away from me."

"When was the last time you used drain cleaner?"

Silence. Then, "Drain cleaner? Ike . . . I don't know what that is."

"You pour it in to dissolve hair clogs."

"Eww! I don't even want to think about that."

"You'll have to buy some. Just ask the clerk at the store."

"But . . . I don't have time to go to the store. That's what I was trying to tell you! I have a project due, no food in my apartment, a clogged shower—and I think my neighbor's cat might be dead on my balcony."

He'd laugh, but Lea would start crying and then he'd have to deal with that too.

"Can you please come over and help me?"

For a moment, he wondered what fiercely independent Riss was thinking about his very dependent youngest sister.

"Please?" Lea pleaded.

"I'm in my truck drivin' between Casper and Muddy Gap. So it'll be at least an hour before I can get there."

"That's perfect. Thank you so much! You're the best brother ever! Love you!" The call ended.

He sighed. "Sorry. I'll have to drop you off first because . . . well, you heard."

"Yeah." She stared out the passenger's window. "Do your sisters need your help with stuff like this very often?"

"Lea more than Jen or Kay. But when things go to hell in their lives, or at least they believe that it has, I'm first on the call list."

"What would Lea have done if you'd said no?"

Ike's hand tightened on the steering wheel.

"You never say no to them, do you?" Riss answered for him.

"Not usually."

"What do they do when you're out of town?"

"Wait until I get back," he joked.

Ten minutes passed in silence.

Ike was grateful that Riss had fallen asleep. Now he wouldn't have to try and explain why he gave so much time and attention to his sisters. Nor would he have to admit to her—and to himself—how little they reciprocated. Lea hadn't asked him about Riss, when he knew damn well Jen had spread the news to her and Kay after her visit.

Then again, he wouldn't know how to describe his relationship with Riss to them when he didn't understand it himself. It seemed to change every damn day.

An owl-eyed Riss sent him a questioning gaze when he parked his truck in the driveway. "You'll be all right on your own for a few hours?"

"I'll probably sleep some more." She yawned. "Getting

out of the house was great, thank you. But I hate how tired I am."

Ike helped her out of the truck and into his front entryway. As he unbuttoned her coat and unwound her scarf he said, "Text me if you need anything."

"I will."

But he knew she wouldn't. "I'll be back before supper."

"No worries. Do what you need to. It's not like I'm goin' anywhere."

She shuffled off to her bedroom.

∞

The next day, Riss was determined to make up for lost time in sorting out the JSC paperwork, since Ike hadn't returned until nearly nine the previous evening.

Guilt still gnawed at him because she'd fed herself and crawled in bed.

Some great caretaker he made.

So he'd slapped on a happy face when she suggested tackling the boxes of files.

The woman was a one-armed bulldog, pawing through papers with a single-minded concentration that made Ike feel like a slacker.

Face it: you are a slacker. The more she digs, the more obvious it'll become.

"Ike, is there a master list?"

"Uh. No."

Riss shuffled through a pile of papers. "Here's *a* list." She scanned the words with her pen. "There are a lot of smaller, one-day events that don't have a check mark. What does that mean?"

"That neither of us had contact with the event coordinators in the past year."

Her gaze trapped his. "But this list is duplicated someplace else with the details of follow-up contact?"

"Nope. That's the only list with the info. No need to duplicate it when it's blank."

"It shouldn't be blank. There should be notes on who was the main contact. If there was a secondary contact. The dates you called to discuss next year's schedule. If there wasn't a convo with a real live person, that should be noted. As should the date of the second attempt of contact. And the third . . . and so on."

"In makin' the calls, sometimes the phone number wasn't current and neither was the contact person. I'd reckon about half the names and numbers on that list fall into that category."

"If you'd kept accurate records, you'd have that exact information."

Ike kept his laid-back posture and granted her an easy smile. "Salesmen are notorious for their bad record keeping, darlin'. Say I'm on the road at an event. When I'm chatting with Barbara, the event coordinator, my focus is on selling our services to her. Face time is crucial. I need to make an impression so when I follow up with Barbara, she remembers me."

Riss scribbled on the list and then snapped it in his face. "It took me literally two seconds to jot that down. Two seconds. With my left hand."

"What'd you write?"

"Barbara, first contact and the date. You could also put in personal info, like if she is a ranch woman or a rodeo queen or if she goes everywhere with a three-legged dog."

"Them kinda details?" He tapped his temple. "It's all up here. So it sounds natural and not like I memorized stats from a master list." In a robotic tone he said, "'Barbara Duncan, of the Skyview Rodeo Committee. How are you today? How is your dog Fido? Could we discuss the benefits of hiring Jackson Stock Contracting.'"

Riss didn't even crack a smile. "All right, Mr. It's All Up Here"—she tapped her temple—"what can you tell me about . . ." She snatched another list off the pile. "Marietta Eichenberg?"

"You gonna at least give me a hint on which event she runs?"

"Sure. Sun Valley."

Sun Valley? Where the hell was that? Ike's mind went completely blank. Then his stomach roiled—just like it had in high school when faced with a pop quiz. And also like in high school, he flashed an aw-shucks smile that kept him out of teacher trouble. "Afraid you stumped me on that one, darlin'."

"Okay. How about . . . D. J. Jeffers? Man? Woman? Heads up the Madison County Fair?"

"You sure you're lookin' at the right list?" He leaned forward, resting his forearms above his knees, like he could somehow cheat and see the right answer.

"There are a couple of check marks by the names at the bottom, so that indicates you handled this list."

"Read me one of the names with a check mark."

Riss looked at him. "I did. D. J. Jeffers has a check beside it."

"Nothin' else?"

"Nope."

"Dammit, how did this list slip through?"

"Ike. That's *one* of three incomplete lists. How many more are in there"—she pointed to the stack of papers in front of her—"and in there?"—and then to the four boxes on the floor.

He scrubbed his hands over his face. "I don't have a fuckin' clue."

"When was the last time you pulled information from these boxes?"

"Late fall, before I had to switch gears and start shipping cattle."

Her expression read: *You've been slacking on this for over two months?*

"Then all the prewedding stuff—"

"Kept you too busy to attend to your business? Because I remember you admitting that your part in the wedding party was to show up in a suit and hold the rings."

"Fine. I suck at this record-keeping stuff. You happy now?"

Riss's gaze turned laser sharp. "Why would I be happy? Your disorganization cost me money. JSC only managed to score four events last year."

"Six," he corrected. "We had to use another bull hauler for two events since you were unavailable."

Ike expected her to snap back, but she didn't say a word.

She let the paper in her hand float down to the table . . . like a mike drop. Then she rose from her chair. "My head is spinning. I'm gonna lie down for a bit."

"Do you need—"

"No. I'm good." She stopped halfway across the living room before she turned around. "You need to organize those papers if we hope to get anywhere with them."

He smiled. "I'm on it." The second she was gone, he pressed his forehead to the table and groaned.

Organize them? He thought that was what they were doing. Together.

If he had an idea how to do it himself, he would've already done it.

In the brokering business, he'd paid a secretary to keep his client files organized and up to date. All he had to do to access information was click on the program and the color-coordinated spreadsheet appeared like magic.

Yeah, you were spoiled.

Over the years Ike had gone to great pains to hide the truth he wasn't book smart. In high school he'd struggled to carry a low C average. He hated to read; he hated to write. Even now he spent very little time on the computer. Facebook and social media didn't interest him. If he wanted to sit in front of a screen for hours on end, he'd turn on the damn TV.

People who geeked out over gadgets and technology? He didn't get it—literally; he didn't understand half of what they yammered on about. Ike considered himself lucky that he hadn't needed technical knowledge to start working at Stocksellers all those years ago. He had a diploma, a knack for selling things, a mentor and three sisters to support. That was all he needed to succeed.

When technology first started creeping into the

brokering world, Ike made a good show of embracing it. Then the company began losing clients due to live-stream sales. The personal connection between the stock growers and the brokers didn't matter as much as the bottom line.

He'd barely been a decade into funding his retirement when Stocksellers "refocused" their business plan. At thirty-seven years old he'd been released from the only real job he'd ever had.

It embarrassed him.

It confused him.

It depressed the hell out of him.

Not that anyone—his sisters or his friends—had caught on. They still saw the laid-back guy, the charming salesman, the always-there big brother, the buddy his friends could count on to share a beer with or lend them a hand, and not the unemployed loser.

Ike hid his emotions so well that some days he believed he was okay.

Then there were the other days. The dark ones.

No one knew he suffered from severe insomnia. No one figured out his weight loss was from anxiety. No one knew some days he'd get up and aimlessly drive hundreds of miles.

Speaking of hundreds of miles . . . He pulled his phone out of his back pocket and called Hugh.

But by the second ring, he felt like a pussy asking for advice on how to alphabetize shit.

"Ike. Hey. What's up?"

"Not much. Freezin' my nuts off. How about you?"

"Smoggy here today."

"Now that the weather talk is outta the way, I have a

question. I'm reorganizing the paperwork Renner gave us from previous rodeo events. Not sure if I oughta file them alphabetically by the event name, or by state with subfolders."

"Why would you refile them by state? There are only about ten states that we dealt with. Chronological order of the events, separated by year, is how we did it."

He forced a chuckle. "Guess I don't need to reinvent the wheel, huh?"

"Nope. That said, at this point all my event information down here is potential. When an event becomes actual, then I'll have to create another spreadsheet."

"That's a smart idea," he said, without understanding a lick of what Hugh had just said.

"Why are you digging through that old paperwork again? Didn't you comb through all of the boxes last year?"

Ike had made it through one box and hadn't found anything useful or interesting, so it seemed a waste of time to paw through even older paperwork. "Since Riss is staying here we're backtracking in hopes of discovering some jewel of info we might've missed."

A pause. "If you run into questions about a specific event, e-mail me a copy of the contact and I'll see if it jogs my memory."

"Thanks, man. I appreciate it."

"How're things goin' with Riss? She's been there a week now?"

"She improves every day. We'll see how much improvement when she goes to the doctor next week."

"You're even taking her to doctor's appointments?"

His retort—*Who else would do it?*—stayed unspoken.

Ike knew all she'd have to do was pick up the phone and half a dozen people would be there to help her out.

"This is her first checkup since surgery."

"I wish her well. Bet you'll be glad when she can go home."

Actually no. Turns out I like having her here.

"Speaking of . . . Harlow just walked in so I gotta go."

"Later."

Ike skirted the boxes and snagged a beer from the fridge.

Chapter Thirteen

※

*R*iss's phone rang at eight thirty. She fumbled for it, casting a bleary eye at the caller ID. Why the hell was Jade calling her so damn early?

"Hello?"

"Morning! You up and around?"

"Uh, no. Call me back in an hour."

"Don't hang up. Drop your cock and grab your socks. I'm on my way to pick you up."

Riss released a sleepy groan. Of course that phrase would come back to bite her in the ass. How many times had she barked that same expression at Jade? She stifled a yawn. "Why are you coming here?"

"Ike asked me to."

"When?"

"Just now, after I finished prep work at the Split Rock. He and my handsome hubby are rounding up some cattle that got spooked by coyotes and he asked me to bring . . . ah . . . something to him."

"Something," Riss repeated, pushing herself upright. "Like what? I can't imagine Ike would keep anything here that he couldn't borrow from the tack room at the Split Rock."

"Are you always so cranky this early in the morning?"

"Yes."

Jade laughed. "Too bad. The truth is, Ike is sending me to pick *you* up."

She froze. "He is? Why?"

"He said you have cabin fever. I'll be there in ten minutes, using Ike's garage door opener, so don't shoot me or anything," Jade warned her.

"Lucky for you, I'm a lousy shot with my left hand."

"See you in a few." Jade hung up.

Riss shuffled into the bathroom and managed to complete her routine before she heard Jade's cheerful voice outside her bedroom door.

"Knock, knock."

"Come in."

As soon as Jade cleared the doorway, Riss said, "You're just in time to help me choose an ensemble for today. Should I go with the Chanel sweater set? Or the Prada pantsuit?" She paused. "Oh right. It'll be polyester floral shirt number three and yoga pants. Again."

"Which is why Ike told me to grab this." She held up a dark gray fleece jacket. "It should keep you warm."

Riss unhooked the sling and pulled her baggy T-shirt over her head, leaving her topless.

Modest Jade blushed when faced with Riss's bare

breasts. "Does Ike help you get dressed and undressed every day?"

I wish. Riss's thoughts rewound to the first couple of days she'd stayed here and Ike's unintentional eroticism when he helped her and how she'd declined his help because his touch had been too much to handle. "Nope. I'm fairly self-sufficient now. With the exception of bras. I'm skipping them." Of course, her struggle to get just a simple shirt on made a complete liar out of her and Jade had to step in and help.

Riss eyed the fleece zip-up. "I'll roast in that if I'm wearing a coat."

"Not where we'll be."

"Which is where exactly?"

"Outside. It's a balmy ten degrees, the sun is shining and fresh air will do you good," Jade chirped with entirely too much enthusiasm. "Now hold out your cast so I can slip this jacket on."

Ike's scent surrounded Riss—the starchy aroma of laundry detergent and the cool crispness of the outdoors. Man. That was one of her favorite things about Ike's daily demand of hugs: being enveloped in his scent. And his heat. Feeling that hard body against hers and knowing physical contact was something he only needed from her . . . made her feel a little smug.

"Did you just sigh?" Jade asked.

Rather than confessing the truth, Riss went on the offensive. "Maybe. I don't get why you're forcing me out of the house."

"For precisely that attitude. The Riss I know and love isn't content sitting still. You're always out doing something. 'Homebody' is the last term I'd use to describe you and yet here you stand, acting agoraphobic. If you truly don't want to go, I won't force you. But I thought it'd be fun to hang out for a few hours."

Riss sighed again. "I hate when you use logic on me."

"I know." She smiled. "Let's get the rest of your outerwear on and hit the trail."

∞

Riss could admit it was a gorgeous day outside.

The sun shone. The air was crisp. The snow sparkled and crunched under her boots.

She'd always loved cold weather—it was sort of a requirement of living in Wyoming. But there was something humbling about surviving blizzards and facing icy winds and frozen ground for months on end. Sometimes she believed living in harsh conditions made her appreciate the fleeting months of summer more than people who lived in places with mild temps year-round. But the truth was, she wouldn't trade her snow boots, sweaters, gloves and jackets for shorts and tank tops. Give her a winter day like today, and all seemed right with the world.

"This time I know what that sigh meant," Jade said.

Riss glanced over at her as they trudged through the partially broken crust of snow that marked the path between the main barn and the closest corral. "You heard that? Even through those ridiculous earmuffs?"

The tops of Jade's tiger earmuffs bobbed as she nodded. "You're happy to be outside."

"I am. Thank you for bringing me." Riss stopped, tilted her face to the sky and basked. "It's so quiet out here."

"Until we run into the guys yelling at the cows and each other."

"But even with that, there's a sense of peace. The cold weather just magnifies that feeling of isolation." She refocused on the landscape. Drifts of snow weren't only pure white. As hard as the wind blew, the red dirt was bound to leave its mark, so the mounds varied from ivory swirled with streaks of tan to the murky gray hue of cement. The lack of trees, structures and anything resembling civilization reinforced the sensation that not much had changed in a millennium or longer, besides a few fences and roads. How old were the root structures in the tall grasses popping up through the snowbanks? How many cycles of seasons had the skeletal sagebrush bushes survived?

Few besides hard-core Wyomingites would see the beauty here. Tourists—hell, even most residents—preferred the "prettier" places in the Equality State, like Yellowstone National Park, Jackson Hole, the Tetons and the Bighorns. But Riss loved the vast emptiness of the topography between Rawlins and Casper. In sections she could see across the horizon: red dirt, blue sky, clusters of gray scrub oaks and sun-bleached grasses waving in the always-present wind. Then the road would wend through a canyon, and she'd find herself surrounded by granite-striped rock walls that absorbed the sunlight and gave off a sinister vibe. But eventually the walls crumbled, creating plateaus where the horizon-sky was once again visible.

So she admired Renner Jackson for thumbing his nose at convention and building the Split Rock Ranch and Resort amid this odd slice of heaven.

"Sorry. I could blather on about earth, wind, sky all day. Blame it on my Native roots."

"Is it stupid that I forget you're part Native American?" Jade asked.

"Nope. Some people don't believe I have any Indian in me at all. It's weird how genetics work. Lonnie and Louie have dark hair and brown eyes, while me'n Lloyd have green eyes. The origin of my red hair is a mystery."

"It'll be interesting to see if any of my Asian and Spanish features get passed on to kiddos that Tobin and I might have." She grinned. "Speaking of hot baby-daddies . . . there's my man."

Riss turned to see four men on horseback headed across the field.

Her stomach did a slow roll. Lord. Was there anything sexier than a cowboy, all duded up in hat, boots, chaps and shearling coat as he sat atop a magnificent horse that kicked up puffs of snow with every hoofbeat?

Yep. Four cowboys decked out like that and headed her way.

But she only had eyes for one cowboy in particular.

The lone blond.

The one laughing and gesturing with his gloved free hand.

The one who looked as comfortable atop a horse as the men beside him, despite the fact he hadn't been ranch-raised like all the rest of them had been.

The one whose broad shoulders straightened a little when he caught sight of her.

She sighed.

"I know, right?" Jade said beside her. "I don't know that I'll ever get used to the fact that not only is Tobin mine, but he's the real western deal. He embodies the modern-day cowboy whether he's out checking cattle on the range or he's checking genetics in the lab in Casper."

"I've run into my share of wannabes, Jade. You don't gotta explain the appeal to me." And no doubt Ike was the real deal too. It'd been several months since she'd seen him in this cowboy role . . . and damn. How had she blocked out how much it suited him?

Because Ike Palmer in jeans, boots and a black hat, sitting astride a horse, with a bundle of rope casually hanging off his saddle, was powerful enough to make any woman drop to her knees.

In the snow.

Her heart beat a little harder as the men approached.

"Ladies," Renner Jackson said first as the posse stopped just shy of the fence. "Gorgeous day."

"It sure is," Riss said.

"How's your arm?"

"Still broken. But I've been getting excellent care." She sent Ike a grin.

"Glad to hear it." Renner wheeled around and addressed Ike. "Thanks for your help today since I know you've got other responsibilities."

"No problem. Felt good to be outdoors." He smirked. "Even if Streeter poked fun at my cattle call."

"Is that what that godawful noise was?" Streeter said. "Shoot. I thought you were rustlin' in them bushes lookin' for wild boar and using your mouth as a pig whistle."

Both Streeter and Tobin snickered.

"My approach must've worked since I rounded up, what . . . nine missing heifers to the Hale brothers' combined six?" Ike retorted.

Silence.

Ike said, "I thought so."

"Or maybe no one wants to point out how good you are at beating around the bush," Riss said sweetly.

"Dude. Total burn," Tobin said, giving Riss an air fist bump.

Streeter's gaze moved between them. "I thought you guys were in a truce or some damn thing."

Riss wondered who he'd heard that from. Gossip-lover Tobin? Or had Ike mentioned it during the live-stock checks? "We are. This is us bein' nice."

"I'd hate to see you bein' nasty."

"I can deal with nasty Riss just fine." Ike backed his horse up, but his eyes remained on Riss. "You'll stick around while I deal with Sparky?"

"Sure. I'd offer to help, but . . ." She waved her cast in the air. "I'll just snowbathe in the sunshine."

"Be careful. Don't venture too far. Stick to the places that are shoveled. The snow is slick in spots."

She gasped. "Really? Wow. Thanks for the warning. Maybe the Split Rock should put out a bulletin that ice is slippery."

Ike flipped her off.

Streeter appeared taken aback by that gesture and looked to Tobin, who just shrugged.

Jade insisted on going into the barn to help Tobin with his horse, which brought a soft smile to Streeter's face. He seemed like a sweet guy and was genuinely nice to his sister-in-law, which earned him brownie points with Riss.

So while they headed into the barn, Riss wandered

down the path that curved behind the arena into the spare gravel parking lot.

In her head, she understood that having dedicated indoor space to house a semitruck—aka the main engine—was a luxury, but it squeezed her heart a little to see JSC's Peterbilt parked outside, the top of the cab and the hood covered in snow.

Which caused her to wonder . . . when was the last time that Ike had even started it?

Riss cautioned herself to let it go, to walk the other direction, but her feet didn't obey. She stood next to the running board, which was surprisingly snow free.

That had to be a sign, right?

So she carefully used her good hand to grab onto the side mirror bracket and hoisted herself up, stepping onto the running board. From there she could peer into the cab itself, even if it did give her a momentary pang of guilt for being a Peeping Tom.

The inside of the cab was a wreck. Filled with junk. Crumpled wrappers from fast-food joints littered the floor on the passenger's side. A water-damaged cardboard box, overflowing with paperwork, took up the entire passenger's seat. Her gaze moved to the thick layer of dust coating the dashboard and the gray film that nearly distorted the windshield glass. The floor mats on the driver's side were caked with mud and straw—or possibly cowshit and straw, given this was used for hauling livestock.

But that wasn't an excuse. There was no excuse for the cab to be this filthy. It was sheer laziness not to clean the inside, especially if it wouldn't be in use for a while.

Her anger mounted.

Despite the stinging pain inside her cast, she decided to try to open the door. She hopped down off the running board, reached up and jerked the door handle hard with her left hand.

The door popped right open.

Riss climbed in the driver's side, twisting her body beneath the steering wheel, trying to see if this model had an interior hood latch. There were so damn many different makes and models of semis she couldn't keep them all straight as to where the hood latches were located. Given the state of the interior, she felt compelled to inspect the engine to determine if it suffered from general neglect too.

She noticed a fuel receipt beneath the seat. She pulled it out and squinted at the date.

It was for fuel . . . over a year ago.

Surely this rig hadn't been sitting here unused that long? Even if JSC hadn't been hauling rough stock to rodeo events, Renner Jackson had to use this to transport his livestock to sale barns or feedlots or meatpacking plants.

Now she really needed to see the maintenance logs. Too bad truck mechanics didn't attach an oil change reminder to the windshield, like lube jockeys did for personal vehicles, that detailed the date, mileage and reminder for the next oil change. She scooted forward toward the glove box and a familiar voice boomed behind her.

"What in the hell do you think you're doin'?"

She jumped and whacked her cast into the gear shaft.

"Motherfuckingsonofawhore! Jesus Christ, Palmer.

What the fuck is wrong with you that you'd sneak up on me like that?"

"What the fuck is wrong with you that you're crawling around inside a truck cab with a broken damn arm when it's ten degrees outside? If you were cold you should've come back into the barn."

Riss glared at him. "Really? I'm not an idiot who climbed into a cold cab to get warm."

"Then what the hell are you doin'?"

"Lookin' for the DVIR." When Ike gave her a blank look, she said, "The driver-vehicle inspection report. When was the last time this rig was used?"

"Why?"

"Because I want to know, that's why."

"What are you tryin' to do, Riss?"

She cautioned herself not to assume the mess in the cab was his. But she could assume that his truck maintenance record keeping was as poor as his event record keeping. She took her time getting back into a defensive position, secretly liking that she towered over him when she stood on the running board. "I'm tryin' to prove that I care. Did you know the cab door was unlocked?"

"It's standard policy for all vehicles at the Split Rock in case they need to be moved quickly."

"Even in the winter?"

Ike shifted his stance. "Why?"

"So anyone who works here has access to this vehicle?"

"Again, Riss, what's the point of this?"

"I wanna know who's been out joyridin' in this. That's the only explanation for it bein' left in that condition." She used her head to indicate the mess behind her. "Which brings up my next issue on maintenance."

"I don't see how that's any of your concern since it ain't like you'll be drivin' it anytime soon," Ike bit off.

Her jaw dropped. "I cannot *believe* you said that to me."

"I cannot believe you're snooping around tryin' to show me up, hell-bent on proving I'm doin' everything wrong."

"You're the one who asked for my help with JSC, dickface. And this goddamned semitruck is part of the company."

"Now we're back to name-callin'?" he demanded.

Riss inhaled. And exhaled. "No. Sorry. That was uncalled for." To give herself a break, she returned to the driver's seat, dropping to her knees before she patted under the dashboard.

"What in the hell are you doin' *now*?"

"Lookin' for the hood release. Sometimes they're inside the cab." Her gaze challenged his. "Do you even know how to get to the engine, Ike?"

"Yes. I'm not a fuckin' idiot," he said crossly.

"So? Where is it?"

"Back to the same old Riss." He laughed harshly. "Like I'm gonna let you poke around a greasy engine with a broken arm? No. Way. So I'll just deal with your smug face and admit I don't know the last time this thing was serviced. I haven't driven it since our last rodeo in Powell."

"Ike. That was last August."

"As I'm perfectly aware." He looked away, toward the

main barn. "There are two sets of keys that anyone who works here has access to. And you're right that I wouldn't have left the cab lookin' like that if I'd been the last one to use it. So obviously someone else did." His troubled gaze met hers. "I ain't about to go in and ask who."

Riss used the steering wheel to support herself as she reseated herself.

"I'll also admit that I haven't had this serviced since at least a month before Powell. So again. Go ahead and point out how goddamned careless and clueless I am. I'd just rather you didn't bring it up in front of everyone else, okay?"

"Ike. I wouldn't do that to you. Ever. This is between us."

Ike's face relaxed with relief. "Thank you."

She studied him for a moment as she debated.

"What now?"

"You have keys?"

"Yeah. Why?"

"Let's start 'er up and see what she runs like."

His eyes turned shrewd. "Two things are gonna happen first. One: I'm helpin' you outta the driver's side because *I'll* be the one to 'start 'er up,' not you. Two: I'm helpin' you into the passenger's side because there will be no climbing over the seats for you, monkey girl."

"Fine. But I expect you'll put that box in your pickup right now, because I think it contains service records. We need to go over them tonight."

"Deal."

A minute later he pointed at her from the passenger's doorway with the box tucked under one arm. "Stay put while I do this. If I come back and find you've moved even one mean red curl? I will paddle your luscious ass, Riss. I ain't jokin'." Then he slammed the cab door.

She snickered. *He thinks my ass is luscious, huh? In that case, I might be persuaded to disobey and let him try the paddling thing . . . one time.*

When Ike returned and opened the driver's-side door, Riss said, "Catch!" as if she intended to launch herself at him.

The man dove for her like a world-class outfielder.

"Awesome reflexes, cowboy."

"That paddling threat still holds true, sweet cheeks."

Thankfully he didn't get pissy about her fake-out. Ike granted her the you're-in-for-it-now grin and stepped up on the running board. Hooking his arm around her waist, he said, "Hold on."

And he literally meant "hold on"—the man didn't let her feet touch the ground when he carried her around the front end to the other side.

Not that she complained, since those big strong hands were firmly clamped on her ass cheeks . . . until the sadistic jerk buried his icy cold face in her warm neck and laughed when she shrieked.

"Not fair!"

"You deserved that. Now up you go."

Once they were both situated, Ike shoved the key in the ignition and moved the shifter to neutral. Then he pumped the gas a couple of times, tapped the roof twice and cranked the key.

Nothing.

The engine turned over after the third attempt and they both whooped.

Ike turned the heater off so Riss could listen to the clicking and ticking as he revved the motor.

"How's it sound?"

"Okay." She pointed at the gauges. "How's the oil pressure?"

"Seems a bit low at idle."

That was what she was afraid of. "Ike, buddy. There's no way around the fact that this engine needs to be serviced. Especially if it's gonna be sitting outside for the foreseeable future."

He scowled at her. "I can't afford to put the money into it now. And please don't lecture me about the importance of maintaining equipment."

They were at a standstill.

Or were they?

Riss dug her phone out of her pocket and dialed.

"I'm serious. Don't set up a service appointment I can't keep," Ike warned.

She held up her finger to keep him from talking as her brother came on the line and she put him on speakerphone. "Hey, Lonnie."

"What's the occasion that I'm getting a real call from you and not a text?"

"Business."

He sighed loud enough that she knew Ike heard it. "What business?"

"Palmer is doin' you a solid by lookin' after me, so I need you to repay the favor by takin' a look at his rig. It's been out at the Split Rock, someone drove it, we don't know where or what they were hauling. It's running now, it sounds good to me, but I'd like for you or

Lloyd to check it out in your spare time." She paused. "No rush."

"You know I ain't gonna say no. But we don't have a lick of space for an extra vehicle to sit around outside the garage. Especially one that's not a rush job."

"I can drive it—I mean *Ike* can drive it—wherever is easiest for you."

"Lemme think . . ." She heard him cover the receiver with his hand after he shouted to Lloyd. A minute later he was back on the line. "Drive it to your place. If it's nothin' major, we can fix it there. If it needs more work, I'll call and let you decide the next step."

"Thank you, Lonnie. I appreciate it."

He grunted, "Gotta go," and hung up.

Riss dropped her phone back in her pocket before she looked at Ike.

The muscle in his jaw flexed. "You didn't have to do that . . . but I'm glad you did. Thank you."

"You're welcome. If you wanna head over to my trailer now, we can ditch this and return to your place in my car. I'd bet Tobin would be happy to drop your pickup off at your house since it's not out of the way for him and Jade."

"You think of everything, don't you?"

She shrugged. "I try."

"Okay. Just . . . give me a second." Ike sent her a sharp look. "You need help getting buckled up?"

"Nope."

"Sit tight. Gonna do a final check before we take off." Then he hopped out.

Riss went through the same mental checklist he probably did before hitting the road. And she could admit that she missed the smell of diesel. The vibration of the rig as it idled. She glanced longingly around the cab and clenched her right hand, promising herself she'd be back in action soon.

Ike clambered back in. "Everything looks good."

"Then let's hit it."

He readjusted his hat. Then his side mirror. Then hers. Next was his seat.

"Christ. Let's go already."

"If I hear you mutter *if you can't find it, grind it* even one time, I will gag you. Understand?"

"Now who's actin' violent with the spanking and gagging threats? Got a Fifty Shades fetish, Mr. Grey?"

"Only if I can use rope."

Yowza.

"Stop distracting me, Riss."

"Nervous about drivin' with me ridin' shotgun?"

"Are you serious? I'm fuckin' terrified."

His honesty floored her. "Why?"

"Jesus, woman. You're a pro; this is your damn life, your livelihood and what you live for. You have thousands more driving hours than I do. I've worked events with you, watched as you backed a fifty-three-foot trailer between a couple of chutes like it ain't no big deal. You do it time and time again and think nothin' of it. You're a goddamned expert at your job, Riss, the best driver I've ever seen. So I'd be a fool if I wasn't intimidated havin' you sitting next to me, judging every shift, every turn and . . . well, every damn move I make."

Silence hung between them like a rusty chain.

Riss swallowed hard before she spoke. "That's the

first time you've ever praised my professional abilities, Ike. Thank you."

He sighed. "I'm sorry it's taken me that long. Don't make it any less true." He turned and his gaze hooked hers. "I hate that the injury is keeping you from doin' what you love. It's gotta be killing you, watching me sitting where you should be."

"Maybe a little. I'm thinkin' we could even things up between us by swinging by the fairgrounds. You could let me broker a deal for next year's ranch rodeo."

Ike laughed. "No fucking way, because if anyone could pull it off, it'd be you. You outdoing me on one skill is enough for today, thanks."

"So let's hit the road. Wow me with your driving skills, Palmer."

And surprisingly . . . he did.

Chapter Fourteen

❧

$\mathcal{T}$he next morning, a bleary-eyed Ike was shuffling through the kitchen to start coffee, when he heard, "You'd better have more than one insulated coffee mug, Palmer, or I'm goin' back to bed."

He jumped and spun around. "Motherfuckingsonofacocksuckingwhore! Jesus Christ, Thorpe. Why would you sneak up on me like that?"

Riss smiled. "Payback, baby cakes, for you doing that to me yesterday."

"Whatever." Ike snagged the glass carafc, rinsed it and filled the coffeemaker's tank with water. After adding fresh grounds and hitting BREW, he faced her again. "Why're you up at the crack of nothin' anyway?"

She shoved her left hand in her back pocket and shrugged. "I thought maybe you could use company when you checked stock. I think it sucks you hafta do it by yourself all the time."

Thrown off by her sweetness, Ike didn't respond. He just blinked at her.

"Or not. I guess with a busted arm I'd be pretty worthless as a gate opener, huh?"

"Luckily for you, there are only two gates. So I'd be happy to have you ride shotgun."

Riss's shoulders relaxed. "Cool. But I wasn't kidding about the mug. I needs me coffee."

"As I'm well aware after livin' with you for a week. I gotcha covered on the mug front, sweet cheeks."

She smiled.

He smiled back.

When Ike realized they'd been staring at each other with goofy grins for longer than the norm, he also realized that things had changed between them yesterday. When she broke eye contact first, he pushed back from the counter. "Let's get you bundled up. Coffee oughta be done by then."

"Are you tired of helpin' me with every little stupid thing?"

"Nope. Especially since you argue with me less than you did at first." He paused for a beat, then added, "I like havin' you around, Riss. You make me . . ." He stopped, embarrassed because he'd been close to confessing his loneliness.

"What?" she prompted.

"Nothin' that won't keep. Come on, let's get you ready," he said gruffly.

For once, finishing his chores went by way too fast. Ike found himself making up an excuse that he needed to run into Rawlins just to keep Riss with him. She appeared to be enjoying his company, chattering away with random thoughts and observations that had him laughing, cringing and just plumb tickled to see this vivacious side of her coming back to life.

Plus, she amused the hell out of him. He'd caught her regaling the clerk in the paint section of the hardware store with an alternate reality of how she injured her arm. This time she detailed her mishap of driving an ATV across frozen Flathead Lake on her way to her cousin's ice fishing camp. He dragged her away from the male clerk's rapt attention for the clerk's own good, since the perverted motherfucker was looking for Ike to kick his ass due to his inappropriately intense focus on Riss's amazing tits—not on her story.

After a quick fast-food lunch, they returned to Ike's place. He insisted after so much activity that Riss needed to rest. She argued. But he herded her to her bedroom for a nap anyway.

That night, they watched old westerns. By the time the second movie ended, Riss had finished her popcorn and most of his. She decided he made a better cushion than the couch and curled up on her left side, with her butt pressed against his hip and her legs across his lap.

Ike watched the third movie alone, content to stroke her leg and occasionally brush her hair from her face as she softly snored next to him.

The next morning, once again Riss was up early to accompany him on his livestock check.

And the morning after that. Ike had been looking forward to another night of cooking supper for Riss, and then binge watching more episodes of *Jessica Jones* on Netflix, but that afternoon, while Riss napped, his sister Kay called, completely freaked out. Her heater wasn't working, the maintenance guy had the flu and she swore she smelled natural gas. So Ike scrawled a quick note for Riss and drove into Rawlins to deal with the situation.

Ike didn't leave Kay's apartment until five hours later. He'd spent most of his time waiting with his panicked sister for the gas company to show up. Kay hadn't offered him food, so he was starved and cranky. Plus, he worried that Riss would attempt to cook for herself—a nearly impossible task since the woman couldn't even use a can opener—since he wasn't around and she'd be as hungry and annoyed as he was.

But there was a strange pickup in his driveway. He parked in the garage and entered the kitchen to find Riss sitting at the table with her brother Lloyd, drinking beer and playing cards, an empty pizza box between them.

Riss smiled at him. "So you didn't blow yourself up fixing Kay's heater. I wondered since I hadn't heard from you."

"Funny. I had to call the gas company to figure out the problem." He glanced at Lloyd. Talk about disconcerting, looking into green eyes identical to Riss's though they held none of the warmth or humor hers did.

"Well, Lloyd called with good news about your semi and I mentioned bein' hungry, so he showed up with food. Now I'm reminding him why he hates playing gin with me. But we can switch to poker and deal you in, if you'd like."

Ike's stomach rumbled. "Maybe after I eat something."

Riss's eyes narrowed. "You rode to Kay's rescue, spent hours with her and she didn't bother to feed you?"

He shook his head.

"Dude, that sucks. It's a good thing I saved you some pizza." She pointed with her beer bottle. "It's in the fridge."

Little things like this . . . Ike hadn't realized how much he needed someone to give that to him until Riss did. Her thoughtfulness humbled him; he was supposed to be looking after her. He gave her a soft smile. "I appreciate it." He met Lloyd's gaze. "Thanks for bringing food."

"Gotta make sure my little sis is getting what she needs and she knows I'm just a phone call away if she isn't."

Lloyd's meaning wasn't a threat, but the intent very clear; Ike was on notice.

Later that night after Lloyd had left and Ike and Riss were more or less snuggled up on the couch, he sensed she had something on her mind.

"Darlin', your tongue is gonna be bloody if you keep bitin' back what you wanna say to me, so spit it out."

"I hate that your sisters take advantage of you. Seems like all they do is take and don't give anything back. My brothers are bossy and nosy as shit, and yes, they do things for me if I ask. But I do things for them too, yet, that's not all we are to each other."

"I see that. But things have always been this way between me and them." He stroked her back. "I don't know how to change it. Ain't like I was gonna tell Kay to man up and figure out the issue herself when there was a chance it could be a life-threatening problem. Your brothers wouldn't leave you to deal with something like that either, sweetheart."

"I know." Riss made a low-pitched purring sound when he pressed his fingers more deeply into her spine on a slow downstroke of his hand.

For just a moment, Ike imagined that sexy noise vibrating against his throat as Riss arched into him, their naked bodies sliding together as he moved in and out of her body, right here on the couch, with the TV on in the background, both of them so crazy for that intimate connection they couldn't make it to a bed.

"You okay?" she asked.

"Yeah, why?"

"Sounded like you growled."

I did. It's the sound I make when I can't have what I want. "Just clearing my throat."

"I'm tired. I think I'll call it a night."

"Okay. I might stay up and catch an episode—"

"You are not watching *Jessica Jones* without me!"

That gave him the response he'd wanted; Riss to stay snuggled up with him for another hour. "Fine. But if you fall asleep and start snoring, I will carry your ass to bed."

She snorted. "Hand me the damn remote."

And sure enough, Riss conked out. He hit pause and watched her sleep before closing his eyes . . . just for a moment.

Hours later, Riss woke him up, her arms flailing about and nearly clocked him in the head with her cast. "What happened?"

"It appears we fell asleep in front of the TV." Then the alarm on his phone started pinging.

"Jesus, Ike. Is it really five a.m.?"

"Yep." He discreetly brushed his lips across the back

of her head before he shifted to sit up. "Go back to sleep. I got this."

"No. Way. You promised me steak and eggs after the stock check chores this morning, remember?"

Yeah, but I wasn't sure you would. "Well, get movin'. I'll start the coffee."

"Can you help me sit up? Feels like I'm fallin' into a sinkhole."

"Hang on."

As soon as he freed her left arm trapped against his chest, she used it to grab onto the back of the couch. She balanced on one knee as she straddled Ike's lap.

The expression on her face when they were this close had him holding his breath.

"It's not fair that you look like a million bucks even with bedhead and rumpled clothes." She slid her palm up his chest, over the cotton barrier blocking her from direct contact with his skin. Her hand continued its ascent until the tips of her fingers connected with his neck. She paused to trace the line of his jaw and then scraped her nails through the scruff on his lower cheek. "I like that this is darker than the hair on your head."

"Yeah?"

"It's sexy. Everything about you is sexy."

Ike shook her shoulders slightly. "Riss, darlin'. Wake up."

Those sleepy green eyes met his. "What?"

"You're paying me compliments and touching me so obviously you're not fully awake."

"I was fully awake when you kissed the back of my head about two minutes ago."

Ike blushed.

"I'm fully awake now. Fully aware of you in ways that I shouldn't be, Ike Palmer." After she dropped that bomb, she actually dismounted from his lap like she was getting off a horse. "Go start the coffee or something." She hustled down the hallway.

He definitely wanted to start something, but it wasn't a pot of coffee.

∞

The next couple of days Ike and Riss fell into their new normal routine. Doing chores first thing, then running errands, then he fed his patient and forced Riss's afternoon nap, which she fought him on but ultimately ended up taking anyway.

A phone call from his sister Jen that his niece and nephew missed him kicked in his guilt. He hadn't seen Mikayla or Elijah for a couple of weeks. He agreed to hang out with them while Jen attended her continuing education class.

Riss said nothing about Ike being on babysitting duty. She informed him that Louie might be coming over, so he would take care of dinner.

Before he left for Rawlins, Ike paused outside Riss's bedroom door to ask if she needed anything. But he could hear through the opening she was on the phone—speakerphone—with someone.

A male voice said, "You'd only get half of the money, but it's still better than nothin'."

Riss responded with, "I know and I appreciate your out-of-the-box thinking, Louie."

"Just think about it. I'm pretty sure Tito will be okay with it. But we can talk more tonight." Louie paused. "Dickhead ain't gonna be there, is he?"

Ike's jaw tightened. *Dickhead? Really?*

"You mean Ike? No. He's been roped in to babysitting duty."

"Good. I ain't in the frame of mind to make nice with him." A pause. "He's treatin' you good, right sis?"

"Very good. Too good maybe."

That caught Ike's interest.

"What's that mean?"

"We spend so much time together—we've gotten close."

"How close?" Louie demanded.

"Falling asleep watching TV together kind of close. Doin' chores together kind of close. He still bosses me around constantly, which annoys the piss out of me. But he is sweet and thoughtful."

"And . . . ?"

"And nothin'. We're just friends. That's it."

Ike couldn't tell if she was complaining.

"I don't give a shit how hard you try to convince me you were kidding about bein' involved with him, I know there's something goin' on between you two. That kiss wasn't just for show. That kiss was the real deal."

"I know."

"You do?"

"Yeah, but we're both denying it. It's easier that way."

Ike was absolutely floored.

"Look, can we drop it? I just wanna chill out tonight with you and ignore all the complications in my life. I miss your stupid face."

Louie laughed. "I miss your stupid face more. See you in a couple of hours."

He knew he should skedaddle before he got caught eavesdropping, but he couldn't believe that Riss considered him just another life issue to deal with.

Why?

When a text buzzed asking if he was on his way, he quietly slipped out, his thoughts pulled in a million different directions.

After a long night of playing Legos and Barbies with his niece and nephew, all Ike wanted was another beer and his bed.

So it made zero sense that he bypassed the fridge and the staircase to the second floor and wandered down the hallway to her room instead.

She'd left the door cracked—which he took as an invitation.

He ducked into the room and sauntered across the carpet.

Immediately she struggled to sit up. "Ike? What the devil are you doin' in here?"

"Just checking on you. I didn't mean to wake you."

"You sure?"

"Will I sound pathetic if I admit I'm at loose ends?"

"Yes. How dare you interrupt my much-needed beauty sleep." She pointed. "Remove thyself from my chambers at once, scoundrel."

"Never a dull moment with you, Thorpe." Then he sat on the edge of the bed. "You should get up. I don't think my heart could stand it if you got any prettier."

She leaned closer and sniffed. "Aha. You have been drinkin'. That explains the sweet-talking."

"One beer. That's it. I'm just sharin' the gospel truth."

"You are a silver-tongued devil," she murmured. She yawned and stretched her left arm above her head, giving him a peek of the creamy skin between her belly button and her hips.

He had an image of running his mouth along that strip of skin, over and over, until she squirmed like crazy and arched into him, begging for more.

"Ike?"

His gaze snapped back to hers. "Uh, yeah?"

"You're staring at my panties."

Busted.

Her eyes glittered with a challenge. "If you want more than a peek at my panties, just ask."

What would Ms. Smarty-Panties do if he called her bluff? Still act bold? Or retreat?

Time to find out.

"Thanks for the offer, darlin'." Ike ripped the covers back and crawled across the mattress until he was looming over her. "I do want a better look. Roll over so I can see if there's lace covering your cute butt or more of that sexy see-through material."

"Jesus. I was kidding!"

No you weren't.

"What has gotten into you?"

You. You're under my skin in a way you've never been. I'm as afraid of acting on this attraction as I am of just ignoring it.

"Ike?" She placed her hand on his chest. "You okay?"

Her simple touch rocketed through him, short-circuiting his brain. "No. I'm . . ." He locked his gaze to hers. "Literally seeing you in a whole different way. Did you know your eyes are flecked with gold? Makes that beautiful green stand out. I never noticed that before." His gaze searched her facial features, from her broad forehead and the arch of her eyebrows to the freckles spattered across her nose and her apple cheeks to the curve of that sensual mouth accentuated by her full lower lip. Before, he'd only noticed the stubborn set to her jaw, not the cute dimple at the end point of her chin.

"Are you tryin' to seduce me?"

Maybe. "I'm just admiring what's always been there."

"I'm the same as I've ever been."

"I know. Which is why it's so goddamned confusing that this feels new even when it's not."

"Well, cowboy, this"—she gestured to him being on all fours above her—"definitely isn't the same old, same old." Her lips curled up. "And while I've got you all het up like this, admit that kiss to convince Louie we were together wasn't solely for his benefit."

"*That's* what you and Louie talked about tonight?"

"One of the things. You did a damn good job convincing him, because nothin' will deter him from the idea that we're really together. Now, confess, Palmer. That kiss . . . ?"

Ike groaned. "It felt real, okay? But don't bring up that kiss when I'm this damn close to your lips and I'm tryin' like hell to remember you're a guest in my house. An injured guest."

Riss's smile faded.

"What?"

"The way you flip-flop between hot and cold with me is frustrating as fuck."

"Part of my charm . . . isn't that what you always

say?" Ike chuckled when she swatted at him. "So the offer to see the backside of your panties is off the table?"

"Ya think?"

He bounced off the bed. "Come into the kitchen for a midnight snack."

"I'm not hungry."

"Do it anyway to keep me company."

"No. Stop bossing me around. You're not one of my brothers, Ike."

"But for the time being I am your keeper. And when I say you need to eat, it's because you need to eat. When I say you need to rest, it's because you need to rest. So quit bein' a pain in my ass—get that cute ass up and into my kitchen because there's some stuff we need to talk about."

"At midnight? I don't think so."

"Where's your sense of adventure?"

"It's coiled in the corner ready to strike because you interrupted an awesome dream."

He played his trump card. "I'll bake cookies. Soft, rich, warm, gooey chocolate chip cookies. Isn't that tempting you a little?"

"It's more tempting every day to murder you in your sleep," she grumbled.

"Come on, Riss. Please."

"No. I'm tired, you've been drinking, add in a late night sugar buzz and we might be tempted to do something we'd regret when we're wide awake, sober and not riding the sugar train."

"That's kind of what I'm hoping will happen."

Ike laughed when the pillow she whipped at his head missed him.

"Fine. Go back to sleep. Don't say I didn't offer."

"Offer me what?"

"Whatever you want."

Riss studied him for several long moments. Then she said, "You can't give me what I want."

"Which is what, sweetheart?"

"My real life back."

That sucked the wind right out of his sails. "I'm tryin' to help you create a new normal."

"Yeah, good luck with that." She rolled over and pulled the covers over her head.

Chapter Fifteen

✂

"𝓡iss, will you get a move on? We're gonna be late."

"Yeah, I'd really hate to miss the doctor poking and prodding me."

"Let's hope they're done fast and I'll take you out for tacos to celebrate."

But she wasn't done complaining. "I don't know why they scheduled an appointment. It's not like they can see through the cast to check if my bones are healing."

Ike helped her into her coat. "A clinical follow-up visit is standard after any surgery."

"There oughta be a standard online questionnaire to fill out. If any of my answers are hinky then they can call me and see if an appointment is necessary."

"*Hinky*? Is that an official medical term?"

"Bite me, ass-hat."

Lashing out, her tell for nerves. He let it slide.

"Hold on to my arm and slip your boots on."

Grumble, grumble.

"Besides, I think they're just taking out your stitches today."

Riss lifted her head and glared at him. "Why do you know more about my medical treatment than I do?"

"Someone has to pay attention, darlin', because you obviously don't."

Without a word, she turned and walked away.

Fuck. He did not want to do this with her today, but the woman was a master at self-sabotage. Ike followed her into the guest bathroom.

She'd upended her toiletry bag and was rifling through the items, tossing them into the sink one by one.

"What in the hell are you doin'?"

"Looking for my scissors." She dropped a tube of lip-stick into the sink.

"I already said your hair looks great; there's no need for you to follow through with your earlier threat to chop it all off right now," he joked.

Her eyes met his in the mirror. "The scissors are to take my stitches out."

"Riss, you are not takin' out your own stitches."

"You're right. I'm not. *You* are."

"Enough." He spun her around and caged her against the countertop.

"Move."

"Not until you tell me what's goin' on with you today. You've been in a shit mood since you woke up."

Something vulnerable flitted through her eyes and disappeared. "Don't be nice, don't be reasonable, just let me be."

Then it clicked. Their conversation last night. Riss

didn't know how to act around him, so she acted like she always did—came out swinging. "I meant what I said."

"I know. And it's thrown everything off, okay? It's thrown me off balance and I'm already struggling with one working arm, so back off."

His eyes narrowed. "Was that an attempt at a joke?"

"A lame attempt, apparently."

"Baby, talk to me. Please."

"See, that? That right there is confusing me. Calling me *baby* when you're so sweet and your concern for me so genuine that I get this melty sensation inside."

"Melty sensation is good, right?"

"I want to believe it is." Her eyes were troubled, but she didn't look away from him. "Then you change completely. Bossing me around. Telling me how things are gonna be instead of asking. So half the time I get the sexy, flirty Ike I want to bang into next week, and then I get Ike the big brother, who mansplains everything. I'm confused and I just want some time alone, in my own damn house, to sort everything out."

Ike's brain had gotten stuck on *bang into next week*.

Oh hell yeah, and this counter was the perfect height for him to spread her thighs wide as he decided if he'd devour her with his mouth first or just drive his dick into her.

"Then you get that look," Riss said, bringing him back to reality. "And if you say *what look?* I will knee you in the 'nads."

Ike stepped back, and wily Riss slipped away and stormed out of the bathroom.

When he tracked her to the foyer, she was attempting to put on her coat.

"Goddammit, Riss. Stop. You're gonna hurt yourself."

"Then it's a lucky thing I'm goin' to the doctor."

He grabbed the edges of her coat, using them to pull her closer. "So now you *want* to go to the doctor?"

"Yes. Because I realized she can clear me to return home."

His guts tightened into a knot and he might've yanked on her coat a little harder than he meant to. "You know what? You're right. It's sucked ass every day you've had to be stuck here with me. I told you if you hated it at the end of two weeks, and if the doctor cleared you, you could go." He tugged the poncholike scarf down over her exposed cast. "So let's go find out."

"Ike. It hasn't sucked."

"Then why are you so fired up to leave?"

"Because I'm confused about how things have changed between us."

That was when Ike let his gaze find hers. He'd wondered if she would acknowledge the shift in their relationship or if she'd ignore it.

Question was, should *he* ignore it?

The bigger question: was that shift situational?

"You've already told me several times that nothin' can happen between us while I'm staying with you."

"Do you want something to happen?"

"If I did, I'm not sure I'd tell you," she retorted.

"Don't start talkin' in circles. Christ." He grabbed on to her coat lapels again, stopping her retreat. "You're the one person in my life who I can be fully honest with."

"Then what do *you* want, Ike?"

"Fuck it. I want this." He clamped one hand on the back of her head and slammed his mouth down on hers.

The instant their tongues touched and their passion caught fire, her caution fled and she threw all her energy into the kiss. Driving him wild with her soft moans and sucking mouth.

Ike hadn't imagined he'd be a guy who got hard from control. But he loved that Riss couldn't use her hands or that sinful body of hers to push him to the edge.

And holy fuck, did the woman kiss his face off.

His damn lips tingled.

He forced himself to let go of her.

They were both breathing hard and unable to look at each other.

With the doctor's visit looming, he shouldn't have kissed her, because now they'd talk the damn kiss to death on the hour-long ride to Casper.

"Riss—"

"Don't."

"Don't what?"

"Don't apologize."

Shit. He'd been about to do just that. "Then don't put those walls back up. I'm as confused by this as you are."

That was when the pounding on the door started.

The glass panels allowed a glimpse of a hulking figure in a bulky coat peering in at them.

"What in the world is he doin' here?" Riss said, trying to distance herself from Ike.

"How can you even tell who that is?"

"I recognize my brother Lonnie's coat."

Ike reached over, unlocked the dead bolt and opened the door.

Then Riss stomped past him and got boot to boot with her brother. "Spying on me much?"

He snorted. "I knocked. More than once."

"We were just—"

"I saw what you were doin'. At least you had clothes on. Now come on. We gotta git."

She just stared up at him. "What?"

"Your doctor's appointment," he prompted her. "I texted that I'd pick you up."

"All your text said was 'DR @3 TUE.'"

Lonnie pushed his hood back—likely to better glare at her.

Ike forgot that Riss looked nothing like her brothers until they were side by side. Lonnie's darker hair, skin, eyes and sharp, hawkish facial features showed more than a hint of his Native American ancestry.

"Yeah, and here I am," Lonnie said.

"I was supposed to decipher that to mean you'd pick me up?"

"What'd you think it meant?"

"I thought it was a reminder!"

"Jesus, Riss, it *was* a reminder that I was coming to pick you up. You can't drive. How else are you gonna get there? Order a cab?"

"I thought since I'm a grown woman, you'd assume I'd get to the doctor on my own. God. I'm not twelve. I'm perfectly capable—"

"Of takin' care of yourself, yeah, yeah, yeah, I've heard that before. But you *can't* take care of yourself right now, can you? So I'm here to drag your stubborn ass to the doctor. Because we both know you'd blow it off if you could."

"You took time off from work to do this?" Riss demanded.

"Yep. Now gimme your arm so I can help you into the truck because the walkway is slippery as shit."

Déjà vu hit Ike hard.

You've acted like this dozens of times with your own sisters. And now you can see that you've been treating Riss the same way.

"Go back to work, Lonnie. Ike is takin' me. We were just on our way there."

Lonnie finally acknowledged Ike's presence with a scathing look. "I got this."

"Since she's stayin' with me, I'm driving her."

"Nope. That's why *I'm* takin' her. I need to hear from the *doctor* that she's healing. Just because she's in your house don't guarantee she's getting any rest."

Riss smacked him on the shoulder. "Lonnie, you asshole."

Now Ike understood Riss's automatic response to come out swinging, because *he* wanted to punch her brother. "At least since she's been stayin' with me—in her own private room, with a private bath—she's been rested, bathed, fed and clothed."

"Omigod, you two. Shut the fuck up. Gimme the damn keys. I'm driving myself to the doctor."

Both Lonnie and Ike snapped, "No," at the same time.

"Then figure it out now," Riss huffed. "It's fuckin' freezin' out here."

Lonnie said, "My truck's already warmed up. Let's go."

Ike glanced over to see Lonnie had parked his dirty dually sideways across the cement slab, completely blocking the garage door so Ike couldn't get out.

Jesus, this family was belligerent.

But so was he.

He slipped his arm around Riss's waist. "Looks like Lonnie is drivin' us to Casper."

"Us?" Lonnie repeated. "There's no room for you, bud."

"You have a quad cab, *bud*—there's plenty of room."

Lonnie looked between Ike and Riss. "Whatever. But he sits in the back."

Ike let go of Riss for one second to shut and lock the front door and Lonnie was right there, herding her to the passenger's side.

The hour-long drive to Casper oughta be real fun.

∞

But the ride was eerily quiet.

After Lonnie pulled into the doctor's office parking lot, he said to Riss, "You've got your insurance card?"

"No. Dammit, I left my purse in Ike's foyer."

"So you can't pay the co-pay either?"

"I was a little distracted by—"

"Yeah, I saw firsthand what was distracting you."

"Shut up. The two of you fuckers arguing while I stood there and froze is what distracted me. Besides, they can bill me for the office visit."

Ike said, "No big deal. I'll cover it."

Lonnie scowled at him. "Riss is on the shop's insurance plan. I'll handle the paperwork and the payment."

Surprisingly, Riss didn't argue. Because, not surprisingly, she followed her own agenda at the patient check-in desk.

"Hey there"—she squinted at the receptionist's

name—"Wanda. I hope you're havin' a better day than I am."

"Is there a problem?" the bored-looking woman said.

"With this damn cast I'm more helpless than I'm used to. So the two angry-looking dudes behind me decided the best way to 'help' me today—when we were already running late—was getting into a testosterone-fueled argument about who was the most qualified to drive me to my appointment. Which means, while playin' referee between them, I left my purse with my insurance card and my credit card at home."

Wanda angled her head to look around Riss's shoulder. "I can see where they'd both be distracting."

"I'm pissed off at both of them, so I do not want either of them coming into the exam with me. I'm pretty sure if you took my blood pressure right now it'd be off the charts."

Ike said, "Hey, that's not—"

The receptionist held up her hand, stopping his interruption.

"Can you help me out? Please?"

Wanda said, "Of course. Our patients' welfare is our priority." Then she picked up the phone and started punching buttons.

"Who are you calling?" Lonnie demanded.

Riss whirled around. "I hope it's security and they toss you both outside in the snowbank to cool off."

"Riss, darlin'—"

"Don't. I mean it. Back the hell off."

"You heard her," Lonnie said.

"That includes you, dumb-ass."

Ike's glee at Lonnie's smackdown was short-lived. If neither of them went into the exam room with her, they'd have to take Riss's interpretation of the doctor's advice, which, knowing her, could be a total fucking lie.

The concerned look Lonnie gave Ike indicated he'd just realized that too.

"Seriously, sis. I need—"

"Your ass kicked," she hissed. "Both of you. So why don't you settle this like *real* men and beat the fuck out of each other in the parking lot. Because obviously the guy with the least amount of bruises when it's over is the one who cares about me the most."

"Ya don't gotta be so sarcastic," Lonnie drawled.

A door opened and a female voice called out, "Riss Thorpe?"

"Go on, honey," Wanda said. "They'll take care of you back there and I'll take care of them."

"Thank you so much."

Then he and Lonnie were left alone with Wanda. Her bored expression? Gone. She had a glint in her eye that meant they were totally fucked.

"Dr. Frost is running behind today. You have two hours until Miss Thorpe is finished. There's a coffee shop across the street."

"We can't wait here?" Lonnie said, gesturing to the empty waiting room.

"Absolutely not. I suggest you ignore Miss Thorpe's advice to settle your differences in the parking lot because if I see one fist flying I *will* call the police."

Definitely mean.

"If you are determined to pound the snot out of each other, there's a boxing club two blocks off Main Street."

"Where's the closest bar?" Ike asked.

Her eyes narrowed. "As you are Miss Thorpe's caretakers, I strongly advise neither one of you return here with booze on your breath. Is that clear?"

"Yes, ma'am. Thanks for your help," Ike said, tacking on his most charming grin.

"I'm familiar with that smarmy salesman smile and it won't work. Now. Get. Out."

Lonnie snickered. But he was the first one out the door.

The icy wind had Ike hustling to climb in the passenger's side of Lonnie's truck. "I'll be glad when this cold snap is done."

Lonnie cranked the engine. "Where to?"

"Not in the mood for coffee."

"Me neither. The boxing club is a good option."

"You really wanna fight me, Thorpe?"

"Fuck no. I work out there, so the owner wouldn't care if we killed time watching practice. It's loud so we don't gotta worry about our conversation bein' overheard. And it's always warm."

Humid and reeking of sweat, Ike thought. But it beat sitting in the truck. "Let's go."

∞

There was one sign—a cheap plastic one from the 1970s—with a stylized boxer outlined in black that marked the entrance to the club. The building itself was a warehouse; metal siding scratched and dented, rusted in spots. Weeds lined the chain-link fence that disappeared down the left side. The high windows above the door were dirty on the outside and looked to be covered in moisture on the inside. The only other indication this space wasn't abandoned was the security camera above them and the fancy keypad beside the door handle.

Lonnie punched in a code and the lock popped open.

That familiar gym funk—sweat, vinyl and dampness—filled the air. Ike stomped his boots on the rug and looked around the waiting area.

Off to the left side were wooden benches, long lines of wall hooks above them and a few metal lockers anchored the corners and part of another wall.

"No outerwear inside the gym," Lonnie said. "Club rules. Pick any spot out here to hang your stuff."

"Boots come off too?"

He shook his head. "We'll be in the bleachers, not walking across the mats."

An attractive brunette with fake tits spilling out of her sports bra manned the check-in desk. Her eyes lit up when Lonnie approached. "Hey, stranger. Haven't seen you in a while."

"Because I avoid the newbies during Gym-uary. I'll be back when their New Year's resolutions fail."

"Cynical. But you're still cute."

"Back atcha, Brandi. Look, I brought a guest to get a feel for the place. We'll just hang in the bleachers, cool?"

"Sure. He's gotta sign in, though."

Ike scrawled his name in an oversized ledger as thick as two telephone books.

"Great. I'll let Rocky know you're here."

Rocky?

Lonnie caught Ike's amusement. "As a matter of fact, the owner was named after Rocky Balboa."

After passing through a concrete hallway, they entered the main part of the club. Ike didn't take time to look around until after he'd followed Lonnie to the top of the bleachers.

Six rings filled up the space, three of them in use. On the floor a dozen guys milled about, working speed bags, jumping rope, running on a treadmill. In the back corner was an entirely separate weight room, completely glassed in. Ike whistled. "This is some boxing club."

"Serious boxers train here from all over. I've been coming here since high school."

"Did you ever bring Riss?"

"I tried. She did develop a decent uppercut."

"I can attest to that."

The heater kicked on, masking the thud of gloves and coaches yelling.

"So how do we do this, Palmer? Do I ask what gave you the right to take my sister away from her family when she wasn't in any shape to tell you to fuck off? Because if she hadn't been drugged up, she wouldn't have let you get within a mile of her."

"You're so sure of that?" he said coolly. "We do work together."

"Rarely. You were forced to spend time together during all the prewedding crap. But she's never hinted that you're in a 'secret relationship.'" Lonnie snorted. "Louie is a dumb-ass. Can't believe he fell for that."

"He fell for it because he was happy to see Riss leavin'. Outta sight, outta mind. She became someone else's responsibility. Louie didn't care who was watchin' over her, as long as he didn't have to do it." Ike paused. "Tell me I'm wrong."

"You're not. But you're assuming that me'n Lloyd felt the same about it as Louie and that ain't true. I don't appreciate you talkin' shit about how we neglected her 'basic needs.' We were at the hospital and dealt with her medical stuff—not you."

Ike knew continuing along these lines of accusations, he and Lonnie would come to blows. "Why did you call Jade?"

Lonnie looked at him like he was a moron. "Because she's Riss's best friend."

"Did Riss ask you to call Jade and let her know what happened?"

"It was a little goddamned hard for my sister to dial a phone when she left it in her trailer."

He remembered Riss saying Lonnie had chewed her ass for that oversight.

"When I retrieved her cell after they released her from the hospital, she lost it. Took me a couple hours to figure out she'd hidden it on purpose because she didn't want me calling anyone or anyone contacting her. She was embarrassed about getting hurt. *Embarrassed.*" He scrubbed his hand over his jaw. "She said she'd handle telling people about her 'little accident' in her own time frame. Meanwhile, she's out of the hospital one damn day and me'n Lloyd and Louie are getting phone calls up the wazoo demanding to know what happened. It seemed Larissa's buddy who was visiting her grandma at the hospital saw Riss in the cafeteria and started passing news of Riss's hospitalization around to their other friends, assuming she'd want their help, sympathy and support, right? Not my stubborn goddamned sister. That girl's pride has always been an issue between us. So when Aunt Bernice lit into us about not contacting *her* . . . that was the last straw. On the third day of Riss's recovery, I called Jade, not because I expected she'd offer to take Riss in, but I hoped she'd talk some sense into that pigheaded girl." He sent Ike a menacing look. "But instead, Jade tells you and the two of you conclude that we're holding Riss against her will, starving her and denying her basic hygiene. You figure it's your job to charge in, in your white pickup, and save her. Because it's easier for her to manipulate one guy with a hero complex than her three brothers wise to her scheming ways."

Lonnie finally paused to breathe. "That's the truth, but it's probably not the way you heard it."

Ike's jaw hung open. Too pissed off to speak, he stood and walked to the end of the row. He closed his eyes and inhaled a few deep breaths before he'd calmed down.

The bleachers wobbled as a kid raced up the steps and handed Ike two bottles of water.

"Good timing, kid."

Ike rejoined Lonnie and tossed him a bottle.

"Thanks."

Neither spoke as they watched the action below them. Ike appreciated the distraction so they didn't have to look at each other.

"Maybe you don't know this, but Riss and I mended our fences a while ago. The last time I saw her after the wedding? She hugged me good-bye. So we were on good terms then." Ike took a drink. "We're on different terms now."

Lonnie remained quiet.

"I was there when Jade got your call. She was pretty freaked out when she told us what happened . . . so I'll admit maybe I didn't catch every detail. Maybe Jade exaggerated Riss's situation, but I believed her concern was genuine."

"Why?"

"Because she was ready to order a hospital bed and move Riss in. Bein' a newlywed just back from her honeymoon . . ."

He sighed. "Okay. Point taken."

"Riss hadn't given Jade a good impression of life at the Thorpe brothers' place, which Jade shared with me. I thought I'd show up at your house and give Riss the option of stayin' with me."

"You just *happened* to show up when the weakest link was the only one on duty?"

"Easier to deal with one brother than three. Anyway, seein' Riss in that kinda shape? No way was I leavin' her there."

"You make it sound like we locked her up and beat her."

"There's the problem, Thorpe. You're making this about you. Your pride. As the oldest, you've made the hard decisions for your siblings. I know exactly how it is. You struggled to keep a roof over their heads and food in their bellies. You prayed there'd come a day when you weren't awake at night worrying about fucking everything up."

Lonnie tilted his head to scrutinize Ike. "You weren't just selling me a line about knowing how it is."

"No, sir. Then something like Riss's accident happens and you're back in that place where you think you have to decide what's best for her. So you can try and convince me that only giving her cast-off men's clothes was a safety measure to keep her in the house. Ditto for not allowing her any personal items. But where that scenario fails . . . none of you were willing to give up your personal space. You expected *her* to adjust and that put her recovery in jeopardy."

"Damned if I do, damned if I don't," he bit off. "What's your angle for volunteering to take her in? Sex?"

"We're not sleeping together."

"No shit. If you were fucking she'd be in a much better mood."

"Are all of you so blunt?"

"Pretty much. I take full blame for that. Hard to be a role model when you're a punk-ass kid yourself. Lloyd, Lou . . . even Larissa started to talk like me after Dad died. Truth was, I'd rather have them mouthing off than mealymouthed. My dad was one of those quiet guys who figured things would get better if he didn't make waves. So he took shit, kept his mouth shut and nothin' ever got better. The only unexpected thing he did was die when he was fifty-five."

"How old were you?"

"Nineteen. Worked three jobs and lied my ass off to make sure they didn't split us up." He squeezed the water bottle. "Native kids have a high rate of foster care. I wasn't gonna let that happen to my family. No one would ever convince me my brothers and sister would be better off with strangers than with me. I ain't gonna tell you it was easy. But we stuck together."

"You're still together," Ike pointed out. "Riss is the only one who's struck out on her own."

"Lloyd joined the air force right out of high school. Saw some crazy shit. He came back different. So I wasn't supposed to take him in after you got him fired from his first job outta the service? Fuck that. It's his house too. And Louie . . . he's a thirty-three-year-old frat boy. But he's got a good job, pulls his weight, pays his fair share. So as long as he's doin' that, I'm fine havin' him around." He sighed. "Riss had enough of living with the three of us, and I'll admit any guys that came around we were pretty clear on what we'd do if he crossed the line with her. So yeah, she grew up too fast. Always had a million irons in the fire, figuring out how to squeeze another nickel out of a dollar. I'm proud as hell of her. And the last thing I'd ever willingly do would be pass her off to someone else. That said, I knew we weren't set up to take her in and I was workin' on a solution when you swooped in."

"I'm not sorry she's been with me the last two weeks." Ike took a drink of water. "I don't think she wishes she woulda been somewhere else either."

"I know."

"How?"

"Bernice. She gets off calling and telling us how well Riss is doin' with you. So much better than she'd be doin' with us."

Ike frowned. "That's a dick move. Why would she rub it in?"

"'Cause we've gone head-to-head on what was best for Riss since a week after my dad died. She wanted to take Riss in. Just her. Not Louie. Not Lloyd. Not even me. Pissed me off. I think she even went behind Uncle Bob's back." Lonnie looked Ike in the eyes. "I never told Riss about that so I don't know why the hell I'm telling you."

"It's a test to see what I'll do with the information. If I use it to drive a wedge between you two because you kept this from her. No matter how she finds out, it'll hurt her, so yeah, I'll pass on passing it along."

Lonnie didn't respond right away.

After a bit he said, "Put yourself in my shoes, Palmer. Your youngest sister is injured, facing major recovery time, and a guy you don't know shows up and takes her away for 'her own good.' How would you handle that?"

Jesus. He hadn't thought of it that way. "Honestly? Not as well as you have."

"Your sister ain't any more precious to you than my sister is to me."

"I get that."

"Last thing I'll say is fuck you for your assumptions about my so-called neglect of her basic needs. Riss hadn't showered because she wasn't *supposed* to shower for seventy-two hours after they put the cast on. She refused to eat the healthy meals I cooked and convinced Lou to go to the C-Mart for cupcakes and corn chips because she *prefers* to eat processed crap."

Fuck. "I apologize for my assumptions about you."

"But?"

"But nothin'. I've said what I intended."

A match started in the far right ring. After the

second round, Lonnie started commentary on what the opponents were doing right and wrong. After the match ended, Ike said, "You know a shit ton about boxing. Just from hanging out in the club?"

"Partially. I spent a lot of years and hours here, dreaming on making it big. Made it to the Golden Gloves championships three years. Won all three years too. Then reality set in and now I keep up with it because I still love it."

"What happened? You get injured or something?"

He shook his head. "After my dad died I couldn't train and work and take care of my family. So I had to choose."

"And boxing lost."

"Yep." He stood and looked at his phone. "It's been almost two hours. We'd better go."

When they were in the freezing cab of Lonnie's truck, Ike said, "What's your cell number? You can hear directly from me how Riss is doin' instead of thirdhand from Bernice."

Lonnie rattled off the number, then said, "Don't forward memes. I hate that shit."

"Got it."

Ike had hoped Lonnie would just let him go in and retrieve Riss, but nope, they both went in.

Wanda looked them both over and frowned. "Why are you two here again?"

"You said to return in two hours. So is Riss finished?"

"Miss Thorpe finished an hour ago."

Shit. Now she'd chew them out for being late. "Then where is she?"

"With the friend who picked her up."

"Which friend?" Lonnie snapped.

"I don't know. She called someone for a ride and left. But she did give me a message to pass along."

"Which is?"

"She'll find her own way home."

Chapter Sixteen

❧

*T*hanks for rescuing me, Jade."

"I'm glad you called so I can see for myself that you're on the mend." Jade turned out of the parking lot. "Where to?"

"The closest bar."

She laughed.

"I'm serious. I need an hour or two of loud music and regular people enjoying happy hour and life."

"All right. But I'm not familiar with the bars in Casper."

"The Friendly Ghost is downtown."

Jade shot her a dubious look. "Right. It's next to Richie Rich's Bank. I'm not nearly as gullible as I used to be."

"This time I'm not yanking your chain. There really is a bar in Casper called the Friendly Ghost. It's in one of the old stone buildings that's supposedly haunted."

"You've been there?"

"Not for a year or so. Book club met in the back room a few times when we didn't have other options."

Jade put the car in park and pulled out her cell phone.

"Are you calling Tobin for permission to go to a bar?" Riss asked her, slightly horrified.

"No. I'm looking up the address on Google Maps."

"Uh, you're not in New York anymore. How about if we do this the old-fashioned way and I give you directions?"

"That'll work."

It cracked Riss up to ride with Jade. She took driving seriously. Using her turn signal. Hands on the wheel at ten and two. Never venturing even one mile above the speed limit.

Riss prided herself on being a safe, aware driver. Driving big vehicles gave her a different perspective, an impatient one. She knew she made a lousy passenger, because she hated being a passenger. She'd rather be behind the wheel. It took every bit of her control not to critique Jade's snail-like pace.

"There it is," Riss said, pointing. "Looks like there are parking spaces out front."

The frigid Wyoming wind practically blew them inside the building. The sign by the coatrack read:

Wipe Your Boots And Seat Yourself

"It's usually warmer in the back," Riss suggested.

Jade chose a booth in the middle section, fussing over Riss as she helped her remove her outerwear and then insisting she sit on the side that allowed her to rest her cast on the table and against the back wall.

Happy hour special was two for one so Riss ordered two margaritas. Jade, considering herself the DD, opted for soda.

"This is a cool place," Jade said. "I'll have to come back with Tobin."

The exposed rock, scuffed wood floor and two-story ceiling hit the mark between hip and vintage. The second floor above the curved bar was an open dance floor, where the upstairs drinkers could watch the people sitting in the booths and tables below.

"It's a serious party bar. They don't serve food, they don't have TV for the sports crowd, so I'd avoid it on the weekend."

"Then it *is* a meat market?"

"Yep. It's a younger crowd than the bars I've taken you to in Rawlins."

Jade sent Riss an arch look when Riss sucked down half of her first margarita in one swallow. "Thirsty?"

"Stressed."

"What'd the doctor say?"

"That I still have a broken arm."

"Riss. I'm serious."

"So am I. She went over the list of answers I gave the nurse and asked if I needed refills on pain meds." She smirked. "Which I immediately said yes to. With me not workin', I might have to resort to selling them for quick cash."

"Omigod, don't even joke about that!"

"You're too easy to tease, New York. I'd think a married woman wouldn't be so gullible."

"Bite me. What else did the doctor tell you?"

"Evidently the danger of my brain leaking out passed, so they snipped my stitches. My head is fine."

"Eww. Gross visual. Did it hurt to get the stitches out?"

She shrugged. "It pulled some. I'll be happy to wash my hair on my own again."

"What else?"

"The doc did say I could ditch my babysitter. So I'll be back at my trailer as soon as it's livable."

"That's great! What about driving?"

"An automatic is okay." Riss assumed that was the restriction. The doctor hadn't specifically said no driving, so in her mind, that meant yes.

"But your big-girl toys aren't automatic. So she didn't clear you to go back to work?"

Riss shook her head. "Not even light duty."

"I have no idea what 'light duty' means to a truck driver."

"It's essentially fifty percent of my job." Riss raised her glass for a toast. "If I can't drive I might as well drink."

"You drinking a lot at Ike's house?"

"At every opportunity and with unrestrained gusto."

At seeing Jade's immediate concern, Riss felt guilty for her breezy response. "I'm kidding. There's a whole lot of nothin' goin' on at Ike's. And no, I'm not picking fights with him to entertain myself."

"A whole lot of nothing?" Jade repeated. "That's not what I heard."

"What did you hear?"

"That you've been doing livestock checks with Ike every morning."

"So?"

"So in rancher culture, a new woman riding along with her man to open gates means you're going steady, you're sweet on each other . . . in other words, you're involved."

Riss sipped her margarita. "Well, they're wrong."

Jade folded her arms on the table. "So what happened today?"

"Lonnie pulled a surprise visit to shuttle me to the doctor. He and Ike had words. Stupid male pissing contest words. The three of us had a super fun drive into Casper afterward. I refused to let either of them come into the exam room with me. When I finished early . . . I called you."

"They'll blow a gasket when they find out you bailed on them."

She furiously stirred her drink.

"Riss?"

"They were being assholes, treating me like I was a stupid kid one moment and like I wasn't there the next. They'll call when I'm not in the waiting room. I won't be ornery and refuse to tell them where I am. I just needed a break."

"Talk to me." Jade reached for Riss's hand. "For reals. No judgment."

"This injury has made me question things about my life." She knocked the salt off the rim of her glass with her straw into her drink. "I pride myself on my independence. I never imagined my stubbornness would result in loss of that independence. I'm worried I won't be able to drive again."

"The doctor warned you that could be a possibility?"

She shook her head. "I looked at the rehab lists of dos and don'ts. Even if my arm and my hand heal perfectly? There's a minimum of two months of PT. Two months in which shifting a semi is not allowed. Two months in which unloading a semi is not allowed. So I'm facing four and a half months without income. I don't have enough in my savings to tide me over. I can't ask my brothers for financial help—not out of stubbornness, but they're havin' their own issues tryin' to keep the garage afloat. And my dire financial outlook doesn't include the medical bills that'll start rolling in soon."

"I hate that I don't have any advice to give you, when you were so . . . instrumental in helping me find part-time jobs that allowed me to stay here with Tobin."

"Instrumental." That brought a quick smile. "I love me some good puns."

Jade peered at her intently.

"What?"

"You always have a backup plan. Is that why you're panicked? Because this time you don't?"

Riss shrugged. She had two ideas percolating. Her first option that Louie had brought up made the most sense, and the fact she hadn't thought of it herself proved how much this injury had rattled her. The other option was so far out of left field it came from another galaxy. Sharing that one would convince her friend that she'd finally cracked.

"This is what sucks about the current system. Catastrophic injury can render you jobless and homeless within a matter of weeks. Then if you're persistent enough to decipher which government agencies might be able to help out, you'll suffocate in paperwork before you go completely broke."

She tuned out her ranting friend. While she'd love to blame someone else for this predicament, she'd brought it on herself. Logic dictated she solve it herself.

"Sorry about that tangent. Let's get back to you. And Ike." Jade waggled her eyebrows.

"That's a short convo; there *is* no me'n Ike."

"So the two of you aren't . . . ?"

"Fucking? Nope."

"But . . . you're alone in his house twenty-four/seven."

"We're roommates, Jade. That's it."

"There's no personal interaction?"

"Of course there is. The man cooks for me and won't even let me do the dishes. We watch movies or TV every night—even if it's late, like after his sisters have demanded his immediate assistance. We talk until I can't keep my eyes open and I swear he'd carry me to my room and tuck me in if I let him."

Jade opened her mouth. Closed it.

"Don't do that," Riss warned, snagging her second margarita. "Spit it out."

"That's not *nothing*, Riss. It sounds like you are getting more involved with him every day."

"Even if I am, I don't trust it."

"Why not?"

"What if bein' in close quarters has temporarily amplified feelings that will vanish once we're not sharing living space? Which is why when he's kissed me—only twice, mind you—afterward it's like he remembers, 'Oh right. This is just Riss. I got caught up in the moment of bein' overly friendly.' It hasn't gone any further than some suggestive verbal exchanges, a hug here and there. Once I'm outta his hair, I doubt we'll stay in contact." The thought of not seeing Ike every day caused a sharp pain in her chest, but things couldn't stay as mixed up as they were now.

"Jeez, Riss. I hadn't expected to hear that. In fact, I'd psyched myself up to hear all the dirty details."

Riss raised her glass. "No one is more disappointed in the big suckfest that is my life than me. So entertain me with gossip."

She laughed. "Okay. Can you believe that Harlow is pregnant? Isn't it exciting?"

For the next half an hour they talked about their friends, book club, home projects Jade had started and TV shows. Normal conversation with her BFF that she'd desperately missed.

Jade left to use the restroom.

Riss's phone rang with a call from Ike at 5:12—exactly two hours after she'd heard the receptionist order Lonnie and Ike out of the doctor's office. She wouldn't be petulant; this last hour with Jade had soothed her ragged edges. She answered, "This is Riss Thorpe."

"Where in the hell are you?" Ike demanded.

"At the Friendly Ghost with Jade."

"Why didn't you text me that you'd finished early?"

"Because I needed some girl time."

A pause, then, "Girl drinkin' time? How much have you had?"

"Is there a point to this phone call besides tryin' to make me feel guilty?"

"You should feel guilty. Your brother and I—"

Riss ended the call and shut her phone off. Listening to him rant would only demand she respond in kind. She'd had enough. Of all of it. This was why she didn't date: she couldn't be disappointed if she didn't have any expectations.

Jade slipped back into the booth. "Was that Ike?"

"Yeah. Can I ask if it'd be too much trouble for you to give us a ride back to his place? Lonnie doesn't need to make the drive since he's only ten minutes from home here."

"Of course I'll take you."

"Thanks."

"He's on his way here now?"

She nodded.

"I already paid the bill. And before you argue, it was, like, six bucks. Total."

"Thanks. I don't know what I was thinking ordering two drinks." She smiled sheepishly. "I actually don't have my purse with me or any money."

"I think you were pretty rattled. You're still rattled. Are you sure you're okay to go back to Ike's place?"

"It's not like I have another option." Riss carefully slid out of the booth. "My turn to use the can."

Everything took so much longer with only one working arm. So when Riss exited the bathroom, Ike and Lonnie had arrived.

Yippee.

They both looked at her warily.

Riss dealt with her brother first. "Since Jade lives closer to Ike's place, she's drivin' us back to Muddy Gap."

"That'll work. What'd the doc say?"

"Great news! I'm on the mend enough that I can move back into my trailer."

"Did the doc put that in writing anywhere? Or are we supposed to take your word for it?" Ike asked.

She ignored that barb. "Think that buddy of yours would have time to fix the pipes anytime soon? I'm ready to go home."

"I already had him fix everything," Lonnie said.

"You did?"

"Why didn't you tell me that when we were talkin' earlier?" Ike asked.

Lonnie spared Ike a look. "Because you didn't ask." He may as well have said, *Because it's none of your business.*

"How much do I owe you?"

"Nothin'. I'm happy that I got to do something for you, since you don't ask for help."

Riss grinned and hugged him. "Thank you! I cannot wait to go home."

"Me'n Lloyd and Lou will swing by every day and check on you." He lowered his voice. "You need me to come get you in the morning and drag your stuff over there?"

"I'll do it. Ain't like she's got much."

Way to say that with such feeling.

Even Jade's eyes narrowed. Then she inserted herself between Riss and Ike. "Let me help you with your coat."

"Maybe she oughta do it herself since she won't have anyone to help her when she's back home."

Lonnie dragged Ike out of earshot and they exchanged terse words.

Riss didn't want to know what that was about.

When Jade said, "Ike's in rare form," Riss didn't acknowledge that either.

She convinced Jade to hit the McDonald's drive-thru on the way out of Casper.

Sullen Ike sat in the back seat and declined a tasty double cheeseburger.

His loss. Riss ate both of them. And his fries.

Then she asked Jade about the honeymoon and there wasn't a moment of dead air during the rest of the drive to Muddy Gap.

At Ike's house, he thanked Jade for the ride and bailed out to unlock the front door, warning Riss to stay put.

She flipped him off.

Just like old times.

"I'd offer to stick around and run interference, but I have to clean the hair out of the shower drain."

Riss laughed. "Ain't like this is my first go-round with him. I'll be fine." Or she would be as soon as she called in reinforcements. She fired off a quick text.

The front porch light clicked on, distorting Ike's shadow across the snow.

He was solicitous, hooking his arm around her waist to keep her from falling.

Even after they'd shed their outerwear inside his foyer, neither one spoke.

Riss retreated to her room. Even one-handed it wouldn't take long to pack up.

She heard the doorbell and Ike's surprise at seeing Bernice.

Then Bernice knocked on her bedroom door twice before she entered.

Riss waved from her spot on the bed. "Thanks for coming on such short notice, Aunt B."

"Your text surprised me, to be honest."

"You thought I would've figured out one-handed hair washing by now?"

"Something like that." She jerked her chin toward the closed door. "You and Ike fighting?"

"Yep."

"So I'm a time killer?"

"Partially." Riss blushed guiltily. "I got my stitches out today. The PA was distracted by my babbling so she might've missed one. You're more familiar with the top of my head than I am, so could you check?"

"Sure."

"After that I could use a wash and a style."

She harrumphed. "Anything else, *milady*?"

"Not unless you wanna shove that stuff in a suitcase for me."

Bernice whistled. "That musta been some fight."

"No, I just got cleared to go home."

"*Can* you go home?"

"Yes, Lonnie had the pipes in my trailer fixed."

Her e-cig paused in front of her mouth. "Did you ask Lonnie to do that?"

"Nope. He just did it as a surprise. And I cannot wait to be back at my own place."

"You sure you're ready?"

"After today I'm more than ready. I'm not cleared to drive for work, so I need to figure out how I'm gonna pay my bills."

She puffed on her vape pen. "We've all been there, girlie."

"Some of us more than once."

Strawberry-scented air drifted over to her.

"Does Uncle Bob know you're still smoking?"

"Honey, as long as we've been married, there ain't a lot of secrets between us."

Riss looked at her. "So, this might sound weird, but have you always known when he's keeping something from you?"

Bernice exhaled. "If he was really good at keeping things from me then I wouldn't know he was, would I?"

Typical Aunt B response. "Forget it." Riss headed to the bathroom.

"Riss. Wait."

She turned around.

"Sorry. It's easier to go for the smart-ass answer."

How well she knew that.

"Bob . . . he knows I never really quit smokin'. I don't smoke in the house and he doesn't complain. Sorta our don't-ask-don't-tell policy." She angled her head toward the door. "You think Ike is keeping something from you?"

Even if she suspected that, she wouldn't share her suspicions with the woman who owned the biggest gossip gathering spot in the county. "I got to thinking about that saying ... a lie of omission is still a lie. But is it really? If a person opts to keep something to themselves, and it's their truth, then it's not a lie."

She blinked. "That's a circular argument. A secret can be a lie too, so you can go round and round with this and make yourself crazy. So stop."

"I'll try."

"You really okay, doll?"

I don't know. I hate the direction my thoughts have taken. Nothing is simple. Nothing is as it seems. "I'm trying to be."

"Well, get yourself stripped and in the tub."

"I'm not gonna miss you bossing me around."

"You ain't getting rid of me that easy. I'll be over to check on you every other day, so don't be waltzing around buck-assed nekkid."

"Little cold for that this time of year."

She blew out another stream of air. "Who's takin' you home tomorrow?"

"I imagine Ike will get saddled with that. Why?"

"'Cause your uncle keeps asking me what he can do to help out. Personally seeing you settled in at home would give us both peace of mind."

That would be easier. "I'd want to leave super early, while Ike is checking stock at the Split Rock, so, like, six a.m.?"

"Bob is an early bird. That'll work fine." Bernice set her e-cig aside. "You need help covering up your cast?"

The nurse had given her a fancy inflatable plastic cover for her arm that she could slip on without help. No time like the present to test it. "I'm good."

Bernice didn't chitchat, which was unusual. Seemed like she had something on her mind.

When she was combing out Riss's hair, she said, "I kept something from Bob once. 'Course, when he found out, he blew his top. I didn't apologize because, at the time, I didn't feel like what I done was outta line."

"He disagreed?"

"Yeah." She smoothed both her hands over Riss's scalp. "Want me to French braid this? It'll stay for a couple of days."

"Sure."

Riss prepared herself for Aunt B to yank hard as she braided, but she kept adding product to smooth the constant state of frizz that was Riss's hair.

"Can I ask what you hid from Uncle Bob?"

Bernice's motions stilled. Then she sighed. "It's probably time you knew anyway. I've always been surprised that Lonnie never told you. Always been a little ashamed to tell you myself."

A bad feeling surfaced immediately. "What?"

"After your dad died, and everything was up in the air, I told Lonnie I wanted you to come live with me'n Bob."

"Why?"

"For some reason I had it in my head that Lonnie wouldn't raise you right. As the only girl living in a house of boys—young men—they'd expect you to cook and clean and do laundry and basically be their servant. I worried with no female influence you'd become—"

"A doormat or a tomboy," she finished angrily.

"Yes."

"Did you feel vindicated when I turned into a tomboy? Like you could've somehow prevented it?"

Bernice abandoned the braid and moved to stand in front of Riss. "Lemme finish, then I'll let you tear into me." She paused, but she kept her eyes on Riss. "I was wrong. Lonnie had enough to deal with without fearing that his aunt was gonna take his sister away. He said you—all of you kids—were his responsibility and he'd do whatever it took to keep his family together."

"Lonnie never expected me to do more because I was a girl. Neither did he ask me to do less because I was a girl either."

"I know that now. Back then, I had a self-righteous streak as wide as the Yellowstone River. I'd conveniently forgotten you'd spent most of your life without your mother's influence and living in a house full of testosterone."

"My brothers drove me crazy sometimes, but I can't imagine growing up without them. I hated when Lloyd joined the air force. Seemed like we had another big hole in our family." Something occurred to her. "Is your rift with Lonnie why we didn't spend holidays or birthdays together?"

She shrugged. "Partially. Bob and your dad didn't have the usual upbringing so they didn't have holiday traditions. No surprise Lonnie limited the amount of contact I had with you after that. For a few years I was pissed off, but as the years have gone on, I've kept my distance because . . . I was ashamed." Her eyes filled with tears. "Lonnie raised you right. All of you. I was wrong to think I could do better."

Riss stood and gave her aunt a one-armed hug. "I'm glad you told me. I won't pretend it doesn't tick me off now, but with all the shit I dealt with today, I'm gonna put it aside to think on later." She stepped back. "You need to tell Lonnie what you told me. He gave up his dream to keep us together."

"I will." She swiped under her eyes. "Now let's get this hair finished."

"Take your time."

"Still not ready to deal with Ike?"

"I don't know that he's ready to deal with me."

∽

Riss ventured into the living room three hours after Bernice left.

Ike was staring at the TV with the sound muted.

"Hey."

He looked over at her. "Hey. You hungry?" He rose to his feet.

"Don't get up. It's fine. I'll just grab a piece of fruit."

"I'll heat up some soup. Sit."

Riss didn't want to make a big deal of this, but . . . would he even recognize his behavioral pattern?

Ike stopped. Faced her. "I did it again, didn't I?"

"Yeah. But you realized it before you got the pan out and started cooking."

"Sorry. Let's try this again. Riss, darlin', what could I fix you to eat?"

"Nothin'. I'll grab an apple."

"Would you like it sliced?"

"Yes. Thank you."

"Are you sitting at the breakfast bar? Or taking it to your room?"

"I'll sit."

She watched him wash the apple and center it in the pie-shaped slicer, gently pushing down until the core separated and the apple was in eight slices. "What time are you planning to leave tomorrow?"

"In the morning. Uncle Bob is taking me home."

Ike's frustrated gaze zoomed to hers. "I said I'd take you."

"Which I appreciate. But Bob felt bad about not doin' anything for me, so this will make him feel useful."

"If that's the way you want it . . ."

"It is." She attempted a lighter tone. "So what're your plans once the houseguest from hell is gone?"

His hand movements were smooth and controlled as he arranged the apple slices. "I'll head to the big stock show in Rapid City." He smiled as he slid the plate to her. "Maybe I'll make a few lists."

Riss smiled back. "I swear it helps to see things differently when it's literally spelled out in black and white."

"I agree." Ike snagged a notebook and a pen. "Let's list all the things that went wrong today."

"Don't be an ass-hat."

"I'm serious. We fucked up and I wanna know how to fix it."

"Why?" She snatched an apple chunk and bit into it. "I'm leaving tomorrow."

"We can't let things stay as they are between us. Surely you see that?"

She chewed her apple and swallowed. It was unnerving that Ike's gaze only left her mouth to dip down to sweep over her neck. As if he wanted to take a bite out of her.

Yes, a big old bite. That sucking mouth seeking out all the shiver-inducing spots as his teeth scraped against her skin would be equal parts heaven and hell.

"Riss? You gonna answer?"

"Do you wanna make this list as a scorecard? To see who was more at fault today?"

The guilty flush to his cheeks gave her the answer.

She pointed at him with an apple slice. "Not the best use of a list. And I doubt you're prepared for how one-sided—my side—it will be."

Ike leaned across the counter and neatly bit off half of the apple slice between her fingers. "Prove it."

Smarmy jerk. "Fine. Items one through ten: Ike making decisions for me without my consent and treating me like a child."

"You can't have one example equal to ten items."

"Why not? I have at least ten separate examples."

He flashed his teeth. "Name them."

"Gladly. One: Riss, get up.

"Two: Finish your breakfast.

"Three: Go put your sling on.

"Four: Stop dawdling; you'll miss your appointment.

"Five: Hold still.

"Six: I *am* going to the doctor with you.

"Seven: You'd better not be drinking.

"Eight: *I'm* taking care of her.

"Nine: Do. Not. Move. I'll be right back.

"Ten: Make her do it herself."

Ike blinked at her.

She pointed at the open notebook. "I don't see you writing any of that down."

"I'm tryin' to mentally combat your list with my explanations, but every damn one of them sounds more like an excuse." He shoved his hand through his hair. "I'm sorry. Christ, I'm so sorry for treating you like—"

"One of your little sisters?"

Ike scowled. "Ain't a single sisterly thought comes to my mind when I look at you, Larissa. I thought that kiss today would've proven that beyond a doubt."

"All it proved is there's chemistry between us. Whether it's real or whether it's a proximity thing . . . neither of us can answer that right now."

"Is that what your girl time with Jade was about?"

"Yes." Her gaze clashed with his. "These past two weeks have been confusing. Not to say they haven't been good, but I'm leaving here with more questions than answers."

"About us?"

"About everything. But yeah, whether there could be an 'us' is a biggie. I can't be objective while I'm here, when you annoy the piss out of me one minute and the next all I can think about is kissing you again."

"Well, darlin', we're on the same page there."

"So . . . truce again?"

"Again?" Ike walked around the end of the breakfast bar. "We're on day ninety-three of the original truce. Nothin' has happened so far to break it."

"You've kept track of how many days it's been?"

"Yep. Now c'mere and gimme a damn hug."

She laughed. "Gonna twist my arm if I say no?"

"You won't say no." He pulled her against his body, those strong arms encircling her. "You like this."

"I do." She rested her cheek on his chest. "Thanks for taking me in. I've no doubt the reason I've been cleared to stay by myself is because bein' here allowed me to rest and heal much faster."

"You're welcome."

As with so many of their hugs, neither of them wanted to be the first one to let go.

"Gonna miss you, sweet cheeks."

"Gonna miss you too, cowboy."

Riss didn't look at him as she disentangled from his embrace and went to bed.

Chapter Seventeen

❧

*T*hree weeks had passed since Ike had seen Riss.
They'd texted a couple of times, not much beyond a quick check-in on his end to see how she was faring.

It bothered him that she hadn't asked what he'd been doing.

At the end of January he'd attended the Black Hills Stock Show and Rodeo in Rapid City, South Dakota. During his brokering years it'd been an annual event for him. He'd made a lot of deals and contacts, so showing up and hanging out at the Stockman's Bar seemed like old times.

Except it wasn't.

His former clients were happy to talk about their families, their mutual acquaintances and the weather . . . but the cattle business? Not so much. And it hadn't been just one or two clients that'd reacted that way. They all had. Like Ike had abandoned them.

He hadn't, but disclosing *now* that his position had been eliminated *then* would make him look desperate. And desperation was bad for business, especially in the sales game, where confidence equaled success.

His mentor, Augie, always reminded him: *selling yourself is the most important aspect of any sale.*

Ike had taken his mentor's advice as gospel. That wisdom coupled with *don't disclose your personal problems* had proved to be a winning combination.

Would things be different for him if he'd confessed that leaving Stocksellers hadn't been voluntary?

It certainly hadn't helped that the *Quad-State Live-stock News* had reported Ike's departure from Stock-sellers, Inc., in the same paragraph that listed him as one of the new owners of Jackson Stock Contracting—two changes in his life that had happened nearly four months apart.

So it had been five very long days in South Dakota. And just to reinforce his feeling of futility, Ike had attended the rodeo all four nights. He'd crossed paths with the Sutton family several times over the years, so he'd scored a chute pass that allowed access to the pens, the competitors, behind the scenes.

Sutton Rodeos, an offshoot of Sutton Cattle Company—a family-run business with one hundred–plus years raising livestock in South Dakota—was listed in the top ten stock contractors in the nation. Not only did they supply the rough stock for the ten-day Black Hills Stock Show and Rodeo, they were the promoters for the entire event.

There was no way JSC could compete with that.

According to the Sutton Rodeos brochure, they were contracted for fifty-six other rodeos—small and large—across the Dakotas, Nebraska, Minnesota and Iowa in the upcoming year.

Again . . . there was no way JSC could compete with that.

When he'd contacted Hugh to share the rundown on the two official meetings he'd managed to set up, Hugh's main topic of conversation was Harlow's ultrasound and how freaky-cool it'd been to hear the baby's heartbeat.

That was when Ike spiraled into depression.

Not even a last-minute booking for a one-day rodeo in central Nebraska bolstered his spirits.

He'd continued on as he always did, rising at the crack of dawn to feed stock. Checking in daily with his sisters. Watching hours of mindless TV. Sleeping entire days away.

The paperwork he'd promised to organize sat on the dining room table untouched.

He hadn't gone to the store in weeks; he'd eaten all the frozen meals and canned goods on hand, but he had no clear memory of cooking for himself.

He hadn't hopped in his truck and taken a long drive to try and clear his head because no matter which direction he went, he felt as if he was on the road to nowhere.

So he may as well just stay home, since he couldn't outrun that feeling even sitting on his couch.

He'd even been too melancholy to restock his whiskey and beer supply. The upside to that was he hadn't been drinking until he passed out every night.

On a whim, on an unusually warm February day, Ike

decided to hell with texting; he'd just show up on Riss's doorstep.

Ike got an eyeful of her jeans-clad ass first thing as he parked next to her 4Runner.

See, the day is already looking up.

She scooted out of the back end of the vehicle, brandishing a dust cloth.

He sauntered over, his grin immense. Sunlight reflected in her hair a fiery red. A smudge of dirt streaked her forehead. Concern flattened the lines of her mouth. She wore denim overalls, a University of Wyoming fleece jacket and purple ropers.

"Riss, darlin', you are a sight for sore eyes."

She snorted and some of her wariness faded. "Hey, Ike. You out and about spreading that cowboy charm to invalids on this sunshiny afternoon?"

"You are the first and only stop for me today, hot stuff."

"Really?"

"Yeah. I missed you. Hell, I even missed your vulgar vocab. Now c'mere and gimme a damn hug."

"Pretty cocky to assume I'd just run into your arms the moment you showed that handsome face."

He shrugged. "You can skip over here if you'd rather."

She laughed. "Ass-hat." She walked toward him. "Fair warning that I probably reek."

"Don't care." Then Riss was in his arms and everything seemed better. Brighter. Clearer.

All too soon she squirmed away. "You have time to come in for coffee?"

"I'd like that."

"Cool. Lemme just close this." She stood on tiptoe to grab the handle of the hatchback.

"Whoa. Let me help."

She jockeyed for position. "I got it."

"Are you even supposed to be doin' this kinda stuff?"

"Probably not." Riss slammed the door and spun to face him. "You gonna lecture me before putting me in time out?"

Low blow.

Ike said nothing since apparently she was still pissed off.

Closing her eyes, she inhaled a long breath. "I'm sorry." She exhaled. "Reflex with you."

"Wonder if there'll come a time when a snippy, snappy smart-ass response ain't the first thing that exits our mouths when we're together?"

"I'd say a cold day in hell, but I'm pretty sure that was here last week." She started toward the house.

Ike had only been inside her trailer once before and hadn't bothered to look around. So he felt . . . well . . . blind for not noticing the vibrant colors everywhere. Rich reds, deep purples, dark greens, bright blues. It was as if he'd stepped into a sultan's oasis.

"Wow. This is awesome."

She grinned. "Thanks. I wanted to feel like the king of my castle when I came home . . . even if my castle is a trailer."

His gaze moved from the purple couch to the turquoise armchair. The fancy fabrics looked easily stainable. Maybe this space was just for show.

"Have a seat."

"I'm afraid I'll wrinkle it or rip it or spill coffee on it."

She pointed at the couch. "It's crushed velvet. It's durable and I've had it stainproofed. I wouldn't have put any of this furniture in here if I couldn't use it."

"Okay."

"I'll get the coffee."

Ike waited to see if Riss removed her boots before he stepped on the plush rug.

Nope. He was good to go.

He sat in the corner of the couch next to a floor-to-ceiling bookshelf crammed with books. Everything in this space spoke of the owner. Vibrant, funky, well-ordered, warm and soft, but with unexpected edges.

No wonder she'd been so eager to get home. And he was really glad he'd never asked her what she thought of his place.

Riss handed him a mug that read: **Dear Pumpkin Spice—Fuck You**.

He chuckled. "Tryin' to tell me something?"

"Nope. It was my white elephant gift from our book club Christmas party."

"Sounds like a fun book club."

"It is."

He tipped his head toward the bookshelf. "Have you read all of them books?"

"Most of them." She scowled at her cast. "I've had more time to read lately and I didn't enjoy it as much as I imagined."

"What else have you been doin'?"

"This and that."

The way Riss avoided his gaze when she sipped her

coffee, he figured she'd been doing stuff she shouldn't have been. So he let his gaze continue to roam around the room. "Does that thing actually add heat?"

She turned to see where he was looking. "The fake fireplace? No, it's just for show. I picked it up at an estate sale for next to nothin'. I refurbed it intending to sell it, but it turned out better than I thought, so I kept it. Plus, come on, a plastic log with a red lightbulb behind it to simulate fire is the best idea evah."

"That, it is." He couldn't remember ever feeling so awkward around Riss. It was as if being welcomed into her personal space he'd gotten an intimate peek into more than just her living room. "So is that a hobby of yours? Buying stuff at estate sales and selling it?"

"I'm invited to some of them so there's loading and delivery options on-site for people who buy big stuff like furniture and appliances. I tend to go for the stuff that's prepriced that won't be auctioned off. That way I don't fall in love with a piece and then it's sold for out of my price range."

The oddest sense of sadness flowed over him. He hated that Riss had pined for things she couldn't afford.

"Tools are usually the best deals. Cheap to buy, fast turnaround to resell and make a quick buck." She set her cup on the coffee table. "But you didn't swing by to hear my estate sale philosophy. What's goin' on with you?"

"Same old, same old. I drove up to the Black Hills for the stock show."

"Anything interesting happen?"

And like she'd opened the overflow gates, everything poured out of him.

Everything.

For once Ike didn't temper his tone. He didn't mask his anger about the sharp downward spiral his livelihood had taken. He lamented the ugliness of a corporate bottom line. He admitted his fear and uncertainty about his future. He bitched about his sisters' continued dependency. He placed blame—a reaction he usually avoided. After getting up to refill their coffee, he began to pace.

As he paced, the hopeless feeling that'd been clawing at him for over a year to get out . . . finally did.

When Ike eventually ran out of steam, his throat was dry from talking, but his shoulders weren't bunched up around his ears. The tension in his neck and back and jaw had lessened. And now that the things he'd been afraid to admit were out of that dark space inside him, his words pushed out into the ether, no longer weighing him down, he felt . . . free.

He stopped in the middle of Riss's kitchen, threw his head back and laughed. Then he shouted, "Goddamn, that felt good! Like fucking fantastic! Like I've been cleansed."

That was when he realized Riss hadn't said a single word during his catharsis.

Or was it a metamorphosis?

He should've paid more attention in school.

Regardless, he was damn near giddy with relief.

His gaze sought Riss's and he expected to see happiness, pride, maybe even excitement on her face that he'd had this breakthrough, but she was staring intently into her cup.

Shit. Maybe he'd pissed her off by bein' so loud.

"Hey. Sorry if I got a little carried away."

"It's fine."

Fine? It was way, way more than just fine.

"Riss?"

"Yeah." She lifted her head and glanced at the clock across from her. "I'm a sucky hostess." She stood and walked right past him to set her cup in the sink. "Coffee's gone, but do you want a glass of water or something?"

"Water? What the fuck? I want you to be happy you were here with me when I had this life-changing moment."

Riss's gaze finally connected with his.

But he didn't see joy or pride or even amusement. All he saw was anger.

"A life-changing moment, Ike? That's what that was?"

"Yes." He paused and studied her, confused as fuck.

"So tell me . . . how are you going to change your life?"

"What do you mean?"

"Now that you've had this great epiphany, what's the first thing you're gonna do when you leave here?"

"I don't know. I'll probably go to the grocery store."

"And tomorrow? What will you do differently tomorrow than you did today?"

He frowned at her. "What's with the third degree?"

She shrugged. "*You're* the one who called this a 'life-changing moment.' I'm just asking when you intend to carry it out."

"Intend," he repeated. "I just acknowledged to myself—and to you—what I'd been afraid to admit out loud. Can't that be enough?"

"No. Acknowledging it is not the same as acting on it. Not at all."

"So I'm supposed to know what action to take right fucking now?"

"Ab-so-fucking-lutely you're supposed to know that *right fucking now*. If you don't, then it's not a god-damned 'life-changing moment,' is it?"

Who was this woman sucking away his joy with every barbed word?

"If you get up tomorrow and do the exact same thing that you've been doin' the last week, or month, or year, or decade, your life doesn't change. And I don't know anyone that needs a complete life overhaul and an honest wake-up call more than you do, Ike Palmer!"

Riss had yelled that last part . . . and that flustered the hell out of him. He'd seen her annoyed, exasperated, mad, but he'd never seen her like this: her entire being pulsing with fury.

"Whoa. Where is this anger comin' from?"

"From me! From here!" She smacked herself in the stomach with her good hand. "My gut instinct is never wrong. And right now it's telling me that you don't have any intention of ever following through and making this be the life-changing event you're bragging that it is!"

"Fuck that, Riss. And fuck you. You don't know . . . you've got no right to assume anything about me, or what my future actions will be."

"Future actions," she said harshly. "That's because you have no fucking concept of the phrase 'immediate action,' because you've never in your life had to act on instinct. You've never been forced to make a decision you might regret."

"I just told you that I got fired from bein' a cattle broker!"

"While that sucks, and I hate that you felt the need to hide it from everyone, how did getting fired impact your life?"

Ike found it difficult to speak he was so goddamned mad. "Impact my life? It changed everything in my life."

"You lost your job. But did you lose your truck?"

"No, but—"

"Did you have to sell it because you couldn't afford the payment, gas or insurance?"

"No."

"Did you lose your house?"

"You know I didn't."

"I also know you didn't have to put it on the market and sell it at a loss and move in with your sister."

"What does—"

"Did you lose your health insurance?"

Since she knew the answer, he didn't respond.

"Did you lose your retirement fund? Did you have to cash it out to put food on the table? Or pay medical bills?"

He scowled at her. "No."

"So essentially, nothin' changed when you got fired except you weren't getting a regular paycheck."

Breathe, man, just breathe.

"And you didn't have to take immediate action either, did you? You weren't at McDonald's the next week applying as a fry cook because you didn't have the cash to pay your cell phone bill."

"Do all of these sharp-edged questions have a point?"

"Yes. You claim you lost everything. But all you did was give yourself the luxury of more time—a year and a half—to actually fail."

"Jesus Christ. I didn't expect you—of all people—to be judgmental. Especially when I opened myself—"

"Yes, you opened yourself up to this! You wanted me to pat you on the back and congratulate you for finally admitting that you were depressed because you got fired. Yay! Good for you, now you know why you've been sitting on the couch the past year and a half. Yay! You're human and can shove all that macho bullshit aside and accept you lost a piece of yourself when you lost the job. But goddammit, Ike, you took the path of least resistance when you went all in with JSC. Which might've been a good choice had you not doomed it from the start with your apathy."

"My apathy."

"Apathy, indifference, laziness."

Laziness?

Blood roared in his ears.

The silence stretched tighter and tighter with each second, like a cheap rubber band pulled past the break-ing point.

He managed to say, "You think I'm . . . lazy?"

Riss's cheeks turned bright red. But she kept her eyes locked to his and her chin up when she said, "Yes."

Ike's entire world tilted. No one had ever said that to him. Called him that. He'd never been that.

Lazy.

Obviously Riss was off her fucking rocker with jeal-ousy that she had to work three times as hard as he did for half as much.

Obviously she was grasping at straws to make him feel like shit.

"Ike," she said softly.

He looked up from staring at the tips of his boots to see her standing closer.

When she tried to put her hand on his chest, he flinched and said, "Don't."

"Please listen to me."

"Are you gonna apologize?"

A slight shake of her head. Then, "But I will clarify."

"I know the goddamned definition of that word, Riss. Ain't a whole lot you need to clarify for me."

When he tried to retreat, she grabbed a fistful of his shirt. "You need to hear it in the context I intended it."

Ike barked a laugh. "Are you seriously tryin' to tell me I took 'you're lazy' out of fuckin' context?"

"Yes."

Jesus. Why was he still here listening to this?

"We've known each other for two years. I'm not talkin' about hating each other in passing or my misperception of you because of the shit that went down with Lloyd. I'm talkin' about the two years since we first had to interact with each other."

"Your point?"

"I didn't know you as Ike Palmer the cattle broker. I've only known you as Ike Palmer, a co-owner in JSC."

"A lazy guy with the luxury of time on his hands to fail," Ike said sarcastically.

"So let me repeat that all together. I've only known you as Ike Palmer, an apathetic co-owner in JSC."

He wanted to protest that he'd always been so much more than that.

But how would she know that? She could only judge him on how he presented himself now.

He couldn't deny Riss's point about context.

In the short amount of time she'd known him, he had just floated along. At first he'd been gung ho about cold-calling rodeo promoters and committees, anxious to line up events and prove their stock could go horn to horn with any other stock contractor's. In hindsight, the constant stream of rejections had weighed on him. Because in all his previous years as a salesman, he'd never failed.

So it'd gotten easier not to do anything. No one checked up on him. Ike told himself he was waiting for Hugh to return and really take charge. He convinced himself he wasn't a self-starter and that had somehow become a free pass to explain his failure.

Failure he'd blame on Hugh being in Cali, or the shitty economy, or entrenched stock-contracting companies not giving them a chance—or a combination of all three. His feelings about his position at JSC ran the gamut from resentment to guilt to who-gives-a-damn. Nothing about the business had ever given him a sense of purpose or even a glimmer of happiness.

Riss hadn't come up with those theories in a fit of nastiness to hurt him.

For the past two years she'd seen him in action—or inaction. For two weeks she'd seen exactly how he spent his days . . . wallowing in apathy.

Fuck. Me.

I am lazy.

I *am* lazy.

I am *lazy.*

No matter where he put the emphasis the context didn't change.

I am lazy.

He took two steps back from her.

"Ike?"

"Give me a minute."

She nodded.

He turned and faced the living room. Bright colors, full of life and hope and promise, all mixed together to create a beautiful kind of chaos.

Then all of a sudden the space closed in on him and he couldn't breathe.

In two steps he sailed out the door.

Air, sunshine and wind greeted him. An icy breeze eddied around him, both bracing and breath stealing.

Kind of like Riss.

Tough love. She said she'd give it to him when he needed it—but least expected it.

Yeah, she'd done that all right.

He laced his hands together and set them on his head. Restless energy had him walking in circles in front of the carport as his thoughts reordered themselves, morphing from indecipherable to scrambled to circular to linear.

Riss's accusations found their way into his head too. *You've never in your life had to act on instinct. You've never been forced to make a decision you might regret.*

Maybe the time had come.

He dropped his arms and moved his head side to side.

Standing in front of Riss's fleet, he noticed one was missing.

Footsteps crunching on the gravel stopped beside him. "Hey. You all right?"

"Yeah. Where's the bull hauler?"

"I sold it."

Shocked, he faced her. "What?"

"I sold it."

"Why?"

"Because I needed the money. Bein' out of work with bills piling up . . . I've had to make some hard decisions. That piece of equipment has always gotten the least amount of use so it was the first to go."

"Riss. I'm sor—"

"Don't be. It'll keep me in the black for a few more months. But JSC will have to hire someone else as I'm officially out of the bull-hauling business."

Ike watched the dead grass blowing in front of the metal carport supports. "So that's it?"

"What?"

"I have an epiphany, which you immediately dismiss. Then I learn you're outta the stock-hauling business, which means we're no longer coworkers. So I hop in my truck and you wave good-bye with your cast?"

"Is this where you demand a hug?"

"Maybe. It feels like an ending."

"It is. But we'll see each other." She smirked. "We'll always have the memories of our time as roomies."

"God, I hated that."

"Seriously? It was your idea that I stay with you!" She whapped him on the arm.

Ike caught her by the wrist and moved in front of her. "Lemme put this in context, sweet cheeks. I hated that you were injured. I hated that we fought like siblings. I hated the way you left." He set her palm on his chest. "I hated the promise I'd made not to kiss you again."

"You did?"

His eyes searched hers. "Wanna know the real reason I never made a move on you?"

"Because you were . . . lazy?"

His jaw dropped.

"I was kidding!" She paused. "Too soon?"

"Ya think?"

"Sorry. I'll be serious now."

"I didn't make a move on you because it'd matter too much if you rejected me."

Riss dug her fingers into his pectorals. "Your heart raced when you said that."

"Because it's hard as fuck telling you this, when I'm still smarting from when you told me earlier what you really thought of me."

"Funny, I don't remember admitting out loud that I wanted to see this hot cowboy face smirking between my tits as I'm riding you like a fucking pony."

Cock . . . instantly hard.

Hopes he hadn't fucked this up . . . definitely soaring.

He placed a lingering kiss on her forehead. "Thank you for giving me the kick in the ass I needed."

"Seems weird to say you're welcome . . . but you're welcome."

She shivered and he realized she'd chased after him without putting on a coat. Instead of harping on her for being forgetful, he stepped back and removed his jacket. He settled it on her shoulders and tucked it around her.

Seeing her odd expression, he said, "You looked cold."

"Now you'll be cold."

"Nah, I'll be fine."

"Come inside and—"

"Warm myself by your fake fire?" He grinned. "Normally I'd be all over that seduction ploy, but darlin', I'm gonna have to take a rain check."

"Wait . . . you're leaving?"

"My to-do list just got hella long." Ike traced the curve of her cheek. "See, this smart, sexy woman I'm crazy about told me that life-changing events require immediate action, so I'm setting things in motion."

"Ike—"

He stopped her protest with a kiss. Not one filled with hunger—he'd save those for later. For now, he kissed her softly, sweetly. With care and gratitude and an unspoken promise of more to come.

When she trembled in his arms, he held her tighter until she settled.

Then he whispered, "This isn't an ending, Larissa. This is the beginning." He kissed her one last time and said, "I'll be in touch soon."

Chapter Eighteen

❧

*W*hat in the hell did you do to Ike?"

Startled, Riss glanced up from her phone.

Three big guys fanned out in front of her. Tobin, Renner and Abe Lawson.

"I haven't heard from Ike in over a week." Her gaze moved across each of their faces. "Is he all right?"

"No, he's not all right," Abe said tersely. "He's lost his motherfucking mind."

A loud whistle pierced the air and Susan Williams, co-owner of Buckeye Joe's, leaned across the bar. "Riss. You okay?"

"Everything's fine," Renner assured her.

"Not from where I'm standing. I see three men trying to intimidate one woman, and fellas, that don't fly in my bar. Don't matter how long you've been comin' in here or how much money you spend, I will throw your asses out if you don't back off. You hear me?"

"Yes, ma'am," Tobin said. "They'll take it down a notch. And my wife will be joining us shortly."

The man tossed in "my wife" every chance he got. It was sweet.

But there wasn't anything sweet about the look on Tobin's face right now. That got Riss's back up. "Speaking of your better half . . . *she's* the one I'm supposed to be meeting here. So maybe you oughta tell me if Jade is in on whatever this is too."

Guilt flushed Tobin's cheeks.

Bingo. Jade had no idea what was going on.

Before Riss could really let Tobin have it, Renner jumped in.

"We need to talk and I'd rather do it privately. Please. This is important."

"Fine." Riss picked up her drink and slid off the barstool. "Lead the way."

Renner chose the round table for six in the back and pulled out a chair for Riss.

Susan arrived with bottles of beer almost before the guys were seated. Being a regular had its perks.

Abe Lawson sat across from Riss and gave her the stink-eye as he swigged his beer.

"This ain't much of a happy hour with the three of you glaring at me," she said coolly.

"Sorry. It's just . . ." Renner adjusted his cowboy hat. "So you've had no contact with Ike at all for over a week?"

"No. I did two short runs and a longer one with one of Tito's new drivers. But I had my phone with me the entire time and Ike didn't call or text. Has something happened?"

"It's been a helluva busy week for Ike. He called Hugh and quit the stock-contracting business. Then he called me and said the same thing, reminding me that someone else would have to take over his daily livestock checks. When I asked what was goin' on with him, he said something about havin' an epiphany."

Oh fuck.

"Would you know anything about that?" Abe asked. "Or why he'd suggest me'n the guys—guys he's been friends with since grade school—find another cattle broker because he was done with that too."

Ike had taken the *immediate action* suggestion to heart. He'd completely upended his life.

Riss was as shocked as she was proud.

"We're all wondering what had sent him off the deep end, but Ike ain't answering anyone's calls. Imagine my surprise when Holt Andrews called me." Abe pinned her with a look. "You know where this is headed, right?"

Did you lose your house?

Crap, crap, crap. Her pride slowly slid into panic. They hadn't talked specifics about what his immediate actions would entail, because he'd immediately gone into action.

"Riss?" Abe prompted.

"Dude. I don't have a freakin' clue." She sipped her margarita. "Did Ike ask Holt about putting his house on the market? Ike mentioned it was one of the first homes Holt built when he started his own business."

"Nope. Ike asked Holt for a job."

Riss's jaw dropped. "A job? Doin' what?"

"Honest work."

"Honest work. That's it?"

Abe nodded. "When we tried to get Holt to tell us more, he got pissy and warned us not to harass his newest employee."

"So any light you could shed on Ike's strange behavior would be appreciated," Renner said.

Asking why they believed she had answers would just bring up more questions. Best to keep her mouth shut. She shrugged. "Sorry."

Riss's gaze connected with Tobin's. She recognized his attempt at keeping his expression neutral. Come to think of it, Tobin hadn't grilled her on Ike's recent life changes and choices.

That's because he knows the truth. He's here to make sure you've got Ike's back too.

"You stayed with him after your accident," Abe pressed on. "Did you notice—"

"Ike doin' lines of blow with high-priced call girls as he called in his horse-racing bets to Vegas? Nope."

"No need to be a smart-ass," Renner cautioned. "We're wondering if you saw anything that'd help us help him. Maybe he talked about—"

"Stop right there. If Ike would've felt comfortable enough to tell me personal things in confidence, I sure as hell wouldn't break that confidence and tell you guys."

So much for keeping her mouth shut.

Then three sets of eyes focused on someone behind her.

Jade had arrived.

Riss turned and said, "Thank god that you're here."

Except it wasn't Jade.

Ike had stopped several feet back. But he wasn't looking at her.

"It's odd seeing the four of you together lookin' like you're planning a funeral," Ike drawled.

Just then Jade raced from the opposite side of the bar, making a beeline for Riss. "I'm sorry! I didn't know they planned to ambush you for information about Ike until Tobin texted me."

Talk about awkward silence. No one knew where to look.

Then Ike said, "My friends ambushed you?" as he moved in behind Riss's chair.

Riss had no problem throwing them under the bus. "Yes. It was ugly, Ike. A total shakedown. Abe held me upside down by my toenails while Renner beat on my cast with a stick and Tobin blocked the door. But I swear I didn't tell them about our secret you-know-what."

Renner and Abe were confused by her outburst. Tobin snickered and Jade took two steps back. But the only reaction she cared about was Ike's.

It seemed an hour passed before Ike smiled at her. "Ain't fun bein' a piñata, is it?"

"Ay, caramba."

He laughed. "I missed your crazy alternate realities."

She knew the look on her face said, *but did you miss me?*

His eyes softened. "Yeah, darlin', I missed you too. Now c'mere and gimme a damn hug."

Relieved, Riss stood and faced him. "You're still a pain in my ass." Then she slipped her left arm around his waist and pressed her cheek against his chest.

Ike's heart pounded beneath her ear as he pulled her in closer.

She took a moment to breathe him in. And maybe she indulged in another moment, enjoying how securely and gently those strong arms of his held her. And maybe she figured what the hell, and turned her head in to the curve of his neck to feel the warmth of his skin on her lips.

When Riss raised her head, she felt Ike's friends' curious stares boring into her back, but her full attention was focused on Ike. Specifically on the sexual heat darkening his eyes.

Holy hell, the guy gave good smolder.

"This is gonna be intense, sweet cheeks, you sure you're ready?"

God. He had the cutest freakin' dimples. She just wanted to nibble on them.

"Fuck yeah, I'm takin' a rain check on that look," he murmured. Then after bestowing that charming smirk, he kissed her nose.

"Eww. What am I? A puppy?" she said, letting him face her forward.

Ike kept his arm draped across her shoulders. "Still got questions?"

Renner and Abe, who had been so concerned for their buddy's state of mind, each wore a silly grin.

Renner said, "Nope. Now it makes sense."

Abe just said, "Yep, total sense," and pushed to his feet.

Riss had never felt more flustered. But not in an embarrassing way.

"This don't mean you're off the hook, Palmer," Abe

said. "Call me next week when you're more . . . settled into these changes and we'll catch a beer."

"I'll try."

Renner stopped in front of him. "We need to schedule a conference call with Hugh to hash this stuff out."

"I've made my decision. I'm only interested in fair compensation. You've always been up-front with me. Do I need to worry that's changed?"

"No." He clapped Ike on the shoulder. "I'll be in touch."

When Riss glanced over at Tobin and Jade, Jade mouthed, "Call me," and blew her a kiss as they took off.

Once they were alone, Riss said, "Why aren't you surprised by this ambush?"

"Because I ambushed the ambushers. Come on. Let's sit."

Ike chose a table for two in the farthest corner. He situated Riss and sat across from her. "Is your arm all right resting there?"

"Yes. Now would you please—"

"You drinkin' the usual, Ike?"

He glanced up at Susan. "I'm on a budget these days, so PBR."

"I'll have the same," Riss said, hoping to hurry her along.

"You seem impatient," Ike said.

"Ya think? I don't hear from you for over a week. I'm waiting for girl time with Jade to pump her for information about you, only to be ambushed by your buddies, who inform me you tossed in the reins for JSC, you ditched your few broker clients and you're working construction."

Ike smiled at Susan but didn't respond until she left. "You're surprised?"

"Yes!"

"The 'life-changing' conversation ringing a bell?" He sipped his beer, but those intense blue eyes never left hers. "Or didn't you believe I'd follow through with it?"

"I hoped you'd take action. A text letting me know what was goin' on with you would've been nice because I was worried."

"Sorry to make you worry but I wanted to have this conversation in person." He threaded his fingers through hers. "How was your week?"

"Not as exciting as yours."

He smiled and swept his thumb across her knuckles.

Gooseflesh broke out and she suppressed a shiver. "So construction, huh?"

"Holt complains about guys quitting all the time so I figured he'd have immediate work. It's part-time for now, but I got a couple other things on tap. I'm mostly doin' gofer and grunt work. That's about all I'm qualified to do at this point. But . . . I like it. Feels like I've accomplished something at the end of the day."

Wasn't a hardship to study Ike's handsome face looking so happy and content. "You look good."

"It's a start." Ike lifted her hand to his mouth and kissed the inside of her wrist. "You are a menace, Larissa Thorpe. I think about you all the damn time. I like that you crack me up, piss me off, force me to look deeper, not only at myself, but everything around me." His gaze roved over her face with reverent leisure, as if he was seeing her for the first time. "You make me want things."

"What kind of things?"

"Everything-about-you things. I wanna hear your laughter, earn your trust, hold onto your secrets, your brain and rock your body." He briefly closed his eyes. "Fuck, do I wanna feel that body of yours all over mine."

She could barely breathe when Ike leaned even closer.

"I want every sweet, dirty, funny, sassy, mean, sexy part of you. I will prove to you that I'm the man you need. So as of right now, you and me are dating."

"Dating?"

"Yep."

"You're telling me we're dating. You're not asking."

"Nope, because you don't date. I'm giving you something no other guy has."

"And what's that, cowboy?"

He grinned. "No choice."

"Omigod."

"Exciting, isn't it? Us officially being a couple."

Tell him to shove his dating edict. What right does he have to take away your choice?

"I see them gears grinding, Riss. You want to tell me off. But it bugs you there's a bigger part of you that wants this because you *know* we'd be dynamite together. And not just in bed." Ike dragged his mouth back and forth across her wrist. "Although I cannot wait to test that theory."

The damp heat of his soft lips teasing her skin sent electric shocks through her entire body.

"God, it's a fuckin' rush when you look at me like that."

"Like what?"

"Like a dare. Gets me hard instantly."

"Ike."

"Larissa. I know what you're gonna say next. And it's okay that dating scares you. It's healthy to admit that *I* scare you."

"Whoa. Back up. I'm not scared of dating. And I sure as hell am not scared of you."

Ike blinked those baby blues at her.

"I'm serious, Palmer."

He said nothing. Just studied her, exhibiting patience as he waited for her to confess.

"It won't work. This whole reverse-psychology scheme."

"What scheme, sweetheart? Talk to me."

Argh. Gentle, understanding Ike was as goddamned sexy as she feared.

Riss froze.

Feared? Her subconscious piped in with the word *feared*? Because maybe . . . possibly . . . there was some truth about the being-scared thingy.

Fuck. That.

"The scheme where you taunt me about bein' scared, and you expect me to deny it—which I absolutely am— and then you challenge me to prove it by dating you."

His expression didn't change one iota. But he did sigh.

"Busted you, didn't I?"

"No. But he warned me not to get my hopes up."

"Who warned you?"

"He said you live to deliver the smackdown."

"Who told you that?" she demanded. It wasn't like

she had other boyfriends that Ike could swap "the trouble with Riss" stories with.

"Your brother."

"My brother? Which one?"

"Lonnie."

"You were . . ." She took a breath. "You've been talkin' to my brother Lonnie. About me."

Ike bestowed a dazzling smile. "Well, now, darlin', that is a little egotistical. Lonnie and I have a lot in common. But yeah, I did talk to Lonnie about you."

This wasn't happening. Ike and Lonnie almost came to blows! Two times. And she hadn't heard from Lonnie that "Ike was an okay guy" or anything. In fact, she hadn't heard from her brother at all.

Because apparently he'd been spending time with Ike.

Riss let go of Ike's hand and sucked down half of her beer.

"Better?"

No. "What did you say to Lonnie about me?"

"I asked him if I could date you."

She dropped the bottle.

Which Mr. Lightning Reflexes caught before it hit the table.

"Careful, darlin'. Don't wanna get that cast wet. Beer on it the next few weeks would stink to high heaven."

Spots danced in front of her eyes. Her hearing went wonky.

"Riss," Ike said sharply. "You look like you're gonna pass out."

She managed one nod.

Then Ike was next to her, right in her face, his hand

curled around the front of her throat. "Breathe, Riss. Lemme hear you."

Her reflexes kicked in and she inhaled deeply.

"Good. Let it out."

Keeping her eyes on his, she exhaled.

"One more in."

And she returned to a normal, functioning, breathing human being. Jesus. What kind of person is so idiotic they forget to breathe?

A person who is scared.

She, Larissa Thorpe, was scared.

Of dating.

Specifically of dating Ike Palmer.

Shit. Ike had nailed it.

What was wrong with her?

"Oh no. No, no, no, no, no, no, no, no, no, no. Don't panic. Riss, please. Focus on me."

Her focus immediately fell to his mouth, which was moving. But why wasn't it moving on hers? She could totally focus on that.

So she leaned forward and kissed him.

Ike didn't freeze up, or take over. He just made a deep hum and kissed her back.

Riss swept her mouth back and forth over his. Tasting beer on his lips. Tasting him as her tongue ventured in to lick the underside of his upper lip. She'd never kissed a guy with lips this full and lush. She could feel his pulse pounding as she pressed her lips harder against his.

While she explored his mouth and reveled in his restraint, Ike kept his fingers around her neck.

It was sexy, possessive and yet, oddly soothing.

She ended the kiss with soft smooches and nuzzled his cheek.

"You okay?" he said gruffly.

"Never better." She smiled against the corner of his mouth. "I like kissin' you."

"And I haven't even brought out my tongue A game yet." He nipped her bottom lip. "Come on, sweet cheeks. Say you're on board with this."

She laughed. "Fine. You win. Yes. I'll date you."

Chapter Nineteen

❧

*I*ke had been prepared to pull out every romantic feat he'd seen in movies and on TV to convince Riss they needed to take their friendship to the next level. But all his scheming wasn't necessary.

Suck it, Lonnie; your sister likes me for real.

He kissed her again, just because he could.

"Can I tell you something?" Riss said softly.

"Anything."

She curled her hand around the side of his face and slid her fingers into his hair. "Even with zero dating experience, I can pretty much guarantee that I'm the kind of woman who fucks on the first date."

As his brain—and his cock—tried to process that, Riss softly blew in his ear, destroying any coherent response.

Fuck yeah. More of that. Tons more of that.

"I love that noise you just made," she murmured as

she licked the shell of his ear. "A sexy little growl that your cock would make if it could talk." She sank her teeth into his earlobe and tugged. "Yet I imagine your dick has its own way to communicate."

"It does." Ike turned his head and captured her sassy mouth in a teasing kiss, rather than the blistering soul kiss they both craved. He held her chin in his hand, forcing her to focus on his eyes. "But not here. What's between us is *only* for us."

That surprised her.

He didn't explain. He didn't care if she believed his resolve to keep even their kisses private was because of his shyness. He had to set this apart from what she was used to if he had a prayer of keeping her interest.

That was when Ike noticed the odd look on her face. "What?"

"You're not banning PDA because you're embarrassed to be seen with me?"

"Nope." He rested his forehead on hers. "I'm a selfish bastard. All your sexy noises, molten looks and fuck-me vibes . . . are now mine."

She shivered. "If this is what it's like to date you, I'll need to buy new underwear since those kinds of sexy promises are liable to set my panties on fire."

"Then you'll have extra pairs I can tear off when I'm desperate to fuck you."

"Are you desperate to fuck me now?"

He grinned. "Yeah, baby, I am. But—"

Riss placed her fingers over his mouth. "Please don't insist on some kind of dating rules."

"You'd hate that, wouldn't you?"

She blinked at him without answering.

"There are no rules for what happens between us except we both have to be into it."

"So no minimum of 'five dates before we can fuck' or anything ridiculous like that?"

"Not on your life, sweet cheeks."

She granted that flirty smile that made his heart race. "Good."

"How's tomorrow night for our first date?"

"Tomorrow night I'll be in Sydney, Nebraska. I'm supervising Tito's newest driver. But I'm not busy tonight."

"Of course you're not, because I have to attend my niece Mikayla's President's Day program in"—Ike glanced at his watch and swore—"an hour. So I've gotta get goin'."

"Walk me out, then, so you can kiss me good-bye in private."

After donning their outerwear, Ike tossed some bills on the table and followed Riss outside.

She stood next to a Jeep he hadn't seen before.

"Where's your Toyota?"

"Even though it was an automatic, I couldn't drive it. Lloyd found this one for me in Denver." She tapped the window on the passenger's side. "Check it out."

Ike bent down and peered through the glass. "European style with the driver's side on the right. Awesome." Her brothers really did look out for her.

"I know. Since it'd been used for rural mail service it has a ton of miles on it, but we got it cheap. I won't keep it longer than I have to, but now I can drive myself again on my own. Which makes my brothers and Tito happy since they're off the hook for ferrying me around."

He stepped in front of Riss, herding her against the

door. "You shoulda called me. I'da been happy to take you anywhere."

Riss fiddled with the collar of his coat. "You were a little busy last week hand-grenading life as you knew it."

"True. Tonight will be the first time I've seen my sisters since I informed them of how my life changes will affect them."

"Oh no, Palmer. What did you do?"

"Made some executive financial decisions regarding Lea's future education. I'd already paid for this semester of school, which includes her rent. But that's it; the cash cow has dried up. Lea had better figure out how to make this third career change work, or find another way to fund it because I'm out."

She stood on her tiptoes and put her lips next to his ear. "Hearing you laying down the law gets me hot." She snickered. "Unless you're trying to lay down the law with me, 'cause them's fighting words."

"I like fightin' with you." He turned his head and fit his mouth over hers, indulging in the hot and hungry kiss he'd been dying for.

The world around them went still, allowing his focus to boil down to Riss kissing him back with equal ferocity. And this was some heady shit.

She ripped her mouth free from his. "Go. You're already getting these panties wet."

He loved how she held nothing back. "Here's an idea . . . Maybe you should come with me."

"Not. A. Chance. Face the family fire on your own." She pecked him on the lips one last time. "But I will want all the juicy details when I see you for our date on Saturday afternoon."

"You're setting up our first date?"

"Unless you have a conflict?"

"No conflict." He pressed his lips to her temple. "No conflict Sunday either, so maybe you oughta pack an overnight bag." He blew in her ear. "And extra panties."

⚭

Ike barely squeaked into the auditorium before the lights went down. Jen had saved him a seat in the second row next to Mikayla's grandma Alice. No sign of Alice's son Mikey—aka Jen's baby-daddy number one. Lea sat on the other side of Kay, in the farthest seat away from him. His four-year-old nephew, Elijah, squirmed off his chair and crawled around Alice's legs to climb into Ike's lap.

Elijah was a quiet little boy, still at the sweet and snuggly stage, so Ike tucked him against his chest, knowing that these moments would be gone pretty soon.

Ike had been to enough of these programs over the years that he zoned out when Mikayla's class wasn't on stage. It'd been a crazy week. He'd dropped into bed every night exhausted, but exhilarated. Opening up to Riss and taking a hard look at who he'd become forced him to admit to himself that he wasn't the man he wanted to be. Even if none of his family and friends understood his need for change, he felt proud of himself for the first time in a long time.

Maybe he'd known on some level that taking Riss into his home would force him to face the truths he'd been avoiding. Now he felt like he'd been given a second chance.

Clapping started, pulling him out of his own head. He shifted his leg before it fell asleep and noticed Elijah had conked out. Ike glanced up and saw Alice smiling at him.

She whispered, "You're so good with him and Mikayla. You should have a couple kids of your own. You'd be a great father."

He smiled and said nothing, although he saw Lea talking to Kay and rolling her eyes.

The program lasted about an hour and they waited in their seats for Mikayla to finish backstage. As soon as Elijah woke up he returned to Jen's lap.

Lea ignored him.

Tough love, Ike.

"Uncle Spike! You came!" Mikayla yelled as she raced toward him, blond pigtails bouncing, her colored paper beard hanging by a string from one ear.

He caught her and managed to block a groin shot. "You were excellent on stage as always, Micky-D."

"I wish you'd stop calling her that," Kay complained. "The kid is gonna get a complex when other kids start using it."

"When she tells me to stop, I will."

"I like it," Mikayla declared. "It's our thing, huh, Uncle Spike?"

"Yes, ma'am."

"Are we gonna get ice cream now?" she asked.

"You deserve it," Alice said. "But Grandma's got an early day tomorrow. I'll see you this weekend."

Mikayla hugged her good-bye and addressed her mom. "Are we goin' to DQ?"

"Yes." Jen looked at him over Elijah's head as she zipped his coat. "See you there."

So much for his plan to head straight home.

Since he hadn't eaten supper, Ike ordered a burger and two orders of fries, knowing Mikayla and Elijah would demolish one order.

At the table for six, Ike ended up sitting between Mikayla and Elijah, with his sisters lined up across from him like judge, jury and executioner.

"So what's gotten into you?" Kay asked.

"Maybe the better question is who *he's* gotten into," Lea retorted.

Ike smiled, refusing to take the bait. He dug in his pocket and pulled out a handful of change, which he passed to Mikayla. "Why don't you and Elijah play that racing game for a bit."

"Come on, E. The grown-ups wanna gossip," Mikayla said with the world-weary wisdom of her eight years.

As soon as the kids were out of earshot, Jen jumped him. "You're working construction? What happened to your partnership in the stock contracting business?"

"Renner and Hugh will buy me out or we'll decide to end operations and sell off the few assets. In the meantime I needed a job so Holt hired me."

"Why can't you get your old job back with Stocksellers?"

He looked at Lea, her dark brown hair hiding the stubborn set to her jaw. "Because I was fired, although I believe they used the term 'downsizing.'"

"Fired?" Kay repeated. "You never told us that."

"I never told anyone that because I was embarrassed. Thirty-seven and unemployable. Not my proudest moment. The contracting business is a bust too. So I'm throwing all my failures out at once." He slurped his milk shake. "Fun, huh?"

"Why did you say 'unemployable'?" Lea asked. "Can't you, like, . . . get another job as a livestock broker with a different company?"

Ike shook his head. "There was a three-year non-compete clause that I hadn't paid attention to. But I can go outside the five-hundred-mile radius they set. And I could broker deals for half a dozen of my longest-standing clients for a period of two years . . . with fifty percent of the profit going back to Stocksellers. Oh, and I had to sign an NDA about that."

"What made you decide to tell us this now, almost two years later?"

Before Ike answered Kay, Jen said, "It's her, isn't it? She had something to do with this."

Her. She. Jen's way of trying to rile him up by not giving Riss's name importance. "Riss had a lot to do with this."

Three pairs of eyes widened.

"I thought you hated her."

"Nope."

"Are you living together?"

"Nope."

"So you're with her. As in . . . ?" Kay prompted.

Lea said, "They're talking as well as fucking, which isn't a step in the right direction, from what I can tell."

Ike set down his cup. "Riss and I are dating. Deal with it."

Another set of exchanged glances between them.

Lea totally ignored Jen's warning and opened her

mouth. "That's it? Deal with it? You're not gonna lecture me about being respectful toward her?"

"I'm done policing your behavior, Lea. You've been an adult for a decade. If my expectations about respect haven't sunk in by now, then I doubt they ever will. If you're hell-bent on disrespecting her when you meet her, *Riss* will take you to task on it, not me."

"What bothers me is that you told your new girlfriend about all this life-changing stuff and you couldn't be bothered to tell us. We're family, Ike. We should've been told first."

"Maybe you should've asked."

None of them had a smart retort for that.

Ike stood. "I've got an early day tomorrow. I'll say good-bye to the kids on my way out."

Dismissal shocked them into silence.

Too bad he hadn't tried that years ago.

Chapter Twenty

❧

On Saturday afternoon, Ike tried not to call Riss a dozen times to see exactly when she'd be over.

He might've peered out the front window a time or ten.

He might've checked his appearance in the hallway mirror once or twice.

He might've popped half a package of breath mints.

He might be just a little anxious.

Riss wasn't the only one with no history of dating.

He hadn't done the girlfriend thing since high school . . . before his mother died. And dating hadn't been an option when he'd had guardianship of his sisters.

By the time he had his own place, he'd already established his preference for one- or two-night hookups. The few times he'd had overnight female guests in his house, he'd seen the calculating looks as they mentally redecorated and replaced his office with a nursery.

No, thanks.

He wasn't sure if he even wanted kids. And he sure as hell hadn't discussed the possibilities with any of the one-offs who'd warmed his bed.

Was that something he and Riss would have to address down the road?

When the doorbell rang, his heart raced, and he nearly tripped over his own damn feet to get to her.

Riss smiled tightly. He recognized the anxiety dogging him showed in her face and her posture, given her white-knuckled grip on the duffel bag.

"Hey, hot stuff. I'm glad you're finally here. Come in."

"If we're leaving right away to go on the date, I'll keep my coat and stuff on. It's a pain to take off."

Crap. Had it been his responsibility to come up with a specific plan for this date?

She gave him a once-over. "We won't be stupidly awkward with each other now that we're dating, will we?"

"No. But I ain't gonna strip you to the skin the second you're in the house, so you might as well come in while I'm getting ready."

She actually looked annoyed. After she stomped the snow from her boots, she came inside and dropped her duffel bag on the bench.

And for some stupid reason, Ike began to babble. "I know we said no dating rules, but it's probably best if we take this slow. No pressure, go with the flow . . ."

"Live-in-the-moment kind of a thing?" she supplied.

"Yep."

Riss snorted. "Dude. You are the least spontaneous guy I know. You are so set in your ways it's ridiculous."

Ike snagged his shearling coat from the coatrack. "I

was the least spontaneous guy. I threw a hand grenade into my life, remember? I oughta get credit for that."

"Fine, I'll grant you that. But that doesn't mean you'll suddenly become Mr. Go-with-the-Flow."

"You're wrong."

"Prove it."

Of course she challenged him first thing. "How?"

"No matter what happens today, you follow my lead."

Do not panic. "I'll follow your lead . . . within reason."

"See?" She whapped him on the arm. "You're already qualifying it. If I wanted to date a grumpy old man, I would've let Jim Barnes take me out. He's asked me, like, fifty times."

Jim Barnes. One of the seventy-something regulars at Buckeye Joe's. As if. "I'm nowhere near Jim Barnes's age."

"Word on the street is he doesn't even need Viagra."

"Neither do I."

Riss opened her mouth, likely to retort "Prove it" again, but he placed his fingers over her lips. "Woman, when will you learn this shit doesn't work with me? This whole taunting tactic to goad me into tearing your god-damned clothes off to prove how badly I want to fuck you." He inched closer. "That is a given. But we're doin' the date thing first. So suck it up and grow some damn patience for a few hours."

She smiled. "There he is. The bossy, pissy Ike I know and like. You started to worry me that you'd become sickeningly nice now that we're dating."

"God forbid."

As Ike settled his black Resistol hat on his head, Riss said, "Do you mind driving?"

"Not at all. Where are we goin'?"

"Casper."

"What's in Casper?"

She smirked. "The scene of the crime—aka our first date."

"You preplanned something?"

"Of course I did. Something really thoughtful."

When her smile widened he fought another surge of panic. But he managed to smile back. "By all means, darlin', let's get this date started."

The only difference on this drive to Casper was that Riss held his hand the entire time. As soon as they pulled into town, she said, "We have some time to kill so let's go to Runnings."

"Sure." He shot her a wry look. "I'm worried a trip to Runnings is setting a precedent that I only take you to the best places. Where could I take you on the second date that could possibly compare?"

"You could take me there again. I love that store. Where else can you buy clothes, ropes, corn chips, salt licks, toys and baby chickens? It's one-stop shopping at its finest."

"You're familiar with their rope section?"

"Wouldn't you like to know."

Yes, sweet cheeks, I surely would. I might be mechanically challenged, but when it comes to ropes . . . I've got all sorts of tricks.

"What's that smirk for, Palmer?"

"Wouldn't you like to know."

"*Tssssss.* I feel that burn."

His usual manner of shopping—get what he needed

and get out—wasn't how Riss did things. She wanted to shop. Take her time, look around.

And since he worried she'd lift something she wasn't supposed to—like the portable generator he caught her eyeing—that meant he was shopping too.

Which he hated.

Or he thought he hated it until he'd experienced shopping with her. The crazy woman made the mundane fun.

So far they had two bags of circus peanuts, a roll of camo duct tape and a rain gauge in the cart—none of the items made sense, nor had Ike chosen any of them.

They'd managed to pass through the "As Seen on TV!" aisle without adding anything new to the cart and now they were in the women's clothing section.

"What about these?" she asked.

Ike homed in on the black panties she'd draped over her cast. "You honestly need a pair of underwear with 'Sinday' spelled out on the crotch?"

"I don't *need* them. I said I like them." She tossed them back in the bin and pulled out another pair. "Do you like these better?"

He squinted, because he couldn't possibly be reading that right. "'My other ride is a cowboy.'" Their eyes met. "Oh hell no. I never wanna see them words across your ass."

"Even if you're the cowboy in question that is my ride?" she cooed.

Ike slipped his arm around her waist and brought her body to his. When he felt the weight of those luscious tits pressing into his chest, rational thought vanished.

Riss was soft and warm and they fit together perfectly. Why were they in the damn ranch supply store when they should be rolling around in his big bed?

"Stop growling at me, Ike."

"Then stop taunting me."

"It's your fault."

"What did I do now?"

"Dressed like that for our date. All hot, cowboyed up in a long coat, boots and jeans and this tight shirt that shows off your muscled arms. And then, you just had to go and put that black cowboy hat on, didn't you?" She bit her lip. "I needed a distraction because banging you next to the water softener pellets wasn't an option."

A slow smile spread across his face. "So teasin' me with images of you wearin' nothin' but them panties is a distraction . . . for *you*?"

"Yes. It levels the playing field. I feel like now you're lookin' at me the same way I've been lookin' at you. And for that, I deserve a reward."

"What kind of reward?"

Riss's gaze moved to his mouth. "A kiss."

"Right here, right now, in the ranch supply store?"

"Yes, because you didn't even kiss me hello at your house. I'm pretty sure that violates a dating rule. So to make it up to me, you have to violate your personal 'no PDA' rule and mack on me immediately."

Her logic made no sense. "Hold that thought."

"Am I such a bad kisser that you don't wanna kiss me again?"

"God no." He slid his hand up to curl his fingers around the nape of her neck. "Didn't we agree to take this slow?"

She broke eye contact. "I don't recall."

Ike chuckled and whispered, "Liar."

Her entire body trembled against his.

Since whispering in her ear elicited that reaction, he did it again. "Riss."

"Mmm?"

"Tell me you believe I wanna kiss you more than anything."

"Uh . . . I guess you do."

He brushed his lips across her ear. "You guess? You don't know?"

She tried to squirm away. "If you truly wanted to kiss me more than anything, you would've done it by now."

Ike's hand, still on the back of her neck, pulled her back. "I've jacked off thinking of your mouth on mine, and kissing you all over when it'll lead to more than just kissing. But, sweet cheeks, standing in the women's clothing department at Runnings, with underwear dangling from your cast and cameras recording us, is not the place that kiss is gonna happen."

"Okay. But as far as I'm concerned? Going slow is for the birds and I'm gonna do something rash to turn this G-rated date into triple-X-rated territory the first chance I get." She patted his cheek. "Now let's finish shopping."

"We're not done?"

"Not by a long shot, bud."

Riss took off and Ike had a hard time keeping up with her.

"Hey. Slow down. The floors are slippery."

She whirled around and almost smacked him with her cast. "My god. I'm not an eight-year-old girl running by the pool! I'm perfectly capable of walking around on my own, jackass."

Jackass.

Then Miss Perfectly Capable slipped.

Ike lunged for her, catching her around the waist.

Her fingers dug into his biceps as she righted her balance.

Ike chose the high road and didn't say *Guess bein' a jackass ain't so bad when I save your ass from hitting the concrete.* Instead he murmured, "You okay?"

"Yes. Thank you."

He waited to see if she'd tag it with an insult, but Riss merely squeezed his arm and sighed.

"What?"

"You're such a big, strong man. These muscles of yours make me absolutely weak in the knees."

That threw him. And her sexy little smirk . . . Nope. He was not getting a hard-on in the ranch supply store. No way. No how.

Riss led him to the back of the store.

He smelled them before he heard their high-pitched cheeping coming from the warming pens. She bent down and stuck her hand inside. Immediately a small brown-and-russet-flecked chick rushed to her hand.

"Hey, little fella. How would you like to come home with me?"

Ike crouched down beside her. "Looks like you missed the section in the roommate rules about no live poultry allowed in the house."

Riss angled her head. The look in her eyes was both coy and mean. "Is that what we are, Palmer? I bring an overnight bag and we're back to bein' roommates?"

"Brought that one on myself, didn't I?"

"That's not an answer."

"Because you already know the answer. We're dating."

Her gaze fell to his lips. "So I don't need to be back here picking out a new chick for you?"

He laughed hard enough to scare all the chicks away. Christ. He might not survive this woman. "Nope. I'm good with the chick I've already got."

She rested her good hand on his shoulder, using him to push herself upright.

Which put her crotch in his face.

Directly in his face. If he angled his head just so, he could have his mouth on her. Maybe even get a whiff of her scent.

"Hey."

He tilted his head back. The look in her eyes didn't bode well for him. "What?"

"No kissin' those lips either, cowboy."

He couldn't believe she said that.

Yes, you can. Her unapologetic lewdness is one of your favorite things about her.

She laughed. "You brought that one on yourself too."

Ike stood. "You done?"

"Nope. I wanna go look at the fish."

When they were close to the multitude of fish tanks, he said, "I know what you're doin', Riss, and it ain't gonna work."

"I have no idea what you mean."

"Askin' me first if you can have a baby chick, knowing full well I'd say no, so then askin' me to buy you a fish won't seem as bad."

"Are you always so suspicious?"

"I'm wise to female manipulations, courtesy of my three sisters."

Riss tossed her head. "Bet you never bought them a fish either."

"Nope. No pets."

"Lord. Now you sound exactly like Lonnie."

"I'm takin' that as a compliment."

She leaned forward and tapped on a tank. "Look at these white ones with the long flowing fins. Aren't they cool? I think they're called angelfish."

An employee moved in to stand next to Riss. "They're called kissing fish."

"Then god knows we don't want those because they might give me ideas."

Unbelievable.

"Can I help you with something else?" the middle-aged woman asked.

"Do you sell snakes?"

The woman jumped back. "Uh, no. We don't."

Ike wondered what the hell Riss was up to now. Probably a test to see if he could go with the flow.

"That's too bad. We were hopin' to look at a couple of snakes for inspiration."

"Inspiration?" the saleslady repeated.

"Yeah. I just love snakeskin, don't you? How it looks. How it feels."

"Ah, no, not really."

Riss pointed to her broken arm. "I love it so much I even asked the surgeon to create a fake snakeskin cast. She thought I was joking and I woke up with this ugly thing on. I reckoned snakeskin would be appropriate since I busted my gol-durn arm chasin' coral snakes in Texas."

You oughta be a Texan with the tall tales you come up with.

"Are you from Texas?" the saleslady asked.

"Yep. Me'n my hubby, Clem"—Riss jerked her chin toward him—"are from Texas hill country and are up here visiting my brother. How do y'all stand the cold? We about froze our naughty bits off."

The saleslady gave a nervous laugh. "We're used to it."

"Well, the cold sure keeps the snakes away. I was hopin' you might have a rattlesnake I could look at."

"I'm pretty sure it's illegal to sell rattlers."

"I hear ya. Coral snakes, water moccasins, copperheads . . . they're everywhere in Texas so nobody is fool enough to buy one."

"Aren't coral snakes dangerous?"

"They're deadly poisonous. But that red and yellow is so damn pretty together that I'm determined to have my tattoo be an exact replica."

"Tattoo?" the woman repeated.

She leaned closer to the woman and mock-whispered, "I'll admit I'm a vain woman. I cried buckets when I saw pictures of what my skin will look like after bein' in this cast for months. All white and wrinkly and scaly. Not to mention the surgical scars."

The woman paled.

"But then I said to myself, 'Bootsie, you just gotta cowgirl up. This ain't the end of the world. Turn that scaly skin into body art.'" Riss smiled. "Lucky for me Clem is a tattoo artist. The third best in the county. He's promised to ink me up as soon as this blasted cast is off." Riss gestured to Ike. "Clem, sugar pie. You still got them pictures on your phone of the snakes we rounded up?"

"Sorry, *Bootsie*. I left my phone in the truck."

"Shoot. I don't suppose you'd fetch it so we can show this nice lady what I'm talkin' about?" Riss asked sweetly. "Since she seems so interested."

The only thing that interested this poor woman was escaping from the crazy Texas snake charmer. "No, dumpling, I'm not gonna *fetch* it. You've taken up enough of this nice lady's time. We need to hit the road."

A forlorn look crossed Riss's face. "But we haven't checked out the rope selections yet."

And . . . they were done.

Ike discreetly grabbed a fistful of Riss's shirt and tugged her toward him. "Let's get you bundled up, babe."

She giggled. "Ain't he sweet? Makin' sure my lady bits stay warm."

The saleslady said, "I hear my manager calling," and fled.

Ike hissed, "Not another word," in her ear as he grabbed her coat off the cart. Feeling ornery, he zipped her cast inside her coat, turning it into a straitjacket.

"Hey. I can't move."

"I know."

"Why are we leavin'? I had stuff in my cart. We didn't buy anything."

"*Clem* forgot his wallet." He plastered a smile on as he herded her to the front of the store and outside.

Big, puffy snowflakes floated down. They were covered by the time they reached his truck.

"*Clem* and *Bootsie*? The tattoo artist and snake lover from Texas? Really, Riss?"

"Pretty great that I came up with those backstories off the cuff, huh?"

"It's not great. For Christsake, I can't show my face in there ever again."

One auburn eyebrow winged up. "You hang out in the fish department at Runnings on a regular basis?"

"No, but I sure as hell can't now."

She grinned as wide as he'd ever seen. "Now who's bein' dramatic?"

He made a growling noise.

"Besides, admit that was fun. And you did go with the flow, so I'm impressed."

He studied her.

"What? It's exciting bein' someone else."

Ike continued to stare. Not because he was mad; but because he'd become mesmerized by her. The snow clouds muted the sunlight. With the dreary gray skies as a backdrop, Riss's red hair was vibrant as fire. Her green eyes danced with mischief. Her cheeks were pink, giving her skin a beautiful glow. And those lips . . . lush and curved into a devious smile. She took his breath away. He'd never seen anyone brim with so much life.

She made him feel more alive than he had in years.

And he wanted to drink her down, letting some of her joy fill the empty spaces inside him.

He cupped her face in his hand. "No, sweetheart, it's exciting bein' with you." Then he kissed her.

As soon as their lips touched, Ike's hunger for her roared back to life.

This wasn't a slow, getting-to-know-you kiss, even when it should have been. He pushed past his preconceived ideas of slow, sweet, gentle seduction and plowed full steam ahead, ravishing her mouth.

Riss melted into him, trusting him without question.

His hands tightened on her head, keeping her where he wanted her, where he needed her. Breathing her in as their tongues twisted and twined together. Their lips constantly searched for a better fit that'd allow an even deeper kiss. A more complete connection.

When Ike's frozen fingers reminded him that he'd forgotten to put on his gloves, he let their lips part.

"No," she breathed, "I'm not ready to stop."

He smiled and continued teasing her kiss-swollen lips. "Don't get greedy. There'll be more of that. A whole lot more."

"Thank god." Riss licked the inside of his bottom lip. "I'd kill for full lips like these."

"Baby, you can have mine whenever you want."

"Not that I'm complaining, but why did you suddenly decide it was all right to kiss me, Mr. No-PDA?"

He whispered, "Clem can be a spontaneous guy. It's Bootsie's favorite thing about him."

She laughed.

Ike tilted her head back. He loved seeing that hazy lust darkening her eyes, knowing he'd put it there. "The truth is you looked so stunning standing in the snow, them fiery red curls haloing this pretty face, I couldn't remember why I'd been holding back. So I didn't."

Riss stood on tiptoe to reconnect their lips in a

tender kiss. A soft glide of parted lips, followed by a lingering press of her mouth to the corner of his smile as she nuzzled his cheek.

It wasn't a kiss packed with the sexual aggression he'd expected. Instead she'd shown tenderness that he hadn't been capable of.

Easing back, he rained soft kisses down her chin and up her jawline. "This wicked mouth might do me in."

"I promise my tongue on your cock will be a religious experience."

"Of that, there's no doubt." His thumb swept over her nipple—not that she could feel it through her coat—as he cupped the weight of her breast and squeezed.

"Ike."

"Yeah?"

"I'm seriously afraid my clit is gonna freeze to my panties if we don't get in the truck."

Never a dull moment with her.

Once they were in the truck, he said, "You gonna tell me where this date is takin' place?"

"Sure. The Ramada Plaza."

"The Ramada Plaza is a hotel."

"I know."

"You set up our date night at a hotel?"

"Not the whole night. Just a couple of hours." She smiled—smirked, really—and patted his arm. "Is that a problem?"

Fuck no. "Not at all. It's just unexpected."

Riss laughed. "You have no idea. Let's go."

Chapter Twenty-One

～

Riss said, "Park by the conference center entrance."

"We're goin' to a conference? For our first date? Really?"

And Riss didn't say another word, ignoring Ike's harrumphs and complaints. As he preferred, she waited for him to help her out of the passenger's side. She paused at the outer door and looked at him.

"No matter what, follow my lead, okay?"

"More Bootsie and Clem?"

She snorted. "Watch and learn, Mr. *Quad-State News* Cattle Broker of the Year. Pretty prestigious award, dude."

Ike's gaze turned sharp. "Where'd you hear about that?"

"I did my research on you, now that we're dating."

"Worried that you were dating a loser?"

She stood on tiptoe and poked him in the chest. "Not at all. I just figured *you* needed a reminder that the sales game has been your life and obviously you excelled at it."

"Christ, Riss. This isn't one of those pyramid-scheme, get-rich-quick meetings?"

She motioned for him to open the door and she strode across the lobby to the registration table.

There were three people in line ahead of them, which allowed Ike to read the banner on the wall behind the desk:

Need A Career Change?

**Let Us Help You Navigate
A Path To A Better Life!**

**Welcome To
Global Communications Outreach!**

"You've got to be kiddin' me," he muttered behind her.

"Not even a little bit, cowboy. It'll be good for both of us to listen to their spiel."

"What are they selling?"

"Employment opportunity packages. But as a salesman I'm sure you're immune to high-pressure sales tactics."

"So?"

"So, keep an open mind. And a closed wallet."

Ike stepped in front of her as the line moved forward. "No bullshit. Why are we really here?"

"You hand-grenaded your life, and my life could use

a helping hand. It's a two-hour seminar addressing those issues, followed by a buffet."

"A buffet."

"Yep."

"How much did this cost?"

"Nothin'. It was free for the first fifty people who signed up."

He leaned in. "You signed us up for this for the free food, didn't you?"

"We're both on a budget, so this kills two birds with one stone—food and entertainment on our first date."

"Why is this the first I've heard that we're on a budget for these dates?"

She rolled her eyes. "Common sense. Neither one of us has extra money, so it's only fair that we both have to stick with a free- or cheap-date rule."

"You said no dating rules, Riss."

"Maybe we need one rule—my rule," she retorted sweetly. "Think of it as a chance for you to be creative when it comes to choosing what we do on *your* date night."

Ike slid his hand up the front of her body. "Oh, I know exactly how my date night is gonna play out."

"Next, please," the woman chirped from the registration table.

"Help me off with my coat," Riss said. "And watch and learn, baby cakes."

"Woman, you are a menace."

Riss smiled brightly at the stylishly coiffed fifty-something woman, who said, "Name, please?"

"I'm Jimmi Sue Jones. Jimmi with an 'i.'" She gestured to Ike. "That's my husband, Ike Palmer. He oughta be on the list too."

She skimmed the list and highlighted both of their names. "Great. There you are. Next I'll need your IDs, please."

Riss's face fell. "Oh no. Where's my purse?" Then as she searched her coat, she accidentally dropped it on the floor. When she went to retrieve it, she banged her cast on the edge of the table—hard enough to make a loud noise, but not hard enough to hurt.

But the woman didn't know that.

"This blasted cast! It's such a pain in my rear. I was so busy trying to hurry so we wouldn't be late that I musta left my purse on the floor of the mudroom." She aimed a teary-eyed gaze at Ike. "I'm sorry, baby, that we drove all this way from Rawlins for nothin'. I was really hoping to find other job options now that I'm laid up with this stupid cast."

Ike seemed at a loss for words.

"Oh, honey, I wouldn't keep you from getting the help you need," the woman said. "As long as one of you has a valid ID, I can admit you both, bein's that you're married." She frowned. "You said your last name was Jones?"

Riss gave her a sheepish look. "Me'n Ike have only been married a month and I'm not used to my new name yet, since I haven't had occasion to write it since the accident."

"What happened, if you don't mind me asking?"

"Well, it's sort of embarrassing . . . but we were on our honeymoon in Playa del Carmen—that's in Mexico—and we went on a Mayan pyramid tour. Not the one they call 'Chicken Pizza' but Coba, the one that you can still climb. I insisted on climbing it, made it to the top and everything. Anyway, on the last five steps down, my foot slipped on loose rock and I tumbled ass over teakettle to the bottom."

The woman gasped. "That is awful!"

"It was. But Ike picked me up and carried me four miles back to the tour bus. Four miles! Lord, we were a mess. I got a gash on my head that bled all over us and my arm was obviously broken. And Ike is yelling at people to get out of the way . . ." She sent him a grateful smile. "It was romantic. Made me realize how lucky I was to marry this man—"

"We'd be plumb grateful if you'd let us attend this meeting." Ike whipped out his wallet and pulled out his ID. "She's been goin' on and on about this seminar changing her life."

"We're usually sticklers on requiring IDs, but it's up to my discretion, so I'll cut you two a break. Sounds like you need one."

"As long as it's not another broken arm I'll take it," Riss added.

The woman laughed and jotted down Ike's information. Then she handed them lanyards, buffet tickets and two prospectuses.

Riss said, "Bless you." Before she could add anything else, Ike took a hold of her upper arm and led her away.

He chose seats in the very last row. After draping his arm across the back of her chair, he put his mouth on her ear. "How convenient for you that I'll have to deal with telemarketers since you used my real name. Why didn't you show them your ID and make up a name for me?"

"Because you would've blown it for both of us."

"Bullshit."

"No offense, but Ike . . . you have no imagination."

"Yes, I do. I went along with the Clem and Bootsie bit, didn't I?"

"That's the difference. You went along with it. You didn't come up with a believable story on your own."

Ike gently blew in her ear. "I came up with a believable story for Louie."

Riss turned her head until they were mouth to mouth. "But now we're in a relationship so I'm disqualifying that one."

"For fuck's sake. You always gonna change the rules?"

She smirked. "Probably. Besides, that woman wouldn't have believed you left your ID since men always have their wallets. I've legitimately forgotten my purse half a dozen times since I got this stupid cast."

"But your purse is in the truck."

"She doesn't know that. Anyway, here we are. About to learn all the secrets of getting ahead in life."

"I'm not takin' notes for you," he warned.

Riss sent him a sideways look. "Dude. We're here for the buffet, not the seminar, so I don't give a damn if you fall asleep until they open the chow line."

"Good thing I'm wearing my hat." Ike kicked his legs out in front of him, pulled his hat down to hide his face and crossed his arms.

Well, that sucked. Now she wouldn't get to sneak looks at that handsome face. Before the truce she took pleasure in dismissing Ike because he was almost pretty, with his longish blond hair and full lips. But now, she

290 ~ LORELEI JAMES

liked looking at him as she tried to find ways to make him smile. He had more smiles than a man had a right to, all of them different. She challenged herself to categorize each one.

"Stop staring at me," he said softly.

"Ego much?"

"You like the way I look, sweet cheeks. You admitted that much to me less than an hour ago. I like lookin' at you too so we're even."

"Except you've seen me naked several times."

Ike lifted his head and gave her the smile she called I-can-make-you-beg. "Just say the word and I'll strip. I won't even insist you keep your hands and mouth to yourself."

"I've only got one hand."

His grin widened. "Not a problem. You already told me you could go lefty on yourself. I figured you could go lefty on me too."

She opened her mouth. Closed it.

"Welcome, ladies and gentlemen, to the Global Communications Outreach Program! I'm Eric, one of seven team leaders here tonight to assist in starting you on the road to success."

Her gaze moved to the guy in the front of the room wearing a suit. And the two guys beside him.

Holy crap. They were all hot. Was that how they sold the program? By hiring good-looking dudes and putting them in expensive suits?

"I'll warn you, Jimmi Sue, not to flirt with the seminar leaders. I'm a possessive fucker when it comes to my sweet, sexy wife."

Her stomach flipped and her chest tightened at hearing his gruff tone that wasn't playful at all.

Thankfully the program leader saved Riss from responding. "Before we get to the nuts and bolts of how Global Communications can change your life, let's watch this short video featuring our most recent success stories."

Two hours later, Riss's stomach grumbled loud enough that Ike heard it.

He leaned over and said, "How soon before the brainwashing is over?"

"It looks like they're setting up the buffet in here, which gives the leaders a chance to corner people one on one before and during the meal."

"After we've gorged ourselves on free food, got a plan for politely passing on access to their exclusive training programs for five easy payments of one ninety-nine, ninety-nine?"

"Bathroom breaks? I'll go first and then you follow five minutes later? We'll meet by the pool?"

"Nope. Gets me hot and horny seein' my wife in action creating alternate realities."

Riss ran her finger across the brim of Ike's cowboy hat. "Then it's a good thing I have a brand-new box of condoms in my purse to service those hot and horny needs of yours."

Ike's eyes turned molten. "You seriously have an entire box of condoms in your purse?"

"Yep. I'm fully prepared now that we're dating."

He made a growling noise.

"What?"

"Later."

The group leaders opened the buffet and that was when Riss realized a buffet wasn't the brightest idea with one arm.

But Ike came to her rescue. "Tell me what you want and I'll load up your plate."

"You think I'm an idiot for choosing this, don't you?"

"Not at all. Some of the advice wasn't half-bad."

Riss pointed to the mound of mashed potatoes. "I thought you slept through the whole thing."

"I was resting my eyes, not sleeping, and yes, there is a difference." He slid two pieces of roast beef on her plate and smothered everything with gravy. "What else?"

"Meat and potatoes are good for now."

She devoured the first plate. And a second plate. The third plate she filled with desserts and French fries.

As soon as she threw in the napkin, Eric, the program leader, joined their table.

He shook Ike's hand. "I'm so glad to see a married couple here." He pulled out his notebook and stack of brochures. "Genie out at the front table told me your story. All the leaders were fighting over who got to approach you first."

"Too bad you got the short straw," Ike said, flashing a sharklike smile.

Under the table, Ike's hand landed on her knee and slowly moved up the inside of her thigh.

"What job did you used to have, Mr. Palmer?"

"I was in sales."

That startled Eric. "What did you sell?"

"Things that most people don't need."

"Interesting." Eric smiled at Riss. "And you, Mrs. Palmer?"

"Uh . . . I was a truck driver." Wait. She needed to make something up, not tell him the truth. But how was she supposed to think when Ike's fingers were stroking so so so close to where she needed them stroking?

Eric said, "You? A truck driver? For real?"

"Yep."

Ike slid closer—acting as if he was interested in the brochures—so he could cup his hand over her core. Then he slipped his hand into her pants.

Dammit. Why had she worn yoga pants? She should've worn jeans. Then he'd have to work on getting them undone.

If you don't want him fingering you, why are you widening your thighs and tilting your pelvis closer to his hand?

"She's had her CDL since she turned nineteen, haven't you, sweetheart?"

"Uh-huh." Ike started doing a press and slide maneuver with his thumb that made her skin twitch.

"Once you're recovered, you can return to truck driving, right?"

Ike's middle finger slipped down to her opening, gathering the wetness on the tip of his finger and sliding back up to rub and tap her swollen clit.

"Yes! Right there."

Eric frowned at her.

"I think what my wife is sayin' is she loves it so much that she can't imagine anything better." Ike gently pinched her clit, over and over.

His posture was so relaxed as he leaned across her that if she hadn't felt his fingers working her, she wouldn't have paid attention to where his hand was.

And she needed that hand to stay exactly where it was.

"Well, I don't know that I can help you," Eric said and kept talking.

But Riss had tuned him out. She looked at Ike as he moved his tongue across his bottom lip in the same rhythm he stroked her sex. When he bit down on his lip and squeezed her clit, she had a mini-O.

"Oh god," she said and rested her head on her forearm on the table. Squeezing her thighs together as Ike continued to torment her through the small pulses.

What the hell? She'd come in, like, thirty seconds.

Shit. Her thoughts scrolled back to the conversation they'd had about being quick on the trigger as an indicator of bad sex.

"As you can see, the loss is overwhelming to her, so could you give us a minute?" Ike said to Eric.

"Of course. I'll just leave this information here."

As soon as he left, Ike's mouth was on her ear. "Look at me."

"I can't."

"Baby, people are starting to stare. And we don't want anyone else comin' over here. Lift your head."

"Move your hand."

He chuckled. "Unclench your thighs."

As soon as she did, Ike's hand returned to her knee. She raised her head and met his gaze.

Ike put his fingers over her lips. "They won't try and hard sell us now. So let's go with your plan of sneaking out one at a time. You first. I'll meet you in the front lobby in five minutes."

Riss nodded. She gathered her coat and draped it over her shoulder. She didn't look around the room as she left, she just hightailed it into the bathroom.

Thankfully no one was in there.

In the mirror she noticed her bright eyes and the color on her cheeks. What in the hell had Mr. No-PDA been thinking, fingering her in public? Granted, if Eric hadn't picked up on it as he sat across from her as she had a mini-O, then chances were that no one else had either.

Why had he done it? Boredom? To prove a point? Overwhelmed by lust?

Okay, maybe that one was reaching. And dissecting Ike's motives now was pointless.

After Riss wended her way down the hallways to the front lobby, she noticed Ike at the front desk.

As soon as he saw her, he beckoned her over.

"There's my sweet Jimmi Sue. Good news, darlin'. I earned a free night's stay through their rewards program. So we don't have to drive back home. We can finish our date night in style."

"Really?"

"Absolutely." Ike leaned in the clerk's window. "I hate to ask this, but can you give us your most secluded room? My wife's a little . . . loud, if you know what I mean."

The male clerk shot her a look.

"Ike!"

"What? You know it's true. And we don't have to worry about the kids overhearing us tonight so I want you to really relax."

"I have a suite in the far corner of the second floor. Empty meeting rooms below it this time of night."

"That would be fantastic. Is there an upcharge for a suite?"

The guy smirked at Ike. "Happy to make it complimentary for you."

"Thanks. You da man, Gino."

While Gino reworked the room info, Ike said, "I found your purse in the truck." He draped it over her shoulder.

Her purse . . . with the box of condoms.

This was shaping up to be an awesome date.

Chapter Twenty-Two

~∞~

*R*iss and Ike didn't speak on the elevator ride to the second floor.

But Ike held her hand and rubbed his rough-skinned thumb across the inside of her wrist.

She shivered with anticipation. She could feel it pulsing from him too.

Once they were in the room, Riss tossed her purse and coat on the dinette table and took in the suite. The space consisted of a kitchen and a living area with a desk, sofa, two chairs and a large TV. Through the set of folding doors was the bedroom, with a king-sized bed, two side dressers and a wardrobe. Frosted glass surrounding a deep soaking tub separated it from the bedroom as well as the bathroom with a walk-in shower.

When she turned around, Ike was leaning in the doorway watching her. Her heart skipped a beat or ten. "Nice suite."

"Glad Jimmi Sue approves." He cocked his head. "C'mere, sweet cheeks. Don't be shy."

"I'm not shy. Just . . ."

"What?"

Riss couldn't stop her fear from rushing out. "You got me off in, like, a minute so I was paranoid you'd bring me up here and leave me hanging as punishment, warning me not to judge people—men quick on the trigger—too harshly like I'd done before with . . . you know."

"First of all, I'd never do that. You and I have always bullshitted each other, but I've never purposely hurt your feelings, not when we were frenemies and I sure as fuck won't do it now that we're dating. I don't care about any other man you've been with, or the issues they might've had."

"Then why did you finger me in a room full of people, Mr. No-PDA?"

He hitched his shoulder—a tiny show of his nerves. "I didn't like the way Eric was lookin' at you. As far as he knew, you were my wife. So when I glanced over at you, I saw this gorgeous, vibrant woman, and I wanted to do something crazy and unexpected like you do to me. Even though I touched you in public, it felt sexy and private."

She moved until she stood toe-to-toe with him. When his gaze went to her throat, she wondered if he could see how hard her pulse pounded.

He reached out and cupped his hand beneath her jaw. "You nervous, beautiful?"

"I'm anxious." She nuzzled his hand. "And curious."

"Since we've eaten and been entertained, this now becomes my date. I got this room—for nothin', which fits the cheap-date rule. And that means I call the shots. But I'm a team player, so I'll let you pick where in this suite I fuck you first."

A wave of heat rolled through her body. "Did that look just incinerate my clothes?"

"Nope. But getting naked is an excellent idea. Right after you c'mere and gimme a damn hug."

Riss walked into his arms, tipping her head back and offering her mouth to him.

His gentleness—always a welcome surprise—gave way to hunger. Ike had her pushed up against the wall with his tongue buried in her mouth and his body plastered to hers.

It'd felt like days instead of hours since Ike had given himself over to the electricity that sizzled between them. When he said he was all in . . . he was all in.

"Choose," he urged, as he trailed kisses up and down her throat.

"Is it lame if I say the bed?"

She felt him smile. "No, baby. Not lame at all." He breathed in her ear. "Is it rude that I just wanna get us both naked as fast as possible?"

"It's necessary, not rude."

Ike kept kissing her as he started walking her backward toward the bedroom. He stopped when they reached the edge of the mattress and he switched their positions. He unhooked her sling and tossed it aside.

His look of concentration as he lifted the stretchy top over her head and down her cast made it hard to breathe. Ike was both cautious and impatient as he slipped his fingers beneath the lace edge of her camisole top, exposing her belly, her rib cage and her breasts. He left the cami dangling from her cast in his haste to get his mouth on her nipples.

She groaned and let her head fall back, trusting that he'd keep her upright.

"Do you know how goddamned hard it was to have these beauties right at mouth level the first night you stayed with me, and I couldn't do anything but wonder how your nipple would feel as it hardened against my tongue like this?" He flicked his tongue around and around before blowing on the tip.

Riss trembled and dug her fingers into his shoulder.

"I tortured myself imagining every sexy noise you'd make when I caressed them. When I squeezed them. When I sucked on them. When I bit them. When I pinched them. When I slid my cock here and fucked them."

"Yes. To all of it."

He buried his face between her breasts and placed sucking kisses on the inside swells. "So fucking gorgeous. God. I'm never gonna let a day go past where I don't absolutely worship these."

"Anytime you want. I love the way the rough skin of your fingertips scrapes across my skin."

"I won't shave for a couple of days and I'll see how you like havin' my scruff dragging across them." He demonstrated with his chin. "Leaving red marks and tender nipples so every time the tips brush against your shirt, you think of me."

"Ike."

"Kick off your boots, sweet cheeks. I need the rest of you."

These boots were pull-ons with zippers on the inside.

They were fairly easy to get on and off herself . . . as long as she was sitting down. "I need to sit to do that."

"Then let me." He stood and switched their positions, settling her on the bed while he dropped to his knees in front of her.

Ike made quick work of removing her boots and his own. Watching her face, he popped the pearl buttons on his western shirt and let it flutter to the floor. Then he yanked the T-shirt he wore under it over his head, leaving him bare chested.

Riss might've forgotten how to breathe. His arms and shoulders were well-defined—which she'd suspected because she had squeezed his muscles a time or ten. But the definition in his chest? The thick mat of dark blond hair that spread out nearly to his nipples and then disappeared down his flat belly into the waistband of his jeans? That made her mouth water.

"Riss, darlin'?"

"Jesus, Ike. You haven't spent all of your time watching TV. Where did you get those pecs and abs? And can I lick them right now?"

He laughed. "You can lick and touch to your heart's content. But right now I need to strip you outta them britches."

"It's not like you haven't seen that the rug matches the drapes." She hooked her finger into his belt loop. "I haven't seen this part of you."

"You gonna be disappointed if my dick size is average?"

As Riss looked into his eyes, she realized for maybe the first time—or maybe it was the first time that she'd actually cared—that men also had body image issues.

"I'd only be disappointed if your dick wasn't hard and ready to get an intimate introduction to my pussy."

"Darlin', that ain't ever gonna be a problem where you're concerned."

She traced the thick ridge behind his zipper until he groaned and pulled away.

"Lift up." Ike's hands tugged hard on the sides of her yoga pants until they were to her knees, then he slipped them, and her black lace underwear, past her ankles and over her feet. Still in his jeans, he rested on his haunches and pushed her knees open, his gaze glued to the red triangle of curls between her thighs.

Slowly, he stroked his fingers up the backs of her calves, and then the outsides of her legs to curl around her hips. "I'm gonna take my time eating this sweet cunt, but I ain't patient enough to do it now, so we'll put a pin in that for later." His hands glided up her body as he stood, stopping on his way to make her head spin with a blistering kiss.

As soon as he was standing, he peeled his jeans off.

Of course the man preferred boxer briefs because they were sexy as fuck.

In the next instant they were gone and she was a foot away from his cock.

Riss licked her lips and said, "Gimme." Maybe it wasn't the biggest dick she'd seen, but it had decent girth with a wide head. She liked that he was circumcised and that he kept his bush trimmed. He angled himself close enough that she could swipe her tongue across the slit for a small taste of him.

Then Ike was gone, searching her purse for the box of condoms.

She scooted into the middle of the bed and somehow flung the covers aside so she had the cool sheets on her back, sending goose bumps skittering down her legs and up her belly to tighten her nipples. Somehow through the roar of blood in her ears, she heard the rip of plastic and her heart kicked up another notch.

Warm, velvety soft lips started kissing the inside of her left ankle and traveled up her shin, across her knee, zigzagged across her quad to the innermost portion of her thigh. He pressed his mouth on the upper rise of her mound and straight up her belly, over her sternum and between her breasts. "I love the taste of your skin on my lips. Sweet and musky with the tiniest hint of coconut."

He balanced on his knees and said, "Will it hurt you if I put your cast above your head? With the back of your hand against the mattress?"

"I don't think so. But at this point, I don't really care. You'll just have to make me feel good enough to forget about it."

"That I can do." Ike gently moved her arm so the bend in the cast framed her head.

"I wish I had both hands to touch you," she admitted.

"If I had a dozen hands to touch you, it still wouldn't be enough," he murmured.

His deep voice rumbling in her ear was nearly as potent as his words. "Ike."

He moved between her legs, all the while kissing her, nuzzling her, turning her inside out. His hands, his mouth, his body: everything was focused on her. In that moment when he pushed his cock inside her, his eyes owned her too. Intently watching her face as he rocked into her, filling her slowly, as if savoring the connection of their bodies.

"Baby, I gotta ask if this is workin' for you."

"It'd be workin' a lot better if you'd move like I know you want to." She nibbled the cord straining in his neck and flicked her tongue across the pulse beating beneath his jawline. Her left hand mapped the contours of his muscular arm as he held himself above her. "Show me every dirty thing you've imagined doin' with me."

"There are so many. But let's start here." He eased out and snapped his hips, ramming into her so completely that she felt his balls slap her ass.

Once she caught her breath, she said, "Yes. Like that. Again. God, that feels so good."

"Yeah, sweetheart, you feel perfect. Hot and wet and tight." He reached down and gripped her hip. "Tilt up a little more."

Just that tiny adjustment made her eyes roll back in her head.

He groaned. "There it is."

Then Ike's mouth returned to hers as he switched between long, slow rolls of his hips and hammering thrusts that drove the breath from her lungs.

Her body tingled in a continuous wave from her toes to her tits. She closed her eyes and let him drive her through the storm. His kisses were crazy hot, or slowly sweet. Kisses on her lips, a brush of his hot mouth up and down her neck, his tongue following the line of her collarbone, his teeth sinking into the tops of her breasts as he sucked the delicate flesh, as if he couldn't decide what part of her deserved his feast of attention next.

When that first little buzzing started in her tailbone,

she latched onto his ass cheek, pushing her pelvis up to catch every bit of that delicious friction.

"Ike."

"Yeah, baby?"

"Please keep doin' that. Don't switch back and forth. It's too intense."

"Too intense in the best possible way."

"That too. God. Just think," she panted against his chest, "we could've been doin' this the past two years instead of arguing."

"Next time we argue, we'll turn it into a hate fuck." He groaned. "Jesus, Larissa, I don't know how much longer I can hold out."

"I'm right on the edge."

"What will get you there?"

"Just don't stop."

Ike pushed up higher, watching his body moving in and out of hers. Then his gaze ventured up, stopping at her breasts. Each thrust sent her tits bouncing and a grin creased his face. "Hot as hell, darlin'. Every move of this body, every glorious inch of you." He urged her to tilt her head, giving him access to the underside of her jaw. He licked and bit and nipped at that sensitive skin, all while keeping up a steady, smooth rhythm.

Then he blew in her ear and growled, "Come apart for me. I wanna feel this wet pussy pulsing around my cock."

"Oh god."

"That's it, Larissa. Give it all to me. Don't hold back. Wrap your legs around me."

The next time he put his mouth on that spot below her ear and gently bit down, she exploded. Gasping, writhing, moaning as her sex throbbed deep inside where she felt the contractions to the tips of her nipples. She babbled words of praise for his cock and his stamina and his amazing lips until he slammed his mouth down on hers. Kissing her stupid as she spiraled down from that point in space and time where she existed only as a vessel of pleasure.

Then as the last pulse faded, those lean hips began to jackhammer into her.

When Riss canted her pelvis and squeezed her inner muscles around his cock, he buried his face in the pillow next to her ear, and his guttural grunts vibrated against her scalp, sending another round of gooseflesh pebbling her skin.

Ike slowed his movements and then stilled completely.

She swept her left hand down his sweat-dampened spine and he trembled beneath her touch.

Riss kept caressing him as he regained his composure. She licked the dimple in his chin when they were face-to-face again.

"Let's do that at least a million more times."

She grinned. "You are ridiculously amazing in bed, Ike Palmer."

"And you, Larissa Thorpe, rocked my world to the point it'll never be the same." He pressed soft kisses on the corners of her smile. "Thank you."

"Of course you have to one-up me on compliments on your sexual prowess." She traced his beautifully full lips with the tip of her tongue. "For now, I'll hold back any more praise until you prove your tongue game is all that when your face is buried in my pussy."

"I love this dirty-talkin' mouth." Keeping his eyes open and on hers, he kissed her with a mix of tenderness and wonder.

Ike lowered her cast and slowly rolled them to the side. They'd lost the connection of their bodies, but they remained chest to chest, with their legs entwined.

As Riss watched him kissing her breasts, stroking her belly, whispering endearments against her skin, and saw the pure enjoyment he took in her body, she felt reborn. This didn't have to be a night where she crammed in as many sexual positions as she could and got off two or three times because her chance for partner-produced orgasms would be gone in the morning. She could look forward to Ike figuring out all the different ways to drive her crazy, to make her moan, to make her beg, even when she'd never wanted to open herself up to that kind of vulnerability with any man. But being with Ike, she knew she could be the lover he needed.

"What are you thinkin' about so hard, sweetheart?"

"Honestly?"

A tiny flash of fear showed in his eyes before he banked it. "Yeah."

"I'm glad this isn't a hookup. I'm glad I don't have the mind-set of . . . 'We've scratched the itch, satisfied the question of how hot it'd be between us.' I'm happy to imagine how we'll spend tomorrow together. And next week, and next weekend." She ran her fingers through his hair, loving the soft moan he made and how he angled his head for more. "It's a new feeling. And I'm not scared of it."

Ike's eyes were so serious when they hooked hers.

"That's awful damn close to a declaration of intent, Larissa."

"I know. I gave you a dose of tough love in hopes you'd see that you were wasting your potential. I'm not the type of person who can dish it out and refuse to see my own flaws. I will go out of my way to change things when I'm backed into a corner. And usually that change means I fall back on the tried and true."

"So falling back on it now, because you're scared of how not temporary this feels, would be . . . ?"

"If I kissed you good-bye in the morning and treated you like a one-night stand. I don't want to do that."

"Thank god."

"That's not to say I won't fuck up somewhere down the line, Ike, because that's what I do."

He shook his head. "Not anymore. We can call each other on our bullshit. That's what our previous antagonism was about. Testing each other to see if we had the guts to look deeper."

Riss nuzzled the patch of hair in the center of his chest. Breathing him in, taking a break from the intensity in his eyes, she admitted, "I want to ask you to be patient with me even when I know how ridiculous that sounds."

"Won't sound so ridiculous if I ask you to do the same with me?"

She smiled. "I guess not."

He kissed the top of her head. "Let's put that whirlpool soaking tub to good use."

"Good plan."

While the tub filled, Ike grabbed a plastic dry-cleaning bag out of the closet and covered her cast. "Just be careful because it ain't watertight."

"No splashing around."

"There goes my plan to fuck you wildly in the tub."

Ike stepped in first and lowered until the steaming water stopped at his armpits. He held his hand out. "The only way to keep that cast outta the water is if you sit on my lap."

She snorted. "And we'll talk about the first thing that pops up?"

"Fine. I'll behave."

"Don't make promises you can't keep, cowboy." Stepping in, Riss dropped to her knees, facing away from Ike. He curled his hands around her rib cage and pulled her back to his chest with her ass resting on his thighs. She could prop her cast on the edge of the tub, but that meant Ike's arm had to go underneath, which put his hand directly over her mound.

"I'm likin' this a whole bunch. Your soft, wet skin sliding against mine." His mouth moved to her ear. "You don't know how many times I imagined bustin' in on you when you were lounging in the tub in my guest bathroom."

His deep voice in her ear tightened her skin and he immediately reached across to toy with her hard nipple.

"I wanted to catch you playing with yourself, getting yourself off with that waterproof vibrator."

"What would you have done if you'd caught me?"

"Oh, such dirty, dirty things, Larissa."

God. She loved it when he said her whole name in that wicked tone.

"The first time I would've propped you on the edge of the tub and made you slip that vibrator into this sweet cunt."

His middle finger started stroking her slit from her clit down to her opening.

"I would've held you up with my hands gripping your ass as I sucked on your clit."

When Ike said the word *clit*, he began rubbing the pad of his finger back and forth, while his other hand pulled and pinched her nipple.

"I would've used my lips and teeth and tongue until this little pleasure pearl was plumped and hot. Making you come against my face so many times." He sucked the slope of her shoulder, flicking his tongue as a demonstration. "So many times that you'd be so wet, Larissa, that those sweet juices would be running down your leg. And when that piece of plastic wasn't enough to satisfy you, I'd pull it out, spin you around, bend you over the edge of the tub and plunge my cock into you."

She forced herself not to squirm because pressing her body weight into his dick might hurt him if he wasn't ready.

And she wanted nothing to break this dirty fantasy he was sharing.

"I'd hold on to your tits as I fucked into you. Pinching your nipples to that knife's edge between you wanting me to stop and you begging me to squeeze harder. I'd leave love bites from the nape of your neck to the ball of your shoulder, sucking and biting as you bucked beneath me. I'd overwhelm you by showing you over and over how I can give you every spine-tingling, hair-raising, belly-twisting sensation you need to come hard enough to pass the fuck out in my arms."

"God. Ike. Yes."

He kept leisurely stroking her clit. "Or my other

fantasy. Mmm. This one I jacked off to at least four times." He angled his head to her other shoulder and peppered kisses up her damp skin, stopping behind her ear. "Same scenario. I strip and join you in the tub, making you stand with your cast braced against the back wall. Your skin is still wet from your bath and you smell like coconuts. It drives me crazy. I need to taste you."

Riss was dizzy with the possibilities and suspected she wouldn't survive when Mr. Dirty Talker finally put that wicked mouth on her pussy.

"I'd turn your trusty vibrator on high and make you push it deep into your pussy, making you hold it there while I spread your cheeks wide and eat your ass."

Her clit spasmed beneath his finger.

He chuckled in her ear. "You like your sex a little on the filthy side, don't you?"

"Yes."

"Then I'd drag it out. Licking and sucking that tight muscle. Getting off on making you squirm and fucking loving that you let me do anything I want to you. When I sense that vibrator has pushed you to the edge and you start to come, I'd wiggle my tongue into your ass to feel those powerful contractions."

All she was capable of at that point was a whimper.

"Then when your legs are still shaking, and that vibrator is still lodged in that swollen pussy, I'd slick up my cock and drive it into your ass, balls deep. I wouldn't last long—anticipation and the sheer sexiness of you craving dirty raw sex with me has me worked into a frenzy. The vibrations would tease the front of my dick as your tight channel milked me dry. I'd stay buried deep, so you could feel every jerk of my cock as it unloaded."

She turned her head and sought his mouth, needing something to anchor herself after he'd plunged her headfirst and panting into his fantasy.

Then he broke the seal of their lips to whisper, "Let's get outta the tub. This position isn't good for your arm."

Arm. What arm?

He laughed. "Up you go, darlin'."

Riss barely remembered getting out of the tub. She followed Ike into the living room, plucking up a condom on the way. She put her hand on his chest and shoved him to a sitting position on the couch, dropping the condom on his leg. "I can't do this one-handed, cowboy, so lemme see how you handle yourself."

Ike ripped the package open with his teeth and rolled the condom on.

Bracing her hand on the back of the couch, she straddled his lap and watched as he reached between them to align his cock.

She sank down on him slowly. Savoring every inch of that hardness. Shifting her hips side to side until his dick was in as far as she could force it.

His hands skimmed her waist and circled her rib cage, ultimately homing in on her tits. "Fuck. Me. Jesus, woman. I'm half-afraid I'm dead and bein' with you is just a dream of the afterlife."

"I'm real." She began to ride him. "I'm sorry I can't touch you, but I need my good arm for balance."

What a rush to drive Ike crazy as she savored this intimate connection between them. Stopping with his cock half in, half out, bearing down on just the tip with her inner muscles, waiting for him to beg in that gruff tone for her to *motherfucking move*. Learning his reactions and pulling out her best arching, hip-rolling moves. She worked him, crazy to see those beautiful blue eyes roll back in his head and hear that throaty groan of masculine satisfaction.

But he didn't relinquish all control. He gripped her head and bent her backward, motorboating her breasts until she giggled.

Playful sex with Ike loosened that trust she'd been so reluctant to give, because she knew he hadn't shared this side of himself with many people either, let alone lovers.

The playfulness vanished when he brought her mouth to his for an explosive kiss that left her clinging to him. Panting with their lips pressed together, they breathed the same air and she almost came again from the pure eroticism of the moment.

"Christ, Larissa. I'm about to crawl out of my damn skin."

"Tell me what to do."

"Just hold on." Ike clamped his fingers onto her hips and pumped his pelvis up. The rapid countermovements of their bodies pushed him closer to that surge of release. Every muscle in his body tensed and he groaned against her throat . . . until that moment he roared.

She nestled her cast behind his neck so she could run her fingers through his hair as he caught his breath.

After he'd leveled his breathing, his lips trailed across her jaw. "Sorry you didn't come. Spread your knees so I can remedy that."

Keeping their bodies connected, Ike ran his index and middle fingers up and down her pussy lips, focusing on those tender tissues and avoiding her clit. Until the hitch in her breathing and the clenching of her thighs had him redirecting all his efforts to that needy bundle of nerves.

"That's it," he breathed in her ear. "I wanna feel you. I wanna hear you. I wanna know I can give you exactly what you need."

"You do. More than I ever imagined, Ike."

Then he finished unraveling her with the precision of a master.

Her sex throbbed and pulsed and she let her head fall back, until she felt as if she was falling for real. She jumped and scrambled upright.

"It's okay, I've got you." Then Ike stood, as if it was no big deal that he had a full-sized woman clinging to him like a limpet. He lowered her onto the bed and kissed her forehead. "I'll be right back."

After ditching the condom, he crawled in on the opposite side, snaking his arm around her waist and keeping her head beneath his chin. "I'm whupped. Let's take a breather."

"Okay. But . . ."

"Whatever it is, Larissa, it can keep for a few hours, can't it?"

"Mmm. I guess." She yawned.

Ike didn't answer and she knew he'd already started to drift off.

Chapter Twenty-Three

❦

*G*etting smacked in the face with a cast was a horrible way to wake up.

One second Ike had been sawing logs, the next he was gasping in pain.

"Ike? Omigod, what did I do?"

Riss scrambled to turn on the light on the nightstand, but Ike was already up and headed toward the bathroom. The light briefly blinded him and he had to press his face into the mirror to see anything.

Holy fuck. She'd whacked him good. His eye socket had already puffed up, as had the section of skin between his eyebrows. His left eyebrow had a small cut and blood dripped down the side of his face.

He reached for a towel just as Riss entered the bathroom.

"Oh, you're bleeding, I'm gonna be sick." She swayed

and he pushed her against the wall with his forearm across her chest.

"Breathe. I'm fine. Facial cuts and head wounds bleed a lot, remember?"

"No, I don't remember because my head wound knocked me out! We have to get you to the ER, Ike."

"Riss. Stop. Right now. Breathe."

"I can't believe you're so goddamned bossy that you're telling me to breathe when you're bleeding all over the damn place."

He knew that would redirect her attention.

"How about if you sit your ass on the toilet and let me look after you."

"Fine. Get a washcloth and run cold water over it."

"Still bossing me, jackass. Sit."

By the time she got his face cleaned up, the cut had crusted over. But he'd have one helluva black eye.

"Stay put. I'm gonna run and get some ice and a bandage."

Ike caught her by the wrist. "Don't forget to put some clothes on."

"Do I have to? It's four in the morning. I doubt anyone is around the ice machine."

"Clothes. On," he growled. "In addition to me not wantin' other guys gawking at your naked glory, I've left love bites in some pretty awesome places that I don't expect you'd want anyone else to see."

She blushed and snagged a robe off the back of the door. Then got frustrated when she couldn't put it on without his help. After she was covered, she grabbed the ice bucket and sailed out of the room.

He managed to last fifteen minutes with ice on his

eye before he tossed the ice pack aside. Riss shoved aspirin down his throat to try and stave off a headache. After she put the ice pack in the sink, she went into the living room portion of the suite. Ten minutes later when she hadn't returned to bed, he went looking for her.

She'd maneuvered herself into a prone position on the couch.

"What are you doin' out here, sweet cheeks?"

"Saving your handsome face from further damage."

That was when he noticed she was crying.

"Riss. Baby. Don't. It was an accident."

"Why do shitty weird accidents always seem to happen to me?" She paused. "I mean, *you're* wearin' the brunt of it, but you wouldn't have a black eye and a swollen face if we—"

"Hadn't spent the previous six hours rolling around naked together lost to everything except mind-scrambling sex?" He perched his hip on the edge of the couch. "We were both exhausted and in a happy place when we drifted off. You stayed with me for two weeks. I know as well as you do that you're supposed to sleep in that sling. Now I get why."

"You're not mad?"

"No. But I will be if you don't get your ass off this couch and back in bed next to me."

"Need a damn hug?"

He shook his head. "I wanna be body to body, skin to skin with you the rest of the night."

"You have to help me put the sling back on."

"Sure." He wiped the tears from her face. "But how have you been getting the sling off and on by yourself at home?"

"Louie rigged me up a hook thingy. It works great. I told him he should make a bunch of them and try to sell them on *Shark Tank*."

He pressed a kiss to her bare shoulder after she stood. "For now, you've gotta put up with my help."

Riss turned her head and brushed her lips across his. "I'll take it."

After they were back in bed with her weapon firmly lodged against her belly, and her body tucked into his, he said, "So tell me, what alternate reality have you created to explain my black eye?"

"Nothin' yet." She paused. "Why? Do you have one?"

"Yep. I knocked you out of the way and jumped in front of a speeding car."

She snorted. "Lame. Try again."

"Some dude was eyein' you in the bar. I warned him, he didn't heed it and we settled it the Wyoming way, except his old lady was pissed off and she took a swing at him and I got caught in the crossfire."

"Better. But you've gotta be the hero in your own story."

"Such as?"

"Such as . . . you were in the grocery store and this little kid was crying in the produce section. You thought his distress was because he couldn't find his mom, but after talkin' to him, you discovered he was trying to learn to juggle. So to show him that fruit wasn't a good choice, you juggled apples and one smacked you in the eye."

Ike laughed. "You get a gold star for comin' up with that off the cuff."

She kissed his pectoral. "Stick with me, babe, and I'll learn ya all of my tricks."

"Can't wait."

After a leisurely breakfast the next morning, they returned to the room and Riss showed Ike just how sorry she was about the black eye.

On her knees.

It was such a fucking stellar blow job that he could've pulled a Johnson and shot his load in less than two minutes. There was something inherently sexy about watching a woman who loved sucking cock. And Riss built him up, giving him a running dialogue with every lick, suck and stroke. So by the time she did let him come, he roared with primal satisfaction and had to sit his ass down he'd gone so weak in the knees.

During the hour-long drive back to his place, Riss crashed with her head on the armrest console and Ike stroked her cheek.

He parked in the garage and led a sleepy Riss inside.

"You know something?" she asked with a yawn.

"What?"

"Not once during the time I stayed here with you did you take me upstairs and show me your bedroom."

Ike frowned at her. "That can't be right."

"You were so determined to keep that line of propriety between us—most of the time—that I didn't ask for the grand tour. I figured if you wanted to show me, you would."

"I want to show you now."

"Thank god."

As a single guy, Ike didn't use all the extra rooms in his house, especially those on the second floor. He hadn't even filled them with junk; they merely remained empty, except for the room he'd turned into a personal workout space. He had questioned Holt about putting the master suite on the main floor while they were in the planning stages, but Holt pointed out he'd have a much larger space on the second floor than on the main floor, so he'd kept the only dedicated guest room on the main floor.

Riss stopped inside the doorway to his bedroom. "Whoa. Look at the size of that bed! I just wanna crawl in right now."

"Go ahead. I've imagined how you'd look between my sheets."

"I hope I live up to the hype."

"No hype." He nuzzled the back of her head. "The reality has already been ten times better than the fantasy."

"Wanna crawl in with me and take a nap?"

"Hold that thought. We'll circle back after I show you the master bath. I'll warn ya. No soaking tub. I'm a shower guy." Although, after last night he could see the appeal of a giant tub.

Riss took in the space. "I like this. Clean lines. Lots of storage. My bathroom is so tiny in my trailer I can barely turn around." She stepped away and trailed her fingers along the top of the slate-colored vanity. "So using your guest bathroom was a real treat."

"Stay with me tonight."

Riss sauntered back to him. "I can't. I've gotta be at Tito's at the ass crack of dawn tomorrow." She walked her fingers up his chest. "You sure I can't interest you in a quick catnap? My pussy needs a rest. Or petting."

"Let's go back downstairs for a bit first. It'd be too tempting to never let you outta my bed once I finally get you in it."

Ten minutes later as they were sipping cranberry juice in the kitchen and snickering about their other cheap-date ideas, the doorbell rang.

"Please let me get it," Riss said and skipped off.

Ike laughed. The woman literally skipped.

"Well, hello. I'm not surprised that you all showed up at once, but I'm sure Ike will be thrilled to see you."

Before Ike reached her, Riss yelled, "Ike, your sisters are here. Hide the dildos and the porn."

"Dildos?" Jen repeated. "That's not funny. Good thing my kids weren't around to hear that."

"That's why I said it. We're all adults. It's not like I was serious anyway."

Jen huffed out her annoyance. "Where is my brother?"

Ike turned the corner and stepped into the entryway. "I'm right here."

Three gasps sounded at seeing his swollen face and black eye.

"What a surprise that you all descended on me at once." He beckoned Riss to his side and draped his arm over her shoulders. "Riss, you've met Jen. That's Kay to her left and Lea to her right. This is my girlfriend, Riss."

Riss gave them a little finger wave. "Heya."

Lea stomped up to Ike. "What happened to your face?"

Ike looked at Riss, silently prompting her to create an alternate reality that'd leave his snoopy sisters' mouths hanging open in shock.

"Believe it or not, when I rolled over in bed last night, I accidentally hit him with my cast."

Wait . . . Riss told them the truth?

Jen moved in beside Lea. "I doubt that's true since you 'stretch the truth a tad,' isn't that right?"

Riss sighed. "I suppose I deserved that."

"That's really what happened. We forgot to put her sling on after . . ." *We fucked for the fourth time last night* wasn't something he could admit to his sisters, as proud as he was of that fact. "After we called it a night."

"And this sucker is super uncomfortable to wear naked anyway."

Ike chuckled. "I'm not crazy about how it rubs against me either."

"Why didn't you say something?" Riss demanded.

"Because that would've sent you back to tryin' to sleep on the couch. And we'd already established that you sleeping away from me wasn't happening." He kissed her temple. "It's fine, Riss."

All three of his sisters gaped at him.

Then they huddled together and started whispering.

And they kept whispering and shooting looks at him and Riss without bringing them in on the discussion.

"You know what?" Riss shrugged her shoulders, forcing Ike to drop his arm. "I'm too damn old to wring my hands, hopin' you all like me, as you rudely discuss me as if I wasn't standing right fucking here." Riss looked at Ike. "I'll be in the kitchen." She turned on her heel and disappeared.

Since his sisters had become adults, Ike rarely yelled at them. And he had to dig deep to fight that urge now. "Let's get one thing clear. Your rude behavior is not welcome in my house. That includes dropping by unannounced, insulting my girlfriend and me."

"Ike. We're worried about you. Don't deny you've changed everything since you hooked up with her."

"Last warning about insulting me and her in my home. She is not just a hookup."

"Whatever. But you have to admit you've been acting completely out of character. Especially since all we knew of her before was your mutual hate-hate relationship. We don't hear from you for two days and when we check on you . . . we see you've got a black eye. Which you're both laughing off. The only way we'd be more concerned is if you told us you'd 'run into a door.' If the situation was reversed and one of us had started acting this way? You'd freak out and demand answers."

Kay had a point.

"And we don't like that she's cut you off from your family. None of us have heard from you since the night of Mikayla's program," Jen said.

"When we tried to talk to you that night, you got pissed off and left," Lea added. "We can't talk to you about her at all."

"Talk to me?" Ike repeated. "All I hear are accusations. Once you get to know Riss, you'll like her."

"We're hoping she is a passing phase and we won't have to get to know her," Jen retorted.

"If you would've told us you were interested in dating, there are a dozen women we'd be happy to introduce you to," Kay said.

Ike was so dumbfounded that words failed him.

That was probably the only reason he heard the garage door open.

Shit. Riss was leaving.

Can you blame her?

Ike didn't plow through his sisters and take the shorter distance to Riss's car via the front door. Instead, he spun around and raced through the kitchen and out the garage.

Riss was already in her car.

Dammit. He tried to get in on the left side, but she'd locked the door.

He beat on the window. "Riss. Open up."

She shook her head.

"Come on. Please."

She rolled the window halfway down. "What."

"Look. I know you're upset—"

"Upset?" she yelled. "I'm furious."

"At them?"

"At you! At myself."

Stunned, he said, "What the hell brought this on?"

"Even when we were frenemies or whatever, I wondered why a hot-looking, successful guy like you wasn't married at your age, or at least in a relationship, or hell, even divorced. So now I know why."

Please don't say something that you can't take back or I can't forget.

"Your life is already crowded with women. Now I have to wonder whether there's room in your life for a woman besides your sisters."

"Of course there is. Please don't leave mad like this."

"Mad? Too late. I don't give a damn if they like me. I thought it was enough that *you* liked me."

"Riss—"

"Instead I had to listen to them tell you how horrible

I am for you. And when one of them suggested they could set you up on a date with someone better than me? I didn't hear you leaping to my defense."

"Because Kay's suggestion shocked me, okay? Before I could tell her to get the hell out of my house, I heard the garage door open. I worried that you'd take off before we could straighten this out."

"Well, you don't need to worry. There's nothing to straighten out. You can date whoever the fuck you want. Now move your ass because I'm leaving." She started to roll up the window.

"Goddammit, Riss!"

She threw it in reverse and maneuvered her way around Jen's minivan like a NASCAR driver. Then as soon as she hit the road she was gone.

He yelled, *"Fuck!"* at the top of his lungs.

Before he went back inside to grab the keys to his truck so he could chase her down, his sisters raced out of the house.

They looked scared.

"Ike?"

"Are you happy now?" he demanded. "Is it your goal that I should spend all of my years alone? It wasn't enough that I didn't date and avoided relationships while I was raising you? Now that I finally found a woman that I'm crazy about, you take it upon yourselves to try and destroy this relationship?"

"But we're concerned—"

"For me? Bullshit. You're concerned for yourselves. If I'm with her then I won't be at your beck and call. And FYI? Your claim that 'we were worried, we hadn't heard from you in a few days' is total bullshit too. I don't have a single missed call from any of you. Not one. No texts either. I can count on one hand the amount of times the three of you have just dropped by my house and it's only been when you've wanted something."

"That's not true!" Jen said.

"You don't want it to be true. But it is. And the saddest fucking part of this? The reason you're all selfish and inconsiderate to anyone's feelings and lives besides your own is my damn fault. I'm sorry that it's taken me this long to accept that I fucked up."

Kay was openly crying. "Ike. Please. Don't say that."

"It's time I did. I've had the worst two years of my life besides the year that Mom died, and not one of you has even noticed. Again, I blame myself, but part of me feared that if I told you the truth about my job and the changes in my life, none of you would care. So rather than face that, I saved face and kept my misery to myself."

"You're wrong. We would've been there for you," Lea said.

He laughed bitterly. "Right. You can't be there for me *now*, can't accept that I'm the happiest I've been in years. You wouldn't know how to help me when I was broken and in a dark place. And again, that's my fault. I've done everything for you—all of you—so your coping skills amount to letting *me* deal with the shit sandwich that life sometimes serves up. But no more." He looked at Jen, then Kay, then Lea. "Don't make me choose between family and my girlfriend. I've picked the three of you over everything since I was eighteen years old. I'm almost forty and the time has come that I choose what makes *me* happy." He ran his hand through his hair. "Go home. I'll be in touch on my time frame, not yours."

"Ike. I'm sorry," Jen said.

"Me too," Lea and Kay said at the same time.

"Good." He turned and walked away from them without looking back.

✺

Ike grabbed a beer and paced through his house, his mind running in a million directions.

He waited two hours before he felt calm enough to deal with Riss. Not that she'd been in the wrong; that was why he needed a clear head. Thanks to Lonnie, Ike had prepared himself for Riss to have a mini freak-out after she realized they were in a relationship. Without going into too much detail, Lonnie had indicated that Riss was a master at self-sabotage.

But her abrupt departure was his fault. He needed to grovel in a big way as well as assure her that he'd stand up for her—for them—from now on.

When he went to grab his keys, they weren't on the hook by the door where he'd left them. Weird. He always hung them up first thing.

But he had been distracted by Riss, so maybe he'd shoved them in a coat pocket.

Nope.

They weren't in the foyer, or his bedroom or his bathroom.

Nor did he find them in his living room or kitchen. He even checked the ignition in case he'd left them in the truck.

He had an extra set, but he wanted to know where

the hell his regular set was. A niggling suspicion started and he picked up his phone. He texted Riss.

ME: Were u mad enough to hide my truck keys before u left?

He didn't get a response from her for ten minutes.

RT: Yes.

Great.

ME: U wanna tell me where u hid them?

Twenty minutes went by this time before she texted him back.

RT: Not really.

Stay calm. He tried to call her, but she wouldn't pick up.

ME: Riss. Please tell me where they r so I can come over and we can talk.

RT: I don't want to see u that's why I hid ur keys. Besides I'm not @home.

ME: Where r u?

RT: Family time w/my bros.

Yeah, he was not gonna face the wrath of the Thorpe brothers today.

ME: Fine. We'll talk tomorrow. Where r my keys?

RT: Same place as our relationship. I put them on ice.

Jesus. Seriously? Ike opened the freezer and saw his keys on top of the ice cream.

ME: Thank u. Have a good night. I miss u s

An hour passed and Ike knew he wouldn't hear from her again.

But that gave him plenty of time to plan his next move.

Chapter Twenty-Four

~

*T*ito canceled Riss's run with the newbie driver the next morning. But she couldn't make herself go home. So Tito put her on the clock as an hourly employee—beggars couldn't be choosers when it came to earning a paycheck.

She cleaned the office and the bathrooms. She filed paperwork. Made a list of supplies. Answered the phone and looked longingly at the comfy chair where Dianne the dispatcher usually sat.

Being a dispatch operator for a trucking company wasn't an easy gig. Some dispatchers had a god complex—they could give you jobs or take them away. With smaller outfits like Tito's, there was no forced dispatch, meaning Riss could turn down a load. And Tito worked closely with Dianne so she didn't have all the power, like with the larger companies, where if you pissed off your assigned dispatcher, you'd find yourself at the bottom of the pecking order.

Tito specialized in short hauls. Most of his drivers had two or three overnight trips a month and could be home with their families at night. Although Tito had been a driver for thirty years, he'd only been running his small, independent company for five years. He claimed he was too old to have huge ambitions to take on tons of clients. But he kept the door open and new clients seemed to find him. Since supply and demand didn't take weekends off, neither did Tito's drivers. And since Riss didn't have a family with a spouse and kids, she preferred to take the Friday, Saturday and Sunday runs. The pay was slightly higher, which meant she could afford to take two weekdays off for the dedicated runs for Desert Plains.

Or that was how it used to work. She wasn't sure how much longer Tito could hold off on hiring a replacement driver. Riss had seen the stack of applications—those were just the ones drivers sent in, not an open call to fill a specific position.

"I hate to waste your talents doin' office work, but damn, girl, the place always shines when you get done with it. Dianne doesn't do nothin' except sit behind them glassed walls."

"She has a dedicated position and she's never had to adapt to anything else."

"Is that what you're doin'?"

"Yep. I appreciate you keepin' me on, even when I know any day you might change your mind. As much as it's gonna suck, T, I want you to know I won't blame you. Business is business."

Tito sighed. "That's why I adore you, Red. And that's why you'll land on your feet no matter what."

"Thanks."

He pointed at her cast. "How much longer?"

"I've had the cast on six weeks. The doc indicated it'd be on the full eight weeks, maybe twelve. I guess my bones are brittle for my age, which I never considered. So I've been takin' calcium supplements."

"Any idea about what rehab entails?"

"Not until the cast is off for good."

The phone rang and Tito toddled off to answer it.

Someone pressed the buzzer to the delivery door, which was odd since most everyone just walked into the shop. Riss wandered over and pushed on the bar that opened the door. She said, "Come on in, you don't need a formal invite," before she looked up to see who it was.

Ike stood framed in the doorway.

Riss was so stunned it took a moment to notice that he held a bouquet of flowers.

"If I don't need a formal invite, can I come in before these freeze?"

"Ah. Yeah. Sure." She stepped aside. And Ike had her crowded against the wall before the door slammed shut.

"Is there someplace we can talk?"

"I am workin', Ike."

He didn't glance around the empty garage and say, "Workin' on what?" He just retreated. "I don't want to get you in trouble. What time do you get done? I can come back. Or I can meet you someplace. Whatever works best for you."

His willingness to compromise and his eagerness to

fix what happened the day before . . . how was she supposed to maintain a bitch-on-wheels attitude when faced with that? She couldn't. She didn't want to. "It's close to quitting time and the dispatcher is off today so we can use her office." She heard Tito yakking on the phone as they crossed the concrete floor in silence.

Once inside, she left the office door open.

Ike set the flowers on the desk.

She intended to put the desk between them, but Ike had other ideas. His cold hands framed her face. "I'm sorry for yesterday. I handled it all wrong."

"With your sisters?"

He snorted. "It's obvious I've been handling things wrong with them for years. And that means I didn't do right by you. For that I'm truly sorry."

Riss waited for him to tack on an excuse or an explanation, but he didn't.

"Riss. Say something."

"That's it?"

"Umm . . . I guess. I've never had a girlfriend so I don't know if I'm doin' this groveling thing right."

"Well, I've never had a guy grovel or bring me flowers so I'm kind of at a loss what to do next too."

"So let's do what's familiar to us." He dropped his hands from her face and stepped back. "C'mere. I need a damn hug."

She laughed and was in his arms in the next heartbeat. She buried her face in his neck, searching for the scents she associated with him, the icy cold of winter, the warmth of wool and clean tang of his laundry detergent mixed with his aftershave.

"Baby, I'm sorry," he whispered into her hair.

"I know. I am too. I shouldn't have stormed off and hidden your keys."

"You shouldn't have answered the damn door."

"If you would've crawled in your bed with me like I suggested . . ."

"Good point. Another mistake I'll never make again." His lips trailed soft kisses down her hairline, stopping at her ear. "How is it that we've only had one date and I already feel like you know me better than anyone?"

Her heart turned over. "I don't know, but now I don't feel like an idiot asking you the same question."

"I dreamed of you last night," he whispered. "Of your body twined around mine. Skin to skin as I was buried balls deep in you." He nuzzled the skin below her ear. "We weren't moving. We weren't sweaty and frantic driving each other higher as we tried to get off. We were just as close as a man and woman can be. Lost in all the perfect ways we fit together."

"Ike."

"I woke up and you weren't there. And if I really concentrated I could still catch a whiff of your scent on my skin. But I didn't want the phantom scent of you, Riss. I wanted the real you. The you that only I get to see."

"I'd dismiss that as just another one of your smooth-talkin' lines, but I know you now. You are as overwhelmed by this as I am."

"Yes. So come over tonight. Or I'll come to you."

"So we can come together," she teased.

He groaned. "If you're tryin' to get me hard, Larissa, it's workin'."

She tipped her head back and met his gaze. "You

wanna level the playing field, kiss me. Your kisses make me wet."

Ike's growl rumbled against her lips and he brought his mouth down on hers. Then they were kissing like crazy. Hands didn't wander. Their bodies didn't grind together. Their focus was solely on this moment between them that had changed everything. This passionate connection was just a bonus.

"What in the hell is goin' on in here?"

Tito's bellowing broke the spell. Riss's entire body, which had been flushed with arousal, now went flaming hot with embarrassment.

Ike kept a firm grip on her with one hand even when he turned to face Tito. "Hello, sir. You must be Tito. I'm Ike Palmer."

"Red, is his black eye your doin'?"

"Accidentally. I'm about as graceful with this cast as I am with a club." She bumped Ike's hip with hers. "Ike here was my cranky male nurse and is now my boyfriend. Ike, this is Tito, my boss and ruler of this trucking empire."

Tito rolled his eyes, but he did finally offer Ike his hand. "Ike, is it?"

"Yes, sir."

"So you decided you'd have a better chance with the beast when she's minus a working arm?"

Ike smiled. "You might say that. I'm just happy she's givin' me a chance at all."

"Smart man." Tito motioned to the flowers. "You already get yourself into the doghouse?"

Riss expected Ike to hedge. But he didn't.

"Yep. So I'm sorry if me stopping by during working hours is breaking some kind of company rule."

"Only if you're breaking her rule. But that lip-lock indicated that wasn't the case."

Tito looked at Riss. "Marlon just called."

"What'd he want?"

"To know when you'd be back to work. He's got a load of pieces he just finished they're waiting for in Omaha. His son took his last delivery and showed up with four broken sections. So he had to bring back the broken pieces, Marlon had to fix them and now he's got twice the load size, which means the dry box his son borrowed ain't big enough."

Riss held up her cast. "Tito. I'm sorry. There's nothin' I can do. If you have to assign Jerry or Dickie, then I understand. But I can't even drive an automatic transmission, so no solo runs."

"Too bad. There's a two-thousand-dollar bonus for the driver if the statues are delivered by Friday."

That was when a lightbulb went off in Riss's head.

No solo runs, but she could team up with someone.

She blurted out, "Ike has a CDL."

Ike looked at Riss as if she'd lost her mind. "What does that have to do with anything?"

But Tito saw the same potential solution that Riss had: she and Ike could partner up. "You have a CDL," Tito said. "Current?"

"Yeah. Class A. But the truth is I've not driven much since my last renewal and DOT physical."

He cocked his head at Ike. "You ain't pulling my leg, right?"

"No, sir. I spent over a dozen years as a cattle broker.

Set up more than my fair share of loads. And even had to drive a bull hauler myself a time or twenty. Why?"

"We could take the run," Riss said excitedly. "You and me. Co-drivers. You'd drive and I'd co-pilot." She looked at Tito. "What do you think?"

"I don't know, Red."

"But Ike has drivin' experience. You keep Marlon happy and I get a paycheck—that I'd be happy to split with my co-driver."

Again, Ike stared at her as if she'd gone plumb mad. "You'd trust me to go on a run with you? You'd be happy ridin' shotgun?"

"Not happy. I'm always gonna want to be behind the wheel." She squeezed his biceps. "But I've convoyed with you when we were hauling rodeo stock and I've recently ridden with you. I know you're beyond competent behind the wheel. I trust you."

"That testimonial is a good enough job recommendation for me," Tito said.

"What's this Marlon guy manufacture?" Ike asked.

"He casts concrete. Everything from angels for gravesites to birdbaths to garden benches. He's contracted to a garden center distributor in Omaha and it's his busy season."

"What kinda rig do you drive for something like that?"

"One with really great air shocks because that concrete weighs a fuck ton," Riss said.

"Meaning what class?"

"Usually class 7 flatbed trailer. Since the concrete pieces are built to be used in the elements, keeping them covered from the weather ain't a factor. The bonus is the pieces are loaded inside with a forklift and un-loaded inside with a forklift."

Tito's eyes narrowed at Ike. "Do you have experience with a flatbed?"

Ike scratched his chin. "What's the full length with the semi?"

"Around the fifty-three foot maximum."

"How long is the JSC cattle pot?" Riss asked Ike.

"In the forty-foot range." Ike exhaled. "So to be honest, I'd need drivin' time to get used to the extra length."

"I'd be happy to go out with you," Tito said. "I spent many years on the road with my girl and I can share how to handle her quirks and the tricks that make her purr."

Ike froze. "Jesus, man. Tell me you're not talkin' about Riss."

"No, he's talkin' about the Kenworth!" Riss exclaimed. "Remember the semi I drove to Kansas? That's Tito's prized W900L. And it sounds like he's gonna let us take that to Omaha."

Tito nodded. "Need something that's got enough power to handle that load."

Riss jumped up and down. "This is so freakin' cool! Thanks, T."

"Don't thank me until golden boy proves he's got the mettle to handle her." Tito walked over and pulled open the top drawer of the filing cabinet. "He oughta be in the system by Thursday as long as all the paperwork is filled out today." He handed Ike a packet of papers half an inch thick. "Lots of repetition. The one I'll need you to fill out first is the background check. I can put a rush on it, but the insurance company requires it for all new drivers."

"Understood." Ike gestured to the desk. "Is it all right if I start doin' this here?"

"Yep. I'll take your driver's license and social security card to make photocopies for our file."

Riss tried to contain her excitement as Ike handed the cards over to her boss.

When Tito left the room, she jumped up and down. "Omigod. I don't know why I didn't think of this sooner."

"Because you are an island and never ask anyone for help," Ike said dryly.

"Will Holt give you time off?" She paused. "We may have to stay in Omaha an extra day before we can pick up a return load. So it might be Tuesday morning before you can slip on your tool belt and hard hat. Will that be a problem?"

He gave her a tight smile. "I'll handle it." Then he snagged a pen and moved behind the desk to start filling out paperwork.

Riss unwrapped the flowers from the plastic and brought the bouquet up to her nose. The petals were velvety soft and vividly colored: dark red, deep pink, creamy white tipped with crimson. A droplet of water on the inside of a pink rose sparkled like a prism in the light. She inhaled the delicate perfume, which was different from the earthier aroma of the red ones. Her gaze scanned the bouquet and she counted each bloom. A dozen.

When she glanced up at Ike, he wore the softest smile.

"You like them."

"I love them. I've never gotten flowers before."

"Seriously?"

She shook her head. "No dating, remember? How about you? Do you give out roses all the time?"

"Never. The last time I bought flowers was when Jen had Elijah."

"Is it horrible of me to say I'm glad?"

"No more horrible than for me to admit I'm happy to be the only man to have given you flowers."

"Hurry up and fill that out. I wanna get out of here so I can show my appreciation for how well you grovel, cowboy."

While Ike pushed through the paperwork, Riss was so tempted to flip through the maintenance records to see the last time the W900L had been serviced. The semi was one of fourteen that Tito owned. He'd been fortunate enough to buy an old warehouse, so none of his vehicles had to sit outside in the elements. Riss wandered into the garage—a generic name for the bays that housed the different semis.

A few of Tito's drivers had their own rigs. But as much as Ike and everyone else considered her a self-starter, at heart, she really wasn't. Her lone purchase of a Peterbilt tractor barely two years into her trucking career nearly bankrupted her. She'd had to spend a year as a long-haul driver for a trucking conglomerate to earn enough to pay off the loan—even after she'd downgraded to an older semi.

That was why she hadn't pushed the issue with JSC. She could've picked up jobs here and there—and she had—but she'd actually lost money working for herself rather than taking a weekend run for Tito or dedicated runs with Desert Plains.

Three of the five trailers parked on her property didn't belong to her. The flatbed and stepdeck were a third hers; Lonnie and Lloyd owned the remaining two-thirds and they also owned half of the dump truck. Again, she'd made more money renting out the double-decker bull hauler and the small dry box for daily or weekly lease rates than she'd earned contracting for loads.

So she'd run the gamut from working long haul for a big company to working for small owner-operator companies. She'd taken the shit runs to add miles and increase her safety rating, but she'd never found a company she wanted to stick around with long enough to become a senior driver, until she went to work for Tito.

She remained in Wyoming because there'd been enough short-haul jobs to make a living. When Lonnie bought the garage she promised she'd help out, teaching him how to run a bookkeeping program, doing pickups for their fledgling tow truck business. She worked enough hours to qualify for health insurance. The real bonus was that both her brothers understood her bargain hunter mentality. They too scoured auction announcements, haunted junkyards and subscribed to online liquidators for deals where they could utilize their skills and make a quick buck.

Riss wondered if Ike could accept the part of her that would ditch stability for adventure. Not "pack up and move to Costa Rica" type of adventure, but taking on a challenge just to see if she could do it. She certainly had numerous failures under her belt—more of those than successes.

Would Ike want a life partner who defined unpredictable?

She froze. Whoa. Life partner? Where the hell had that come from? They'd had one date and she'd started thinking long-term? People didn't do that.

Did they?

You see yourself being with him for the long haul. No man has ever captivated your interest as much as he has. And he's become more real since he stopped wallowing in what he used to be and focused on what he could be. It was important he'd taken your advice to heart after he'd shared his frustrations, failures and resentments with his life. A man who talks isn't a rarity. But a man who truly listens . . . that's what you've always waited for.

But she couldn't take credit for anything more than telling him what no one else would. Ike had been so closed off. So much more "I can handle this" than even she was. Ike reminded her of Lonnie. The responsibilities they'd taken on far too young in life. The fierce love they had for their siblings, even when neither of them chose to confide in their families about their struggles.

And Ike had followed through on his promise to find a way to make this relationship work. He'd let her storm off yesterday, which, in hindsight, had been over-the-top dramatic for her. But she'd known if she'd stayed, she would've lit into his sisters and she hadn't been sure how he'd react. Regardless if what she'd said was true. He'd given her time to think about the changes they'd face as a couple—but not too much time. Ike had figured out when to push her and when to leave her be.

But if Ike hadn't come to her, she would've gone to him.

The classic Kenworth W900L was parked in a place of honor. This had been Tito's pride and joy the last decade he'd spent on the road. Riss loved the longer nose of this model even when the hood was a bitch to deal with for a woman of her size. The first step up into the driver's seat was a killer, but the interior was the best designed on the market. Even to this day.

Some of the newer models, like the Kenworth T680, had all the bells and whistles in the sleeper cabin— almost to the point it resembled a luxury motor home. But this classic ran well, especially with the engine updates for improving fuel efficiency. Tito had overhauled this semi three times and he still had a soft spot for the rig that'd allowed him to expand.

"She's still a beaut, ain't she?"

Riss smiled over her shoulder at Tito. "That she is. I'm not just sayin' that to butter you up, old man."

"I know, Red. I know." He stood beside her. "Lots of memories. Lots of miles."

"Do you miss it?"

He shrugged. "Some days. But my back don't ache like it did. My wife actually likes me again. After I'd spent so much time away, she'd gotten used to doin' her own thing. I'd gotten tired of doin' everything by myself, but we worked through it."

"Your son have any plans to take over this empire when you retire?"

"Nope. He's gonna be an engineer." Tito paused. "So that's your fella."

"Yeah."

"First time you've let any guy hang around here."

"First time I've let any guy hang around longer than a night."

He snorted. "I'm gonna let that one lie, bein's I'm old

enough to be your dad. But I'll say I'm happy for you. Got too much to offer to spend your life alone."

"Thanks, T."

"You trust him with my favorite?"

"I wouldn't have suggested he drive it if I didn't."

"I wasn't talkin' about the truck, Riss."

"Oh." She felt a burst of happiness she didn't bother to hide. "Thanks."

Tito put the keys in her hand. "I'm headed home. I'll trust you to put Ike's paperwork on my desk and lock up."

"I will."

"See you in the morning."

Not long after Tito left, Ike's boot heels echoed across the concrete.

Riss remained in place, damn near holding her breath until he finally reached her.

"So you have a lady boner for this truck?" Ike said as he tucked his body behind hers.

She leaned against him. "It's such a classic. And it's comfy."

"Those ten days we spent together hauling stock with Hugh and Harlow, you never invited me into your comfy, classy sleeper cab." Ike nuzzled the side of her neck. "But I didn't see you dragging other lucky cowboys into your lair either."

"Borrowing a luxury sleeper cab made me protective of it. Technically it's a work vehicle, but when the truck is parked, that rear space felt sacred."

"Will you show it to me now?"

Riss grinned. "You betcha." Maybe she had an extra spring in her step as she hopped onto the running board. She opened the door and crawled inside, heeding Ike's warning to be careful. Now that she was finally on the downhill stretch with this stupid cast, it'd suck if she set her recovery back with carelessness.

Turning sideways, she lowered onto the thickly padded bench seat that served as the couch. Even when this unit wasn't in regular rotation, it didn't have a musty odor. The scent of oranges hung in the air, from a hidden air freshener or a lingering remnant from the cleaning service.

The cab jostled and she watched Ike duck as he entered.

His gaze started at the padded ceiling with button-tucked headers, the height of 1990s luxury—following the line down the padded walls to the flat-screen TV hanging above the built-in table, past the microwave and mini-refrigerator inset behind the passenger's seat, stopping to where she'd settled in the living/sleeping area.

He whistled. "Red seems an odd choice for an interior color. I'd think Tito would've wanted a soothing blue or pale green."

"Kinda feels like you're in a Wild West whorehouse, doesn't it?"

"If I gotta pay to play, then I'm in."

Ike ambled toward her until she had to tip her head back to look at him.

Oh lordy. Hunger and greed glimmered in his eyes. No man had ever looked at her that way. And her body responded immediately. Her skin went hot and he soaked her panties without saying a word.

Still watching her response to him, he traced his knuckles down the left side of her face. From the outer edge of her eyebrow, down her temple, over her cheekbone and then following the line of her jaw to the tip of her chin. He repeated the exploration on the right side of her face with the same thoroughness. Then he brushed the pad of his thumb across her cheekbones and the slope of her nose. "These goddamned freckles are sexy as fuck. I wanna kiss every single one."

Riss kept quiet, opting not to jokingly point out the freckles dotting her chest, shoulders and belly would need equal attention so they weren't jealous of the freckles on her face.

Ike gripped her chin between his thumb and forefinger, forcing her head back, allowing him to move closer. "My fresh-faced and feminine Larissa. The dirty, dirty things I wanna do to you in this sleeper cab would make you blush so hard them freckles would all but disappear beneath the heat of your skin."

God, she loved the purely sexual side of this man.

He teased her mouth with soft, slow passes of his lips and tiny bites as his hand kept her head where he wanted it. "Gonna give me what I need, baby?"

"What's that?"

His free hand slipped between her thighs and he stroked her. "This pussy on my face."

She released a happy little hum. Ike hadn't gone down on her Saturday night or Sunday morning because they'd run out of time.

"You created a monster, girl, when you confessed no man has had you in any way in this sacred cab. I'm gonna be the first"—he bit down on her bottom lip—"no, make that the *only* man who's gonna take you every way and then some. Startin' right now."

Ike tugged her to her feet. "Pants off."

Riss might've set the world speed record for one-handed boots, socks, yoga pants and underwear removal.

He'd made himself comfortable where she'd been sitting. His rough-skinned hands circled her hips. "Hop up, darlin', and brace yourself against the wall above me. I noticed there's a strap hanging down on the left side. I suggest you hold on to it."

"You want me to stand while you . . . ?"

"Devour this juicy cunt? Yes." Ike's thumbs slid down and pulled back the flesh protecting her clit. "As soon as my tongue is on you, you won't know if you're standing or sitting, 'cause, baby, I'm gonna send you flying."

The man had better have an impressive tongue game, like, porn star—*lesbian* porn star—impressive, Riss thought as she stepped up, placing a bare foot outside of Ike's jean-clad thighs. Reaching for the strap, she pressed her sling and the side of her face into the velvet-paneled wall, feeling more awkward than sexy.

"Scoot that right foot out a little farther. That's it. Perfect." Ike dragged his mouth across her abdomen and he relocated his hands to her ass.

Riss waited, body tense, jaw tight, her anticipation . . . dwindling.

Then she caught a whiff of Ike's scent. The one she'd discovered Saturday night when he was so hard his cock was about to burst. Had he already gotten so worked up by the idea of making her come with his mouth that he'd had to free his cock from his jeans?

Tempting to lean back and check, but with her luck she'd lose her balance and . . .

HOLY FUCK! was her last coherent thought as Ike Palmer enslaved her and proved he was an oral sex god.

No, he proved himself to be *the* oral sex god.

His mastery with that wicked, wet, whipping, winding, wandering tongue was unparalleled in the history of the world—or at least in her personal sexual history.

Riss held on to the strap and let go of her sanity. Her legs shook, her insides quaked as she tried to prepare herself.

But nothing could've prepared her for the lip-gliding, tongue-flicking, mouth-sucking, teeth-nipping deity who made her come the first time within a minute. Then he made her come again with just four hard sucks on her clit and BOOM, she hit orgasmal orbit.

Ike's mouth was on a mission to enslave her. Those lips. That tongue. Wait. Had he grown another one? Because how else could he do . . . that? Where it felt like he was licking her in two places at the same time.

"Oh, please, don't ever ever ever ever stop doing that," she begged.

He growled against her wet and swollen tissues as he ate her without mercy. The combination of stellar tongue action and the vibrations of his hungry growls against her sensitive tissues sent her spiraling into orgasm number three.

Before she'd regained any semblance of composure, he eased back to sweet kisses and soft smooches, lovingly pressed on the rise of her mound, the creases of her thighs, up and down her slit, until she realized that sneaky fucker hadn't eased off at all; he'd been ramping her back up.

Way up.

A return-trip-to-orgasmic-heaven kind of up.

Her tits shook, she sweated in places she didn't have glands, her toes cramped from curling in pleasure so many times, her scalp tingled, her throat opened up so she could moan as she shattered with orgasm number four.

When she came to, she was no longer standing, but sitting on Ike's lap.

She blinked at him. "Whoa. What happened?"

"You gonna get pissy if I say that I made you come so hard that last time that your knees buckled?" Ike said, trying—and failing—not to look smug.

"Why would I get pissy? Dude. I have no words for how fantastically lucky I am that you . . . that you can use your mouth . . ." She snickered, feeling half-sex-drunk. "See? No words."

"Riss Thorpe speechless. Write that on the calendar," he teased.

She kissed him, licking the taste of herself from his lips, then gently sucking the taste from his tongue. The kisses and touches continued, as neither was in a rush to stop this intimacy that was so new to both of them.

"Can I ask you something?" Ike murmured in her ear.

"Mmm-hmm."

"Think we'll survive livin' in close quarters of the truck cab, eatin' together, sleeping together, workin' together for at least four days without a break?"

"Are you worried?"

"Only an idiot wouldn't be a little concerned."

"Think I'll drive you crazy?"

"Baby, that's a given. I just don't wanna blow it with you, okay? This is too important."

She felt the same way. "It's important to me too, Ike."

"I'm so fuckin' relieved to hear that." He kissed the top of her head. "Let's get cleaned up before our date."

"What date?"

"The one I decided on before I showed up to grovel." He nipped her earlobe. "And while feasting on your sweet pussy for the past hour was damn near a religious experience, I'm starving for real food."

"It's gotta be cheap," Riss reminded him. She disentangled herself and reached for her clothing. That was when she noticed Ike's jeans were undone and his cock looked . . . lonely. "Hey, I could always snack on some cowboy sausage as an appetizer." She smirked. "Don't want him feeling neglected."

"Thanks, darlin', but not necessary. He got his. He'll be fine for a while."

Riss froze. "You—"

"Got off about thirty seconds after you did when I had my first taste of your pussy. I didn't even have to touch myself, Larissa. Never had that happen before."

"Are you embarrassed?"

He stood, tucked his cock in and zipped up. "Are you kiddin'? It was fuckin' hot as hell." Ike's gaze fell to her groin and he growled. "Get dressed or I'm liable to see if I can get it to happen again to both of us."

As Riss locked up the building Ike accompanied her. "So tell me about this date."

"Bingo night, baby, at the R&R Senior Citizens Center in Rawlins. Buy one card, get one free. So there's cheap entertainment. And it's 'Moo Monday' at DQ so burgers are a buck."

"Damn, Palmer, I'm proud." She settled his cowboy

hat on his head and smoothed her hand down his chest. "You're serious about making changes."

"I'm serious about a lot of things these days. You're at the top of the list."

She kept fussing with the buttons on his shirt, unsure what to say.

He crouched down, forcing her to look at him. "Come home with me tonight after we kick those senior citizens' asses at bingo. I'll even throw in a ride to work in the mornin'. It'd be an economical decision to carpool since we're goin' to the same place."

"Playin' on my thrifty sensibilities . . . that'll earn you brownie points, cowboy."

"That's what I'm hopin' for."

Chapter Twenty-Five

∽

*I*t'd been an interesting couple of days since Riss's epiphany about them teaming up to take this run for Tito.

Since Holt's side projects had finished, Ike had been laid off until the construction business picked up, so this driving partnership couldn't have come at a better time.

Tito rode along as Ike familiarized himself with the Kenworth. They'd driven into Casper, allowing Ike to practice backing up into tight dock spaces—apparently similar to their unload point at the distribution center in Omaha—because it'd been a while since Ike had un-loaded anywhere besides an open field. Then they'd driven highways, both interstate and rural, into the mountains and then back down to the plains, until shift-ing and speed control felt natural. It gave him a sense of accomplishment to polish his rusty skills, even when he understood the rig would handle differently loaded down with concrete than just coasting along as an empty flatbed.

Early Friday morning, he and Riss hung around the shop, waiting for dispatch to sort out a last-minute pickup/drop-off load before they reached North Platte.

Ike's presence as a new hire—and "Red's" boyfriend—had caused a stir among the other drivers. Even Tito's wife, Esme, had stopped by to meet the man who'd broken Riss's "no dating" rule. Ike loved watching Riss in her element, talking smack with the guys while maintaining a professional boundary. Ike followed her lead when they were in the shop even as he wondered how their dynamic would change when they were alone.

He and Riss had discussed possible conflicts the past four days—and nights—since they'd spent all of them together. Riss's concerns were that Ike would ignore her advice when it came to driving scenarios; he'd revert to his former bossy-big-brother behavior and talk over her instead of listening to her.

Whereas Ike's major concern was the professional side of their relationship would overtake the personal aspect. They'd relapse to constant arguing, which would lead to them needing time apart—not an option when they shared less than one hundred square feet of space twenty-four/seven for the next four days.

Then again, the amount of time they'd been together had only increased their desire to experience more time doing couple things. Monday night, after finishing their bargain burgers, they headed to the R&R Senior Citizens Center for bingo. Fun-loving, outspoken Riss had gotten some nasty looks from their somber-eyed, gray-haired matronly tablemates. She'd maintained an even keel when the curmudgeonly bingo callers rechecked her winning bingo cards four times to ensure she hadn't been cheating. And just to be ornery, Riss had tucked her winnings into her bra.

However, Riss's laid-back attitude vanished when two ladies tried to slip their granddaughters' phone numbers to Ike during the last coffee break when Riss had gone to the restroom. When Riss returned and confronted them about their sneaky behavior, not only did they not apologize, they defended themselves, claiming that Ike and Riss hadn't "acted" as if they were in a relationship.

In the past, when Riss emitted that mean little laugh, Ike might've warned bystanders to run before he took off himself.

But now when he heard that sarcastic trill of Riss's laughter, his dick immediately went hard.

Riss showed everyone in the room exactly what kind of relationship she and Ike shared when she settled herself on Ike's lap and kissed the crap out of him.

Somewhere behind them the timer had dinged, indicating the third round of bingo was about to start.

Riss hadn't cared.

For once, Ike hadn't cared either and another protective wall crumbled between them as he'd given himself over to her very blatant PDA.

But someone had called security—not until after Riss had demonstrated her excellent lap-dancing skills.

Several attendees had booed as a security guard tapped her nightstick on the metal chair to break up the show.

As the security guard herded them past the bingo

callers' table, Riss had yelled, "I've been thrown out of better joints than this! And just so you know, the bingo payout at the Casper Senior Center is twice as much as it is here. Check it out for yourselves online if you don't believe me!"

That'd nearly started a riot.

As soon as they cleared the outermost edge of the building, Ike had Riss pressed against it, his mouth hungry on hers, his hands everywhere, his thigh between hers, his need for her overpowering and immediate.

She moaned, "Yes, yes, yes," as she ground her sex against his leg.

Wrenching her yoga pants to her knees, he spun her around, angled her forward and fucked her hard and fast. His shearling coat kept their exposed bits covered from the cold and any prying eyes, but he wouldn't have cared if the whole damn town had been watching them. Ike had never felt a burning need to claim a woman like he had in that moment with her. Her impromptu lap dance had increased his lust, but what had sparked those embers was when Riss had straddled his lap, planted her mouth on his and left no doubt they were very much intimately together.

Ike had never known what a fucking rush it was to belong to one woman, so he'd gone a little crazy showing Riss just how much he'd loved it.

And she'd loved it too.

"Ike?"

He blinked and the memory vanished. He glanced over at Dianne, the dispatcher, and offered her a smile. "Sorry. Thinkin' about a million different things. Could you repeat that?"

"Sure. Your first pickup is with Ingrid Olaffson. She claims you know her?"

"I know of her. I mostly dealt with her husband, Olly, over the years."

Riss moved in closer. "What's the load?"

"Hay. Load at the Olaffson Ranch in Chugwater, offload at the Winspahr Ranch in Gurley, Nebraska."

"How far does that take us off route?"

"Not at all," Dianne said. "Still goin' south on I-25 until you hit Chugwater. Then you'll head east on WY 313, and slightly south on 385. Then you'll head straight south to hit I-80 at Sidney and continue to North Platte as planned."

"Good. We're ready to roll."

"I'll tell Dave."

Not a surprise at how quickly Riss had jumped in to assert her dominance to Dianne. Or was that a reminder for him that in this temporary driving partnership, she was the senior partner?

Then Riss was in his face. "Is it a coincidence that you're familiar with the person requiring a last-minute haul?"

"No. I put the route and load capacity on a page I used a few years back for Stocksellers. You know, one of those pre-Craigslist rural catchall web pages where people buy, sell and trade items and ask for and offer help. I used my name and my former affiliation with Stocksellers, but gave Tito's Trucking as the contact number. I'm actually a little shocked my former clients still use that web page."

When Riss continued to stare at him oddly, he let her. Then she smiled—grinned, actually. "Lookit you, cowboy. Showin' me up on the first damn day of our partnership. Bein' a self-starter, a team player, a work hustler, a load broker. Dude. I'm so damn proud right now I could bust my buttons."

Ike grinned back. "Glad I could do something to make you proud." Then his gaze dropped to the front of her buttonless shirt. "Buttons or no buttons, them beauties are for my eyes only, so I'd appreciate it if you'd keep the button bustin' until we're alone."

She didn't even check to see if anyone was watching before she stood on tiptoe and kissed him, in that sweet, drugging way that made his head swim.

Tito's shrill whistle sliced through the air. "Thorpe and Palmer. Your rig is ready."

Riss groaned against his mouth. "That ass-hat has probably been waiting to break a lip-lock between us since he knew we were locking lips."

As they stood outside the bay, Ike said, "You gonna let me help you in? Or will *Red* rip me a new one for even offering?"

Her eyes softened. "It's an extra-big step up into the Kenworth, so I'd appreciate your help in and out with this busted arm. But thanks for asking and not assuming." She slid her hand up his chest, just like she did when they were about to get naked. "Call me *baby*, sweet cheeks or even twatwaffle, but never call me *Red*. That's not who I am when I'm with you."

Wham. Love hit him with the force of a runaway truck.

The world as he'd known it cracked and crumbled around him, then just as quickly rebuilt itself into something stronger and better.

Had she noticed that everything had changed?

Tell her.

She tugged on his hand. "Let's go, partner. I cannot wait to start on this adventure with you."

∞

The first two hours Riss rambled on about her experiences as a young solo driver, which included the lean years when she had to work other nondriving jobs between freelance runs. How a few times she'd left employers high and dry because a last-minute hot load had been offered and she'd needed the money and to prove herself. Given the work ethic Lonnie had raised her with, she'd always felt guilty quitting last minute, but driving was her career, not just a temporary job, unlike the other positions she'd taken to make ends meet.

"What about you? Had you always known you'd end up in sales?" she asked.

"I'd had a knack for selling things, starting when I was a kid. I'd buy discounted candy on the weekend and sell it on the school playground the next week for a profit. A small profit, mind you. As I got older, I became the go-to guy for finding a way to fulfill a need and I'd pocket a finder's fee. Anything from cash to a part-time job that paid cash, to a week's worth of lunches, to surplus groceries."

"What kinds of needs were you fulfilling?"

"Say Tim needed a ride home after basketball practice and Jim was looking for someone to help his sister clean stalls during calving season. They traded rides for work and they owed me a favor and a referral. It's strange to think about how well that system worked back then. That's how I ended up doin' so much ranch hand work. So two years after my mom died and I'd exhausted all my options for finding a local job with a regular paycheck and flexible hours, Abe Lawson and Bran Turner introduced me to Bernie Stack, who owned Stocksellers, and he hired me. For the first two years I did all the grunt jobs; whatever they needed, I did it."

"Such as?"

Ike reached for the Big Swig in the cup holder and swallowed a mouthful of Diet Mountain Dew. "Cleaned out cattle pots and bull haulers. Hauled garbage. Ran the snowplow. Delivered hay. Hung around the offices and salesmen as much as I could. So when the receptionist took sick, who did they ask to man the call center?"

"You."

"Yep." He grinned. "And did that come back to bite them in the ass. Like I said, since I'd done everything, I knew way more than anyone gave me credit for. On my own, I set up a meeting with a new client, put on my best clothes, borrowed Abe's truck and showed up as a rep for Stocksellers. I brokered a deal—with Dan Hale, Tobin's dad, ironically enough—and brought it back to the office."

Riss smirked at him. "No balls, no glory, eh?"

"Exactly. The other salesmen were livid. They demanded I get cut out of the deal and fired. Bernie refused. Instead, he assigned me a mentor, Augie, who was two years from retirement. He said if I was up to speed when Augie retired, he'd make me a full-time broker."

"So I can fill in the blanks for the success you had the next dozen or so years. You obviously rocked your job, Ike. How in the hell did you end up getting shitcanned?"

"Ever heard of second-generation failure in a family-owned business?" She shook her head. "It's what started happening at Stocksellers. Bernie Junior—aka Junior—took over after Bernie Senior had a heart attack and was forced to retire. I was the last broker Bernie Senior had hired all those years ago, so my coworkers were quite a bit older than me. Junior began implementing video technology that basically cut the salesmen out of the process, keeping the commissions for the company. None of them older guys needed Junior's shit or needed to learn new tricks so they retired, leavin' me the lone survivor. That played right into Junior's plans to downsize."

"Any idea what's goin' on at Stocksellers now?"

Ike slid his hands up and down the steering wheel. "Just rumors. Junior abandoned the company's existing clients to work with the bigger cattle operations. Last summer someone mentioned Stocksellers was struggling, but I tuned them out, bein's I had my own struggles to deal with."

Riss reached out and ran her hand up Ike's arm. She didn't offer platitudes, just her silent show of support.

His need to shout these strange, wonderful feelings of love for her made the slow crawl from his heart up his throat. Just as the words reached the back of his tongue, her cell phone rang.

He swallowed the words back down and the moment was lost.

∞

Three hours after leaving Tito's they turned off the paved road onto the gravel road that led to the Olaffsons' place.

"The instructions were to pull up next to the haystacks

outside the fence. I'm guessing we won't be four-wheeling this eighteen-wheeler across the frozen tundra to get to those stacks." Riss pointed to six large, misshapen mounds in the distance, half-covered by tarps.

"The loader is already out." He frowned. "Five rolls are all we're takin', right?"

"That's what the bill of lading says."

Ike downshifted. "Best direction to park this? Alongside? Or back end facing?"

"Alongside would mean less overall movement for the loader." She shot him a glance. "I'm assuming I don't get to run the loader?"

"Nope. That is a model I'm familiar with, so as long as it starts, we oughta be good." Ike inched along the fence until the truck was lined up.

Riss clapped to commend his parking effort.

He donned all of his outerwear and jumped out of the cab, skirting the front end to help Riss out. She didn't even fuss when he zipped up her coat, flipped up her hood and slipped on her left glove.

A parka-clad woman waved and crossed the driveway. When she reached them, she threw her arms around Ike. Then she stepped back and lowered her mink-lined hood. "Ike Palmer. Have mercy. You're twice as handsome as I remember. You make an old widow like me wish I was much younger."

Old widow his ass. Olly hadn't been in the ground a year yet, from what he'd heard. "Miz Olaffson, you'd give any woman a run for her money in the looks department." No doubt that was why she'd removed her hood, so he could see how well she'd aged, even in the harsh, less-flattering winter light.

"I'll admit I was surprised to read you're running a trucking company now."

Ike heard Riss snort behind him.

"No, ma'am. I *work* for a trucking company."

"None of this 'ma'am' stuff." She squeezed his biceps, letting her hand linger on his arm. "Call me Ingrid."

"I was sorry to hear about your husband, Ingrid. Olly was a great guy."

"He was. I miss him terribly. It's . . . lonelier than I imagined it'd be."

Riss stumbled forward and Ike shot an arm sideways to catch her. "Careful, darlin'. I don't need you breaking anything else."

Ingrid took notice of Ike calling Riss *darlin'*. Bundled up in the oil-stained men's Carhartt jacket that nearly reached her knees, with her head covered by the oversized hood, her gender wasn't immediately obvious.

"I am suffocating in this. Could you please give me some breathing room?"

Ike pushed back her hood; those wild red curls of hers went *sproing* and haloed her beautiful face. Then he undid the coat zipper so her cast was visible. "Better?"

"Yes. Thank you." She smiled brightly at Ingrid. "Hello, Ingrid. I'm Riss Thorpe. It's nice to meet you."

Ingrid's answering smile was brittle at best. "Whatever did you do to your arm?"

Riss looked at Ike. "It's kind of embarrassing, isn't it?"

Come on, alternate reality girl—make this one good. "I keep tellin' you. It wasn't that bad."

Riss refocused on Ingrid. "I broke it snowboarding trying to impress my man. I took an easy jump and landed wrong."

"Well, baby, I was impressed." Ike kissed the crown of her head. "And you're bein' far too modest. You could've gone pro on the snowboarding circuit. That 'easy' jump was a ten-eighty at twenty-five feet off the half-pipe."

"Such a shame," Ingrid murmured. "Those triples are so hard to land. Where did this happen? Olly and I took the kids snowboarding all over Wyoming and Colorado several times a year when they were growing up, so I'm familiar with the winter sports areas."

"Oh, I doubt you've been to this one," Riss said.

"Why would you assume that?"

"Because it's on the backside of a small mountain on the Shoshone Reservation. It's a spot not known to outsiders since it's part of a sacred site. But as a member of the tribe . . . I've been goin' there for years."

Damn. Ike had been sweating her answer on that one.

Ingrid's skeptical gaze took in Riss's vivid red hair, her green eyes and her freckled, ivory skin. "You're Indian?"

"Yes, ma'am. My dad was half Shoshone; my mom was white; which makes me an quarter Shoshone with enough Native blood to enroll in the tribe, which I currently am." She tossed her curls. "Let's get back to the business at hand. Has that loader been used recently?"

Ingrid looked at Ike, not Riss, which annoyed him.

And it annoyed Riss, apparently. "We're here to load hay, which we can't do if the loader isn't working. And no, forklift maintenance isn't in the contract. So if it ain't workin', save us all a bunch of trouble and say so now and we'll be on our way."

"As far as I know my son-in-law used it last week."

"Good." Riss looked at Ike. "Need my help getting set up?"

"No. But don't go too far in case that changes."

Ingrid left and didn't return until the bales were racked and stacked.

Of course Riss rechecked his tie-downs.

While she did that, Ike had Ingrid sign the paperwork. "I know this seems like an odd work order, but you're delivering this hay to my daughter. She's seven months pregnant with her second child. Her husband is in the army reserves and he's at a mandatory training camp in North Carolina for two weeks. They believed they had enough hay for the horses until he returned home and could load up the rest of these stacks—which are theirs—but she's about to run out. With her pregnant, and her daddy gone, and so many of our neighbors retired and moved to Arizona, I knew I had to find help." She gave Ike a watery smile. "I'm happy I saw your ad. You are a lifesaver."

It hadn't been an ad, but he didn't correct her. He and Riss needed to get back on the road. "I'm glad it worked out for you and the hungry horses. Take care, Ingrid."

"You too, Ike. It's awful nice of you to let your girlfriend ride along, but I'd keep an eye on her. She seems bossy about your business and it's a little off-putting."

"My business?" Ike laughed. "*Riss* works for Tito, not me. I'm currently unemployed. She's nice enough to let me partner with her." He tipped his hat and bestowed his most charming smile. "If anyone else around here needs extra help, we'd appreciate the referral."

Riss waved to Ingrid as Ike helped her into the passenger's side.

After the rubber hit the road, Riss spoke. "Lucky thing that this is a super short haul. The straps Tito sent are shitty. So are the tarps. If I'da known we were hauling hay this first leg when we left this morning, I would've stopped by my place and brought my own straps. We might be screwed if the wind blows hard the next hundred miles, since we've just got a single layer of bales."

"I think we'll be okay. But I hear ya on using different straps in the future." As soon as he said it, he shot her a sideways glance. Would she get pissy that he assumed they'd be driving together again?

Riss was pissy. But not for that reason. Finally, she said, "Why do some women feel entitled to flirt with a guy right in front of his girlfriend? Total dick move."

"I agree. She never acted like that when Olly was alive. So it's not like I've had to fend off her advances in the past. If that'd been the case, I would've declined this load."

She brooded out the window for the longest time before she spoke and even then she wouldn't meet his eyes. "On an attractiveness scale, Ike, you're, like, a twelve. On my best days, I'm maybe a five. I'm good with that. But other people see the seven-point difference between us and assume we're just friends or whatever, because a dude who looks like you could do way better than a chick who looks like me."

"Riss—"

"Hear me out, okay? If those assumptions would've happened once, I'd laugh it off. But that's the third

damn time this *week* people have given me that attitude
when they realize we are together. It sucks. Mostly because I don't blame them for the assumption."

Ike was floored by her matter-of-fact statement. And
really fucking annoyed. And really fucking pissed off. He
forced himself to take a drink of soda and reached deep
for that well of patience before he responded. "So you're
gonna use the ridiculous excuse that other people think
I'm too good-lookin' for you to break it off with me?"

Riss laughed. "Hell no. You like me as I am; I like me
as I am. So I'm not gonna head into Sephora for a make-
over to try to bring myself up to a seven; neither will I
buy expensive clothes that'll camouflage my body flaws
to give me another bump on that number scale. I'll just
deal with the nastiness and now the jealousy that we're
a couple the same ways I always have." She looked at
him and gave him the most devious, most glorious smile
he'd ever seen. "I will mind-fuck with them and then
we'll laugh about it. In bed."

God. I love you, Larissa Thorpe.

The sound of someone laying on the horn jolted him
out of the moment the same time Riss yelled, "Eyes on
the road, Palmer, eyes on the goddamned road!"

Shit. He'd drifted into the other lane as he'd gazed
awestruck at the woman he loved. That rolling,
butterflies-taking-wing sensation in his belly wasn't
from nearly clipping a garbage truck but from another
reminder that this woman was perfect for him in every
way that mattered.

"Tito will fucking kill you if you put a single scratch
on his rig," Riss warned.

"I know. Sorry. I'll refocus."

She was quiet for a few beats. "You're not gonna blame me for distracting you?"

Ike patted the steering wheel. "*I'm* behind this. Any driving errors, including those I make when I hear my woman's fearsome determination to tell people who question our coupling to fuck off . . . are mine. Period."

"Might make a driver outta you yet."

"I'll just ask you not to blow me when we're movin' down the road. I lose all ability to think when your mouth is on my cock, sweet cheeks."

"As it should be, cowboy. Safety first." She propped her sock-clad feet on the dash. "But when this rig is stopped for the night, look out."

He laughed. "Gonna be a long goddamned day."

∞

Unloading at the Winspahr Ranch was uneventful and they stayed on schedule.

Riss had packed lunch and snacks, so they didn't have to stop until they reached the next pickup point outside of North Platte.

The building had a huge bay door that'd been opened as soon as the customer had seen the truck turn onto the gravel road.

Ike's anxiety surfaced in all its blood-pumping, palm-sweating, ball-tightening, teeth-clenching glory as he lined the truck up to back through the open door. He hoped to hell he didn't fuck this up and embarrass himself in front of Riss—and Riss in front of this Marlon guy—as he watched his positioning in his side mirrors, forcing himself to go slow.

Almost, almost . . . yes. The brakes let out a whoosh of air when he put the truck in park. He had to wipe his forehead on his sleeve he'd sweated so much in the past two minutes.

"Ike."

"Yeah."

"Baby, you did great."

"Thanks. Christ. I don't know that I took a breath at all."

"It's gonna be hard for these guys to breathe if you don't cut the engine and kill the diesel fumes."

Shit. So close to getting it right. So. Close. He groaned. "Forget one tiny thing . . ." He turned the key and the cab went quiet. Sometimes he forgot how damn loud the engine was.

"Two things I gotta warn you about with Marlon and this pickup. First, Marlon is a cheap motherfucker. He's gotta be desperate to get this load delivered if he's offering a bonus. I don't gotta tell you it'll be an extra fast live load. He'll put every piece of concrete on the flatbed himself. His son Marlon Junior will try to engage you in small talk. Don't fall for it. I know it's second nature to you salesmen to offer that personal touch in getting to know your clients, but don't engage with any of Marlon's employees either."

"Can I ask why not?"

"Without seeming . . . uncaring, Marlon Junior is a special-needs guy. He helps out when he can and he's pretty good about half of the time. It'll seem that his dad is kind of a dick to him, but as Marlon Senior has raised the boy pretty much alone, he knows the best way to deal with him."

"Jesus. What else?"

"Ever given any thought to the importance of knowing how to look busy while standing around doin' nothin'?"

Ike shook his head.

"Marlon will take note of everything you do—and don't do. If he feels like you were fucking off during your nondriving time while he was loading his pieces—and yes, I understand that is his demand to literally do all the heavy lifting himself—he will complain to Tito. Tito is a businessman; he'll get paid regardless and he'll be willing to go along with Marlon in denying payment of a bonus if Marlon can back up his claims. So don't talk with the employees. Don't help yourself to the free coffee and doughnuts. Find a broom and act like you're sweeping up concrete dust after Marlon moves the pallets to the flatbed."

What a bunch of crap. But Riss had survived this scenario enough times he'd do exactly as she said. "Got it. What else?"

She squirmed. "You can't give any indication that we're a couple. And yes, I realize this is in direct conflict with what we just talked about, but Marlon is old-school. Women shouldn't be drivers. He respects me because I've proven him wrong over the years by bein' twice as tough. So I need to retain all the control of the details about this load, especially since I've got a broken arm. Okay?"

How she willingly dealt with this macho bullshit day in and day out surprised him. "So you're sayin' I'm supposed to shuffle around with a broom in my hand, lookin' all handsome and shit, keeping my charming, chatting mouth closed and my lustful gaze off my beautiful girlfriend?"

"Uh . . . yeah."

"That sucks. I love watchin' you turn into Red, truck-tough, mouthy broad. Gets me hard."

"Save it for later." She exhaled. "Here we go. Stay put for a sec and keep the windows rolled down, 'cause I already see a problem I gotta take care of."

"Just don't hurt yourself getting out."

"I'll be careful." She opened the door and all but jumped to the ground.

In the side mirror, Ike watched her walk the length of the flatbed, stopping at a pair of sawhorses and a plastic tarp about ten feet behind the bed. Then she yelled at someone out of Ike's view. "Goddammit, Marlon. Move this shit off the scale. You're not loading anything until I know I can weigh it."

That sneaky fucker had tried to cover up the scales? To see if he could get away with overloading the truck? Or to see if Riss wouldn't think to check that and then he'd have a legit reason for denying her the bonus? What an asshole.

"Sorry. Junior! Paxton! Get that stuff moved off there now!"

As soon as the area was cleared, Ike could see the scales. It killed him to wait for Riss's signal on what to do next, but he managed.

"Palmer!" she yelled. "Back it up another ten feet. Then bring me the clipboard."

"As you wish," he mumbled and did her bidding.

It was damn near impossible to keep his focus off her as she morphed into the larger-than-life Riss that he remembered from the first time they'd met. While her over-the-top behavior had a specific purpose to get Marlon to fall in line—the old guy defined cantankerous—Ike couldn't help his smug sense of satisfaction that he knew the real Riss, not this ball-bustin' stranger.

Everything played out as she'd said it would. The entire process from start to finish lasted two hours. Ike even slipped in a bathroom break when Marlon was busy yelling at his son.

Once Ike pulled onto the interstate, Riss relaxed. But he was wound tight. The distance to the drop-off point wasn't far, but for him, driving a rig loaded down with concrete was the most difficult aspect of this run. The return load to Cheyenne was empty oak barrels for aging whiskey.

As if Riss sensed he needed to concentrate, she didn't chatter.

After they'd cleared the weigh station two hours later, Riss said, "You're doin' great, Ike."

"Thanks."

"Gonna make a driver out of you yet," she teased.

High praise coming from her.

He would take things one step at a time and hopefully nothing would go wrong in the next three days to make her change her mind.

Chapter Twenty-Six

❧

*T*oday was the day.

Or so she hoped.

After twelve long weeks, Riss was supposed to get her cast off.

She'd spoken to all three of her brothers via speakerphone last night, assuring them Ike was accompanying her to the doctor. Suspicious fuckers made Ike confirm it because apparently they still didn't trust her.

But she wondered if she'd even know how to act without the clunky thing weighing her down. She'd gotten so used to compensating for it she'd probably hit herself in the face and end up with a black eye.

Ike had left for work early, but not before fucking her so thoroughly she couldn't crawl out of his bed.

Cocky jerk.

When she woke up, she debated on going home but

decided that since she had a couple of changes of clothes here it'd be a waste of time.

She tidied up Ike's place, and that killed all of ten minutes because the man was a total neat freak.

So when he came home for lunch, he found her napping on the couch.

"I wonder if I forgot how to work," she mused as Ike fixed them both sandwiches.

"I doubt it. It's too ingrained that two months ain't gonna change much of anything. Hell, most people would've taken the injury as an excuse not to do anything."

"How is the construction business?"

"A little slower than Holt would like."

She paused with the sandwich halfway to her mouth. "Has he mentioned cutting your hours?"

Ike shrugged. "It's a week-by-week thing. If it doesn't pick up, I have no doubt I'll be the first guy off the clock."

"You don't seem bothered by that."

"Nothin' I can do. This is a reality check so I'd have to find work someplace else."

Ike might act like it was no big deal, but Riss knew his tells. He was worried.

"Well, good thing we're still practicing cheap dates. I found a coupon code online for 'buy one, get one free' coffee and scones at this hip new coffee joint in Rawlins."

"Yeah, I know. My sister Lea started working there, remember?"

Riss choked on her sandwich. She had forgotten that.

Ike's sisters had pushed to get to know Riss and he'd

granted them one afternoon at the mall, where Mikayla and Elijah could burn off energy on the climbing wall and she and Ike could leave if things became too tense. They'd managed to coexist peacefully for a few hours, but Riss would be hardpressed to call it fun.

On the other hand, Ike now had become tight with Riss's brothers. Lonnie was teaching Ike to box twice a week and in the afternoons Riss spent at the garage going over the books, Lloyd was teaching Ike car repair basics. There was something seriously sexy about seeing that blond hair beneath the hood of a car and engine grease on his hands.

While Ike changed clothes, Riss loaded the dishes and for just a moment, she had to stop and remind herself this was her life now. Being part of a couple. Learning to balance family and friends and jobs. Before, the very thought of this type of domesticity would've had her slinking out the door.

Ike returned to the kitchen doing up the last button on a baby blue and red plaid western shirt. "You ready?"

"Why are you all dressed up, slick?"

"I have been slacking on my appearance if you think this is me dressed up." He kissed her nose. "I'm only recently a sweats-and-hoodie-wearing guy, yo."

She snickered. "Our next foray into creating an alternate reality, I wanna see if you can make me hot in public by acting like an urban douchebag. You know. Like you used to be when we were frenemies."

He swatted her ass hard. "I'm all for it . . . if it drives us toward hate fucking."

Ike insisted on helping her with her coat "one last time."

She figured he'd be equally disappointed if the cast didn't come off today.

They held hands on the drive to Casper. She'd fielded phone calls from her brothers—triple-checking to see if she truly was on the way to her appointment—and Jade, who was so over-the-top happy that Riss wouldn't have been surprised if she'd been performing herkies during the call. Aunt Bernice called to remind her to call after the appointment. And Tito called—Ike's cell phone, oddly enough—to make the same request.

At the doctor's office, Wanda was sweet as pie to Riss but gave Ike the stink-eye. Even his charm and arsenal of smiles didn't thaw her attitude. But Riss enjoyed the hell out of watching him try to win her over.

This time she let Ike wait in the exam room with her. He said nothing as she paced the enclosed area. He had developed an innate sense of when to order her around and when to keep his mouth shut.

A nurse—or maybe it was a PA—took them to a different room, where they put hospital gowns on over their clothes as well as protective face shields.

"How much plaster you plan on throwing on us?" Riss joked.

"The mask is to block some of the smell from your arm being encased in plaster for three months," she said with no humor at all.

When the high-pitched whine of the saw started, Riss wished she would've asked for earplugs.

Ike held her hand and her gaze as the techie ran the saw. When the pressure in her arm vanished, indicating the cast was off, Ike grabbed her chin and said, "Focus on me," during the next step of cleaning the plaster and stench away.

Then were the X-rays.

So Riss didn't get a complete look at her arm and hand under full lights until she returned to the exam room.

It didn't even look like her arm. It looked like a diseased appendage. Wrinkled. Chalky white. No muscle definition at all. Just a weak, limp noodle crisscrossed with surgical scars.

Her hand hadn't fared any better. In addition to the pasty color, she had red scars where they'd pinned her bones, or re-fused her bones, or whatever the hell they'd done.

So not only didn't it look like her arm, it didn't feel like her arm. She could open and close her hand, but not easily and not without pain.

The doctor sailed in and oohed and aahed over her handiwork while Riss remained in shock. She heard little over the roaring in her head. And she glanced at Ike to see him nodding at the doctor.

". . . the sling for a few more weeks until your physical therapist indicates you've regained some normal mobility."

At least she could hide the hideousness of her arm in the sling.

Riss couldn't focus on the dismissal or the aftercare instructions. Somehow Ike convinced Wanda to take his number as the main contact for the PT people.

Ike put on her coat, just as he'd done at the house, and led her to his truck.

She said nothing. Not a word until they reached the farthest outskirts of Casper. "I wanna go home."

"We are, baby." He kissed the knuckles on her left hand.

"No. I mean my home. I want . . ." She swallowed the tears. "I need to be in my own space, surrounded by my things, and sleep in my own bed."

If that upset him, he didn't show it.

Half an hour later he pulled into her driveway and shut off his truck.

They sat there and stared ahead at her trailer.

Finally, Ike said, "Are you gonna get out?"

That was when Riss realized that she'd gotten so used to him doing everything for her, she'd forgotten even how to open her own damn car door.

She burst into tears.

The ugly kind of tears where her mascara created black rivers that ran down her face, snot dropped from her nose and she hiccupped instead of spoke.

And calm and laid-back Ike vanished. He seemed utterly at a loss for how to deal with her in this state.

She fumbled with the handle on the door—using her right hand, which hurt like a motherfucker—and snatched her purse off the floor. She half ran, half walked like a shambling zombie as she crossed the porch to her front door. Thankfully she'd remembered to put her keys in her left pocket and she was inside her haven within seconds.

She threw off her coat, kicked off her boots and cranked the heat to high on the way to her bedroom. There she stripped down to her camisole, panties and socks before she slid between her flannel sheets and pulled the comforter over her head.

Even as Riss silently berated herself for the stupid tears that didn't solve anything, she cried.

When she realized she was cradling her formerly broken arm to her chest, she cried harder.

Eventually the heat from her tears created a sauna beneath the covers, forcing her to fling them back so she could breathe.

She heard the hallway creak and knew that Ike had followed her inside. Not that she'd expected anything different from him. She glanced up as he leaned in the doorway to her bedroom, a gentleman cowboy waiting for a formal invite into her private space.

He'd ditched his hat and coat. Probably his boots. He studied her with a mix of bewilderment and determination. That was what she loved about him: his hidden complexity beneath what appeared to be a placid surface.

Wait. What? Love? Had she just said she loved him?

Well, duh. This man gets you and still seems to like you anyway. Did you really go into this believing it'd be nothing more than a fling?

"Larissa?" he said softly.

"Don't."

"Don't what, baby?"

"Don't say my name like that when we're not naked." At his confused look she said, "I like that you only use my full name when we're intimate. Before, you said my name in three syllables like . . . La-riss-a . . . when you were pissed off at me. Now it's different. It's like my name belongs to you."

"You gonna let me into that bed so I can hold you?" he demanded softly.

"Yes. But take off your shirt so I don't smear mascara all over it."

"I don't give a fuck about this shirt."

"I do." She sniffed. "You look really handsome in it."

Ike pulled and the pearl buttons popped, opening his shirt. He tossed the shirt on the floor, shucked his Wranglers and slipped beneath the comforter, immediately drawing her body to his.

"Ike—"

"Sh. We'll talk later. Let this be enough for now."

As she drifted off, she murmured, "You're more than enough. You're everything."

∞

Riss jolted awake.

But she had steel bands wrapped around her so she barely moved.

"See? I'm getting smarter. If I lock you down like this, I don't get smacked in the face nearly as often."

"I'm sorry I'm such a wild sleeper."

His lips brushed the shell of her ear. "Well, you're wild in bed when you're awake so you ain't gonna hear me complaining that you're wild when you're sleeping too."

She felt the warmth of his palm on her right forearm and tried to twist it out of his hold.

"No, baby. Don't."

"Ike. Please. I don't want you to see it, let alone touch it."

"Fair warning: I'm about to give you that tough love you're so good at givin' me. So let's get this over with so we can move on." He whipped the covers back and held her right arm close to his face, as if he was inspecting it.

"Dammit, Ike! Let go."

"No. Tell me what's wrong."

"What's wrong?" she repeated. "You can see exactly what's wrong. This . . . appendage looks like it belongs to the Elephant Man! All wrinkled, gray, scarred and useless. It's hideous."

"First off, you're bein' hypercritical. Your arm is supposed to be weak. That means you didn't overdo it during the cast phase. The next phase is physical therapy. You'll learn how to strengthen it. And it'll be back to normal—heck, better than normal—before too long. Same with your hand. You could be facing a year or more of intense therapy. Instead you'll have a couple of weeks."

"That's what the doctor said?"

He frowned at her. "Weren't you listening to her?"

"No. I was too horrified by the big reveal of my Frankenstein arm. I imagined little kids running away from me screaming. I wondered if I could hide beneath a black cloak or if people would think I'm a Harry Potter fanatic. I can't even wear a red cloak because of the whole Little Red Riding Hood connotation and I already have enough people callin' me Red."

His lips twitched, but he didn't stop stroking her arm. "Anything else run through that entertaining mind of yours?"

"I almost made a promise to the universe that I'd stop creating alternate realities, since this deformity might require an entire sleeve of tats to cover it. Sorta seemed like karma coming back to bite me in the ass for becoming Bootsie, even when I'd probably go with a crocodile tat rather than a snake."

"*Almost* made a promise to the universe?"

"I'm weak, okay? I couldn't make a promise I couldn't keep. So I figured the universe was punishing me. My brain couldn't stop obsessing on the nightmare scenario where I'll never regain my arm strength or the flexibility in my hand and I'll have to stop driving trucks entirely. Then what would I do? I mean, the first time I was in the doctor's office when I was so pissed off at you and Lonnie, I saw a flyer that dealt with surrogacy. And I thought that might be an option while my arm was healing, to sit around and gestate someone else's baby. But now I know that's not an option because a couple lookin' to hire a surrogate would automatically dismiss me on account of my deformity outta fear that I might pass that on to the baby."

Ike stopped his tender caresses on her arm. He knocked all the pillows to the floor and rolled on top of her. "Okay, that is enough. Christ. Surrogacy is not a viable career change for you."

"Do you know how much they're payin'?"

"I don't give a damn. You wanna be pregnant? *I'll* knock you up. But that's not the issue, is it? The real issue is you're scared you've already lost your career and part of who you are. Guess what? It happens. It sucks ass. But until you've completed the physical therapy, you won't know the outcome. And refusing physical therapy—because I'm sure you could do the exercises on your own because you probably read it in a damn book someplace—ain't happening. You can call me bossy, get pissy with me, but I *will* hound you to keep those appointments."

"My insurance coverage only pays for one physical therapy session every two weeks," she retorted. "And yes, I did read up that I'll need two to three sessions a week for the minimum length of time that my arm was in a cast. How am I supposed to pay for that without a job?"

"I won't insult you by tellin' you that your brothers would be more than happy to help you out. I'd offer to pay, but I'm short on funds myself. So . . . we'll have to get creative." He smirked. "You any good at hustling pool?"

"Nope. I'm a craptastic pool shark."

"What about gambling? You naturally lucky or have a secret method for counting cards?"

Riss knew at that moment, without a doubt, she was hopelessly in love with this man. He listened to her crazy rants, fueled them with logic and now used the same type of crazy thinking to make her smile.

Tell him you're unlucky at cards but lucky in love.

But she couldn't. Not now. Soon, though.

"Sorry. I have a terrible poker face."

Ike studied her face. The intensity in his eyes had her wondering if he'd read her thoughts.

"What?"

"Yeah, baby, you do have a terrible poker face."

"So that leaves a couple of options. We rob a bank."

"Eh, no. My dad bein' the bank-robbing jailbird in our family . . . not the footsteps I wanna follow in."

"True. We could kidnap a physical therapist. Take really good care of him or her, but keep them chained up when they're not workin' me over."

"They would turn us in after we turned them loose. And we're back to the jail scenario."

She sighed. "I could go to work for a big company as a long-haul driver. I might have enough miles under my belt to qualify for one of those new automatic transmissions. No more shifting; all the controls are computerized right there on the dash with the push of a button."

"If you're drivin' long haul to god knows where, then when would you do the PT that you could finally afford to pay for?"

"Shoot. You blew a small hole in that option, but I am gonna put a pin in it for consideration, because it's the best idea I've had so far."

"If you're considering that, then you oughta consider becoming part of a truck-drivin' team. You'd stay on the rotation until you were fully healed." He twisted a piece of her hair around his finger. "We got along great on the Omaha run."

"That we did."

"We make a good team."

"That we do." Without thinking, she ran her hand through his hair and realized that she'd used her right hand.

Before she could yank it away, Ike clamped his own hand over it and said, "I've been waitin' for you to touch me with both hands." Then he turned his head and kissed her skinny, wrinkly wrist. He glided his lips up the inside of her arm, to the bend in her elbow. Then he rolled onto his back. Shoulder to shoulder, he raised her right arm so they could both look at it. "It's beautiful, Riss, because it's part of you. Even if you end up struggling to adjust to a new normal with this arm, it'll never diminish the beauty inside you."

"Ike."

Then he rolled to his side and kissed her arm, from her biceps down to the tips of her fingers. The gentleness of his kisses belied the heat of them that set her on fire.

On the last pass, that clever mouth traveled across her shoulder and up her neck to her ear. "Larissa," he breathed. "I'm gonna fuck you hard. I'm gonna fuck you sweet. I'm gonna fuck you face-to-face and I wanna feel both of your hands all over me as I'm doin' it. Are we clear?"

"Yes."

Riss insisted on stripping him out of his T-shirt.

And his boxer briefs.

Then she gave him a hand job with her right hand. Using her left hand to stroke his balls and to follow his happy trail up to pinch his nipples. She didn't need to use her mouth on his cock at all. Because her arm worked just fine to get him off as he shot his load on her tits.

Her right hand maintained a firm grip on his hair when he went down on her.

Twice.

Her right arm could hold on to him tightly as he fucked her hard and sweet face-to-face.

Her right arm supported her when Ike fucked her hard and sweet from behind.

By the time Ike was finished with her, she couldn't hold either arm up.

Chapter Twenty-Seven

❧

*I*ke had waited impatiently for Riss to get home from her girls' lunch with Jade.

For the past week, after Riss's cast removal, he'd set the wheels in motion to . . . well, get the wheels in motion.

Tito had taken a liking to him, mostly because Ike had taken a liking to Riss, or more accurately, Ike had fallen head over heels for Riss. Tito had a soft spot for the redhead as well as a romantic streak.

His idea was a temporary solution, but it'd give them both time to think about where they wanted to go from here.

As he paced he squeezed the racquetball—aka therapy ball—that Riss had left after her last PT appointment. While he'd asked to go to the appointments with her, she'd refused. She said she'd be too busy trying to impress him to listen to what her therapist said.

When he heard the front door open and her call out, he counted to ten rather than skipping to her with barely concealed excitement.

She turned the corner into the living room and his heart just stopped. This woman was everything to him. He wanted to spend every moment of every day showing her just how special and precious she was.

Before he could say a word, Riss was off and running her mouth. "I was lookin' forward to a three-margarita lunch with my BFF, planning to be too tipsy to drive so I'd have to call my hot man to come and pick me up, earning the envy of every woman in the bar. But no. Jade didn't 'feel' like drinking, which was totally lame. And there was no way I was gonna get hammered alone so I drank stupid iced tea. So bein' annoyed about the situation, I jokingly asked Jade if she was pregnant—and that's why she hadn't been drinking the last couple of times we'd gotten together. I expected her to laugh it off. But no. She gets this super smug look and says . . . 'So what if I am?'"

"Riss. Baby—"

"Yes, that's exactly it! Jade and Tobin are havin' a baby! She's so damn proud of the fact she got pregnant on her honeymoon because they planned it. I mean, I sort of understand why. Jade wants her kid to know her grandma Garnet before the woman gets too much older and Tobin wants his kid and Streeter's to grow up together."

"Last time I spoke to Hugh? The man couldn't utter a sentence without the word 'baby' or 'pregnancy' or 'kid' in it."

"What in the hell is goin' on that everyone is so

excited about pumping out puppies? Even Geena from book club is knocked up. I tell you, it's a freakin' epidemic. I'm headed straight for the bathroom right now to shower off pregnancy hormones in case they're contagious. And, dude, I'm putting two condoms on your dick—just to be super safe."

He chuckled. "Can we talk about this later? There's something I want to discuss with you."

She got a very suspicious look on her face. "I will warn you that my mood is a teeny bit sour."

"This is gonna sweeten your disposition a whole bunch."

"You're welcome to try and butter me up. But sex is off the table, as I am in a dick-punching, not a dick-munching mood."

The stuff that came out of his woman's mouth bordered on unreal sometimes, but it always made him grin. "Your future as a solo driver is out of your control until the therapist weighs in with your limitations—if you even have any."

She tapped her fingers on the table. "And? This ain't news."

"And this plan is based on your original suggestion and I just ran with it." There'd been more to it than that, could be a bigger payoff down the line, but all she needed to know now was the general outline.

"Ran where?"

"To Tito. I've agreed to go to work for him."

"You did?"

"Yeah, isn't that great?"

"What will you be doin' for him?"

"He initially wanted me to broker better deals on

fuel and tires. But I told him the only thing I'm interested in is driving. With you. He's considered expanding into some long-haul routes as a perk to a select few customers, but he wouldn't commit to researching the idea until he had drivers he could trust."

"Let me get this straight. You've been dealing with Tito, my boss, behind my back, for how long?"

"You're makin' it sound sinister, Riss. I started talkin' to him regularly because he tried to hire me after Omaha and I kept putting him off."

Her mouth fell open. "What? Why didn't I know any of this?"

Why didn't she look happy? "He asked me not to discuss personnel matters."

"Personnel matters? But I'm personnel a helluva lot more than you are!"

"I know. And then when we ironed out the particulars, I didn't want to jinx anything before it was finalized."

"Jinx what? Ike. You're talkin' in riddles. Spit it out."

"You and I will be a drivin' team. While you're in PT I'll bear the brunt of the actual drivin' as you navigate. After you're cleared—think positive, baby—then we'll have a more traditional partnership where we share the time behind the wheel. But the income is split fifty-fifty."

"You're serious."

"Why would I kid about something like this?"

"Because you . . ." Riss seemed too mad to speak. She stood and paced to the door to the garage and back. "Lemme get this straight. My boss offered you a job. Did he offer you *my* job?"

"At first, but I told him I wasn't interested."

"How goddamned generous of you!"

"Maybe it was since I pitched the team option, it kept you from losing your job."

"Anything else you wanna confess? Have you weaseled your way into workin' at my brother's garage too?"

"Weaseled my way in? What the fuck, Riss?"

"Answer the question."

"Why? You already know that Lloyd is teaching me some basic mechanics I should've already known."

"And you're also boxing with Lonnie. So is my brother Lou teaching you how to mix the perfect whiskey soda?"

He held up both of his hands. "Where is this comin' from?"

"From you! When I told you that you needed to make some changes in your life, I didn't mean for you to entrench yourself in all aspects of *my* life and livelihood." She stopped pacing long enough to glare at him. "I can't believe you'd do this to me. If this is what happens when people date, then I want to br—"

"Don't you say it, woman." Ike got right in her face. "Take a deep goddamned breath and think about what you're accusing me of."

"I don't have to accuse you; you've already admitted that you went behind my back to my boss. You've done other sneaky-ass things too."

Now he was getting pissed. "*Our* boss came to me. But I'll play. Name one other thing."

"I can name several. I've looked the other way as you've tried to win over my brothers. And if I hadn't put my foot down, you'd be in the room with me at my therapy appointments."

"So I'm an asshole because I care enough about you to want to get to know your family and make sure your recovery is on track?"

But Riss had started down this path and, as usual, she'd veer off it whenever it suited her, even if it led to a dead end or sent them careening over a cliff. She gestured wildly to the space around them. "I'm here all the time. We've spent exactly one night at my place. One. So were you planning on packing up my shit and moving it here? Without asking me? Will I come home to find a For Sale sign in my front yard?"

He snorted. "Get real."

"Should I ask if you've already brokered a deal and sold the dump truck to Holt? Maybe I have zero dating experience, but I know none of this shit is normal."

"Babe. Neither of us knows normal."

"I hate that you promised you'd stop bossing me around and yet here we are."

"I *have* stopped doin' that!"

"Then what is this?"

Ike forced himself to hold her gaze as he said, "Love."

Her shocked and somewhat angry expression didn't inspire his confidence. "It doesn't feel like love. It feels like control."

Fuck, that stung. But he pushed on. "And you have so much experience with love and relationships to know that?"

"No, but I do have experience with people trying to control me."

That haughty little shake of her mean red curls was the last fucking straw.

"You know what, Riss? You're right. I volunteered to bring you into my home and care for you after your accident because I saw a chance to bring you to heel. It had nothin' to do with my concern that your needs weren't bein' met. So I forced you away from your family and refused to grant them access to you. And while you were here and incapacitated, I demanded you solve my career crises. And when I figured out you couldn't, well then, I got super bossy with you, knowing you'd leave just as soon as you could.

"But that was just another one of my tricks. See, I needed you to feel useful and not controlled so I made up some personal shit about my recent struggles. Then to really convince you of my sincerity, I walked away from a business I owned and took a part-time job that paid slightly above minimum wage. And to further mess with you, I insisted we start dating, knowing I could seduce you and the sex between us would be addictive. Your overwhelming lust for me would overtake your self-control, your common sense and your life. I let you pick a fight with me, so I had to show up where you work and grovel. While I was there I weaseled my way into your boss's good graces so he'd see how awesome *I* am and hear me brag that I'm a much better driver than you, so I could run your workin' hours too. Even your income would be dependent on me. Oh, and then I secretly became buddies with your brothers because I knew I could get them to take my side over yours, and I told my sisters I was done with them because it'd take every bit of my effort to control you, every day, for the rest of your life."

He paused to take a breath. "Does that sound about right?"

Riss stared at him in absolute shock.

"Shoot. I forgot the part where I planned to put my house on the market. So when I move into your trailer, we're working together and living together and you can't ever escape me and my desperate need to control you."

She opened her mouth, but Ike held up his hand.

"Oh no, sweetheart, I ain't done. The best part of this ultimate manipulation is where I confess that I'm madly fucking in love with you and I can't imagine a single day in my life without you in it. Not a single. Fucking. Day."

She made a wounded noise and clapped her hand over her mouth. Her eyes started to swim with tears.

"Don't. You barely shed a tear when you were injured."

"Ike."

"I suspected you were great at self-sabotage, Riss. But I'd hoped I was mistaken." He grabbed his keys off the hook by the door, settled his hat on his head and walked away without looking back.

Chapter Twenty-Eight

∽

*Y*ou, Larissa Thorpe, are the biggest fucking tool
on the planet.

Her fears, her accusations, had all sounded perfectly
legitimate in her head before she started tossing them at
him out loud.

Ike's rebuttal just proved how little she'd thought
things through.

Like that's a surprise.

She should've heeded her dad's lifelong warning—
Girl, engage your brain before your mouth—because
it'd always been her biggest downfall.

She'd laughed it off. Tried to convince herself and everyone else it was part of her charm. Part of being real.

Well, she'd really fucked up this time.

How could she have acted that way to Ike? The only
man who truly "got" her. The only man she'd let get
close enough to her to see through her bullshit.

And what had she given the only man who'd been fool enough to fall in love with her?

Attitude.

Accusations.

An excuse to leave.

Instead of showing gratitude or even joy that the man who absolutely sucked at list making had mapped out a plan for their future . . . she'd given in to her fears.

Even when she knew she loved him.

She literally smacked herself in the head, hating that it didn't hurt enough. And it sure as fuck didn't put her brain back on track.

How could she make this right?

Horror filled her at the thought that she couldn't do anything to fix this. Her pride at never falling into a relationship trap left her with zero skills on how to begin to repair what she'd broken.

Think, Riss.

Ask for help.

No. She had to figure this out on her own.

There's the problem. You admit you don't have the knowledge to fix this, but instead of asking for help from someone who's been in this situation before, you're just going to let the best thing that's ever happened to you slip away?

Who's apathetic now?

Not me. Not ever again.

Riss picked up her phone and scrolled through her contact list. Her first thought was to call Jade. But she immediately dismissed that idea. Jade was a newlywed— now a pregnant newlywed—who'd never fucked up with Tobin. Her skill set was likely as unused as Riss's.

Her brothers were also zero for zero for zero on the serious-relationship front.

And almost as if the universe was giving her a sign, the scroll bar highlighted AUNT BERNICE.

Riss didn't hesitate. She hit call.

Luckily, Bernice answered on the third ring.

"What do you need that has you calling me at two in the afternoon?"

"Your help, your advice, your expertise because I fucked up big-time and I don't know what to do next. It's an emergency, Aunt B, like I-might've-ruined-my-life kind of emergency."

"Take a deep breath, girl, and calm down. Where are you?"

"At Ike's."

"All right. Gimme a minute to close up the shop and I'll be right over."

"No. That's fine. I'll come to you."

Chapter Twenty-Nine

❧

*I*t was beyond pathetic that Ike didn't know where to go after he'd dramatically stormed out.

He'd never been the slamming-doors, running-from-his-problems type.

Maybe subconsciously he'd done what Riss would—gotten pissed and taken off—just to keep her from doing the same.

But he wasn't in the wrong. Riss had figured that out, or he hoped she had, but he still needed time to cool off before he said something he'd regret.

Ike had driven around for almost half an hour before ending up in Buckeye Joe's empty parking lot. Technically they didn't open until four, but he recognized Sherry Gilchrist's Jeep, and she'd let him in early—if only for the chance to be the first one to get the gossip on his morose state.

The front door wasn't locked.

Sherry was singing along to the jukebox as she stocked ice. When she saw Ike ambling toward her, she released a little shriek.

"Good lord, Ike Palmer. You surprised me. What in the devil are you doin' here?"

"Need a place to think and drink. You mind if I just hang out for a bit?"

"No, sugar, that's fine. You need me to call anyone so you're not thinkin' and drinkin' alone?"

"Nope."

"You need a beer? Or something stronger?"

"Beer is fine. PBR."

She raised both of her eyebrows but didn't comment. She cracked the top off two bottles and tossed out bar napkins before placing the bottles in front of him. "I've gotta do inventory in the back. You need another, just help yourself."

"Thanks, Sherry."

He took a long pull off the bottle, swallowed and sighed. Sometimes, there just wasn't anything better than an icy cold beer. Maybe he should drink a dozen of these and dull the edges a little.

In his haste to leave, he'd forgotten his coat and his phone. His phone wasn't a concern since he didn't want to talk to Riss anyway. But he'd shoved his wallet in his coat pocket, which meant he didn't even have a couple of bucks to pay for this cheap beer.

Christ. His life at this moment could be the beginning of a country song lamenting the fight with his woman, bein' down on his luck with no money and literally out in the cold with nothing but his pickup truck.

That thought caused him to crack a smile. Maybe he'd call his longtime buddy Devin McClain, country superstar, and share his tale of woe. Someone should benefit from it.

But Devin would likely laugh his ass off. As would the rest of their friends if he contacted them for advice on his next move with Riss. While it'd taken his friends some time to get to the happy places in their lives, the fact that they were there now . . . he doubted they'd remember being at this "what the fuck do I do now?" stage with their spouses.

He couldn't even call his sisters because he half feared they'd gloat.

That left his options on who to call limited indeed.

Tobin was a newlywed.

Hugh was still sorting out what to do with JSC and Ike knew he wasn't Hugh's favorite person at the moment.

So he felt especially pathetic when he realized that the person he most wanted to bitch about Riss to . . . was Riss herself. The woman had become everything to him— friend, lover, confidant, career counselor, coworker—in such a short time he really didn't know what to do without her.

As he debated on how long he'd have to stay away from his own damn house, the bar door was thrown open with the force of a Wyoming windstorm.

He glanced up as Riss sauntered in.

Wearing his coat.

Snow dotted her hair and she shook herself off before she noticed him, sitting at the end of the bar watching her.

His heart raced when their eyes met. He managed not to grin, or let out a whoop of victory.

Then her chin went up and she took her time erasing the distance between them.

When she finally stopped behind his barstool, and he didn't immediately spin around to face her, she took her time peeling off his coat before she climbed onto the barstool next to his.

Then the crazy woman grabbed his full beer and downed half of it.

She sighed. "You look like a smart guy. So can I ask you something?"

"Sure."

"You ever had a friend who is a complete dumb-ass? You know the type. She thinks she knows everything and she opens her damn mouth and starts talking before her brain can catch up and tell her to shut it?"

Riss paused to down another mouthful of beer.

"I know this woman . . . *Marissa* . . . who does that without thinking. Most of the time her idiocy can be overlooked because there's never any real consequences for her. She says whatever she wants, to whoever she wants, and lets the chips fall where they may because she's not invested in the outcome. She just moves on."

Ike forced himself not to interrupt. To see where she was going with this.

"I mean, she's been actin' this way for so long she doesn't know any other way to act. If she gets cornered, she comes out swinging. Her mind-set is better to be the first person to get a shot in rather than the last. She's lived her life so goddamned proud of the fact she doesn't need anything from anyone. She's in control. And fuck anyone who tried to take any of that control from her."

Riss swung the bottle back and forth like a pendulum, nearly hypnotizing Ike.

"So you'd think this woman is tough. Strong. The type of take-no-shit woman that most women aspire to be. But what people on the outside don't know? Because she lets so few people get close to her? Is that she's absolutely riddled with fear."

"Fear of what?"

"Jesus, too many fucking things to name, to be honest. But she's a goddamned master at hiding them. She fears that by relying on someone—let's say a man—she'll stop bein' able to take care of herself. And then the man will leave because of her dependence. Or she's scared her independence will scare men away. She also fears disappointment that she can't truly rely on anyone except herself. Not even her family is one hundred percent reliable one hundred percent of the time."

"This Marissa person doesn't realize that's an unrealistic expectation? Being let down is part of life. It's how you pick yourself up afterward that matters."

"Yeah, well, I think she knows that's true, but she keeps the bar so high that no one can reach it."

"Sounds like a lonely way to live."

"It is. Do you know she's thirty years old and she's never been in a relationship until recently?"

"That's not the norm, but it's not that unusual. I know this guy . . . *Mike* . . . who's almost forty who's in the same situation," Ike offered.

"I don't know whether to feel sorry for them or to commend them."

"Commend them for what?"

She shrugged. "I'd say for livin' their life on their own terms, no matter what society says about them bein' single. They aren't willing to settle. But the truth is, they're lucky in that they don't have other relationship experiences to fall back on when they fuck up."

"So they can just say . . . my bad? They didn't know any better when they act like a total asshole?" he said sharply.

"No. That sounded a little defensive." Riss bumped him with her shoulder. "I'm just saying there doesn't have to be a cooling-off period. Or a standard amount of time before the person who fucked up can approach the man she hurt and admit she was wrong . . . so very wrong. She let the fear win and that's not an excuse. It's not really even an explanation. It's an embarrassing fact."

Ike looked Riss in the eyes for the first time since she walked in. "She?"

"I. Me." She exhaled. "I'm sorry, Ike. I overreacted. I hurt you. I took something that should've filled me with as much hope and joy as it did you and turned it into an ugly moment. I want to know how we go forward after this. What I can do to make it right again after I acted so very wrong."

He must've looked as shocked as he felt because Riss kissed his surprised mouth.

"Ike Palmer, I love you. You are the best man I've ever known. And it's killing me that I acted so callous with your feelings. Please give me another chance to prove you can rely on me to be everything you need me to be. Because you are everything to me. I can change. I swear . . ."

"Riss. Baby. Don't cry."

"I'm scared that my pride and my big mouth have fucked up the best thing that's ever happened to me."

"It hasn't." He curled his hand around the side of her face. "Thank you for tracking me down and apologizing. And I think you're right in sayin' that we're lucky that the first—and only—serious relationship for both of us means we know what we want. I want you, Riss, as you are. I love you as you are. We will figure this out our own way, okay?"

"Okay." She sniffled. "But I will admit I called my aunt Bernice for relationship advice after you walked out."

"And what was her advice?"

"Go after him."

"That's it?"

She nodded. "She said relationships were like assholes . . . anyone who tells you theirs is pretty and perfect is full of shit."

He laughed.

"This is the most important relationship I've ever had in my life and I'll do whatever I need to, to make it work. I don't want to live a single fucking day without you either, Ike."

"Woman, you can piss me off like no one I've ever met." He wiped away another tear from the corner of her eye. "But I've never laughed as much as I do with you. How did I get so lucky that all the passion, humor and beauty that is you, is mine."

"Good lord, I don't know that I'll ever get used to how easily that sweetness drips off your silver tongue, but I sure do like it." She smirked. "But I do want to one-up you on something, since you one-upped me on saying you loved me first."

"What's that?"

"I want to end the truce. As grateful as I am that it led us here, to getting to know each other, we don't need it." Riss touched his face. "Goddamn, it pains me to admit this, but talking is much more productive than yelling, but I still prefer yelling because it feels more like me."

Never a dull moment with this woman. "No more assumptions either."

"I will try my very hardest not to jump to the worst conclusion first."

"Me too." Ike spun the barstool away and then stood back. "Been a helluva day. We fought, made up, confessed our love for each other, agreed to live together and work together . . . all in the past hour."

"Wait. When did we agree to live together?"

"Uh, darlin', when you said you didn't want to live a single fucking day without me either, that pretty much seals the deal on us sharin' a bed and everything else."

"Dammit, Ike, how has it come down to deciding where we'll settle into this couplehood gig? I remember a time when I couldn't wait to get the hell away from you. When the thought of spending one more minute with you was freakin' torture. And now . . . the thought of not spending every minute with you puts me in a really foul fuckin' mood." She shook her finger at him when he grinned. "Stop that. I'm serious. What super cowboy mojo did you use on me to get me to change my mind about you?"

"They don't call me Palmer the Charmer for nothin', sweet cheeks." He continued to smile at her. "And how many times do I have to remind you that manipulation disguised as goading me won't work? So tell me what else is on your mind."

Riss opened her mouth. Closed it. "Fine, you win, I've got nothin' to add because you've dealt with everything that'd be a sticking point with me. I wanna move in with you. I wanna have crazy adventures with you on and off the road. I want to make you so stupidly happy that you'll never leave me."

"Larissa. I'm too stubbornly in love with you to ever live without you."

"Promise?"

"Promise."

"Good." She closed the distance between them and twined her arms around his neck. "Because I don't know if you're aware that I'm an excellent tracker as part of my Native American heritage. If you leave me, I'll track you to the ends of the earth and cut out your—"

Ike placed his fingers over her mouth. "I thought we were done with the violence and the name-calling?"

"Sorry. I just wanted to remind you of what you're getting into with me, Ike. I've never been in love, so I might get a little intense with the need to prove it to you every day. And I'm not exactly conventional."

"Thank god for that." He rested his forehead on hers. "Can we go home now?"

"Isn't this where you growl, 'Now c'mere and gimme a damn hug?'"

"Riss. Baby, look where you are."

She blinked at him. "What the hell? How'd I get here?"

"This time you came to me, without me havin' to ask."

Riss kissed him. "Because now I know this is exactly where I belong."

I quit."

No no no no no no no, not again.

Streeter Hale practically had to run after his babysitter as she hoofed it away from the house. "Please wait just a minute, Mrs. McCutcheon, I'm sure we can find a better way to deal with—"

That was all he got out before she whirled around so fast he nearly plowed into her.

"I'm done. That's it. I've tried. I've failed. Good luck finding a replacement caregiver. You'll need it since I was your last option at the agency." Through gritted teeth she said, "That child . . ."

Don't you dare say it. I swear I will lose my shit if you call my daughter something like the devil's spawn or a demon child.

"That child . . . what?" he said tersely.

"That child needs a firmer hand." She raised her chin

and glared at him. "I have forty years of childcare experience. In addition to running a daycare and a preschool for twenty-five years, I have four children of my own and ten grandchildren. In those forty years I've never let a child best me. Never. Congratulations. Your five-year-old daughter did what so many others before her tried and failed to do: made me want to quit."

Streeter locked eyes with the older woman, who was a dead ringer for Mrs. Doubtfire. "Can I ask what Olivia did this time?"

"The fact you had to tack on 'this time' is the biggest indicator that there is a problem, Mr. Hale. It wasn't one action, although her drum solo on pots and pans was the final straw."

"I'm sorry."

She harrumphed. "*Olivia* should be apologizing, not you. Stop letting her use her mother's death as an excuse to misbehave—she's not the only child who's lost a parent. Besides, she's five years old, for crying out loud. She'll be starting kindergarten in the fall. The teacher won't put up with her tantrums or her backtalking or her manipulations. And you shouldn't either."

Why don't you tell me how you really feel?

But she wasn't the first person who'd told him that. With her being the sixth childcare provider who'd quit in the past eighteen months . . . he had to admit something had to change. "Thank you for your advice, Mrs. McCutcheon."

She sent him a look that said she didn't believe he'd take it. She shrugged and continued her escape.

Streeter took several deep breaths. Then he counted to ten slowly, six times, before he headed into his house.

The trailer was completely quiet, but the place was a total wreck.

He said, "Olivia. Come out here."

No response.

Louder, he said, "Now. I mean it."

The crocheted afghan on the back of the sofa cushion moved against the paneled wall and he watched his daughter crawl out from behind the tweed couch.

Kid was like a little mouse, squeezing into the tightest spaces.

Her super fine blond hair nearly stood on end from static electricity. His eyes narrowed on her clothing. Not what he'd dressed her in when he'd left the house two hours ago. She'd donned her one-piece mermaid swimsuit, pairing it with her *Frozen* Elsa leggings, the plaid satin Christmas skirt from last year and a beaded metal necklace. His heart stopped as he imagined that necklace getting caught in the loose threads on the back of the couch and choking her. Not to mention the fact she'd somehow gotten into his closet where he'd stashed her mother's costume jewelry—an area he'd warned her multiple times was off-limits.

Pick your battles. Do not give in to your fear by becoming angry and yelling.

That was hard as hell when his little spitfire looked at him defiantly and said, "What?"

"You know what." He pointed to the time-out chair. "Park it."

"But, Daddy—"

"Right now, Olivia Joyce."

Her blue eyes widened. He only pulled out her middle name when she was in deep shit. She dramatically flopped in the chair like a disgusted teen. Tough for a five-year-old to pull off, but she managed it.

"Tell me what happened with Mrs. McCutcheon today."

"She made me sit at the table and color." Her freckled nose wrinkled. "I told her I wanted to play the drums. She said no and when she went to the bathroom I got all the stuff out because she was in there a really really *really* long time."

"And?" he prompted again.

Her bare feet began to swing beneath the chair. "And when she finally came out, she told me to stop beatin' on the pans."

"Did you?"

She shook her head. "Then she tried to *make* me stop, but it's not my fault she tripped over my jump rope and fell down."

Streeter pinned her with a look. "Where was the jump rope, Olivia?"

"Umm . . . I tied it between a chair leg and the cupboard door handle."

"Like a booby trap?" he demanded.

She frowned. "A what?"

"A hidden trap."

"Well, yeah, 'cept it wasn't really hidden. I was just tryin' to keep her from comin' into the kitchen and stopping my drum practice."

He deeply regretted letting her watch that *Drumline* movie a few months back; she'd been obsessed with turning everything into a percussion instrument ever since. "Regardless. Who was in charge?"

"Mrs. McC."

"And if she told you no . . . what were you supposed to do?"

Olivia crossed her arms over her chest. "Listen to her and do what she says."

"And you didn't."

"It's *my* house, Daddy. Why won't she ever let me do what *I* want to do in my own house?"

"We've talked about this a hundred times, Olivia. You are *not* the adult. You are *not* in charge. *You* don't make the rules. You *follow* the rules set by the adults. *All* the rules. *All* the time."

"Even if the rules are dumb?" she countered.

"Yes." Streeter removed his cowboy hat and ran his hand through his sweaty hair. "And now I've had to take time off from work. So get your boots on, girlie, because we're leavin'."

"Mrs. McC isn't waitin' outside until you're done *setting me straight*?"

Good lord. The mouth and the brain on this girl. "No. She quit."

"Oh." Olivia slumped in the chair. "She smelled weird anyway."

His brain cautioned him not to ask, but his mouth was already moving. "What do you mean by *weird*?"

"She smelled mean."

"How do you know what mean smells like?"

"Because it smells like her."

Okay, then. "Get movin'. I don't wanna hear any complaints about you havin' a peanut butter sandwich for lunch again today."

"I'm comin' to work with you?"

Streeter stopped halfway to the kitchen and looked

back at her. "Where else did you think you were gonna go?"

Olivia hopped off the chair. "To Aunt Jade's house."

"She just had baby Micah two months ago, sweetheart. She's busy with him and your cousin Amber."

"But I could help her!"

His sweet sister-in-law Jade was on the very short list of people who could handle Olivia on a regular basis. But he'd been careful not to overstep his bounds with his brother's wife, asking too much of her when it came to taking care of his daughter—even before Jade had two kids under age two.

"I would follow all the rules for her. I always do. Please, Daddy? I'll be good. I promise."

He had a lightbulb moment. "Is that what this has been about? You actin' up so Mrs. McC quits and you expecting that I'll let you stay with Jade instead?"

She looked guilty.

"Olivia, that ain't how things work. You know it. Now while I'm makin' your lunch, grab something to do in the truck cause you're gonna be in there a few hours."

"Hours?" she repeated with horror. "What am I s'posed to do for that long?"

"Bring your coloring stuff."

"Boring," she said with a sniff. "Can I play with your phone?"

"No." Maybe his smile was a little insincere when he said, "Or you could always practice your drumming on the dashboard."

∞

Later that night, while Olivia watched a movie, Streeter scoured Craigslist for potential daycare options. With

Olivia signed up for a half a day at the Learning Center in Casper, and a full day at the upcoming Split Rock Summer Day Camp, he only needed in-home daycare three days a week. Surely there had to be high school or college students looking for a part-time summer job. Without the agency fees tacked on he could afford to pay four bucks an hour more than the standard rate.

He followed link after link until his vision went blurry and his frustration mounted. As he was about to give up, he saw an ad for a babysitters' co-op, which appeared to be run by a woman and six of her female family members. He filled out the form, clicked send and crossed his fingers they'd get back to him soon.

Ten minutes later his phone rang. "Hello?"

"Mr. Hale?"

"Speakin'. Who's this?"

"Marianne Smolen. You sent an online inquiry to Helping Hands Daycare Co-op?"

"Wow. That's what I call a fast response."

"This is the only time of day I can deal with business. So before I get to your questions . . . can you give me some more family information?"

A ball of dread tightened in his gut. "Sure. What would you like to know?"

"You indicated that your daughter Olivia is five and you've been a single parent since she was six months old?"

"Yes. Her mother died when she was a baby." *Please don't ask specifics.*

"I'm sorry. As a single parent myself, I know how hard that is. Do you have other family members helping you out with her care?"

"Olivia spent one day a week with my sister-in-law until she had a baby two months ago. Olivia spends some weekends with her maternal grandparents. The rest of my workin' hours she's either with me or I have someone come in to take care of her."

"She's not new to a daycare situation."

"No. We tried the drop-off type a couple of times and it never worked out. In-home daycare is better for both of us."

"For this summer session you're only looking for part-time care?"

"Yeah. Olivia will be attending two different camps, so I'll only need daycare three other days during the week."

"Living in Muddy Gap is a bit of a drive for us, since we're based in Rawlins."

"I'm willin' to pay for travel time. But they'll need to be here by seven thirty a.m."

"Would you need a childcare provider with her own vehicle?"

Weird question. "Only to drive here. I'm not lookin' for someone to haul Olivia around, just someone to take care of her in her own home when I'm at work."

"Understood. To be clear, the reason we're called a co-op is I have six daycare workers in my employ. Because you'd be a part-time client, I can't guarantee a specific caregiver, but I believe that might serve your needs better given the other information you provided about Olivia."

"Okay."

"You have questions for me?" she prompted.

"What are the ages of the caregivers you're considering for this position?"

"All teenagers, all out of high school and attending college, all with great referrals, which can be shared upon request." She paused. "I'll be blunt, Mr. Hale. This isn't the most economical option for any family. Are you sure you want to proceed?"

Streeter's cheeks flushed. He hated the assumption that he was dirt poor just because he was a ranch hand and lived in a trailer. "Yep. Do I need to pay a deposit?"

"We call it an application fee, which you can pay on-line." Papers shuffled in the background. "I'd like to send a caregiver one day this week. Wednesday at noon?"

"That'll work. Have her call my cell when she arrives at the Split Rock Resort and I'll meet her and show her where to go."

"Perfect. I'll e-mail you an invoice with the pay link. And if anything changes, please contact us. We have a twenty-four-hour answering service."

"Will do."

She hung up.

Streeter stared at the phone for a moment. Then he said, "Huh. I guess when one door closes—"

"I always close the door, Daddy," Olivia interjected.

He glanced over at his daughter sprawled on the couch, wondering how much of his conversation she'd paid attention to. "Most of the time you do."

"Did I get a new babysitter?"

So she had been listening. "Yep. Someone will be here this week."

"Is she old like Mrs. McC?"

"Nope."

She rolled on to her stomach and looked at him. "I heard you tell 'em I don't got a mommy."

"That's something they need to know, squirt."

Olivia crossed, uncrossed and recrossed her ankles as she studied him.

He braced himself. Any change in her life triggered questions about her mother. He just hoped it didn't trigger her night terrors too.

"Can I ask you something, Daddy?"

"Sure."

"If I had my mommy would I still have a babysitter?"

How was he supposed to answer that? "Maybe."

She considered his response for a moment. "Gramma Deenie always tells me that my mommy loved me so so so much." Cross, uncross, recross. "But I think she's lyin'."

Jesus. "Why would you think that, Olivia?"

"Because Gramma cries every time she says it."

"Talkin' about your mom always makes your gramma sad."

"Maybe Gramma was sad because she knew my mommy didn't love me."

He took a deep breath in and let it out softly. The therapist told him to let these types of conversations run their course. Don't correct her. Don't change the subject. Ask her questions and listen to her answers. "You still haven't given me a reason why you think your mother didn't love you."

"Because if she really loved me then she wouldna died."

Streeter moved to sit beside her. He smoothed back her staticky hair. "Darlin' girl, we've talked about this. All the love in the world can't keep anyone from dyin'. My mama loved me and she died too."

She crawled onto his lap and rested her head on his

shoulder—an odd reaction for her, and he held his breath. Several long minutes went by as she fiddled with the buttons on his shirt. "Do *you* think Mommy loved me?"

Such an innocent question shouldn't require him to take a couple of breaths before he answered. "Yeah, sweetheart, she did."

"You love Mommy, right?"

"I did." Thank god she was too young to pick up on the past tense.

"Gramma Deenie said I don't need another mommy as long as I've got her."

He kissed the top of her head. "Well, you needed another babysitter today after Mrs. McC quit."

"I hope this new one doesn't smell mean."

"Me too. Speaking of smellin' bad . . ." Then he sniffed her whole head like a pig searching for acorns. "Girl, you need a bath."

Olivia giggled and tried to wiggle away. "Daddy! That tickles!"

"You sure?"

"Yes!"

He kept doing it. She kept giggling.

This was what his child needed. Just him.

"Come on, in the tub with you." He grabbed her by the ankles and carried her into the bathroom, amid her happy shrieks and laughs.

Later, after he'd tucked her in, he returned to his e-mail and saw Helping Hands had sent another document as well as a payment link.

A document that requested more details about his financial situation.

He couldn't blame them. They were covering their

own asses to make sure a ranch hand earned enough to pay for a part-time private nanny.

Just to be ornery, he filled in the salary he'd earned at his last full-time job, when he'd been part owner at the Hale Ranch.

That seemed like a lifetime ago, although it'd only been four and a half years.

Back then, he'd had everything he ever thought he wanted. A stake in the family business, getting paid to do what he loved. A house nicer than the one he'd grown up in. A brand-new, beautiful, healthy baby girl. And most of all, he had Danica, the woman he'd loved for fifteen years, the woman he'd married, the woman he wanted by his side for the rest of their lives. He'd believed she was happy, they were happy.

That had turned out to be a lie.

After Danica's death, Streeter had been forced to go part-time on the family ranch since his daughter required his full-time attention. After working with his dad and older brother Driscoll his entire life and doing more than his fair share of chores for most of those years, he assumed they'd understand his changed circumstances.

That had turned out to be a lie too.

They'd revised his pay from a salaried position to an hourly wage, claiming that he didn't "need" the money after Danica's life policy insurance paid out.

Streeter had never felt so completely abandoned, so he abandoned them and quit.

By the time Olivia was a year old, Streeter had moved an hour and a half away from the only home he'd ever known to work at the Split Rock Ranch and Resort, job-sharing the ranch hand position with his younger brother, Tobin.

That turned out to be the best decision he'd ever made.

Not only had he and Tobin worked well together, his little brother had become his rock when he needed someone to lean on. When discussions about recouping his share of the Hale Ranch went south, Tobin had accompanied him to the lawyer's office. After their father and brother had grudgingly given Streeter one third of their herd and a cash buyout, Tobin offered his acreage as temporary grazing land.

The temporary solution had become a permanent operation. Streeter had used the payout money from Hale Ranch to purchase land adjoining his brother's. After they'd decided to go into the cattle business together—All Hale Livestock—they'd built a barn and corral halfway between Jade and Tobin's place and the area where Streeter had tentatively platted for a house.

Most days he was content working at the Split Rock part-time and living in a trailer on the property. He appreciated the flexibility in his hours and being part of a community that understood the real meaning of family first.

But some nights, he hated the loneliness of his life after Olivia went to bed, even when he knew it'd take a miracle for his single status to ever change.

Ready to find
your next great read?

Let us help.

Visit prh.com/nextread